WEEP

NO

MORE

MY

BROTHER

WEEP NO MORE MY BROTHER

A NOVEL BY
STERLING WATSON

WILLIAM MORROW & COMPANY, INC.
NEW YORK   1978

Library of Congress Cataloging in Publication Data

Watson, Sterling.
    Weep no more my brother.

    I. Title.
PZ4.W3443We   [PS3573.A858]   813'.5'4   77-28354
ISBN 0-688-03311-3

BOOK DESIGN   CARL WEISS

Printed in the United States of America.

First Edition

1   2   3   4   5   6   7   8   9   10

FOR KATH

. . . his answer was full of deference; but the odious and fleshy figure, as though seen for the first time in a revealing moment, fixed itself in his memory for ever as the incarnation of everything vile and base that lurks in the world we love: in our own hearts we trust for our salvation in the men that surround us, in the sights that fill our eyes, in the sounds that fill our ears, and in the air that fills our lungs.

—JOSEPH CONRAD, *Lord Jim*

PART

I

ONE

"YOU DID GET OUR LETTER?"

"No, sir," he lied.

There was a pause at the other end, some breathing.

The letter lay on the table beside a newspaper clipping. He was not sure how many times he had read the clipping, which was curling at the edges, or how long he'd had it. He'd had the letter for two weeks.

"Know what to think about this mail service nowadays. Do you?"

The voice was calm, atonal. It snapped like shirts hung out on the windy Bradford County telephone line. What would the man be like, Bray, the man whose voice this was? Who were these men who kept prisoners?

"Then we'll be seeing you s'mornin at ten, Mr. Odum?"

"Yes," said Farel Odum, they would be seeing him.

He was twenty-eight years old and he possessed a Ph.D. in Eighteenth-Century English Literature from the University of Florida, newly arrived by mail, and he possessed (less the furniture) the contents of the room in which he now stood with his hand on the dead telephone. Three cardboard boxes full of books, a closet full of clothes, plate and silver to serve one, a full wastebasket and a box of cornflakes, which he had been living on for three days. He had to vacate the premises by eleven o'clock for a new roomer.

He loaded the contents of the apartment into his Belvedere, less the cornflakes, which he left on the kitchen table. He gave his key to the landlord, collected his damage fee (having done no damage) and before getting into his car to drive the old familiar roads northeast from Gainesville to Raiford, he sat down at the table to read the clipping again. It was a routine item from the *Beacon* of Starke, Florida, which described the sentencing of a man to the State Prison at Raiford, only fifty miles distant.

Lester Macabee had been sentenced to five years for the theft of copper wire from a construction site. He had been caught by deputies of the Bradford County Sheriff's Department burning the insulation from the wire in the Starke city dump.

Farel Odum searched his memory briefly, finding for the hundredth time that he could not be sure. He folded the clipping into his wallet, and walked down the stairs to the car.

At the highway's edge, the gray bones of trees were starting to show. Leaves lay in the ditches. He knew these roads, knew how the trees would pass in his side vision darker now, more angular in September, how the little towns would flash beneath his tires in the double-bump of Seaboard Coastline track. In his near memory, each was an image of such clarity as to seem not seen, but chimed.

He shoved his foot into the accelerator, increasing the vented flow of cool air on his face. Thirty minutes later, like a city, the prison rolled toward him on the ruled horizon of this hammock land. Far ahead, submerged block-shapes seemed to stretch and then jump to the surface, swaying in the wind-driven misty rain. Here and there, the sun dropped shafts to promise heat when the rain ceased. He could see the blurry fence, three lines of it, electrified and trimmed with curly barbed wire. Two orange Spanish stucco pillars rose, alone like Druid ruins, forming a gate to the road. A wrought-iron arch hung between them. Passing under, he read the flat-black lettering: RAIFORD PRISON.

Growing, the prison seemed to gather and slump on the land. It loomed and retreated in his eye: five short, unadorned rectangular wings set counter a long center corridor. At each fence corner, and spaced between, were guard towers, faded, sulphur streaked where rain flowed, their tar paper roofs checkered with new bright green patches.

He took the first entranceway, through a maze of cloverleaf

asphalt roads. Confused, unsure which way to turn, he stopped.
"*State your bidnis.*"

The voice came from a speaker box atop the fence to his
right; above it, a sign said:

STOP AT BOX
STATE BUSINESS CLEARLY INTO BOX

There was a rush of static, another click. His signal to begin stating business? He stammered, ". . . interview . . .
teacher . . . ," unsure what the box could see, his eyes searching for the human source beyond. There was a pause, another
click. Behind the drawling voice, as from an old crystal radio,
came a tinny, country sound: "*You got . . .* (You ain't)
. . . *the wrong road . . .* (woman enough to take my man.)
. . . *little buddy.*"

The voice behind the voice was Kitty Wells. He smiled at
the sound, its threading in and out among his memories in the
instant of recognition. That voice (both these voices) had
murmured somewhere within earshot of him all the days of
his life. He shook his head. The speaker box said: "*Gone out
the way you come in an take the firss hard road pass the New
River at the ministration building. . . . Click!*"

Safe behind the last click, he said, "Thanks, peckerwood."

Backing the car, his head was spun by the crisp sound,
"*Click . . . you wekkum . . . Haw, haw, haw . . . click!*"
Fare looked at the nearest guard tower, some fifty yards distant. There he saw through blue glass, the drawn form of a
man who blew a stream of cigarette smoke through an open
port and then waved to him above the black, oiled slash of a
rifle cradled to his chest.

With a burning in his cheeks, he turned north again. Ahead,
he saw more of the same stucco, but there were trees. It all
seemed less severe over here, too, and older. Huge live oaks
mushroomed above the tops of buildings in the distance and
beneath them, through the mists of fences, he saw parked cars,
trucks, forklifts, stacked cartons, the dugouts of a baseball
diamond. Closer, he made out hedges, daubs of flowers, and

the pale blue shapes of men, milling around or walking in long lines. He rounded the last curve toward a smaller, newer building outside the wire.

The morning was dying. The rain had stopped. The asphalt was steaming already. He slowed the car, losing the rush of wind at the vents. He could smell himself. It was a sudden, cutting thing, the stink of apprehension.

Take the first hard road.

The administration building shone in the difference of its modern design, the brightness of its orange and blue colors. It was almost cheery. The buildings inside the wire were not. They looked like certain old schools he had seen: sturdy, earth colored, and decaying.

Walking toward the bright new building, he studied the movement behind the wire. There was a quality of leisure to it he had not expected. He guessed it was some kind of morning break inside. Now the blue figures began forming lines. A steam whistle groaned, and soon the lines began to move.

Women did not belong to his idea of what it would be like, but a big girl with piles of hair asked, "Yes, sir, hep you?"

He explained and then she, and then several other women and finally two men, dressed nattily in pinstripes (where was the gray flannel?) seemed confused, a little resentful at the intrusion of an outsider. What kind of interview? Who with? Who did you say?

"Mr. Odum?"

Fare never thought of himself as Mr. Odum. Mr. Odum had once been his father, but only to strangers, or people he owed money. The time it took to fit this new, serious sound to himself made a space in the lather of politeness on the big girl's face.

"Mr. Odum?"

She turned, bobbing spun-glass hair, rolling cowgirl shoulders and slab ass, toward a near hallway. He followed her to an office bearing a routed plastic nameplate: HAROLD HARKNESS, PERSONNEL DIRECTOR. The cowgirl stopped at the door, handed him a folder, and nodded him in.

Harold Harkness, a large, pale, pudding-faced man, throttled by a purple collar, waited a count of ten before looking up at Fare. Then he rose, as though surprised, and minced around the big, low desk. A burst of executive energy, he swept his hand toward a chair set squarely before the big desk. "Have a seat, Mr. Odum."

There it was again. It had a ring to it.

Harkness shook his hand firmly, expelling it slickly after two pumps the way politicians did, the way his father had done to the clingers after church services.

Now Harkness was making his way hand over hand back behind the desk. He sat, swinging his legs from a lean-back roll-around chair.

"Mr. Bray, the man who called you this morning, will be down in a minute from the school to take you in, show you around. I just have a few things to sound you out on."

Fare nodded, coughed seriously, adjusted the tension in his trousers at the crotch and behind the knees. Harkness was saying, "We're very happy with your credentials. We can't imagine why somebody with a Ph.D. would come out here. We don't even have many people teaching in area right now."

Fare smiled. Harkness eyed him, expecting something. Fare looked at his shoes, fumbled for a cigarette. He thought of the clipping he carried in his wallet. Harkness was asking why he had come. What was he supposed to say? He had come because Lester Macabee was due to arrive from the county jail in Starke any day now. He mumbled something about thinking that prison teaching would be interesting.

"How much have you heard about our recent trouble, the, uh, so-called riot?"

The word "so-called" came out of Harkness in a phlegmy cloud of disgust, like a rotten peanut. Harkness laughed briefly, coughed through an "O" formed by thumb and forefinger, shaking his head the way people do who know the straight skinny about something. Fare thought it must be a loaded question.

"Not much," he said, "too much studying there at the end."

"Wh . . . um," coughed Harkness, "then let me put it to

you this way. Where do you see yourself in the political spectrum? Conservative, liberal, in the middle?" Harkness' phrasing was beginning to sound memorized. There was a slowdown to a concerted effort before "political spectrum." Fare thought of sleeping in the back seat of the Belvedere. He needed a job.

"Oh, I just like to wait till things happen and then do what seems right."

It sounded like a quibble, an evasion. He hadn't meant it that way.

"I see."

Harkness' eyes demanded more.

He said, "I guess I'm a liberal, but I don't condone violence." Now *his* lines came from memory.

Harkness leaned toward him, spreading pale, thick hands on the desk top. "Back when we had our trouble, some of our teachers took it upon themselves to try to straighten things out. I won't go into detail."

That's right, don't give me any ideas.

Harkness continued, "The point is, we expect teachers and all state employees to move within the bounds of our regulations, go through channels. We also expect them to dress neatly and maintain a neat personal appearance. No long hair, no mustaches past the end of the mouth, no flashy sideburns."

"Flashy" was another rotten peanut.

Harkness said, "We think we're being fair, and it ain't fair to those men in there for a bunch of . . . for teachers to go around like inmates and guards can't do."

There was a long silence while Harkness looked as though he was waiting for Fare's true colors to flare forth.

But Fare had none.

"How's my hair?" he asked, attempting a joke.

Harkness smiled, a wrinkle with teeth in it. Hand over hand around the desk to shake and expel Fare's hand again.

"It's all right now," he said, "but tomorrow it'll be too long."

TWO

IN THE GLASS-PANELED CAFETERIA, FARE DRANK A CUP OF coffee with Harkness and watched the main gate, a large, facaded pair of Spanish stucco towers, flanking an office. His eyes moved from the old gate in a wide sweep outward beyond the prison land. In 1969, he knew, men had walked on the moon. Yet, there were people under the press of his eye, in this scarred, firebroken landscape, who did not *know* it even, and people living seventy-five miles to the south and east where the tall rockets towered on the beach and powerful lights brought huge sea creatures up from the depths at Titusville, people whose eyes would blink in disbelief at this hammock land with its hopeless tobacco and peanut patches, its fired chimneys standing, like rockets, undressed of their houses.

Yet this land had been his life, these little towns, sumps of time where nothing quickened a pulse but an act of love or violence. It was from these places that the men he would work with had come.

He left the cafeteria, walked across the parking lot, removed the gate pass Harkness had given him from his shirt pocket and pushed at the heavy barred door.

It was cool inside. He stood in the hush. Four men, two white guards and two black inmates, turned to look at him. The near guard, a sergeant, was fat. An inverted "V" of pale belly flesh was visible between shirt button and belt. He sat at some kind of instrument panel. The far guard, in a barred inner chamber like a lock in a waterway, sat with a tray in his lap. This lean guard bent his head to the tray, then snapped it back harshly, like a dog throwing food to its back teeth.

Something sluiced in the fat sergeant's stomach. His hand covered the "V" tenderly as though the sound itself were pain.

The two inmates were the first Fare had seen up close. The sergeant, whose name tag read "Sgt. Thomas," smiled with turned-down lips, but said nothing. Fare held out his pass.

"I'm supposed to wait here for Mr. Bray."

"Are, are ya?" Thomas turned back to a tray set atop the panel.

Fare looked around for a place to sit, glancing down the walkway into the long hollow of the prison. No one.

The first inmate was a willowy old Negro. His turtle's neck longed to wrinkle the starched blue collar, but lacked the size to do it. He sat on a peeled ladder-back chair, a pair of shoes at his feet. Behind him on the floor were a dozen more, paired by their tied laces. His hands blurred as he honed a black patent leather oxford with a flannel rag, breathing, "chi-chi-chichi-choo." He tossed the rag into a neat homemade shoeshine kit. Behind him on the wall hung a brightly lacquered, elaborately lettered shingle: PLEASE HELP THE SHOESHINE BOY AS YOU MAY BE OLD AND BROKE YOURSELF SOMETIME. Beneath it sat a box into which people had dropped cigarettes, singles and packs.

Fare nodded. The man smiled into the shoe he was shining. The smile seemed to grow on his lips in stages, like a fault in black earth, and above the smiling mouth, pearly teeth, one eyelid dropped him a wink. Fare looked away, digging in his shirt for a cigarette.

After a space he turned his eyes to the other inmate, who languorously swung his legs from a cane table, staring undistracted out through the barred door. He was a big black man, and Fare guessed his blues had begun the day starched too, but his slightest movement caused them to crackle. He swung his legs like a schoolboy, but a threat hung around him in the air.

"Robert." It was the sergeant at the panel.

"Suh." Robert's face ticked, and he turned away from the outside. He slid down and walked to the guard, moving two-fifteen in a way that made the small room seem more cramped than it really was. Sergeant Thomas held out the tray, then rose and tapped Robert lightly with two fingers on the muscle of his arm. Robert turned and spread one hand on the wall, while the other, outstretched, balanced the tray. Thomas knelt and tapped the black nylon socks, squeezed the blue herringbone denim trousers, patted upward along the muscled contours of the thick legs. All this the guard in the inner room watched, still eating.

Now Robert moved to wait at the outer door, holding the tray. His eyes registered nothing. The sergeant unlocked the door and Robert stood in the chamber between the two gates. He moved to a small table, lowered the tray and removed his belt buckle and a silver amulet of a clenched fist from around his neck. He stepped through the metal detector, then turned back to the table and redressed himself. At the far end, he took up the second tray, and was let out the door. The second guard, tall and sallow, released the brass key from the lock and it snapped back to him on a spring-loaded spool belted at his waist. Robert disappeared into the prison, bobbing the dwarfed trays at his sides.

Fare watched all this with fascination, and something inside him said, "You are as much as this. You can do it—do the same as these others do." But suddenly, he was afraid, knowing that he was not like they were, not yet. He looked to flick the ash from his cigarette, but it was gone already. His hands had shaken it away. He thought of the clipping again, and the word "contraband" came to him. He walked to the door and peered deep into the prison again. He tried to seem impatient.

A long way off came a swaying white square, split at the thick chest by an old-fashioned narrow tie. At this distance the man was about as wide as the sidewalk and getting bigger, not smaller, carrying a clipboard. His whole aspect was coming energy. Fare could see the speed at which he walked by the way his tie fluttered.

The fat sergeant at his shoulder said, "At's your Mr. Bray. You can sign in now." With a ballpoint, he pointed to a big ledger. Fare took the pen. He wrote: "Farel Odum—Gainesville—12:15—Teacher," then went back and wrote "Mr." in front of his name.

Finished, he heard the broad, white-shirted man greet the first guard. "Howdy," he said from deep in a machine chest. By the way things got friendly in the gate room, Fare could see that the man Bray was respected. Fare turned his back, smoking. The old Negro to his left stopped popping the rag and watched Bray at the outer door. At the appropriate moment Fare turned, reaching out his hand. "Hello," he said, "I'm . . ." but Bray was saying, "They'll never do it," to the sergeant. "State'll run they butts right off the field. Knock em off the line of scrimmage."

The other said, "I got ten daw-lers of an old man's pay says they can. Hits bad to be poor and hired out for wages, Mr. Bray, but I got it."

"I got you covered," said Bray, pulling out a fat greasy wallet from his pleated serge trousers. His thigh bulged large and hard beneath the thin cloth when his hand stirred for the wallet.

Fare pulled back his own hand. His cheeks pulsed with embarrassment. The old Negro popped again, but not before whispering a chuckle, "thee, thee, thee . . ." Fare cut his eyes sharply in the direction of the laugh and saw, to his utter amazement, that his gaze frightened the old man, who bent religiously back to the shoe.

"You must be our Mr. Odum?"

Fare turned, squaring his feet. A big scarred fist hung stiffly inches from his own belt buckle. Without attempting to meet the face or get words into the space between them, he fumbled for the hand, transferring the sweaty cigarette butt from right to left. It split along the seam, showering the concrete with sparks and wet tobacco shards.

"Thee, thee . . ."

He gave Bray a handful of char and tobacco, shook firmly and then looked up to see Bray's small eyes narrowing at him.

"You sign in?"

"He did," said the fat guard.

"Yes," said Fare.

"This way."

Bray was already leaning his impatient chest against the door while the sergeant hurried to unlock it.

"Ten daw-lers, now," hissed the guard leaning forward, conspiring.

"Lost," said Bray. "An old man's money gone."

They walked fast by the metal detector, through the second door, through an alcove and into Fare's first glimpse of the land inside. He hurried to keep up. On his right Bray pointed out the old hospital, calling it, as the inmates did, the "dope house." Fare looked at the second floor and saw barred casement windows swung open. Out of one hung a limp, bandaged hand, a tattooed bicep. The hand patted the wall softly.

Bray pointed out the exercise yards, the furniture factory, and on their left, the visitors' park, a trampled, fenced area full of picnic tables and vacant concessions, vaguely like a fairground.

They passed under the smokestacked steam plant, the greenhouses, Bray telling him about Rose Festival trophies and false rumors of marijuana growing among caladiums.

The school building was newer than the others, constructed of red brick and stuccoed cinder block. It was landscaped in front with mowed grass, beds of chrysanthemums, hedges of clipped bougainvillea, all ending like the erased forms of a child's pencil drawing in the dirt road spotted with grease spills and rutted by heavy machinery. It was an island in the middle of the hard business of the prison.

At the entranceway Bray did not stop, but kept on striding into the dark, cool, disinfectant-smelling hallway. That smell. God, even here. It was the smell of school—think-sweat, chalk, pee, and disinfectant.

Bray ushered him into an office, past an inmate receptionist who smiled and nodded at them as they passed. Bray said, "Be right with you," and walked out, leaving him standing before a wide, low desk with banks of trophies behind it. Fare pinched himself into a narrow, new-smelling, overstuffed chair.

Outside, faces passed, disembodied, sliding along from the chin up in the glass panels which lined the two interior walls of the office. The glass was set in its moldings at a slant. There was no glare and Fare saw a dizzying array of blue denim movement, broken here and there by the soberer trustee white, or the bright colors of the shirts worn by free men. Already street clothing was beginning to seem strange. His eyes could penetrate every classroom in the building, from wall to wall, wherever his view was not obstructed by blue bodies. He wiped his forehead. It all gave him a cold, naked feeling, especially when he thought why it must be this way, why the need for these slanted interior walls of glass.

Outside, the faces in the slanted glass passed unconnected to fat or thin or muscular bodies. The eyes stared in, unashamed, as though filling up on something. Already he thought he had detected several unnecessary errands. There seemed to be an inordinate amount of traffic. He was being inspected.

Bray returned, carrying his folder. He chucked the folder onto the desk and sat, abstractedly leafing through it. Fare noticed that his eyes intermittently departed their reading to rove the full 180 degrees of glass spread out before him.

"Do you want coffee?" Bray asked.

"Thanks," replied Fare, and Bray seemed annoyed, at time taken from the business at hand, polite, nonsense time.

Time. Since the gate, Fare had felt the heavy, cloying presence of it. Phrases kept occurring to him. Killing time. Wasting it. Making it.

Bray pressed a buzzer. The receptionist stuck his scrivener's face in at the door.

"Inmate Mardis, see bout us two cups of coffee. Tell you what, go down and get some of that filter coffee from Rose in the quipment room."

"Yes, sir, Mr. Bray."

They waited. Fare kept his eyes from the glass, adjusted the flex of his shirt at his belt, tucked some of it back in to make his stomach seem flatter. Bray began pointing things out to him, bringing his eyes back to the glass walls. A hundred yards away stood the plant where the state's auto tags were made, and where, Bray joked, an average of two fingers a week were lost in the presses. "To hear these jarheads talk," he swept his hand at the school's population, "they's fingers dropping like pecans over there. That's the reason we get most of our students. Gets em out of the tag plant half a day."

To their left, across the oil-spotted road, was a machine shop. A tight rein was kept on it, Bray told him. "Things get made in there. Guns, bombs, you name it. We even had some men convert a forklift into a tank and crash the south gate. It was in the Gainesville papers. Course, now them tower guards got armor-piercing bullets, we won't see no more of that."

Mardis appeared with the coffee. "It's not the best, but it's the best in the joint," he said, mostly to Fare. He winked at them, leaving.

They sipped the hot coffee. Fretfully, Bray began flipping through the dossier. He seemed uncomfortable with paper in his hands, like a child who would rather play outside. For some reason, he seemed to find it difficult to begin the interview. He droned a series of polite, mostly random questions. "I see here you got German. I never could get languages. Had to go over to the College of Education to get by. Course I was playing ball at the time. Jew ever play ball?"

"Yes," Fare said. "Some."

Bray sat up. "Odum? Odum?"

His face seemed to come alight. He wrung his hands, and Fare noticed that the scars on the backs of them were full circles and half-moons. Cleat scars. Bray was concentrating fully now. "Odum," he muttered.

"What?" asked Fare.

"Didn't you play some ball out there at, what was it I read somewhere at . . ."

"I went to school at Isle Hammock."

"That's right. Back when they won them four state titles in the Class B. You must be that Odum that was . . ."

"No," Fare said. "That was my brother. Charles Ed Odum."

"That's it. That's the name I remember." Bray's face showed the familiar disappointment now.

"He was one of the real good ones," Fare said.

He imagined it was still the way they spoke of Charles Ed back home. They would stand around the fringes of the field, spitting tobacco juice into the grass, and one of them would say, "That one."

"Which one?"

"That one. There. That Baldry. Don't he remind you of the biggest Odum boy, Charles Ed?"

And another one would hitch up his no-roll waistband and say, "Kindly. He kindly does. With the way he puts his shoulder down real clean like that."

Then the first one would spit again and say, "That Charles Ed. Run right up the middle of your face. He was one of the real good ones."

They'd nod their heads, all up and down the fringe of the field.

Bray was staring into his coffee, clearly disappointed. It had seemed they had found it, the thing that would move the paper out of their way, but it wasn't to be. After a space, Bray said, "That brother of yours must of gone on to be something big at State or . . ."

"No," Fare said. Thinking, he didn't go on to be anything.

They sipped their coffee. Bray shifted uncomfortably. "It's a great sport, but they never tell you about being crippled for the rest of your life from these knees. I tell you when the weather goes wet for three days or more at a stretch I can't hardly walk. Get in there and knock that man's dick off they tell you, for the school, but they don't tell you about the arthur-itis for the rest of your Goddamned life . . ."

Bray stared out the window for a few beats, then repeated, in a more formal tone, almost to the word, the pronouncement Harkness had made about his qualifications, his area of specialization. "So, we're real happy you interested in us . . . surely are . . . state says we got to get qualified people . . ." His voice trailed off. He was an active man caught indoors in an act of convention.

Suddenly he smiled, and Fare could see that he had found

his way onto his own style again. With a jump of the corded muscle in his forearm, he flipped the folder aside like so much shuck.

"What we really want to know, Mr. Odum, is can you *run men*, because, see, that's what it really boils down to is whether or not you can strike a lick when you have to, if you know what I mean?"

"I uh . . ."

Bray's eyes bore in on him. They were amused eyes, rid now of the previous moment's clerical discomfort. They were the eyes of a man in his element. "Now, we have to ask a question like this. It just wouldn't be no good either of us, you *or* me, going through a lot of trouble for nothing, see what I mean, I . . ."

Fare said nothing.

". . . all right, I'll tell you a story. We had a feller in here to run the printshop not long back. He was a perfeckly good printer and he showed us a very good file, just like yours. Oh, he had been a printshop director all over from hell to breakfast, but Farel . . ." Bray leaned toward him, placing both his big hands flat on the desk. "Can I call you Farel?" Bray smiled and lowered his voice as though to talk dirty. "Farel, this feller was a weak stick. It's just as simple as that. And before too long, he had got himself into a blackmail scrape with some of the men in the printshop. You know we got some hard customers around here, some fellers that would just as soon as not cut half-inch washers off of your asshole, and they had just flatly told him to turn his back on some of their activities, and he was doing just that. They was printing contraband driver's licenses for sale; why they even run off some state paychecks before we got onto them. . . ."

"I can run men."

"I'm sorry?"

"I said, I can run men."

Bray's face clearly showed he was disappointed. Fare knew now that Bray had hoped to get rid of him with this story, had sized him up as one who would not answer the question right. Fare sat in the dumb shame of this realization, meeting Bray's eyes with his best "of course I can" expression. Bray took a deep breath, let it out. Again, he was a man beaten by the paper and the words. He could not now deny Fare's right to this position. Nowhere in the civilized structure of an interview, the two of them separated by desk and coffee and words, was there a way to acknowledge that a lie had been told. The papers and their qualifications had overcome the plain truth. In fact, if the papers had said that Fare had stood on the scarry surface of the moon and looked down at this place of imprisonment, Bray would have had to believe them.

"All right," Bray sighed, lurching up awkwardly on arthritic knees, extending his hand to squeeze Fare's. "We give you a try."

After a space, Fare coughed, and asked if he could get an advance.

THREE

FAR ACROSS FROM THE LAKE HOUSE, IN WHAT HAD BEEN Clare's father's peanut field, men were building houses. It was going to be called Blue Pines Estates. Intently, Fare watched the blending orange and yellow shapes of machines and stacks of lumber. A dust of diesel smoke and topsoil was climbing in the sky and it moved toward them across the lake. It rose and floated and fell to the water, and slowly as he watched, the sun moved down behind it. The machines died in single puffs of smoke, but the dust continued for some time to rise and float and fall.

In the pit of his stomach he knew this time of day. He had heard its names shouted, sighed and laughed in exuberance, exhaustion and bewilderment, muttered in the frustration of rain and black darkness.

It was the time of the afternoon when there was no more time, when there was a momentary fault in men's lives and in nature, when gears ceased shifting and wages were paid and the waking sounds of an immense anxiety could be heard. It was the time when work gave way to bittersweet languor and an accompanying listlessness which touched men with an intimation of the last day and the last wage. Reluctant to quit, too tired to continue, they looked forward to nothing but home, the night and taking up in the morning the long stretch of another day. Lying on the dock, Fare felt something of himself go out to the men who were quitting, out in search of the brief serious dusk meetings when he and his father and Charles Ed had debated whether more work could be done, what task could be fitted into the daylight that remained. She moved, intruding.

Next to him on the dock, Clare sat staring at the construction site. She sat with her legs crossed, her weight flowing to her hands and arms straight back from her shoulders to the hard planks. The way she sat, like the hard, tired country wife she might have become, caused her hip bones to protrude, and there was, he could see, a wonderful tension in the coarse cloth of her denim pants across her stomach and pelvis.

He had been driving the old road back, thirty minutes from the prison and his interview with Bray, when he had seen the cutoff to the home place. The fact that it had not changed, its very sameness, the buckshot sign: WELCOME TO ISLE HAMMOCK, the place where the state hard road gave way to the potholed county blacktop like a bloodline going bad, had made him turn. And when he had turned, he had found he had no place to go but here. And once here, he had found that he was curious to see her again. It had been a long time.

"When you start working out there?" she asked.

"Tomorrow." Perhaps he would ask her to let him sleep in the boathouse.

She stared resolutely at the sun and water, while he looked closely at her and was surprised again that something was wrong with her face. Her face was too round, but her woman's trick was to let her hair fall straight both ways from the center of her head, which redrew the shape of her cheeks, eliminating a small crescent on either side. It gave her a fine, long, Spanish face, this common woman's trick, and he liked it.

She had a scar high on her left forehead which looked, even from this distance of a few inches, like a piece of thin white thread laid in a saw-toothed pattern above her eye. She stroked it often, absently, turning it a swollen bluish red. He remembered when she had cut herself, diving into rocks at Poe Springs, how her father had rushed her to the plastic surgeon in Jacksonville, afraid her looks would be marred.

She raised her hand to it now, kneading it, tossing her head to let the sun at her from a better angle. Something in the way she did this took the ten years and swung them inward like a garden gate, and he felt himself stealing in again, upon tenured space.

She had been his brother's girl, yet they had shared her. Young as he had been, she had loved him.

"It sure enough is nice out here," she said.

"It *is*," he said.

With this she seemed for the first time that afternoon to know where she was and who was with her.

"We thought we could keep it for a while longer." She gestured toward the development. "But we can't."

She leaned forward and concentrated on the lakefront and the shimmering water just off the end of the dock.

"Well, maybe you'll move to somewhere just as good."

She stood and ambled out to the end of the dock and spat through her front teeth.

"I doubt it."

"Well, maybe you won't have to leave after all."

"Nope, Mom says."

She looked back at the house and quieted as though Mom might be listening. She sat down again in the same way and he watched as the denim resumed its tense containment of her stomach and the place below, where his hand had once seemed to fit. He wanted to touch it. Hurt it. He watched the mound beneath the cloth move with her breath. Then he stared at her and tried as people did with strangers, through the power of his eyes, to force her to turn the imperfection of her full face toward him. She refused to turn.

"Missed me much?" he asked.

"Some." The way she said it, it might have been a week.

"I'd like to think you missed me."

She looked at him, her lip curled down at the corner, her hands on her hips.

Quickly he said, "I don't suppose it matters much. The way things are."

He waited.

"At first," she said, "but not so much later."

"What about your mother? What does she think about this? I'll bet she still doesn't like me."

"She doesn't. She thinks we were wrong, behind his back

and all. And that you were after the wrong thing."

"I was. I was after it."

She turned to look behind them at the old house, saying, "She doesn't know I was after it too."

"Why didn't you tell her?"

"She ought to known. She's got one."

"It's going to be north of here, up by Live Oak," she began again, telling about the new house they would build. Her father was dead. A powerful man, Fare's own father's contemporary, he had left the two women, mother and daughter, pretty well fixed. But the old woman had not wanted to farm on the backs of hired help and so the sixteen hundred acres of peanuts were to become tract housing. The two women were moving into the middle of an old New Deal tree farm her father had left them. ". . . It's going to have three stories. Mom's room will be on the first floor. The kitchen and living room will be on the second floor and my room will be on top where I can look out at Daddy's old piney woods."

She stood again and walked toward the end of the dock, and then whirled and her face was so consciously formed to be happy that it seemed middle-aged.

"We're going to have a sundeck and . . ."

"What about Charles Ed?"

"What *about* Charles Ed? I told you I don't think about it."

"That's not what I mean."

It was too loud and he looked toward the house and disliked himself for looking. The habit. Why should the exhausted influence of her old mother, her family, bother them now?

"Well, what then?"

"Do you still . . . think about . . ."

"Yes," she said loudly. "Yes, I do."

Her face fell. He had chosen to remember her face as it had been ten years before, flawless save for the scar and still so young as to be not totally hardened into adulthood. Now there was this strange disjunction—her words youthful, her face and body, like his, changed. He could tell her what he planned to do. Maybe that was the reason his hands had turned the steering wheel this way.

She looked up at him now, with the age in her face. "You can't go with someone that long without feeling something. He loved me too. He was just too dumb to say it." (Charles Ed had not been dumb; he had been stubborn.) "He thought to say it would be some kind of giving in and he oughtn't to let it get next to him."

This should have made him feel a tiny triumph, but it only embarrassed him. This honest, colorless description of her feelings for his brother had always appalled, and yes, inflated him. But it was not a division he with his love had put between her and Charles Ed. It was merely a flaw, like a crack in some inaccessible window, that they could never repair. It simply was.

"He'd of hated you," she said.

"Let's be glad he never knew."

He looked out at the lake. He did not believe Charles Ed would have hated him. It was getting dark. Electric light set out against thieves at the construction site gestured softly toward them. It might have been moonlight. It was beginning to be cold. He nodded up the bank toward the house whose heart was her embittered mother. "Let's go into the house."

She said nothing, and so he said, "Here we are again."

"You came easier this way," she said. "I prefer it this way. Like it was secret."

"You always did."

"Piss!" She turned her face toward him. "You know we never had anything together. We could never do anything out in the open. God, how I'd wish just once we didn't have to hide, that we could just once take our time with each other."

Suddenly, she was on her knees. She reached out both hands to him, carefully touching the front of his shirt. She might have been dressing a doll.

"I tried to change it, didn't I? Remember when I asked you to take me to Fernandina down by the inlet where the lighthouse is? To lie out in the sun and drink beer and not

think about anything. Or wait till late and go back into the
dunes and have a fire. Promise me, I said."

Yes, she had said it. But they had both known he couldn't
see her, except as a friend, when the sun was shining.

He knelt too, taking her hands, but she was pushing words
across to him now, one at a time. "I was going along real
good," she spoke mechanically, her face pressed into his
hands, "not getting the letters. It was the letters that ruined
everything. I'd just stop thinking about you and then I'd
get one of those fucking letters and everything'd be ruined
again. You shouldn't of come this time."

"Do you want me to go now?" And he would have gone.
"Do you really want that? For me to stay away, I mean?"

"No, I'm sorry," she said. "I'd die if I didn't see you sometime. If you knew how many times I've nearly come. I don't
know what kept me from it."

He'd kept writing the letters from his furnished room,
sending them sometimes, not getting any answers. Sometimes
he'd written just to remind himself of things.

Theirs had been the last summer, the summer before his
trip with Charles Ed. He had been hired out on weekends
for wages on the new dock and boathouse her father was
putting in. It had been for extra college money. Her parents
had money: a farm and this lake place, boats. Her mother
was educated. She had been his brother's girl. She had started
with Charles Ed a long time back, in junior high when he
had been one of three ninth-grade boys to play on the high
school football team, and she, well she had been what goes
with that. And maybe because everyone expected it, she had
gone. And they had just continued, king and queen of dances,
club president and recording secretary, and more than once
Fare had seen his brother's car gathering dew on the river
road. There had been a kind of envy in Fare in those days
when he put her in the one category with all the other things
his brother possessed. And he felt a cold dislike for what was
possession and only that. But later she had got to be real,
come out of her glittery formal gown, even shed the seamy

smell of Charles Ed's back seat where the interior light was
painted blue. Something in him had made her do this; he could
never let go of that.

"Remember the time when you came down to where I was
working?"

He could have stood and walked ten steps to the spot.

"I just wish we hadn't wasted so much time. It seems like
we had a lot of time together, but really," her voice was full
of incredulity, "it was only just a few days."

He felt that she understood it again, that they could continue.

"Do you see," he said, "how I can spend so much time
remembering? I can rebuild all of it. I can even tell you
what we said, how we felt, and everything. We made promises,
do you remember that we made promises?"

She did remember, because now she pulled away. They
had been touching but now she was only beside him, cold on
the dock.

"I'm glad you've got that," she said, "because we'll never
have anything else."

"You've got it too."

He tried to draw her back.

"I've got to have more than that. That's why I want to
forget all of it. Remembering only makes me want more."

He tried something now, knowing that his time was gone,
and later, it was the only thing he regretted.

"Will you kiss me?"

It was cheap to ask. He should have taken it.

"No," she said, "I don't kiss anybody anymore."

"Sure," he said.

She stood and offered her hand down to him. She was a
big girl and her gesture was not token. He gripped her hand
and for a moment hung from the arc of her strong fingers.

"We'd better be getting back," she said. "It's cold."

"It is nice down here. I hate to leave." He was rising as he
said it. His hands had fashioned this dock and now the lake
was reclaiming it.

She looked out over the water as though estimating its worth. She turned and took the first step that made him follow toward the house.

She said, "I wish Mom could find a way for us to stay here."

"We'd better get back," he said.

They walked up the dock and he felt everything was gone and she did nothing to make it any different. They stood together under the eave of the back door and he shifted his weight around and made a perfect shoe print in the sand by the door. He wanted to tell her that the dunes were gone now just like the peanuts across the lake. He wanted to ask her to tell him she had loved him for himself, not as the part of Charles Ed, the gentle part, that had never existed. But they talked about nothing, and behind their mannered speaking he tried to understand it better, but could understand only that she wanted it over but didn't want to be the one to go in. It was her house and so he made himself go first, but only by giving himself the assurance that she would call him back.

When he had gone too far for any doubt, he turned and watched the eave light go out, and in a moment the bathroom light came on. For a long time he couldn't move and stood watching the glow of lights on the highway, feeling in his whole body the rumble of the big trucks, miles away on 27, highballing for Valdosta.

Then he remembered the night that had put the ghost between them.

He left her, glancing to the right and left and behind, cautious as though closing the gate upon a trespass, unable to shake the habit of his guilt.

FOUR

At the crossroads, Fare turned off the engine. He was nearly out of gas. It was still twenty miles to Gainesville, but even supposing he could make it, what then? He had no place to stay. He got out of the car and sat on the hood, smoking, watching the faint glow of headlights far off at the intersection of 129 and 27. The engine ticked as it cooled. He tossed away his cigarette and lit another. In the Isle Hammock sky some stars were bright and single, others creamy and distant in the band of the Milky Way. Shit, he thought, why not? and got back into the car.

When the headlights plied the columns of tall pines along the lane, and when he saw that the fences were down, their posts little more than stumps; when he heard the weeds rushing under the metal floorboards, he wanted to turn back, call it a bad idea. He had his damage fee, forty dollars. He could turn around, get to a gas station and from there to a night's lodging in Lake Butler. But a curiosity clutched his chest, a feeling close to exhaustion compelling him to look for rest where he knew it had once existed, to lie down in the bosom of the old house. He drove toward the looming shape of the house. He pulled into the circular drive, his headlights sweeping the porch, showing him the broken windows, the tattered screening hanging down from them as though blown outward by an explosion. They had used spray paint.

They had written: GEORGINA SUCKS, CALL 941-8892, CLASS OF 68, BITE ME. The old Belvedere thudded to silence. Through open windows he listened to the sound of the country night. It was like putting your ear to a seashell. The roaring of absolute quiet was penetrated only by the occasional lowing of a cow and the call of a whippoorwill. He reached out and cut the two long poles of light that flowed out in front of him, making the tops of the dog fennels blaze white, and glancing from the tin roofs of the old sheds diffuse into the darkness.

For a long time, he considered getting out, going into the house, kicking at the empty bottles of bay rum, the char of bums' fires, and the sexual refuse of high school kids, all the things that he knew now he would find inside. But he was afraid to go in, knowing that if he did, he would find himself driving again, curling the dust up behind the car, going as fast as he could go, maybe turning up at the prison in the morning, maybe not.

He opened the suitcase which lay on the back seat. He stripped to his underwear, tossing his trousers into the back seat and rolling his shoes in his shirt for a pillow. He would rise in the morning, do his best to clean up, and go to the prison. He lay down in the front seat, smoking, watching his breath as it clouded the window above him, obscuring the stars that glittered through the tall pine treetops.

When he awoke, the sky was dimly alight with a whiteness that made the stars brighter before dimming them. Soon, over the Gulf of Mexico, fifty miles distant, dawn would be a vague glow. He had to get cleaned up. He got out of the car, looked at the house for a moment, then stripped off his underwear and walked fifty yards out into the dripping dog fennels, where he stood shivering for a moment before turning to run back. He stood by the car, soaked, flecked with seeds, wiping himself with yesterday's shirt. He splashed himself with aftershave from the suitcase in the back seat, and dressed in clean clothing. He started the car and slowly drove the short distance from the house out to the secondary road, which gave way to the blacktop south to 27, north to Raiford.

On his left was the south eighty; in its center, the small knoll beyond which lay the pens where the sows had been put to make weight after farrowing. East, under the mushrooming tops of three tall live oaks, lay the little sinkhole. They had called it the dove pond because there they had waited for the doves at sundown. They had stood upright in the deep trenches cut by the hooves of cows coming to drink and shot the doves as they darted in over the knoll to water. He stopped the car and walked to the shred of fence, leaning on a corner post, cursing his wet trousers.

The drifts of ground fog broke like waves at the base of the knoll. For a long time, he stood watching, listening. A rain crow cried. The mist soughed. He felt a burning in his cheeks. He stood without moving until it seemed that he slept standing up by a fire of fat pine in the deep woods. The burning in his cheeks was permanent and good, and he watched the moment when daylight took hold of Mr. Drawdy's pines, dusting their tops with gold. As he turned to the car, he glanced back. The house sat awash in Johnson grass and dog fennels, their tasseled tops lapping at its windowsills. It looked a half-story high. Far off, down the long hollow of the red dirt road, cut like a ditch between high banks of brown weeds, he saw himself coming, still in the dark of the night, driving the old International pickup. Clare sat beside him in the front seat, close, probably holding his upper arm. The truck came on toward him, growing larger. Yes, it was him, was them making it home, but how had they gotten lost?

The truck drew abreast of him, rolling slowly on creaking springs, passing on to the crossroads where it sat idling while its two passengers, an old couple, turned fully around to look at the fool standing by the fence, his trousers darkened to the knee by the dew.

When the truck had passed on, he remembered it. Had he kept it, packed it? He moved quickly, not sure exactly what he was doing, to the back seat, opening the suitcase, rummaging in it. He found a packet of papers, tied with string, in a cardboard tube, his diplomas, three of them. He untied the string, his fingers aching. The string broke. He shuffled the papers, letters, receipts for stocks, finding it at last, folded once, nearly destroyed by time and carelessness. He smoothed it, but did not look.

When he stood by the car again, facing the house, he

looked at the photograph in his hand. Patina had taken it. She had insisted upon it. He stared directly at the picture, and then ahead, at the spot, transmuted by time, where it had been taken. The Odums had not been much for photographs.

They had double-dated that night, and Fare's date, Patina Carver, had brought her camera. They had gone to the party Clare's father had thrown for her birthday. She had been sixteen, Fare seventeen; Charles Ed, eighteen, was going to be a senior in the coming year. Patina had made them pause before getting into Charles Ed's car to drive to the lake. Fare had felt doubly uneasy at being photographed beside the matched set of his brother and Clare, and at being with Patina, who was more attached to the idea of dating Charles Ed's brother, the quiet one (you know), than to Fare himself.

FIVE

THE SHUTTER HAD SNAPPED, ENCLOSING THEM IN THE BLACK box, silvering their images to the film and now, ten years later, they stared out at him, confident in the meaning of that time and its purposes.

Charles Ed had driven a decent distance from the home place, passing the eighty where the old man bounced along at the controls of the crawling corn picker. Then he had reached into the glove compartment and pulled out a pint of Jack Daniel's Black. Fare had seen him do it, and had seen his eyes cross the mirror to check Fare's position in the back seat.

Then, the bottle came turning at him dark in the bright rectangle of the windshield, and he caught it as Charles Ed said, "Wanna kiss the baby a little before we get there?"

Fare held the bottle in his lap, and looked sheepishly at Patina who, only sixteen like Clare, and on her first date with him, stared straight ahead, terrified. Charles Ed's eyes were circling now regularly from the mirror to Fare's face and back to the road. The eyes were smiling as though to say, hell with her, Fare. Fuck them all and the horses they rode in on. Charles Ed was always carefree when he was running things, and so, to see him this way, be infected by his enthusiasm, it was always easier to let him have his head. Fare took the bottle up to his lips and sipped it.

"Come on, Fare," Charles Ed laughed. "Give us a seven-bubble swaller."

Fare bit down the hot, sweet whisky and narrowed his eyes to watch the bubbles break beneath his flared nostrils and jump up the neck of the bottle. At three he turned away from Patina to the window and gagged. He tossed the capped bottle back in the general direction of the front seat. Laughing, Charles Ed caught it backhanded while taking a curve at sixty-five. Without asking, he handed the bottle to Clare.

She took it, unscrewed the cap and tilted it up. The two had practiced this exchange. Fare glanced at Patina again. She held her right hand to her breasts and tapped her fingers there as though to locate the coffers of her virtue. Clare sucked at the bottle slowly, her Adam's apple bobbing. Fare counted seven bubbles. She lowered it, and lowered her head with it, wiping her mouth. When she turned to hand it to his brother, he saw the tears glistening in her eyes. A little of the brown liquid shone on her chin. She wiped the stray drop with a forefinger, and sucked it into her mouth. She watched Charles Ed lift the bottle now, and Fare could not, for some reason, take his eyes from her. A brightness came into the side window behind her shoulders, and her hair, leaping in the wind, caught it in rainbows. He had never before felt so compelled to examine another human being, so conscious of the framing of an event, of its appropriation to memory. In this moment, Clare was beautiful to him for the first time. She looked at Charles Ed with an appraiser's steady gaze, an expression Fare had seen at tobacco auctions. A little smile was operating at the corners of her mouth and then that crazy, dull-eyed happy look came into her eyes as the whisky began to take her.

Charles Ed had gotten off a seven-bubble drink easily, and then established ownership of the bottle, driving with one hand, sipping with the other.

"Give it to Patina," Clare said, her tone imperative.

"Huh, oh yeah, . . ." Charles Ed looked at Clare, his eyes examining her face for a hint at what she was doing. Watching his eyes in the mirror, Fare saw that he wasn't getting an answer.

Clare, not Charles Ed, was taking them somewhere now. Charles Ed passed the bottle back to Patina. She said, "Oh no, not for me." Her pale face flushed in blotches. She tried to hand it back to him, but his hands were back on the wheel. Clare, meanwhile, had turned and sat looking back at Patina, daring her either to refuse or to drink. Damned if you do, damned if you don't, the eyes said. Patina blinked at Clare;

her fingers fussed at her bosom. Fare watched Clare, seeing the hardening outlines of a woman's character. Clare was a full bottle holding an appetite and a certain cruelty; she was vessel of more than ten Patinas could hold in a lifetime.

Patina shrugged in a flouncy way, and lifted the bottle. Fare saw her stick her tongue up into it, let a little whisky into her mouth, making one bubble. Then, not quite stealthily enough, she spit the whisky back out as she lowered the bottle.

"Mmm," she said, barely able to stifle a gag. "Good!"

Charles Ed's eyes flickered in the mirror. Clare sat staring at Patina, and at Fare, her eyes cold and adult.

"Patina," she said, "shit or get off the pot."

"Well, I never!" said Patina, thrusting the bottle toward Fare, looking at him for some kind of support. He did not take it.

"Never, Patina?" cooed Clare, her arm draped languidly across the crown of the front seat, her fingers tapping at Charles Ed's shirt collar. "Not even once?"

Patina squirmed. "I'm sure I don't know . . ."

"Give it back, then." Clare held out her hand. Patina handed it to her. She raised it, looking directly into Patina's eyes, and made the bubbles jump up its neck again. She tossed it to Fare, who found himself drinking deeply, and watching her turn back to face the highway, a gold ribbon coming at them through a canyon of pines.

But not before fixing Charles Ed with an inquisitive stare. A red color crept into Charles Ed's neck and he did not return her look, only reached out his hand for the bottle. They rode awhile, lurching on the curves and enjoying it, and Clare turned back around to look at Fare, ignoring Patina as completely as if she were not there at all. He felt her eyes fasten to his, and he felt his head light with the whisky and felt warm inside, and he smiled at her before Patina reached for his hand, took it into her lap, and said coyly, "Let me tell your fortune, Fare."

At the lawn party, there had been a constant undercurrent

of whispering and the eyes came cutting at them as the word made its way among the cooler kids. The four of them had been drinking. And, of course, it was Patina who made the most of it, dropping into chairs after dancing, bringing the fluttering fingers to her throat and saying, "Man, am I blowed out!"

Whisky usually went into Charles Ed and came out loud talk and horseplay. Fare had liked him the few times before this when they had hit the bottle together. Tonight Fare noticed that Charles Ed avoided the adult chaperones, and that when he did come near them, he straightened himself up and tried to hold his breath. Clare simply did not care how she behaved. She seemed to forget she had drunk the whisky, and watching her, Fare liked this natural way she had of absorbing experience with only the evaluating that came through the appetite. She didn't dangle from strings of platitudes and Bible verses like the other girls he knew.

At sundown, her father came in from the peanut fields across the lake and, delighted to see that Charles Ed Odum had come to the party, walked up to him and asked if he'd like to come go look at the crop.

"Come on go look at the pinders with me, Charles Ed."

Charles Ed glanced at Clare. They had just finished dancing. She fanned herself and nodded to him airily. She didn't like it that her father could not disguise his approval of Charles Ed. Charles Ed plainly did not want to go, but he walked off to get into the pickup truck with the old man, who slapped him on the back a couple of times on the way and said, "You all got good pinders this year too, all bet?" Charles Ed kept looking away, either to Clare or to breathe in the other direction, it was hard to tell.

Watching it, Fare was glad he did not have to put up with such bother. Good pinders too? It was the polite thing to say, but everyone knew the Odums did not do well with peanuts. Charles Ed had to talk to old women about prices when he met them in supermarkets, and had to listen while they said, "Why don't you come on by and carry our Susan out some time?" He had to talk to the men about fertilizers and rain, and the new hog feeders you could get from Smedley with a special new patented feed release mechanism. He had to, because the men knew he was going to farm with his father, and he would have to get along with some of them to share equipment and pool labor. And because he was the running back who had rushed for seven hundred yards last season and who was converting to quarterback this year to lead the team to the Class B finals again. Fare had to admit Charles Ed held up under it well, even seemed to like it. It was a responsibility he bore for all the young men of the county.

When the pickup truck could be seen stopping in the field, a red smear in the dying light far across the lake, Fare looked for Patina, but she was nowhere in sight. He felt himself starting to lose the warm edge of the whisky. He wanted to get it back. Walking to the car, he found that his loneliness was diminished, not increased by Patina's absence.

When he approached the dark shape of the car, parked out in the front yard, someone who was bent over the seat on the passenger side straightened up at the sound of his footsteps and said, "Shit!" It was Clare.

"I can't find it," she said. "Did that yay-hoo take it with him off in the truck with Daddy?"

"Naw," said Fare, liking, yet not liking to be alone with her. "He puts them in the trunk."

"So nobody can steal them?"

"I reckon it's something like that."

He fished in his pocket for his duplicate key, and got out the bottle and they sat in the front seat watching the dark come on. Fare could hear the cows lowing off in the fields and hear the cicadas sawing away, and see the last of the doves darting in to water. Animals were so predictable. It was easy living off them, even when they were predictably hard on you.

They had been passing the bottle for some time and Fare had begun to hear their silences instead of the cicadas. Things had been comfortable at first, but now they were stiff in the silence. She turned around on the seat, resting her back against the dash. She couldn't have been comfortable. Her face was a white cameo in the gathering darkness with its soft, definite features. She leaned back stretching, her neck long and white.

"You're a lot like Charles Ed to look at, but different too. I think you got bigger eyes, and you know what?"

"What?" he asked, looking at her now, and taking the bottle from her.

"I think you're almost . . . pretty. You're almost too good-looking to be called handsome, with those big eyes and lashes most girls don't have, and the dimples you got in your cheeks." She laughed, and took the bottle back. She was enjoying herself, yet not at his expense. There was nothing caustic in her tone. For a moment he had thought she was going to go after him as she had gone after Patina, but he saw now that she was not.

"Almost?" he asked.

"Almost. That's what I said."

He nodded. What the hell, he thought. No girl had ever before said he was almost anything but a moron.

"You're not as hard in the face as he is, either."

She reached out and touched his cheek, then withdrew her hand. The way his cheek kept the hot memory of her fingertips was something he was not prepared for. They drank for a while with the silence coming in again. She sat facing him. At last she said, "Farel Odum," turning her head to the side like a puzzled cat. When she said it again, "Farel Odum," very slowly, her voice doing something rough and deep, the sound seemed to burn him too.

"Yes," he said, thinking, that's me all right, and I'm already tired of it.

"Whatever in the world are you going to do with yourself?"

"What do you mean, do with myself? I'm gonna do what everybody does, I guess."

It was a question he had asked himself, lately, finding he

could not break the habit of answers he thought would please other people. People didn't really want to know anyway.

"You mean farm?"

"What?"

"I said, do you mean you are gonna farm."

"Guess so," but he knew the farm could not support him too.

"Why?"

"Can't dance."

Her face went serious, or at least in the dark it seemed that way to him.

"Why don't you go on off and do something else?"

All the time now her voice was low, distracted as though something in her throat had tightened or maybe come loose. Inside him, the whisky was warming again now, and he felt the edge he had gotten before come back to him, and then pass on to be replaced by something infinitely more pleasant.

When he raised the bottle to take the next drink and felt her leg move to his, he was not sure she had done it. Perhaps he had shifted to her in the act of drinking. When their legs had touched, she looked away through the window so that, with his eyes, he could not ask her whose body had been responsible. To be safe, he shifted away from her. He did not know how long it had been now, since her last utterance. What had she said. Go away? Something about go away.

"Might have to." He cleared his throat. "Daddy says I'm about as much trouble on a farm as good. Fall asleep at the wheel, snatch up fifty yards of fence with the harrow. Did I ever tell you about that?" He could hear the unnatural high ring of his voice, yet he could not stop the flow of words. She shook her head impatiently. ". . . how I was harrowing, and got to woolgathering and turning around one time pulled up fifty yards of new wire before the corner post brought me up short?"

"No," she said, "and I don't want to hear about it. I've heard enough stories on you."

She looked at him with no particular expression on her face. She was not going to laugh with or at him. For some reason, she was bent on keeping this thing serious.

"Haven't you applied to any colleges?" she asked.

"You don't do that until about November of your senior year," he said.

"But you going to, right?"

"Magine. I guess maybe I could work my way through going part-time like Bobby Hayford did. But I don't think Daddy can give me anything."

Fare was beginning to sour on this topic. He didn't like to talk to her about money because her father had so much of it and his father had so little, yet it was there between them, an imperative, would always be there. He decided to change the subject.

"You act like you're trying to get rid of me."

It was almost black dark now, but the clouds above them still held some of the sun's reflected light. He had been told that these rays of light bent themselves as they traveled up across the top of the world. He thought he could see her chin drop to her breast and then come up. She moved and there was her knee again, firm and hot through the fabric of his trousers. He thought he heard the small click of her swallowing, yet he held the bottle in his own hand. Keeping the pressure at him, and looking at him, she reached for the bottle. Not with her hand and arm, but by leaning so that her hair swept past his face and the air that moved with it carried her scent to him. It was not perfume. It was the smell of clean skin and more, the scent of secret skin. He was stunned by it.

He said it again. "You act like you're trying to get rid of me," though he knew now, that for the future of a few moments at least, it was anything but the truth.

She drank and handed him the bottle. He raised it, but it was empty.

"Sorry," she said, shaking her hair, tossing more of the scent.

"That's all right."

The silence was pressing down again from the trees and from the clouds, which were blacker now than the air that floated them and vacant of even the hint of light.

"We better get back," he said, wondering about the time that had passed. He felt her knee stir. He had said the right thing, in a way at least.

She reached out and took the bottle from him. He looked at it.

"Come on, Fare," she said. "Kiss the baby."

He located her voice, low and rough, moving there in the territory between a taunt and a begging humbleness. It had rasped down so that it seemed she had almost sobbed, just then, and now her lips came toward him in the darkness—he heard them open as she drew breath before touching him.

She fell at him, pinning him against the door, her lips losing his, and then finding them, and her tongue coming into his mouth hot and tasting like the whisky and the secret skin. He pressed his own tongue hard against hers, and felt, when he had given it, hers soften and withdraw so that he had to seek it within her.

She had gotten one of her hands inside his shirt somehow, and with its nails she dug at the muscles of his back as though looking for connections, until he stiffened with the pain.

He did not know what his hands were doing, only that they were getting what they needed. When he heard her moaning, and the smell of her was all around them in the car, he came to himself, and broke from her, opening the door and stepping out, painfully aware of himself, tight and unfinished, standing before her.

She shrank back and then he heard her straightening herself. He waited for her, heard the snap of a waistband, but did not look down into the car, for fear he would violate her privacy. When she emerged, her face held the expression with which she had turned to Charles Ed, earlier, out on the road. It was the appraiser's gaze, and standing directly in front of him, she aimed it at him. They could hear the noises from the house. He thought he heard Charles Ed's voice among them, but was not sure.

"Am I all wrinkled?" she asked, looking at him with the look. It was as though he must now pass some test.

"Not too bad," he said. His voice came out a croak. His ears were roaring. The swelling had not abated. She, the cause of it, stood directly in front of him, tossing her hair, patting it.

"We'd better go back apart."

"Sure," he said. He watched her walk away, uncertain what had happened. Then she turned.

"What I said before," she said, "you know, about why don't you leave?"

He said he remembered it.

"Well, I just don't want you around here to make it hard for me. I'm going to have it hard enough as it is."

Then she was just a shape in the darkness, walking erect and taking the big strides she always took. After a space, he saw her emerge in the floodlit backyard, moving across the lawn surely and without haste toward the heart of the dance.

Headlights bore up the driveway at him, and he heard the sound of the radio, then Charles Ed's voice, followed by Clare's father's, "Then, he says to me, sure I will, if you will too! . . ."

The last of it was drowned in laughter.

Fare closed the car door quickly to obliterate the light. He stepped into the darkness behind a tree, and watched as the truck passed. He could still smell her. He lifted his hands to his face and she was on them. He stood in the yard listening to the sounds of the cicadas, the cows, the hogs clattering at the feeders. The trucks on the highways, far off, the near and the far. He thought about what she had said to him.

Why don't you go on off and do something else?

When he walked back into the party, feeling like a criminal under the harsh lights, he learned that no one had noticed his absence. He learned, from Patina, who smiled wickedly at him and motioned to the open door, that Clare had gone off with Charles Ed. You know.

SIX

FOR A LONG TIME, THERE WAS NOTHING. FARE ASKED HIM-
self why. The answer always came accompanied by a memory
of the party and the way he had felt when she had left him
in the yard with the secret smell of her on his hands, and gone
off with Charles Ed. A woman who could do that, he reasoned,
could do anything, and so he did not trouble himself about it
much. Remembering it this way helped him when he thought
of what he had done—to his brother. She had made it happen,
he told himself, and it would not happen again. She could not
make it happen again, not and go off like that after.

He did not avoid her, nor, as far as he could tell, did she
avoid him, but he did not see her much. When the summer
after his graduation came around, and he learned from his
father that he would have money for school, he hired out on
weekends to help build the boathouse and the dock her father
was putting in, and he knew he would see her. They had both
changed. He wondered how it would go, and the more he
wondered, the more he anticipated it. He found that she was
never far from present in his mind. His imagination wrote out
a thousand stories. All of them began when she came down
to the lake to swim and he was there working. They would
look at each other in these stories of his, and his eyes would
say, "Let me see you." Hers would look back at him, "Yes."
It would be the yes which came from the strange appetite.
This was the way he dreamed it, and this was exactly the way
it happened.

Later, he told himself it was foolish to believe that he had
caused it to happen this way by the power of his imagining.
Later, he explained to himself that she and Charles Ed had
been coming apart for a long time.

The football season had been a great success, indeed all of

Charles Ed's senior year had gone as they had expected and better. But the end could be seen coming almost from the beginning of that year.

After graduation, Charles Ed had gone to work on the farm, picking up the slack after the corn blight, and he had done well at it, though he missed the attention he no longer got. When the football season got underway, Fare stood in the middle of the field and watched his brother roam the sidelines with his hands shoved deep into the pockets of his letterman's jacket, a dark scowl on his face. From the field, kneeling with the others in a circle while the Gatorade was passed around and the cheerleaders boomed with the band, he could hear his brother complaining about the team, about the way these new boys played, about their losses, wishing himself one more year.

And watching them lose game after game, there were many people on the sidelines who wished Charles Ed that year too. But there were also those who noticed how shrill he was becoming in his criticism, though he always had praise for his brother Farel. They noticed, too, how often he showed himself in public places with the smell of whisky on his breath and the warp of it in his speech. The year that weaned Charles Ed away from school was not a very good one, and through it all Fare did his best to help, always telling his brother how much they could have used him, drinking with him even though he risked suspension from the team, and bringing him home late from the roadhouses when he could not drive.

Fare graduated from high school at the head of his class of twenty-four, with a sense of hope for the time being, aiming himself at the coming prospect of college. He could think of little he would miss when he left the town and his classmates behind.

Charles Ed and Clare made an engagement. There was an engagement party, and much was made of it in the local news, and once again, Charles Ed was the young man to watch. But the engagement did not last long. It was quietly broken off. They told no one, just called it quits, and put off the time when they would tell about it. Fare had not known himself, until he discovered the ring in his brother's glove compartment while looking for a cigarette.

"What's this?"

"It's at ring I got for her, you know, to get engaged. She give it back."

"What's it doing in here?" he asked.

"It's about as much use now as tits on a man," Charles Ed said. He spoke slowly and without hint of rancor. But there was a fatigue in his voice Fare had not heard before.

Charles Ed and Clare still clung to each other that summer, and when Fare went to work on the dock, Clare was still, in the eyes of their parents and the town, engaged to his brother. But Charles Ed was seeing less of her and more of the Jacksonville women.

One day when Fare was working by himself on the boathouse, as in his dreams, she had come down to the water. The old man he worked with, whose knowledge her father had bought with Fare's muscle, had gone off to pick up a shipment of storm clips, leaving Fare to nail shingles. Later, she told him that she had seen the old man go, and had left the house, knowing it was time, and had walked to the sound of his hammer. She said it was something she had made up her mind to do that night two years before, the night of her sixteenth birthday.

He turned to see her entering the water beneath his ladder. He had been thinking about her, and so now, he thought his imagination had done this in the glare and exhaustion of the work. The sun wrapped her in pieces of broken mirror and he was blinded. So he dropped the hammer into the sling at his waist and turned around leaning back to wipe his eyes on his sleeve.

She was still there, in the flicker of the ripples, walking slowly with her arms held out to the water in an attitude of embrace. She wore a lime-colored bikini. The water made dark patterns on the fabric of the bottom, moved up her torso, lapped at her halter buoying her breasts. When she reached a depth so that the water lifted her breasts, beading at her neck, she took flight in a strong breaststroke and floating, she turned toward him. Something large and coarse like sawdust filled his throat, and he knew that he would not be able to speak. But he looked at her, his eyes naked with the message in them. And she gazed back at the place where he clung to the ladder. Her eyes said their yes.

On his way out that night, carrying his tools, he walked past the downstairs kitchen window, straining to locate her through the screen. She was sitting at the kitchen table husking corn.

"When?"

"I'll come out to the hard road tonight at eight. You be there, can you?"

"Sure," he whispered, and watched her, vague through the window screen, as she turned away to work at the corn.

When the filmy white of her dress moved in the moonlight at the edge of the road, he pulled over and pushed the door open to her. Then a gust of her smell mixed with the smell of the night, and she slid across the seat, not stopping until she was annealed to him, and holding his right arm.

"Where to?" he asked, looking back up the lane toward her house.

"Oh, anywhere," she said. "It doesn't matter. I like to just drive sometimes."

They drove along the moonlit backroads, going nowhere while she held his arm tightly and rested her head on his shoulder for spaces, then took it away, and all he noticed was the warmth that crossed to him so delicately and the way her smell changed with the wind whispering at the vents.

He did not try to touch her. He did not want to just yet. What he wanted to do was let himself be baffled by the act of driving and the strobic play of the headlights down the rows of pines, and to feel the way her hands appraised him. She touched him as he had never been touched before.

When her hands moved on him, he could feel the honest need in them, and the knowledge of him that was passing to her through her fingertips. She wanted to feel him. He realized how little he had been touched in his life, how much of it had been pure collision, just rough handling of one kind or another, how his skin seemed like something put on new when she touched him this way. In fact, that night, and many nights after, he felt a violence in her hands. Would she have tried to force her hands upon him, had he resisted them? He imagined them struggling this way, sometimes, and the image of it, the inverseness of it, gave him pleasure. Yet he did not feel flattered. He might have, had he not felt too much like the book she was reading out of compulsion.

He did not know how long they had driven that night, aimlessly, sliding on the powdery, drifted surfaces of these back roads, when suddenly she said, "There. What's that?"

He slowed the car, focused his eyes beyond her outthrust arm toward a dark hulk under the lee of some oak trees about two hundred yards from the road. It looked like an old house, but it might have been some kind of shed. At this distance, it was difficult to tell in the dark.

There was something familiar about the place. He took her hand, and they got out of the car together on his side, and the smell was gone suddenly into the night. They walked a little way toward it. Then he saw the small, twisted shape of the old cane press that had been his great-uncle Bates', and he knew that they had driven nearly fifty miles, to the north and east toward the Osceola National Forest. This place had been his uncle's, a man he remembered vaguely from childhood— who smelled like blackstrap molasses. The land, and the house, he was certain, were still in the family somewhere, though he did not know exactly where. Perhaps his mother had inherited them.

The front door resisted them, so Fare walked to the back and entered by raising the only window sash that still slid in its tracks. The door had been nailed shut from the inside, but he was able to pry it open to let her in.

Their eyes adjusted slowly to the darkness as they stood in the middle of the room. She was leaning against him. He placed his arm around her shoulders. When they could see, she separated from him and walked slowly around the room, stirring the debris on the floor with her toes, picking up things, snuff cans, drinking glasses, from the counter tops. He watched her, wholly absorbed in the way her body moved, separate beneath the filmy dress. He enjoyed the brassy way she took over this dead space.

They entered a side room. There was a bed, hardly more than a pallet. Seeing it, Fare hoped what he wanted to know could be separated from what he did not want to know. He decided they would go soon. There would be plenty of time, and he could sort things out. She walked to the bed and tested it with her hand, then slapped it to see the dust cloud up. She sat, and removed her shoes. Then she lay down, and beckoned to him, with the motion of arms she had used earlier walking into the water. He sat beside her on the bed.

"Aren't you going to ask me?" she said. He thought her teeth flashed briefly in the darkness. He looked down at her, the outline of her face definite yet shifting, temporary there in the darkness, her white dress luminous on the dark coverlet of the bed.

"Ask you what?" he said, thinking she meant to do it.

"Ask me why I wanted this place, for us to stop here when we passed."

"Why?" he asked.

"Because we have to have a place, and this is a good one. I knew when I saw it. No one is around, and it's dark and quiet, and it smells good, like the woods have come inside."

All he could say was yes.

"And because," she said, her voice changing, "I want to lie down with you and feel you inside me."

He touched her face, tracing her lips with his crude fingers, and it was impossible to know their shape. With his fingers, he closed her eyes. She took his hand in hers and slowly drew it to the place on the plane of her prone body where the small mound rose between her hipbones. She laid the hand there and held it, pressing down, and moving against it from below in a lost, animal way that dazed him a little.

"Fare," she was saying, "do you know what I mean?" She moved against the hand.

He shook his head, dazed. "I'm sorry," meaning that he had not heard her.

"I said, do you know what I mean . . . I want you to be inside of me."

"Yes," he said.

"Can we then?" she asked, her voice wandering again in a country close to desperation as it had that night, almost two years before in the front seat of his brother's car. She was pressing hard against his hand. He took the hand back and made her stop the pressing and began to unbutton her dress.

"Shhh," he whispered like a father. All the while she kept the movement which had begun beneath his hand. She could not stop.

There was not room for them side by side on the narrow pallet. When he stood above her naked, she lay naked, a gift reaching up to him. He paused before going down to her, to keep the moment, lay hold of it forever, before the secret smell enveloped him.

"I'll help you," she said. In her impatience, she was touching herself. His hands began to find the places. It was all mad. She was moving faster. He had never guessed it meant you lost the loneliness.

"You haven't ever, . . ." she said, a kind of sigh.

But he knew that he should cover her mouth with his, and say into the dark hollow of her throat, "No."

And not ask.

SEVEN

ONE DAY, A FRIDAY AFTERNOON IT WAS, HE AND CHARLES ED were working together in the fattening lot. They were building nursery pens for the shoats. Charles Ed had been to a swine convention in Gainesville, and had come back with the idea to build small, movable, sheltered pens to keep the pigs together after weaning, keep them up off the cold ground and concentrated at the new Smedley feeders so that they would make maximum growth before going to the topping pens, at eighty pounds or so. Charles Ed was coming up with a lot of new ideas. He seemed to be warming to the task of comanagement with the old man. Fare had begun to think that the place might come up again, recover from the state it had gotten into after the corn blight.

Charles Ed had always worked hard. All of them had, though it had always been understood that schoolwork must get done. Now his brother worked almost furiously, achieving sometimes in labor the heights of physical inspiration he had achieved in athletics. Fare marveled at him as he always had. Working alongside him, that last summer and into the fall, he had felt the old awe of his brother's quick wit and the old respect for his brother's body, for what it could do. Often as they worked, Fare found himself in the position of the feeder, feeding his brother the necessary materials and tools while Charles Ed created something, or fixed something, always operating at the pace which took him near to danger or to exhaustion, but never crossing the line. It was the old balance. Watching his brother work, Fare felt that he would never lose it. He would always be a spectacle—something for people to stop and marvel at.

The sun was lowering over the live oaks. A pillaring thunderhead in the west hung its blue arms of rain as it marched toward them. Fare knelt, positioning the warped cypress slats as his brother nailed them straight to the floor of the pen. He could feel the small rushes of wind on the sweat of his bent back. He could sense the far-off coldness of the rain with its ozonic smell of high altitudes and lightning, and in it, the faintest promise of winter. Charles Ed felt it too. He straightened, dropped the hammer abruptly and dug into his shirt pocket for a sodden pack of cigarettes.

Fare watched as he found the pack, searched in it for a dry one, then, disgusted, shook them all out into his hand, fingering them around like a man looking for correct change. It was a scene Fare had seen a thousand times. It was one of a thousand like it which would always be the definition of his brother. All around the farm, you could find the crumbled piles of cigarettes from the times Charles Ed sweated them to ruin and then stood, as though discovering for the first time what sweat would do to paper and tobacco, shaking his head in mild disbelief and asking somebody else for a smoke.

"Fare, you got any them pussy cigarettes you smoke?"

Fare got up from the nursery pen floor and walked to the tractor and retrieved a pack of Winstons from the toolbox. Charles Ed reached for one with an expression of distaste on his face. He smoked Picayunes or, in a pinch, unfiltered Camels, and felt himself violated when he had to settle for less. Which was often.

When Charles Ed could not find his lighter and had smeared his fingers red with a wet book of matches, Fare lit them both up with his own lighter. Charles Ed sat by him smoking, breathing more slowly and with his sighs, spitting out sweat and smoke. They watched the weather.

"We better get these power tools back to cover. It's gone rain like a cow peeing on a flat rock," Charles Ed said.

But they sat resting. Fare was a little surprised that Charles Ed wanted to quit. They could nail up a few more slats and work until the rain actually caught them. This was the usual procedure. You worked until forced to stop by some natural barrier like darkness, rain, or, if it were severe enough, a sickness. When it rained on you or darkness fell, you stumbled and groped your way back to shelter secure in the knowledge that you could not have struck one more lick. It was his brother's style.

Charles Ed reached for a couple of two-by-fours, which he wrapped in an empty nail apron. He lay back, resting his head upon the two-by-fours and crossing his legs.

"We had purty good tobacco?" He looked over at Fare.

"Sure did," nodded Fare, smoking.

"Not a brag crop, but purty good, and it got us through them sorry peanuts. An I think things is looking up with the fences and the pens now. If we can go . . . I mean if Daddy and me can go on at this pace to this time next year, we can be looking a lot better. You think we ought to rent them allotments that Patina's daddy got up for sale? Say, Fare?"

Fare watched the doves getting up in dark blots before the thunderhead, flying half a mile in their small, darting formations, then dropping to wait for the next scare. He smoked, wondering how it would go around the home place with him gone, with the old man fading into the religion, with his brother taking over.

"If you can get the labor to cover it, and if *you* can run it, and run *all* the rest too."

Fare realized that he had come down hard on the word "all," when he had said "run all the rest." Now Charles Ed looked over at him.

"You think Daddy's gone go on and slide, don't you?"

"I reckon he is. It looks like it to me."

Charles Ed took a deep drag on the cigarette, letting the smoke drift out of his nostrils and between his teeth. He was smoking too much, lately. Not eating enough, drinking too much. His coloring was not good.

"I don't know whether to get on him about it or not. If I do, he could get righteous and come out here and take over and I wouldn't have the leeway I got now. And if I don't, I ain't got no help, and I don't like the way it does him, you know, the way he don't seem to care about nothing but . . ."

Charles Ed nodded his head abruptly toward what was above them, heaven, or the thunderhead marching toward them out of the Gulf of Mexico, the live oak trees pinwheeling their leaves green, then silver with the cold wind from the storm.

It was time for Fare to say something. But he was thinking about decisions, and about how once they were made, time on the other side of them just seemed to run downhill. It would back up on the nearside so that it seemed you waited half your life, then when the decisions were made, it gushed from the gates and took you with it.

He was going off to college. He did not feel so much a part of all this as he had once felt, and he did not want to make a mark on Charles Ed's plans that he could not be held accountable for. Yet he sensed his brother's need to know what was in his mind.

"I don't know, Charlie," he said. "You don't want to forget how much it means to him to have you around, taking an interest in things like this. You don't want to say anything to bust on that."

"No. That's right. I don't. That *is* right."

They smoked in silence for a while. He had just said to his brother, "Go it alone. Without me." They both knew it. He could feel the grasp of the future gathering up all of the marks he had made upon this place, and moving them out of his reach. He felt suddenly the same strange loneliness he had felt one day as a child when he had wandered out into the fields seeking his father. He had come upon a place whose familiar formations of trees and brush he knew he had passed moments before. He looked down to see his own footsteps. But their toes were pointed toward him, not away, coming out of the distance to the spot where he stood. He had panicked. The farm had seemed enormous, larger than the world; he would never find his father, or the way home. It was as though his entire history, the pitiful small mark he had made in his short life, had been reduced to the sum of what lay here before him, the difference between the last print facing east and the last facing west.

He sat down then and cried, he did not know how long, until he began to look more closely at the footprints coming at him, and saw that they were not his, but his brother's, slightly larger, and he knew that to find his way, he must only turn around and follow his own outward path. The sense he had felt then, seeing his brother's footprints covering his own, both of estrangement and reassurance, returned to him now. Soon, there would be no more of his footprints, no more of his marks.

"You gone come back and help me out summers. At least I can count on that."

"Yes," Fare said. "Count on it."

And he knew that it was true. He would be at his brother's disposal for weekend emergencies, and for the long, sticky, dawn-to-dusk seasons of tobacco, and for dusty, hot days and nights picking corn by headlight on the John Deere gleaner, and into peanuts, driving the wagonloads of green pinders to the shed for air drying. He would be labor. But when the corn was all in the dryers, half of it hauled off to the Lake City scales, the tobacco auctioned, and peanuts gone, he would leave. So, there would be no more of this, of what they were doing right now, no more of it for him. When it came time for the hog pens, the mending of fences, he would always be gone. He would be like the other boys, a few of them, who went to the university. Gone when the slack-up came at the end of August. He took pride in laying the future out ahead of himself so that he would be with them for the hardest times at least. But also, he knew he was approaching the flood-gate and that time, going past, would run hard.

Charles Ed lurched up suddenly, a look of mischief on his face. It was the old look from the wild, lamplit nights in the huddle when he would come up with a new play to get them out of a tight, would draw it with his finger right in the dirt while the coach tore his hair on the sidelines. Now he reached out and forearmed Fare on the shoulder. "Let's get a beer," he said, looking up at the storm. "We earned it."

They jumped into the big John Deere tractor, pulled the

trailer loaded with power tools and hardware to the nearest lean-to shed, and climbed into Charles Ed's car to head for the gas station-grocery.

When they had the beer and sat again in the car, enjoying the first long, sweet pulls that swept away the day's work, they realized that they had no particular place to go.

Neither of their parents tolerated drinking. The community they lived in made no differentiation between occasional drinking and drinking to excess, because the one always led to the other. Both of them had discovered the pleasures of drinking only recently, much later, they knew, than city kids. To their parents, the city was still a bad place. Its excesses had always been held up to them in the form of newspaper clippings, what could happen to them if they were not careful. Still, most of the men and many of the women in the town drank. The cardinal sin was not drinking, but drinking in the open.

They made it their practice to go off to the banks of a little creek that trickled into the Suwanee River about twenty miles from the farm. They had made a considerable pile of beer cans and empty pints and fifths on its banks and they both liked to think of the pile growing as a silent insult to the morality of the town. But Charles Ed had been getting bolder, lately, with his drinking. He was on the verge of doing what the town called "breaking bad."

As they drove now toward the creek bank, Fare could hear it going up the aisles of the supermarket and down the pews of the church. "That Charles Ed Odum done done hit again. Broke bad. I just known he would after he got his head bigged by all that talk about him being the greatest football boy ever around here. I just known it would go to his head. You can't make that much ruckus over a youngun, and him not turned twenty-one yet, and expect no different, can you?"

"Lord no, why my Tommy . . ."

They backed the car to the edge of the creek. Far off they could hear the rush of it making its meeting with the Suwannee River. They could hear the grind of machinery going home for the evening ahead of the rain. Charles Ed opened the trunk and found a half-empty pint of Jack Daniels, and poured a liberal dollop of it into his beer can, swirling the mixture absently in his hand. He held the bottle out to pour Fare's can too, but Fare covered the top with his palm. Charles Ed was getting that look in his eyes and Fare was already thinking about staying sober enough to drive.

When they had each tossed two cans onto the pile before them, the rain came splashing down through the branches to dot the fast surface of the creek. They watched for a while, then climbed into the car. They left the windows open, hanging bare arms out in the cool rain.

At length, Charles Ed said, "You got any more of them queen-sized cigarettes you like to smoke?"

Fare searched his pockets, then remembered he had left the pack in the tool kit of the tractor. He said as much.

"Might be some in the box there," said Charles Ed.

Fare opened the glove compartment. Its latch popped, surprising him. The ring jumped out, landing between his feet on the floor. He reached down to pick it up.

"What's this?"

"It's at ring I got for her, you know, to get engaged. She give it back." His brother's face closed up like a trap.

Fare should have shut up.

"What's it doing in here?"

"It's about as much use now as tits on a man, Fare. S'as good here as anywhere else, ain't it?" The voice was slow, uncharged.

"There ain't any," said Fare, after a space.

"What?"

"There ain't any cigarettes in here."

Fare looked off into the rain and wondered why she had not told him about breaking the engagement. Oh, he had noticed she never wore the ring, but he had thought it was just to keep it from reminding them. She never talked about Charles Ed. She tried, he could tell, not to use what she had learned from him. She tried always to come to him as though her knowledge of it had begun and now grew only with his.

But sometimes her hands or her mouth betrayed what she knew. He wondered why she had not told him. To him, it could have meant asking her to see him openly. Maybe this was what she feared. He did not know what it meant to her. She still saw his brother, though less and less frequently, and she still kept these two halves of her life separate from each other.

Fare shoved his finger around in the litter of condoms in their bright plastic packages and gum wrappers in the glove compartment.

"Not a single one," he sighed. He wished they could go home, but knew that Charles Ed had not yet reached even the halfway point. Soon he would begin drinking from the bottle.

They sat in silence, as the rain thrummed above them. It was like rain on the tin roof of Uncle Bates' old house up in the Osceola Forest. He had been with her there in storms like this. He lay back on the seat, waving his arm out the window in the rain, and letting the cold and the beer bring goosebumps to his chest and throat.

She had sat, that day two years before, a gift and a trap, directly opposite the spot where he sat now. She had leaned back against the dashboard in the near-darkness, and the prominent shapes of her breasts had moved with her breathing, parting the buttons of her shirt at each breath. She had been his brother's girl, younger than he, but somehow much older, sure of herself, seeming to know what she wanted and willing to risk loss to get it, and in one or two minutes she had made the change, taking him into it with her. The change had confused things so completely. And only he seemed to be confused. She did not let on if she was. She came to him as often as possible, her need for him seeming endless and growing rather than diminishing. And Charles Ed did not know, only knew that he had lost something, and could not divine how or why. Yes, Charles Ed was a little confused too, and his answer to it was resting in his hand. He was drinking from it now, and only taking a little beer after, as a chaser.

Absently, he handed it over to Fare. Fare took it, asked himself whether he wanted to go the distance this time or not, and at last fell into step with his brother, taking a long pull.

He looked down at his hands. He still held the ring. Gingerly, he placed it back in the glove compartment. But Charles Ed heard the small sound it made on the metal.

"Give me that," he said, his hand in front of Fare's face, unequivocal.

Fare put the ring into the hand.

Charles Ed was out of the car quickly, and walking at an even pace back toward the creek. Fare jumped out into the cold rain, not sure why he had to watch. He saw Charles Ed's arm cock itself, then the beautiful snake-flick of corded ligament and bunched muscle, and then saw the briefest glint as the ring flashed yellow before striking the surface of the creek with a hundred raindrops.

Back in the car, steaming from the rain, Charles Ed said, "That felt good. Goodest I've felt in a long time."

Fare said nothing. He thought of the money briefly and of Charles Ed regretting it later, but he knew immediately that there would be no regret. The ring was flowing toward its conjunction with the river and the river was sweeping for the Gulf and Charles Ed and Clare were fast now past the gate and into forking futures. Charles Ed turned to him.

"You know," he said, taking a full swallow from the bottle and neglecting the chaser. "She would of been a good woman if I could got her to marry me, long back, when she was fifteen or so. You know, like they used to around here. Like Daddy and Momma?"

Fare nodded, listening, but sure that Clare already had been herself at the age of fifteen, or very nearly so. She would not have consented.

"Course, it would of been impossible to go to high school and all that and be married, but Fare, I got the idea some time, awhile ago, that she was moving off in her head, you know like she does, getting away from me somehow . . ."

Words failed. They faced each other. Fare's cheeks were

growing hot. He sat thinking that he did, did know very well where Clare had been going, where her mind had taken her. But he did not know why.

"She was always a good-time girl, Lord knows . . ."

At this, they both smiled, each of them remembering the break-bad things Clare had done and gotten away with because her father's money made her behavior near unimpeachable. Drunk, she had stripped naked and dived into the Suwanee River from the bridge the night of the senior prom, not once, but twice, and had to be restrained from doing it a third time. And it had been Charles Ed, embarrassed at her nakedness, scared of his own drunkenness, worried about what others were thinking, who had thrown his white tux coat over her to make her stop. Fare had stood by, happy to let her go ahead, knowing her dives were charmed. She had never looked more beautiful to him than she did that night, standing slightly pigeon-toed on the bridge, water streaming from her long hair onto the shoulders of Charles Ed's rented jacket. She had tilted up a beer can, spilling half of it across her chin and winked at all of them standing around her, "All right, shitasses, I'll quit." He had saluted her.

It was the way he always was with her. He sensed it was what she wanted from him, to let her (how could he have stopped her?) take them places. The appetite always held them both in its embrace. It was a powerful and fascinating thing to him, with instincts behind it. She had looked at him that night, and her eyes said she was in it, in the time on the far side of her decision, the one she had made for both of them. Time, taking her, had long ago rushed past the gates, pulling him along too.

"You know, Fare," Charles Ed was saying, "she always liked you a lot. She always would ask me about you. Why didn't we see you more often. How were you doing. What was you plans and such. You know what she said to me once?" Charles Ed looked a little sick now, but playful too with the whisky getting into his voice, and his body suddenly shifting toward Fare on the seat. The red in Fare's face held firmly.

"What?"

"She said . . ." He took another drink, and wiped his mouth on the wet work shirt. "She said that the two of us got . . . how did she put it? She said the two of us . . . had come from the run-down end of the Odum line and you got too much of something and I got too much of something else, and it would of been better to start all over and just try to make one, not two, from the . . . what was the word she used . . . from the remnants, no the *leavings*."

He looked at Fare now, as though for an interpretation. There was hurt vanity in his eyes. But his face, tired, wet, salt-encrusted, getting more like their father's face all the time, said he would suffer an explanation if one were forthcoming.

"Well, what do you think?" Fare asked. "Was she right?"

Charles Ed said, "I'd know if I knew what she meant by it."

"I don't know. I mean, I can't be sure. . . . She's your girl, not mine. . . ." (Later, Fare remembered this statement and regretted it.) "But I think she meant that I'd been a better man for it if I stayed here and you'd been a better man if you left. If we could do both, I mean."

Charles Ed said, "She said she wished you would leave. Feature that."

Fare stared out the window at the rain. "I don't feature it. Cept I guess it's a wish granted."

They were both a little drunk. Charles Ed stared fixedly through the windshield at his own memories, puzzling, swirling the whisky in the bottom of the bottle.

"Not much left."

For a moment, Fare thought he meant with Clare, or with the two of them, or even in all of it, the farm; he could have meant so many things, but he was taking his last drink from the bottle, careful to leave some for his brother.

"Gone now," said Fare, a moment later, smiling weakly and tossing the bottle out the window toward the pile on the creek bank.

Charles Ed sat up, reaching for the ignition key. Then he

got out to piss, shivering, small, hurrying in the rain. Back in the car he said, abstractedly, "I never known what she wanted." He stabbed the key into the ignition. The car's glass-packed muffler boomed in the dripping woods. "Sometimes I think it should of been the both of us that had her. She could of just about handled two. I just never known."

Charles Ed looked over, smiling to show that it was a joke, but Fare knew it was no joke, and he hoped the way he nodded and laughed out the window would not tell his brother that he knew it.

Charles Ed concentrated on the rough, stump-riddled track that led from the creek bottom back onto the hard road.

"I'll say one thing," he said, after a mile or so. His hands left the wheel and groped the air as though to trap some last word. "She was sure a whole bunch of woman."

"Was," thought Fare.

The next day, hung over and cursing the heat, they finished the nursery pen. It was noon. They stood, smoking, looking off to the darkening west for the relief of another storm.

"All done but the welding," Charles Ed said.

"You can do that, can't you?"

"Naw, . . . well, I might take a running jump at it, if you don't mind me fucking it up a time or two."

"Shit, try it," Fare said. "I'll help you."

After dinner they walked back out to the sheds to ready the arc-welder.

As they walked, Charles Ed produced a magazine. He had been reading it before dinner, and he picked it up again from the table. Fare heard him rummaging in the dark recesses of the shed for the welding rods, then heard a loud thump and a curse, "Shit fire!"

Charles Ed came stumbling out into the sunlight. Fare knelt reading the instruction booklet for the arc-welder. Charles Ed was rubbing a blue welt on his forehead. The welt was getting larger.

"Shit fire and save matches!"

"Notch your head?"

"I reckon."

Fare was turning back to the welder.

"Look here, Fare."

Charles Ed stood in front of him, holding out the magazine, cover first, to reveal the headline. DISCOVER AMERICAN THUMB TRIPPING. There was a picture of some hippie-looking fucker wearing an Army surplus backpack and holding out his thumb at the edge of the road. In front of him stood a girl. She was a beautiful girl, and Fare could not help noticing how much, with her dark eyebrows and the intensity of her stare, she resembled Clare. She stood somewhat in the lee of the man behind her, somewhat protected, yet bold.

"What about it?" he asked.

"I don't know," Charles Ed said, disappointed, as though he had expected Fare to perceive something immediately. "I don't know. Let's you and me take some kind of a trip, you know, before you go on off to college."

"Shit, Charlie, you got a car. We don't have to beg a ride with nobody."

His brother looked at him sternly.

"Any fool can sit back at the wheel of a air-conditioned car and just piss himself down the highway. It takes a little adventure in the spirit . . ."

"You been a fool a long time, then, the way you love that car."

". . . adventure in the spirit . . ."

Fare looked up from the bin full of clotted welding rods. He had been trying to sort them by size, to find a few good ones among the mostly cracked or moisture-damaged assortment. It all seemed a long way from adventure in the spirit.

"Is that what it says there? Adventure in? . . ."

"No, hell, I made that up myself."

Charlie the poet, thought Fare.

"Well, shit, why not," he said after a space. "I'm game."

"If these fuckers can do it, so can we," said Charles Ed. "Besides, we might run up on some of this hitchhiking pee-hole." His forefinger stabbed the girl on the magazine cover. "Wouldn't you like that?"

"Sure I would," said Fare. "Same as you would."

When Charles Ed lay dead on arrival in the hospital emergency room in Carrboro and they left Fare with him for a while, he noticed the bump on his brother's forehead. Hadn't the frustration of it caused him to pull the magazine from his pocket, sent the idea of the trip to the surface of his mind? The lump was fading on the flat, waxy plane of the skin. No, Fare told himself. It had not been the bump, not purely that. He was looking too near for the cause. It had been the knowledge that ahead of him, the future held little more than the slow erosion of his flesh by hard work and weather and the necessity, every day of his life, to embrace a smaller portion of hope. It had been that surely, and perhaps also the knowledge that, when he had thrown the ring into the creek, with it had gone the only chance he would ever have to lie in the arms of something to redeem him from it all.

Fare stared at the blue rising on Charles Ed's forehead, watched as it diminished, its color becoming indistinct from the color of the two swollen black eyes which the bullets, coming in from behind, had given him. No man's fist had ever touched this face. Fare took one of his brother's hands in his own and turned it. Examining the knuckles, he saw the damage Charles Ed had done to others in the chips and notches in their blanched flesh. But, he reminded himself, you could not look for a cause too near to you. Causes did not lie in anything so simple as a rising on the head. A picture on the cover of a magazine. Then, like a chill, came to him the memory of the fat man. Of the face foretelling that simplicity of mind which grasped no cause at all save that of gasoline. Gently, he placed his brother's hand back upon the table, but it seemed to him, in that moment, that you could have gentleness in this world only when it no longer mattered much, only when it was too late and you were over the edge.

EIGHT

His mother wore her navy with polka dots. He held her upright by the right arm, while she mumbled on and on behind a matching handkerchief held to her mouth. She did not seem to listen to the words that buried Charles Ed, or even to see much of what went on that day. She had brought the first bowl of pansies, and placed it, humble and absurd, beside the many large, costly arrangements which had been sent, several of them by strangers, with cards signed "A fan." His father stood on the other side holding her left arm, but Fare knew he was holding his father up too.

His father was dressed in his Sunday suit, his bright, unlined, younger-seeming face belying the shock that was surely coming when the full import of what had happened could get through. Fare's eyes were drawn to his father's wrists where the coat cuffs came up short, revealing an inch of pale translucence above the hard, brown hands.

All around in the crowd were similar marks, clan marks. The rashes that had sprung up instantaneously on necks unused to tight collars, the stiff black coats smelling of mothballs, the creak of old patent leather in the silent morning.

The funeral was brief. There was little to remember about it. Fare had turned away when Charlie Brevoort, representing the Quarterback Club, had left the pitiful blue ceramic football by the grave. He had tried to think about a real football, hard and smelling of oil, leaping from Charles Ed's hands and coming surely into his from its long spiraling flight.

Nor was the funeral very well attended. Surely Charles Ed had more friends, could draw more of the curious, the proud, the vengeful and the bewildered than this. But only about fifty people stood that morning on the little rise east of the Mount Horeb Primitive Baptist Church, where the town buried its dead. Fare stood beside his mother, lifting his eyes up and tracking them off to the west a little to the spot where, had it not been for the intervening curtain of dusty pines, he could have seen the land sloping down to the creek bottom, to the place where they had made their pile of empty pints and fifths. He wished he were there now.

He knew why so few of them had come to the funeral. They did not want to believe it. They wanted to keep something alive by simply denying it had died. They could not look at its death, not straight at it. These people who could lance boils, pull calves, castrate hogs, and stick bloated cows could not bear this. They could not bear it because, unlike all the other dirty things they had looked at, this thing was not right. It was wrong.

"He works in mysterious ways," they were fond of saying, but none of them would ever be able to fit this thing into it. "His wonders to perform."

They'd go crazy trying, so they stayed away. And for once, they wouldn't talk about it. He knew there would not be much gossip.

As he stood looking off into the distance toward the creek bed, masked from him by trees, he saw the rising column of dust out on the road. He watched the column as it came nearer, hoping it would be her, rejoicing silently when, at the crossroads, the dust cloud turned toward the church.

Her father's Eldorado, its fancy paint job lashed to dullness by branches and cornstalks, pulled into the churchyard a hundred yards away. He heard the muffled sound of the doors opening and closing.

He saw them get out, Clare, her father and her mother, and saw how her father moved to her side and lightly touched her shoulder. She walked toward the gravesite. She wore white, a skirt and a waist-length jacket fringed with broad strips of lace. She wore a white satin blouse and there was an enormous, almost clownish, white bow at her throat. But for the familiar way her hips rolled as she walked, he would have said for the first time that she did not look good to him.

When she stood opposite him at the gravesite and listened to the last five minutes of the ceremony, he saw that her shoulders moved all the while with quiet convulsing sobs and that her face was streaked with tears. She wiped them at first on a dainty hankerchief, and then mannishly on her satin sleeve.

He hoped that she would look at him, and at the same time feared that she would. He knew that nowhere in the entire realm of human gesture was there anything he could say to her, or anything he could do to make her feel better. He knew it would be pride to try.

So he watched her, careful to avert his eyes when hers might meet them, and later, when he had taken his mother to the car and had walked back with his father's wallet in his hand to give a ten dollar bill to the visiting preacher, she was still at the gravesite. She was the last. Her parents had walked a little distance off to stand under an oak tree near some of their own dead, and to let her have her time.

Fare caught the preacher halfway up the hill, pressed the money into his hand, waved away the perfunctory protests, and walked on up, to stand beside her. His idea was to say nothing, do nothing, only to offer himself. She might want him. It was possible. He had to give her a chance, or later think of her asking, "Where were you?"

When she sensed someone beside her, her shoulders rocked harder, and when she turned so that he could see her face, there was a snarl on her lips.

"Go away, Fare," she hissed, her fists clenching and unclenching.

"I'm sorry," he mumbled, already moving backward.

"Can't you see I don't want you . . ."

When he had driven his mother and father to the lane where the column of dust would spring up behind them and track them all the way to the hard road, he looked back at the little knoll, dotted with the bleached stones. She was still there small and white beside the new, red gash in the earth, her shoulders rocking with sobs.

* * *

Just before going to school for the fall semester, he saw her. He had come home late in the afternoon, tired, to the empty house, or to a house that seemed empty, after picking some very late corn for a man who lived the other side of the river. When the offer had come to hire out on the corn picker, he had jumped at it. It was something he could do by himself. His father had not been working much since the funeral, had only done a little fishing and walked listlessly around the place, kneeling to pray and commenting to himself that he had to get back on top of things. He was growing more and more confused.

His mother lay all day in the bed, getting up only to cook, to serve, to stir the food around her own plate, beseeching Fare to eat, and then going back to the bedroom. She lay in the bed, sighing, shifting one wrist from her forehead to her side, then bringing up the other. She lay with her eyes open, not sleeping, a light on night and day, the blinds closed to darken the room. When people came, she got up and feigned cheerfulness, too well, Fare thought.

When the man had called and said he'd heard the Odums might pick corn when theirs was all in, Fare said that it was already in, and that, yes, he would pick corn. Then the man asked him how he'd like to be paid, in cash or in a percentage of the corn for winter feed.

Fare excused himself to ask his father. The old man had finally been hit by it, just as Fare had known he would be— later and hard. He sat, watching a game show on television.

"Daddy, how do we want to be paid for picking, cash or percentage?"

His father looked up at him blankly.

"Ain't the corn all in, Fare?"

"Yes. Daddy. Ours is all in. This is somebody else's we talking about."

"I don't care how they pay me, Fare. Long's I get what's coming to me."

His father's eyes returned to the television screen.

Fare could not talk to his father without remembering his only question.

"It wasn't nothing you could do?"

"No, Daddy."

Fare went back to the phone. "We'll take cash, if you got it ready, or a percentage of cash and the balance in feed corn." He agreed to meet the man the next day in the field.

Since then, he had regretted not asking for straight cash. The way things were going, he was beginning to doubt his father could keep anything alive through the winter with or without feed corn. He had been picking steady ever since he'd gotten that first job, and would pick, he told himself, until the day when he had to leave for school. If he left for school at all.

He had come home late in the afternoon to an empty house, had searched the refrigerator, finding only a hardened piece of chicken, had gone in to look at his mother, lying asleep with her eyes open and the light on in the darkened room, and had rushed out of the house without stopping to change clothes, heading for Charles Ed's car, then the little bar which was closest, Larup's, up on the Santa Fe River at the 129 bridge. He did not know what he was looking for and felt like turning around before he had traveled a mile, but remembering what he had to go back to, kept on driving.

It was dark in the bar, and the jukebox was wailing loud, and the air-conditioner turned down cold. He stood for a moment in the doorway, feeling the shock of it in his eyes and ears and on his sweat-soaked clothing. He brushed some corn-shuck from his denim shirt and groped his way to a table in the far corner to wait for the waitress. When she had finally come, annoyed at having to serve so early in the afternoon, he asked for a Jack Black and draft chaser, and then said, "Hey, make it a double and you won't have to come back here quite so quick."

She gave him a sour smile.

Four hours later, when the band came to set up for the night, he sat stuporous, gazing down at a pile of paper money and at the sticky rings of the glasses that had come and gone. The waitress had been taking charges and tips from the pile for some time.

When the place began to fill up with people and the live music started, they turned on the strobe lights that made his eyes ache. The dancers flashed on and off out on the floor. When he closed his eyes he saw cornstalks coming at him. They increased and crowded him, jostling his table. He was about to get up and leave when a face swerved out of the darkness and a memory started awake somewhere back in his mind. The face and he had shared some mildly pleasant experience. There was some kind of bond. The face was saying something about seeing the car in the parking lot and thinking for a minute, but of course . . . Then the face was saying, "Hi you, Fare. Mind if I set down a space?"

With an errant hand, Fare gestured the face to take the seat it wanted at his table. The face lowered and scraped its chair and then a hand crossed the face and swiped at a bushy forelock. Fare knew the swipe.

"Fare, it's me, Larry. Larry Bart. Fare, you all right, son?"

"Son bitch, Larry. You son bitch."

Fare was shaking a hand. It was Larry's big, fullback's hand, with the white scars he could not see on the knuckles from fighting and with the cleat marks all over it from the stomping in pileups. Larry had been the goods. Vicious. He did remember that clearly.

"Lare," he said. "You were the goods. You know that?"

"Does a bunny fuck? Course I know it. You was too. We all was."

Larry knew what he was talking about. Good old Larry.

"Wasn't we a bunch of ass-kickers? Wasn't we?"

"Sure," said Larry. "The goods."

"Memmer that night we took Cross City, fourth-quarter drive. We knocked their dicks off, didn't we? Larry?"

Larry was smiling broadly at him. "Sure we did, Fare. Say, man, how long you been sitting in this cut 'n shoot bar?"

"Don't know. What time?"

"I don't know, but Fare, big'un, you just about piss in the face drunk, no offense."

"No fences. Course no fences."

Fare laughed. No fences.

As they talked, he was aware of the faces that pressed themselves into the orbit they inhabited, the two of them swinging slowly, the others smiling their recognition or their indifference, in any case smiling, then sliding away into the music and the flashing lights.

"Why don't you come on with me," Larry was saying, "and I'll drive you on down the road. You can come back and get the car in the morning."

Larry was picking up Fare's money. Fare marveled at how deft his big fingers were with it. Then Larry's chair scraped backward and Larry wanted to dance with him. He was game, and so he fell into Larry's embrace and did his best to keep up until the warm air outside struck him its blow and the music was behind him and Larry had stood him up beside his pickup truck while he tried to get the keys out of his tight Levi's. Behind them, people had come out of the bar. He heard them laughing. One of them said his name, and something about the two dancing queers.

Larry looked up and said, "How'd you like to bite my crank, Williams." His voice had the old meanness in it.

Whoever was Williams must have recognized the meanness, because there was no reply. There was just the sighing sound of the door closing on the music.

They were in the cab of the pickup. Larry had started the engine when Fare felt the pressure of his bladder. "Minute, Larry?"

"Yeah, man?"

"Can a feller shake the dew off his lily?"

"Sure." Larry was laughing at him. "You can shake the rue off your dilly. By all means."

"The goods."

"Right. The goods."

Larry helped him out of the cab and sent him off toward

the edge of the parking lot, where already, he could hear the cicadas ring-ringing.

He seemed to wander a long time, passing between parked cars, using them to hold himself up, feeling some of them warm and others cold and wet with dew. When he found the edge of the parking lot, and the woods, he defeated the zipper and got himself out and peed, but then thinking he heard music in the woods, he wandered away from the bar for a time before straightening himself out and turning back. When he saw the light again through the trees and found the edge of the lot, marked by the white-painted logs, he knew he had circled the bar and come back on the wrong side.

But he knew how to get to Larry, and he was feeling better, and so he took his time getting back. Cars were parked on this side too, and as he passed, leaning on them, he began to sing to himself. "Satin sheets to lie on, satin pillows to cry on, but still I'm not happy, don't you see." God, how he did dearly love Jeanne Pruett. He wished she would come out of the bar there in the distance and walk toward him, offering whatever it was that broke his heart when he heard her voice. She could put it in bottles and make a fortune.

The car he was leaning on was moving. It was rocking with a gentle rhythm. Wasn't it? No, hell, Fare, it's just you. The car is still and you is rocking.

He studied it to make sure, and to reassure himself sang a little louder, and he was very surprised when the legs, white as chalk in the dark inside the car, pulled themselves up and backward, and the torso connected to them struggled to free itself from something, and her face rose above the headrest, and there was the white of her naked shoulders gleaming in the darkness.

She had made it to a sitting position, but whatever it was that had held her down in the seat had not yet righted itself. Fare watched, leaning at the open window, unable to move on, as she began to light a cigarette. She was looking at him. She was smiling the Jeanne Pruett smile, but it was not Jeanne Pruett, it was her. When the head of the man in the back seat with her cleared the level of the headrests and they heard the man's voice say, "Goddamn, girl, throw me why don't you!" she still did not take her eyes from him, nor did she stop lighting the cigarette.

Fare was happy to see her. But then, he realized that something was wrong. Her match flared. The man turned to look at him. He had long sideburns and oiled hair. He was old. Whatever it was was coming to him when he realized that he could still hear Jeanne: "Satin sheets to lie on, satin pillows to cry on, but still . . ." It was not Jeanne. It was him. He was still singing. He stopped the singing and smiled at Clare, and she smiled back and took a quick puff of the cigarette. She was giving him the appraiser's look. He was about to say something to her, sure she would want to hear it, when a big, heavy, hard thing hit him in the mouth.

He had dived from the Suwannee River bridge with her, both of them naked as the truth, had met her somewhere under the dark water, drawing her to him, kissing her deeply, passing his breath to her and taking hers and then he had broken the surface without her and had reached for the bridge abutment. But it had slipped away from him, and he was rolling, rolling with the current.

Rolling, and something was hurting him, and he surfaced again, and knew he had dreamt the dive and that it had not been the bridge abutment, but a man's boot he had tried to hold, and lost. He reached for it again, but it slipped away going upward and he reached for it with his last strength, knowing what that meant. As it came back down, he tasted the hard rubber of the bootheel and then the foot scraped his face. He tried to crawl under the car, but hit the hot muffler and screamed, dove from the bridge again looking for the sheets, the satin pillows.

He knew that he was half in and half out and had to get all the way one way or all the way the other. He surfaced. His hands were pinned under the car, and in the long eternity since the last kick, he tried to brace himself for the next one.

He felt the nakedness of his genitals, his hands could not reach them, he could not straighten himself sufficiently to cover them. He hit upon the idea of turning sideways to shield them, and tried it, but only got the muffler in his face again. He smelled his skin burning, then the blow came and it hurt.

But it had not hit its mark. The pain was in his thigh. Fare heard the kicker's voice, nearly breathless, going, "Pervert! pervert! pervert!"

He pushed himself back out from under the car, took another blow, which passed between his legs, and, telling himself he was not going to be lucky three times, started to crawl up the side of the car. He could hear her struggling with the kicker and see four, then six legs shuffling in the gravel under him, her breathing was hard, the tearing of some garment and her voice, "Stop it, stop it, you asshole!"

Then, as he got his feet under him and turned in a fighter's crouch, both fists balled at the sides of his face, he heard a loud, solid, wet-sounding thud.

Then he heard a heavy thing falling, thrashing, then crawling, the leather of shoes scuffling, and heard the voice that had called him a pervert trying to gag out another word through a mouthful of rubble.

He focused his eyes. One eye tried to hold itself shut against his will, but he opened it with his fingers. It was not his eye. It was too big.

Larry was standing in front of him, his legs spread like he was about to go down into his three-point. The kicker lay at his feet holding his mouth with both hands and moaning, "Theeth . . . by theeth . . ." A personal foul. Fifteen yards.

"Fuck you teeth," Larry said. He was holding his own right hand in his left. He squeezed it tightly and it leapt of its own will, once, twice, then blood jumped from between his fingers. "I'll teach you all about teeth, you cocksucker. S'cuse me, Miss Clare."

"Oh, who cares, Larry, help me."

But it was Larry who helped him, grabbing him from her,

carrying him most of the way to the truck. She stood by the door while Larry stuffed him in and helped him get his arm up over the windowsill to hold himself upright. When Larry pulled the light switch, the dashboard smiled at him, exposing its blue and red teeth. He knew that he could choose to go back and make the dive from the bridge again, but something told him it would be better to stay here. She was really here. In the dream she was only a . . . He could not get the word.

Larry started the engine. She stood outside, still at the door. She had her hand on his arm where it lay on the window ledge.

"Larry," she said. "Go in and get a beer and drink it."

Larry looked at her. He lowered his head a little and stared intently at the smiling dashboard.

"Sure, Miss Clare. Anything you say."

Larry was walking away toward the door of the bar. Watching him go, Fare remembered the man laying over on the other side with his mouth bashed. Larry extended his right hand and shook the fingers once, twice, as though to rid them of water, then pulled the bar door and went in without looking back.

"Fare, please stop it."

"What?"

"Singing that song."

"S'radio."

"No. Fare. It's you."

"I . . . I just."

Never mind she was saying to him, never mind, Fare, it's all right. Don't worry about it. But he wanted to explain it all to her, how he loved her, how they could try it together, just climb up to the bridge again and hold hands, just try it, and then if it didn't work out or if she wanted to, they could wait awhile, to give her time for, for . . . Her smell began to come to him, unbearable and close.

Her hands were moving along his arm, picking as they went at the gravel embedded in his skin. When her fingers came to his neck and started up, he shuddered both from the pain and the memory, and she said, "Oh, Fare, I'm sorry," pressing her eyes, wet, to his arm.

"Did I hurt you?" she was saying, patting at his arm and neck and face with her gentle fingers, spitting on her hand- kerchief and wiping the dirt from his skin.

"No," he said, "I ain't hurt."

He was waiting for her to answer him. Then it came to him that he had not said any of it out loud, and the task of piecing it all together again seemed more than he could face. He decided to try. He had to try.

"We could try it," he said firmly. She would have to listen if he was firm. But the firmness sounded theatrical, coming through his bloated lips.

She put her fingers over his mouth and lay her forehead on his arm and he felt the shape of her face, hot and wet.

"Don't say it, Fare. I know it all. You don't need to say it cause I know what it is."

He was climbing the bridge rail, and beside him, she was asking again, "Did I hurt you?" and he knew that the answer was yes. He looked at her, composing the image of her face in his mind's eye's safekeeping forever.

He could see the dark water down below, and feel the pres- sure of her hand in his. They would make the jump like this, holding hands.

"Wake up, Fare. Fare?"

She was standing there, outside the window. From the other side of the bar, he could hear noises. People had discovered the man who had kicked him.

He closed his eyes and saw the image of two white, parallel objects, moving in a darkness, rising, then falling as though in dark liquid, then a face, her face coming up above the level of the headrest in the . . . You could not light a match under water. It was not water. It was the dark of the back seat of the car that he had seen. He knew what he had interrupted. Knew the thing that was wrong. He looked at her. He held his eye open with his finger. He looked at her. Her face changed as she saw what was in his.

"Back there," he groped, "when I was singing. Why were you? Who was it in there with you? He was on you! Tell me that ain't what I saw."

"I don't know why!" She was crying, her voice pleading. "It just happens. It just happens and I can't keep it away."

"Like with me?" he asked.

She stopped crying, but her lips trembled and her nostrils flared. She was smaller and so far away from him now, and getting smaller all the time.

"No!" she sobbed. "Not like with you. It was . . . it was different. It could never . . ."

Then she was gone, taking the enormity of her smell with her. Maybe she had gone back to the bridge without him. He was not sure. But when next he looked into the window, she was gone. And he heard the bar door open some time later, heard the loud music spill out, and then Larry was sitting beside him saying, "You do like to sing that song, don't you, big'un." And the telephone poles were coming at them, warping in the window glass, toppling down into the darkness behind them. When they crossed the bridge, he looked for her, her long length would be luminous in the moonlight, but he was there alone, on the bridge rail, small and naked, poised for the long drop.

PART

NINE

FARE GOT OUT OF THE OLD BELVEDERE IN THE PARKING LOT.
Because he had cut it thin again, he had to hurry. All around
him, the freemen hustled for the main gate. Some were saying
goodbye to the wives who had brought them. Others, those
who lived on the grounds, emerged sucking their teeth from
the administration building cafeteria. A line was forming at
the main gate. The men who worked in this place were reluctant to enter it. Everyone had cut it thin again.

To his left, east over Jacksonville, some hundred miles distant, as from a deep dive, the sun was buffeting upward
through a brown cloud of industrial exhaust from the Hudson
Paper Company. On good days, the land wind blew this stink
into the Atlantic Ocean. On bad days, this part of North
Florida smelled like the inside of a number-ten grocery bag.
Between the fences, the dogs were stirring. The dogs were
felons themselves who had bitten little children and been sent
here to go mad in these shadeless, routine lanes. They came
out of their hutches to freshen their boundaries with piss.

Fare kept his eyes on the red brick chimney of the steam
plant far within. It seemed to lean dangerously as a dark flight
of birds passed behind it. He saw its gray spit of steam before
hearing the raw burr of the whistle.

"Asthmatic son of a bitch." he mumbled.

A man next to him asked sharply, "What's at?"

"Nothing," he said.

"Nothing it is then," said the man flatly, looking hard at
him.

Fare waited his turn at the metal detector where the entering freemen removed the metal from their bodies to pass
through and then restrung themselves on the other side with
keys, change, belt buckles and cigarette lighters. Penknives

had to be left with Sarn Thomas. If you carried a paper bag or briefcase, it had to be inspected.

The line slowed at the detector. It was already hot enough inside the gatehouse to sour the after-shave on the faces of the waiting men. Fare had brought coffee, sugar and milk substitute in a paper sack. He loosened his belt, removing its brass buckle. He took change, a cigarette lighter from his pocket. In front of him, a man in a fresh blue three-piece suit couldn't get through the detector. Repeatedly he stepped through, and each time, it rang like a telephone. The man was jovial but growing impatient. Fare could see that he thought himself too important to be bothered with this ritual. Fare passed his handful of metal and the sack along to the guard, who carried it past the machine to the table on the other side. The suited man was saying that they could turn him upside down by God if they wanted to.

"Might," said Sarn Thomas.

The suited man laughed a stale laugh.

The guard at the second door called to the Sarn, "Teeth mebbe."

"Mebbe," said the Sarn.

The suited man's face went hard and red. He held up his beltless pants with one hand.

"Yup," summed the Sarn, "teeth. How many filled teeth you got?"

The line of waiting men now snaked out of the gatehouse door, past the trimmed bougainvillea along the entranceway, and into the parking lot. Some of the brown-shirted guards were mumbling about maybe being docked.

Through the window, Fare saw in the distance a group of men working under a shotgun on what was called a sixspot. There were more than six of them, but the title endured. He had been told by McLaren, his clerk, that the guard, or hack as the inmates called him, who stood watch over this sixspot was a strange brooding man who half-muttered, half-sang a refrain, "It's hard but it's fair. You had a good home but you wouldn't stay. Bring me some dirt." All day long, while the

men in the sweated-through blue herringbone denims and
state-issue straws with built-in dark plastic sun visors humped
their brush hooks and slings, he sang this Raiford litany to
them.

Ahead of Fare, the suited man had consented to open his
mouth. The Sarn took it roughly like a horse trader, turning it
toward the bare light bulb.

"I God. I bleeve it is teeth."

"Christ!" bit the suited man. "Machine got no bidnis."

Fare passed through twice, a second time because he had
not removed his college ring. Every once in a while the Sarn
would smile broadly, wink and say, "Teeth!" and all the men
who had been near enough to hear would chuckle some and
then look at their watches. Someone muttered, "Big shots!"
and there were nods of agreement.

Fare began the long ruled walk to the school. All around
him now, the prison was alive with prodded activity. Behind
the hospital, the sick and wounded were taking up places in
the still-gentle morning sun. Some walked slowly, testing feet
or legs, stretching new stitches. A few, waist-deep in drifts of
ground fog, sparred in the good-natured, proficient way that
could turn deadly serious at some signal Fare always failed to
see.

Ahead and to his left, inmate Granger was opening up the
canteen. Its shutters clattered out. The men from O unit
emerged, drifting along the service road past the machine shop,
sullenly, older men whose step in the morning was brittle. As
always, he watched for Lester's face.

The disappointment was a dull pressure in his brain. He did
not know enough about the legal processes that would carry
Lester to Raiford. He had read the papers carefully and they
had made no second mention of him. Perhaps there were cer-
emonies. Maybe they were waiting for a vacancy. Could he
still be sure Lester was coming? Might he have been diverted
to some other place—a road prison, maybe? Or was he still
being processed at the Receiving and Medical Center in Lake
Butler? And all the while, he was troubled by the growing

threat posed by this job. This was alien territory to him. These men had not taken well to him at all.

At the entranceway to the Rock, he saw Sarn Edwards, with his clipboard, walk to the gate. This morning, Fare was slated to count in. He quickened his step to beat the walking line from the Rock to the school.

In the dark recess behind a pool of light at the Rock gate, he saw the gathered faces of the men in the walking line. They stood in twos, each man with the walking partner assigned to him. The line began moving. They came, white men first, about one hundred of them, then black men, a slightly more fluid rear guard. Fare rounded the corner at the steam plant, passing under the stack and cut-mouthed whistle. He broke into a trot, drawing laughter from the approaching walking line, and took his place at the school door, fumbling books and the paper poke.

Two, four, six, eight, raise a thumb is ten. Two, four, six, eight, raise a finger is . . .

"Mornin, fuck boy."

Blood scalded up from his chest to his neck and face. He lost count. He stood on tiptoes to follow the heads with his eyes as they receded down the hallway, blond ones, black ones. Which head had said it? He cooled. Perhaps the words had not been meant for him. He would never know who had said it.

The line passed. Across from him, Ernie Winzinreid, the electronics teacher, stood adding figures on a scratch pad. His head bobbed up, "Two-thirteen. That what you got?"

"Yeah, . . . on the nose," said Fare.

Winzinreid was walking off. "Relax," he said, "they just new-cocking you. Hit won't go on much longer."

He was gone before Fare could reply.

Later, there would be a low grin, eyes that met his with a special boldness, and these would tell him, maybe, who had said it. He knew too that whatever he did about it would depend not on any standard of the prison's (which had a standard for every eventuality), but on who the inmate was. He was sickened a little by this. It showed him the limits of his

courage and of his position, and of what he was officially trying to do in the prison, a vaguer thing than the first two, yet
the thing he was beginning to believe in more than he wanted
to; which was to bring order out of chaos through language.
This was his litany. The fact was, he was beginning to like
this teaching.

He turned from the door and walked down the hall to the
head, removing his cup from the poke. The water here had
run underground, directly across the yard from the steam
plant, and it poured boiling hot from the spigot. He shook
coffee into the cup and held it under the steaming flow. A
black inmate walked in, a look of discomfort in his face, and
walked out. The man would not shit in his presence.

He hated the prison heads. Nothing in the prison could
cause a man to know the hopelessness of his condition more
than these seatless steel crappers, their sides and the walls
around them eaten by the acid urine. He used them only when
he could not get to the staff toilet. He felt guilty of some cruelty when he surprised an inmate drawn down in a heap upon
one of these cold stumps.

He turned to go, but saw the poem again.

> I been in raiford forteen years,
> I beat my meat, i cried my tears,
> chaplin said hel get me out,
> if I wasnt such a scounrul.

It was signed "me." Beneath it was written some of the more
standard shithouse bill of fare—"if you can read this, you
pissin on you foot." He found the spot in the first poem where
the rhyme broke down. Each day he tried to complete the
couplet using words like "doubt" and "lout," but he hadn't
found the right word yet. He stood staring at the poem, his
education failing him again.

He walked to his classroom, a little late, carrying the coffee.
He liked to go in carrying something; it gave him an air of
preparation. Really, he did not prepare. There was no sense
in it. He knew English grammar by heart. He was infallible

within the tight world of its constructs. With this knowledge, seeming to his students a monolith of learning, he settled small arguments, sent one man away a winner, another vanquished, forced to pay a two-pack debt, because, yes, "football," a noun in most cases, is a noun-modifier here, describing "game." Do you understand?

"Yes, sir," they didn't, but his word was a small part of all the law.

He took the count board from Fat Rat Jenkins, who carried it from class to class, and called roll, trying to break the ice that had to be broken every Monday morning after they had spent their weekend in the Rock. A weekend, he had learned, would fade him in their memory—on Mondays he was nothing until he made himself over to them again. Tomorrow, and for the rest of the week, he would have McLaren, who sat at a small desk in the back of the room grading papers, call the roll, but Mondays it was his task. Already he had established a tradition.

"Alford, Clemm, Hartly, Stepps . . ."

"Stepps?" he called, looking up with mock officiousness.

A willowy black hand waved up from a desk top as though called by a silent piper.

"Check it," came a musical response from beneath a shambles of Afro-Sheen, rumpled herringbone, white striped denim asleep in the back.

"Take up thy bed and walk, Stepps."

There was a titter. Things might go well today.

"Stone walls do not a prison make, nor iron bars a jail."

"Sheet," Stepps rose up, words passing through the bruised grape pulp lips. "Three fences sho makes a joint!" Stepps' hand slipped off the desk top and went the rounds of his friends, palm up. Loud pops, crisp against the weekend staleness of the room. Each head rocked a little with a strange bubble of laughter, "Do it, home boy . . ."

A good start. They were with him. Not awake yet, but he knew the tack. Knew that nothing especially vicious to which his white skin would link him had happened over the weekend.

He had made them a part of a good time, better at best than the tag plant, the furniture factory, or a sixspot under a shotgun outside the wire. The school took its life force from such implicit comparisons. You could tell a man what to do, or ask him; either way, he would do your bidding. But asking him, implying his free will in the matter, even making a joke of it, made things easier. Only a few wouldn't play; they had to be told.

Class began with his explanation of "some common errors in pronoun usage," and as though he had pressed certain buttons beneath his shirt front, he gave his talk, its examples, its jokes, prodded its responses, still concentrating on Stepps, with whom he had begun the day.

And they mostly listened or mostly didn't depending upon the feel of their lives during that hour . . .

. . . the old lady wrote, they did owe or were owed, they were fucking or were fucked, they were on the parole list, or would or would not be, they would get a cell change or wouldn't or didn't want one, had a new angle on appeal, were making buck beer, could get 2–4–5, two reefers for five dollars, felony is grounds for divorce and I don't care, he wants to adopt my kids while I'm in the joint, let him, I'll cut off his nutses when I gets out, I am innocent, I am not, I was convicted on my record, I am ashamed, I am a criminal now, though I was not when I came here, I might get cut in the hall between classes, I will cut, shoot, hit on the yard in the evening, I will sneak out tonight and string an antenna for my radio, my sweet, sweet, fuck boy, my flip partner . . .

And so their minds went, far from pronouns, and his voice said, "Case is merely a list. Now the objective case list is composed of pronouns used only as direct objects, indirect objects, and the objects of prepositions," but he knew their minds from long acquaintance, the din of their complaints, and remembered how it had been his first day in the classroom.

"Hello, I'm Farel Odum, and I'm going to be your new English instructor." What else could he say? He had considered and rejected a drill sergeant harangue, "You scratch my back and I'll scratch yours, you break my balls and I'll break yours," and soon had regretted it. He tried to ignore the words which came from behind hands, "newcock," "punk," "my *young* teacher." When he turned his back, someone whistled. He walked to the desk, and giving them a withering stare, began to hand out mimeographed exercises.

Begin work immediately.

Each man had taken a paper from him, looked at it, and as though by prior arrangement each man handed it back to him, grinning, saying, "What I want with this, white man?" or more angrily, "Shit *no*, man!" Finally, he had stood, his face red beyond control, watching them watch him, flicking ash from his cigarette, which from the shaking of his hand held no ash to begin with. And then one man stood, a muscular Negro who later became Ivory Rose. (Fare remembered a brief glimpse of this face in the glass floodgate that first day he had sat in Bray's office.) Rose moved forward as though to bear the sword of all their righteous anger, and behind him papers wafted in small pendulum arcs to the floor or fell crumpled in balls and they all watched to see what Rose would do.

Plunging his ticking right hand into his back pocket, Fare stepped forward to meet Rose, blocked his path. He had been told to keep his class in the room until the bell to change classes rang.

Inmates must not be allowed to wander the halls.

"Where are you going?"

Rose stopped three feet from him, then inched forward extending his glistening arms until they encircled but did not touch him, as though to embrace or strangle him, or merely lift him out of the way, to make him flinch, to draw laughter from the men seated. Then the arms were flexed by stages it seemed, popping audibly, swelling, then falling slowly to slim flanks. And Rose moved closer still, stood with his nose not one inch from Fare's.

"Ah'm gone to empty mah bowels."

"I'll expect you back in three minutes." He kept both trembling hands trapped in his back pockets.

"No man gone tell me how long it take to shit."

"Three minutes or I'll write you up."

"You writes me a D.R., white man, and I shove it down you throat."

"We'll see about that."

Fare's own nostrils were flared. He was putting hot breath into Rose's mouth. His bared teeth grew sticky from exposure to air, and he pressed his face forward, abandoned, closing the distance between it and the black, hot, wet mask by half an inch. A voice said, hush Fare, let me handle this. It was his brother's voice. He ignored it.

"Ah got life, and ah ain't but twenty-nine years old," Rose said, his voice yielding, his vision taking an angle past Fare's heaving shoulders, gone to memory perhaps, to pulpwood loading stations, and red licorice, the smell of woman on worked-out fingers, "and you can take my gain time, tho me on the Flattop and ah still shit ten minutes if ah want to, white man."

Fare felt whatever had been in them both drain away. The issue was seven minutes of crapper time. He wanted to be out of the room, maybe out where these black eyes, sad now, were looking to. But he knew, for the first time, that he had something called appearances to maintain, though it kill them both, and he said, "I'll get a hack if I have to, and sit him down right beside you."

"You get you a goon, you want to, get two, get three, ah kill them all and you too."

The black eyes snapped back to take up the slack, they crackled now burning up the breath that Fare desperately needed. The threat had been the wrong thing. Fare's mind windmilled and in the hot quiet hit upon the thing that put it all back together.

"Come with me," he said, and strode, his back prickling, toward the door.

Walking, he knew that Rose would either follow or hit him, solidly, squarely, with a chair or fist. It didn't matter. Or, would simply stay behind, leaving him to go out by himself.

That might have been the worst thing, for he would have nothing to do but go back then, the room belonging to Rose, not him. But he heard Rose's heavy shoes making steps behind him and in the hallway, before reaching the guard's station, they talked.

They stood staring into each other's eyes as before, but from greater distances. Finally, Fare asked, "You really want this?"

He could see Rose begin to say something, some I don't give a damn thing, but then Rose looked around at the crowd they were beginning to attract. He looked down at his big, black hands, wiped them on his shirt front, flexed them, and looked up. Out of changed eyes, he said, quietly, "I reckon not . . . but doan you push me."

Fare said, "Or you me."

Then Fare held out his hand. It felt foolish hanging there between them. Rose looked around him, at who was watching. Then out of embarrassment, he took the hand. His grip, like some far inner core of him, was soft.

Stepps was asleep again. Now, handing out the exercises, his explanation of pronouns finished, Fare gently woke him. "Stepps, Stepps, wake up and do your work."

He looked into awakened eyes, which were trying now to focus on the hieroglyphs of English grammar before them, and wondered what had made Rose follow him that day two weeks before. And he understood that the prison had done it. Knew that the prison had done it long before he had come.

TEN

WHEN THE CLASS SEEMED ENGAGED BY THE EXERCISE HE
said, "I'll be right back." Down the hall, he leaned in to see
Ivory Rose bent over a hot plate. In repose the black face was
almost impish, the bald head shiny. Rose, who could type,
clerked for the science teacher, Mr. Arthur, in the mornings,
and was Fare's student in the afternoon. He was in Fare's ad-
vanced secondary English class; having never completed high
school, he was studying for an equivalency diploma. He could
write essays as well as many graduate students Fare had
known, and had read more widely than most.
   "Got real coffee?" Fare asked.
   "Not for white men."
   Fare never knew what to make of Rose's hostility. Though
they had become friendly in the way of adversaries who have
settled in for the long term, Rose still bore him a certain dislike for the incident of their first meeting, and bore him, as
well, the general dislike he reserved for all white men.
   "What about octoroons?" Fare asked. He took out his felt-
tipped pen and made as if to color his middle finger black.
"See. I'm one-eighth black."
   "You know what you can do with that finger."
   Rose's voice was a deep rumbling black-dotted line.
   "I'll be back," said Fare.

   At the bell, Fare collected papers, gave them to McLaren,
got his cup, and escaped to Ivory's room. It was a storage
room for the glassware, the ripple tanks, models of solar systems, all part of some past boondoggle, since the science
classes never got beyond the rote memorization of the names
of phyla. But the room had soon come to be known as Ivory's
room, and in it, he carried out his duties as clerk, kept his
typewriter, and wrote his poetry.

It had been the poetry that had overcome the stiffness that existed between them after the truce they made in the hallway that first afternoon. The news of a new English teacher got around quickly, and got around mostly among prison writers. There were many of them, novelists, essayists, epistolaries and poets. Many of them were black and they modeled themselves after Eldridge Cleaver. Most of them were dreary imitators. Ivory Rose was, as far as Fare could tell, pretty good. He wrote an angry verse about being black and down with no hope. In it, he could command the voice of the blue-gum nigger (this was what the white men Fare had been raised among would have called it), which was the voice he had used to speak of "emptying his bowels." He could write third-world political cant pretty well too, but Fare liked him best when he was doing something very uncharacteristic for a primitive black poet. Fare liked him best when he was translating the Horatian odes into street language, and writing what he called Institutional Spillgism, or the language of the American Cream. He was trying, he said, to turn back the madness, by aiming the language of social workers and social scientists at its source. At any rate, they had made peace over poetry.

Fare remembered the day, about a week after they had confronted each other, when Ivory brought him a poem to read. He had been packing his briefcase to leave after the last class of the day, Ivory's class. He could see that Ivory was lingering for some reason. A little fear crowded at him from the back of the room where Ivory sat, smoking, holding a typescript in his hand. When all the other inmates had gone, Ivory approached the desk. Fare looked at the door, measuring the distance to it.

Ivory began in an angry way, "I guess you got one of them Ph.D.'s, ain't you?"

"Yes." Fare lit a cigarette, by the filter. Ivory laughed. It was his last cigarette. He crumpled the pack.

"You can have one of mine," Ivory held out his pack, "if you can cut this R.I.P."

"Thanks."

"Nada."

"Speak Spanish?"

"And teach it."

"Really, to whom?"

"Some of the brothers over in the Rock. Some of them interested in improving themselves."

"That's nice." What an inane comment, Fare thought, and heard the walking line forming up out in the corridor.

"Well," Rose grinned, "idle hands is the Bad Man's workshop; you know what they say."

"Yeah." Fare looked out the doorway at the men in the hall. The line was beginning to move. The word "irregular" came to him. This was becoming irregular.

"Well," he said, "I guess we ought to . . ."

"What I'm really doing," Ivory began. His voice, pitched low, had lost its jivey tone, "is this here. It's a translation. I got onto this Latin from Spanish and got me a dictionary and started looking up the meanings and putting it together in my own way, and pretty soon I liked it. It was like crawling into this dude's mind."

Horace as dude, Fare thought. Interesting. He could not suppress a smile.

"Would you like for me to look at it?"

"Would you like to look at it?"

Fare saw that he was to request that it be given to him.

"Yes," he said, just as Bray stuck his head in the door, scowled broadly and raised up his wrist with its big diver's watch, pointing at the dial with a hammy forefinger.

As they were walking out, more or less together, Rose said, "So you got one of them Ph.D.'s, do you?"

"Yes."

"Know what I think of that?"

"How could I?" Fare was getting a little annoyed at all of the macho gamesmanship.

"I think, Ph.D.'s is like assholes. Everbody's got one."

When they reached the walking line, and Rose fell in with his walking partner, Fare walked beside him.

"Say, Rose?"

"Yeah?"

"Do you have an asshole?"

"Course I do, you fool." But Rose smiled briefly.

"That's funny, cause you ain't got a Ph.D."

That night Fare had read the poem, comparing it to a translation of the original, checking some of Rose's usage against the English. Rose had an interesting sense of what Horace had meant to say, and had used street language without trivializing concepts or clashing images. Fare dug out his Pope, and found the Horatian imitations. He brought them in to Ivory the next day.

Fare liked the storage room. The pace of things was changed in it, not pressurized. Time passed well. Now he went to the sink and dumped the dregs of his instant coffee, rinsing the cup. He sat at Ivory's desk, a spot always relinquished to him, never to anyone else. Ivory had built an aquarium out of enameled wood and one glass panel, and put a few ditch minnows in it. On the walls were posters—one depicted two geese flying coupled, ecstatic grins smeared to their faces; the caption read, "Fly United." Another showed a young Negro man lying O.D.'d in an alleyway with a needle still jabbing his arm. There was a clock above the desk. Its hour hand was rigged to release a gum ball from a glass cylinder each time it passed twelve. The gum balls counted each for a day or a night of Ivory's sentence. It was life for murder, and a long spiraling glass tube full of gum color ran up from the clock to the ceiling. Each day at noon, Ivory emerged from his cubicle and entered the walking line for lunch chewing one half-day of his life.

Pages torn from magazines were pasted below the clock along with copies of Ivory's few published poems. Often, he could be seen through the glass-paneled door, gazing at them. He stood, his back to Fare, pouring boiling water through a piece of coned filter paper set atop a beaker. Now he turned and looked at Fare. Something like care came into his face.

"What's matter with you, man? You *always* look like you seen murder."

Sometimes Ivory had the too formal or too literary way of speaking found in men who teach themselves language. But with Fare, who was educated, he made it a point to speak jive.

"You been havin' the dreams again, right?"

"Yeah."

"Exercise your demons, man. Alls I can say."

"Ex-*or*-cise," said Fare, "That's ex*or*cise."

"Uh-huh," said Ivory, writing the word on a pad, then putting it back into his shirt pocket.

Fare batoned his cigarette down from behind thumb and forefinger.

"How?"

"Don't know, man. You say."

"Don't know either."

"It's a bad thing happened, right?"

"Right."

"Start with that."

"You mean start thinking there?"

"You do too much thinking. It time to *do*."

"Too much doing put you where you are."

"And you come in here to see me. Sides, like the man said, 'To live outside the law you must be honest.' "

"Poeta, poetae . . ."

"What's that, man?"

"Latin for poet."

"S'nother one of you problems. Too many words. Look up there, man." He pointed to the magazine pages. "Just enough, then I quit."

"Quit and do what?"

"Cut, shoot, love, die. I don't know."

"You'd have got along well with my daddy."

"Maybe."

"Surely."

"Got to be a white man," Ivory shook his head.

"He is . . . was."

"Forgive it, but he sound like a neck to me."

"Oh, he'd have had a place for you, all right."

"Thing is, would I of sit in it?"

"Is that the thing?"

"Yup, and you know he put you in one too."

"One what?"

"Place."

"What you mean?"

"You think . . . no, you *do* about it."

Fare looked up at the wall. Ivory had put up something new.

> Between the desire
> And the spasm
> Between the potency
> And the existence
> Between the essence
> And the descent
> Falls the Shadow
> *For Thine is the Kingdom*

"That's not yours, is it?"

"No, that's Eliot. White man, but he said a true thing. I got it up here to remine me. In my poetry, man, I'm gone cut out all those betweens. I'm gone write the one and only true poetry of action for all black men. It's too many these house niggers aroun here sit and talk, talk, talk. The task of the new black poet gone be to incite the brothers up off they butts. God*damn*, but I *do* feel it!"

He raised his arms above his head—black victory at the barricade. Fare was briefly drawn into the scene, saw the rocks and bottles fly, heard the shouts, smelled the fumes. But it all seemed futile. The little room, all the dusty paraphernalia. How could Ivory carve further than this place he had cut out?

Fare looked at the wall again. "I don't get it," though he had heard it explicated in class, more than once.

Ivory dropped his hands and began filling his pipe. He looked sober, bitter. "Most don't. You got to live it."

Fare was embarrassed. He felt the silence growing, forcing him toward the door. His coffee was no comfort any longer. But he wanted to ask something badly enough to break in upon the ground of Ivory's reverie. The black man went off to this place wallowing in pride and self-pity until, often, he could not be reached for days. He called these times "visions."

"Listen," Fare broke in, "what did you mean by all that 'do about it' shit?"

"Simple," said Ivory, aloof, already in a world of mythical black heroism and hurt.

Fare waited, thinking of the dreams. It had been ten years since his brother's death. He had gone through tears to numbness and had come upon the dreams. They had grown, transmuting each year in their month toward some final outcome at which he could only guess. Perhaps there *was* such a thing as exorcism. Perhaps he could do something about it.

"You are a shadow, man."

Ivory's voice was that of a shaman, bent over steamy coffee. He dragged out the word "man" like a taunt.

"All you white motherfuckers are shadows. You got too many words in the world with you now, maaan. Bad words. It's still your world but it won't be long. The words are gone to turn back on you and eat you all up. They gone to start with all the big thinkers first, with the Ph.D.'s, and then they gone eat right on down to the lowest shit-kicking redneck. They might even take as long as the mail takes to get out to the Rock from Starke, maybe as long as it takes me to get my poems through the censors, maaan, but they gone come. The big words is gone eat more than the little words. The abstractions gone fill up till they puke. 'Punitive segregation' gone to turn around and eat. So is 'correction,' but you know what word gone eat most of all, gone eat maybe two, three hundred white men right here on the spot, come the day the words turn around. It gone be 'rehabilitation,' maaan. That word gone eat till it puke, then shake off them fantods and eat some more. Sho nuff is, baby. Maaan. The day the words turn round."

He was silent for a space, but for his breath. He looked at Fare with a cruel satisfaction. Fare felt he was having an idea, an idea about *him*.

"But you my main man, ain't you? My main white man. So I got to tell you what word going to eat you. It ain't gone be none of this institutional spillgism, cause, man, you don't get behind none of that shit anyway. You already got a good rep with the brothers for staying outside the law like we talked. But the word gone get you, man, the word is 'think,' you know, ratiocinate. You just thinks too damn much, you worries, and now, man, you tell me you got some dreams after you ass. Let me tell you, man, I *hear* some dreams come grinding down, man, I want to say it's some dreams walking them hallways late. And you know whose got the dreams, man. I tell you who. It's the fuck boys got the dreams, all the pussy boys got the dreams, man. An you want to know why, it's cause they can't do, they can't do, and when you can't do in this life, it's somebody else gone do *to* you, man, so you see, you time gone come, man. You gone get eat by that word 'think' . . ."

Ivory's black face hung close to his as it had two weeks before. Fare could not say anything. Then it came to him.

"Aren't you leaving something out? The fuck boys, you call them, isn't there something they can do? I mean . . ." He thought of the legions of pitiable soft men he had seen, and could summon no more contempt for them than he felt for himself.

"Like what?"

"Love."

"Yeah, man, but what's that?"

Fare stared at Rose for a long time, at the hurt black eyes and the imp's smile. It was the face of a man who had taken another's blood. It was the face of a man who translated Horace. Fare remembered Rose's handshake, their hands coming together to mate his own shaky resolve to Rose's strange softness. Fare asked himself whether Rose could help him, whether or not they could make some kind of bargain. There was undeniable power in Rose and more. There was the skill to talk about it, the mind to understand it, yet Rose was telling him to stop thinking.

ELEVEN

I<small>T WAS</small> F<small>RIDAY AFTERNOON, AND</small> F<small>ARE COULD HEAR THE</small> faint booming of the presses in the tag plant across the yard. For a week now he had been thinking. Thinking about what Ivory had said. From behind his desk, he gazed across the classroom, above the heads of his students, like penned cattle, gazing perplexedly at their books, toward the tag plant where he saw it. He seemed to see it everywhere now. The special irony of this place was that he had come to find Lester, who had first shown him the fullest mastery of it, what such a mastery could do, and he could see it now everywhere he looked, but could not find Lester.

What he gazed at now on the tag plant loading dock was a single black inmate flattening cardboard boxes. The man, whose muscled chest and arms leaped in the wavy heat, split the boxes effortlessly, holding them at arm's length with a kind of dumb disdain for their resistance, tearing them between fingertips. Huge shards of cardboard fell straight down from his hands like brown leaves in the still air. The hands hung limp, throbbing for an instant, were wiped on the trousers, darkening the white uniform stripe. Then they reached for another box, found a seam, ripped. Above them, nothing that was sentient moved in the blank creating face. Nothing but sweat moved there. Fare saw this in the warp of heat waves. The sound of it, a spaced burring, came to him across the yard, barren and pocked with ant mounds. Watching, listening, his mind fell into step with the motion of the hands, until the separateness of the face from them and their work seemed almost natural. It was, he realized, natural, like predation. It was, as Ivory had said, more natural than thought. It was just one more version of the mute unexamined power that Lester had operated upon the flesh of their father's flesh so efficiently. Tear a box. Kill a hitchhiker.

Fare watched the brown clutter of cardboard increase at the black man's feet until he stopped to gather and carry it to the incinerator.

Think. Or try not to.

From the men before him in the classroom, came an almost audible sigh of combined effort. He looked out and saw no face that was comfortable confronting books, papers. Not a single hand that did not seem about to splinter its pencil. And should the pencils break in these hands, he knew the twist of lips and eyes that would follow: "What have I done?" the eyes would ask in their useless, sorry way. "What am I doing here?"

The men began to finish, bringing their papers, many of them sodden with sweat, to the wire basket on Fare's desk. They looked up from the basket, pleased with themselves, and then held out cigarettes, raising eyebrows a little, until he nodded, "Go smoke."

Singly, they filed toward the hallway, where they produced pouches of R.I.P. and boxes of big kitchen matches, clouds of smoke. It rolled in the hot close corridor until behind it, they became quiet. Thinking.

It was the last hour before lunch and Fare wondered what he would eat, and what they would eat. He tried to remember noon meals on past Fridays. Was there any system? Probably it would be mullet, a battery, simmering mess of meal, grease and bone. For him. For them, the usual beans and greens.

He rose, forgot, and then remembered to lock his desk drawer. In it were his sunglasses, cold tablets, instant coffee; all had been stolen and replaced more times than he cared to remember. He walked through the three adjoining rooms closing windows. It was his duty to "secure" his wing before lunch and at five o'clock. The air grew hotter as he went, and facing the windows, drawing them, turning the locks, he saw the walking line forming at the tag plant. On its pitted front steps and along the shrub-lined walk, inmates milled and shrugged at their fatigue, buttoning blue shirts, shoving them down into striped trousers. He looked for the man who tore boxes and found the broad black face, first in line.

He watched for a smile of satisfaction, an arched eyebrow, anything to tell what it meant to finish another half-day, what it meant to lose your head above those muscles. But the eyes were vague, evasive; one thick hand pinched a street cigarette. That was something, it meant wealth, power maybe. Street cigarettes were money, not to be smoked; they would buy R.I.P. at a one pack to five ratio. The big man now took a last drag, kicked the cigarette hard with a forefinger, loosening the ash. He stripped it, wadding the paper, flicking it away, and ground the filter under his brogan.

Fare pulled the last window to, feeling the shock of its closing in his ears. He opened his mouth, forcing his jaw past its catch. Swallowing, he heard a strange, pulpy, thumping sound. He strained to identify the sound and to locate it, but it was elusive, seeming to come from the very washing of the stale and motionless air. It did not belong to any act he could associate with this time and place and it turned him suddenly cold, a little lightheaded. Where had he heard the sound?

As he moved to the outer wall, he heard the sound twice more, muffled in the heat. He came to his own classroom again. The murmur of talk crossed to him from far away in the corridor. He recognized McLaren's voice. It said, "Fuck that!"

The unspeakable sound neared.

Fare knew he had heard the sound before. As he moved carefully along the wall toward it, part of him went quietly in search of the place and the time from which it would come to him. There had once been a pickup truck, which had been, he seemed to recall, backed up to a slanted trough made of weathered cypress planking. He was a little boy in this memory and he stood somewhere off to the side in the joy of being there in grown-ups' business. But something was getting wrong. A man was climbing into the back of the pickup truck and the man held something in his hands, something heavy in both hands, awkward with it as he climbed. And it was hogs in the truck, three of them and the air was crisp and cold and burnt with his breath, and the man in the truck was his father, the long-ago father, big and strong and young, and the hammer was up at his chest now, and he was trying to get one of the hogs to let him straddle its bristled back in the jostle of the other hogs it was awkward and the man's face said it wanted it done right and the water in the cauldron steamed and the gambling stakes were ready and the men stood around the trough waiting stomping in the cold and the lighterd fire under the cauldron whipped and cracked and one of them it was his uncle Prat said, "Strike a lick, Basil. We got three to do this mornin," and the worried look on his father's face was replaced by an expression of concentration and a single vein clumped in his father's neck and with a swiftness that seemed to violate the very nature of heavy things, the dull rusted hammerhead lashed down and the sound Fare had heard that day he had not heard again until now. It was the wet, deadly, dead-center smack from which there is no recovery, and after which there are only the dreams.

He found it at the back of the room in an alcove formed by two upright metal file cabinets.

The sound came from a yard-long arc of polished steel blade, held like something electric, alive at one end, by the two hands of a tall thin Negro whose passionless face was brightly framed to Fare's eye in one window. He brought the blade down again and again on the swaying head and shoulders of a seated man. Fare knew the man as William Hughes, already dead, who could not read or write, who did not belong in this classroom, who complained incessantly of hemorrhoids, who sat now, legs spread, his face veiled by the thick cords of blood he spilled, falling onto the book, one hand still clutched. Why? Daddy?

The Negro swung the long knife upon Hughes' neck, angling it in to strip trembling a slab of meat from the base of the skull to the shoulder. The cabinets were splashed with bright red gobbets. He rocked the blade to remove it for it

had lodged in bone. The blade fell methodically, rose methodically, gaining speed on the downstroke, its smooth polished
edge sawtoothed now by red blood. It blurred before biting.
The killer stood with his legs apart, and once struck only
with one hand, readjusting his sun glasses flat to his face
with the other. He stood the way a man stands in a field in
the morning, carefully pacing himself for a full day's work,
shifting his muscles from midmorning toward noon. Fare felt
his own legs move to the same wide position.

Sensing him, the tall man turned, and his eyes moved in a
precise inventory of the room before him as he made one
last gratuitous, savage slash. He saw Fare, half-hidden in the
doorway, and both knew their predicament, and each sensed
this sharing. Fare was trapped with two empty rooms and a
dead end behind him.

He and the killer had the same distance to run to the corridor, each his own side of the square room. The Negro raised
the knife as though to throw it, then changed, pushing both
arms up and backward as though grappling the aqueous air.
He began running, to cut Fare off. Fare was running too,
without thought, or decision. He heard the heavy soles of
prison shoes gripping the tiles and felt his own knees rising
and falling, saw the dim hole growing ahead. He threw himself forward like a sprinter arching a tape, and in the same
instant, felt the shudder of a body slamming the wall, recoiling
from it. Behind him the knife blade rang in the cinder block
wall.

He did not turn in the hall, but ran through a confusion
of voices, broken murmurs becoming shouts, the scuffle of
big men getting out of the way, straight toward the back
exit, gathering speed, passing the shoe repair shop, where his
face struck the burnt-oil breath of machinery, until he hit the
fire exit crossbar with a shoulder and forearm and was in
the crystal quiet of fall afternoon with nothing ahead but a
long tract, mowed field, fences, the highway beyond.

It was the same running.

The night dew and the dust made grime in his mouth and

at the bottom he was up and running across the ditch and
across another line of something where the light stopped and
the dark began. He was in the dripping woods, up to his knees
in dead leaves and he heard a car go by in a long suck like a
riptide at night, and then another.

He knelt, not so much to kneel, but because something
liquid in his knees now demanded it. All the cold inside now
became warm and the warm was breakfast, and a yellow,
bitter substance fell, connected to him by ropy strings, then
broke to the grass between his knees. Strings of it held to his
mouth. They blew out in a little wind and wrapped around
his face. William Hughes. He wiped his forearm. Charles
Ed Odum. It was skinned. It was bruised. He breathed, held,
hoped to expel only air, but blurted more puke.

Turning slightly, to the sound of a distant whoop, he saw
a swarm of brown shirts running from the Rock toward the
front door of the school, and into them running blindly now
with the bright blade churning at waist level came the big
killer. The brown shirts scattered, hooting like cowboys, received the blue into their bosom, crouched, expelled dust, and
then hustled the writhing blue spot raggedly back toward the
Rock. Behind them, a curved explosion of light lay on the
ground. It loomed and retreated to Fare's eye. One brown
figure ran back to retrieve it. Holding it at arm's length like
something dirty, a live snake. At the back of the school building, the fire door sighed closed on its greased piston.

He faced the fence, the far field, the highway. Around him
everywhere on the fields, and at doorways—steam plant,
block factory, furniture repair, exercise yard, near and distant—men stopped, small figures in washed-out blue: They
heard the faint sounds of struggle, relayed in the heavy air,
eerily far behind the brown movement that caused them. They
looked from the boiling swarm now making its way through
the Rock's west gate. They looked at Fare, a freeman kneeling
in the grass. He looked back at them, from one group to
another, his eyes bringing defiance, or lassitude, or fear into
theirs. As he watched, they turned back to their work. They

would find out, know it all in a few hours.

At the tag plant door, turning to walk, then looking back again from the head of the line was the big man who had ripped the boxes. He was laughing. He clasped his belly now, as though he might laugh up his guts. He pointed a limp hand at Fare and laughed.

"Got to be something come along pretty soon." Charles Ed laughed thinly.

Fare fought not to see the face.

"Got to," he said.

They sat under an overpass out of the rain. Finally, an old backfiring, missing sound came down the road, echoing like a shout in a pipe, two weak headlights, bouncing long poles of light, an old car. A Buick.

There was something immediately good about this crippled, gypsy thing coming. Fare heard and then saw how different it was from what usually went by bright and swift. They faced each other smiling. The rain had stopped. They stood up from where they had been hunkering beneath the bridge. They were barely visible in the compounded dark beneath the overpass, but eyes inside the car had seen them and it stopped as though they had charmed it. It pulled over, swaying like a stagecoach. They scrambled in, all grateful, fumbling, crushing the TWA flight bag between them. Inside was not what they had expected. Things were very close. There were cracks in the windows, dirty quilts for seat covers. On the floor were piles of dirty laundry and greasy car parts in broken cardboard boxes. Fare tensed at the sight of this interior.

The driver was a big fat man in a dirty white T-shirt, stretched at the neck. His light, curly hair escaped from the T-shirt wherever possible. Tufts of it at his neck made a beard when his chin lowered, which was often, for he seemed to try to hide his eyes. The boys settled, hugging themselves, beating away the chill, and thanking in monosyllables. But there was no answer to their thanks and the driver, who said his name was Lester Macabee, seemed to concentrate too well on the

road ahead. An uneasy conversation began in the car. It was
to the point. The fat man spoke by turning his head back to
look full at them with each phrase. His hands steered, but
his eyes looked back. Before he said his first words, he had
already looked back at them several times, each time fully,
turning his head with the mobility given to certain birds.
Finally, "You boys going to Greenville?"

"Yes, sir," said Charles Ed. He didn't like this fat man at
all. The politeness of his answer told this. The word "sir" was
spoken with the rising inflection of military speech.

"So are we, if we don't run out of gas first," said the fat
man. "We takin Chuckie here in to get dried out, up to the
V.A. Ain't we, Chuckie?" He slapped Chuckie hard on the
shoulder, the way you might adjust the position of a bundle
on the seat. It was the first of this little man the boys had
noticed. Looking over, they could see that he sat with his
back to the door and his legs stretched out on the seat, and
that his feet did not even reach as far as the driver's legs.

Lester got no answer from the drugged Chuckie, so he
reached over and, with a viciousness that was suddenly natural to him and this car and this night, punched again hard.

The boys' eyes focused on the gas gauge. The indicator
lolled to the left with just a slit of light between it and empty.

With his cunning, the man Lester caught their glances and
said, "You boys like to help out with that?"

Charles Ed, the stronger, made a quick glance to Fare
which did as much as a hand placed over his mouth to keep
him quiet.

"No, sir," he said. "Don't guess we can do that."

"Don't expect to ride for nothing, do you?" Lester came
back quick.

"Usually do." Charles Ed, just as quick. This was a point
of honor with him. It was the hitchhiker's right. He paid only
with his company.

Fare was nervous. By now the gas gauge and the "E" line
were one and palpable. They were the only referent in the
black car night. The fat man held the wheel in both hands.

His arms did not lie against his sides, but flexed straight out like stubby wings. Underneath his arms there were dark rings of sweat in the dirty T-shirt. He reached out like a snake striking to slap the other man again. "Wake up now," he said, "you hear!" It was as though he needed a witness.

The old man came up from his sleep with a quick start, spewing like a speechmaker, but saying only, "Ice . . . ice . . . ice!"

After a while his head fell upon his chest. "Lee me alone, damn you, Lester, now."

"Wake up," said Lester. "We got these boys here and they don't want to help for no gas.

"Gas," said the old man sing-songy, "gas-o-line."

Fare wondered. "We got these boys." *Was that what he said?*

"Do, do," said the old man in a bubbly way. "Do em to hell."

"Listen," said Charles Ed, leaning forward onto the seat. "We'd like to help, but we ain't got no money." Fare knew he didn't want to say this, but he was frightened fully now and felt he had to.

Fare looked to the window where, straining, he seemed to see stars of water on distant leaves go by more slowly.

"Nope," said Lester, turning around with his jaw set, the dumb "O" of his mouth a flat line now. "You got money."

"Hell no, we don't," said Charles Ed. He was mad. Losing all control.

"Listen," said Fare, "why don't you just let us out right here?"

"Out!" echoed the old man.

"Okay," said Lester, who was slowing down anyway.

Stars of water on leaves stopped.

Lester jerked the car over onto the shoulder. The muscles in his shoulders came alive beneath the fat. His left hand disappeared between his legs. The car stopped and he turned off the engine. He stayed behind the wheel. They began to get out, though nothing was said about them doing it. First

Fare, then Charles Ed. The two stood, foolishly it turned out, waiting for Lester to crank up. Two cars passed by close together like racers, heading on toward Carrboro. Lester sat still behind the wheel, sinking low, as though lost in the deepest thought he could know.

Then, very quickly, the way some fat men could do, he jumped out on the highway side with such force that the door flew out and came back to hit him. He had a thick, nickel-plated pistol, smothered in both his fat hands and leveled across the car roof at them.

"You boys ain't riding for no free."

The look passed again from Charles Ed to Fare; the eyes said, "Be quiet."

Later, when he thought about it, Fare was always transfixed by the innocence of this decision of Charles Ed's, who, at twenty, thought the world worked. Who did not believe this man would kill them for nothing, for gasoline. Watching, Fare whispered to himself, "Give in. Give in."

But Charles Ed said, gritting his teeth, "We ain't got no money!" Fare did nothing. Then Charles Ed turned and walked, not too fast, down the shoulder of the road, leaving Fare wondering, did he motion me to follow him? Next he saw a storm of stupid misery cross Lester's face.

Or did he go off and leave me? Which is it?

Lester turned the gun toward Charles Ed, rotating his whole body, screwing the tiny gun butt down into the car roof, crouching down to sight from behind it.

"Hey you, boy!" he called. He had now a lax, satisfied smile on his face. It was resolution. The old drunkard, Chuckie, stuck his head out the window. "What now?" he asked petulantly.

Fare said something, some quiet syllable, caught in his throat or lost in the flash and sharp crack, and heard the *ping* of the automatic action chambering another round, saw it drive Lester's hands a full foot back across the roof of the car. Charles Ed, about twenty feet away, turned slowly, angry but all right, just big in the eyes, and then Fare saw a fan of dirty crimson spread across the shoulders of his letterman's jacket. Red lace along his chin. Lester saw too. Charles Ed walked toward them, holding his head carefully erect, his eyes growing with each step, and went on by and stopped, losing his stiffness in a huge shudder. He knelt down, still careful with his head, and reached forward, his hands palms downward, smoothing a trough in the dirt by the highway. Then he bent his shoulders and chest for the first time and leaned over, dripping the red lace from all along his face. He lay himself into the sand.

The calm broken, things quick again, the pistol again twice, loud and close, Fare cursing himself, the infinity of a long arching leap, the momentary dizziness of rolling down the embankment. Streaks of light passed by him striking—phit, phit—among the trees.

The night dew and dust made grime in his mouth and at the bottom he was up and running across the ditch and across another line of something where the light stopped and the dark began. He was in the dripping woods, up to his knees in dead leaves and he heard a car go by in a long suck like a riptide at night, and then another. He waited and grabbed a handful of leaves and rubbed them into his face and mouth, chewing mechanically. Then he spit them out and tried hard with all of himself to fall instead, to die, and see what Charles Ed would do in his place.

"You jack-leg son of a bitch," Charles Ed screamed in controlled fury, and he was on Lester before he had time to turn the gun, faster than Fare, dreaming it, thought he could ever move. He had Lester up against the side of the car and had the gun away and held it, taking his time, up under Lester's chin and there was an outrageous noise rolling down against the trees.

As the old Buick cranked up and caught, Fare heard it backfire twice, and Lester burned it wildly out onto the road. Alone, Fare stood cold still and the mauled leaves spread in a hot green liquid through his fingers.

After a while standing there, he crawled back out to the

edge of the light and saw something falling by stages down the embankment like a bundle of old clothes. Charles Ed was turned around longways toward the road and his head was down in the ditch. A long stretch of white neck was all that showed in the moonlight with his head pitched down this way. Fare knelt, finding his brother's forehead by hand, and pulled out his shirttail to wipe it clean. This finished, his head went down and touched Charles Ed's, warm and impossibly familiar, and he remembered things, times when they had done this in spirit if not in fact. Too drunk to stand unsupported, they had supported each other, or exhausted, with a football crushed between them, wild with laughter and victory under the harsh light in some country end zone. He began to cry.

It took a long time to get Charles Ed back up to the road. It didn't hurt him anymore to hit against things, but they slipped in the dew on this angle, and each time Fare had to cry. The tears fell freely, but not in release, coming from eyes that saw this night as a simple, bitter task. Kudzu vines. Glories closed up until morning. What there was still left to do: Get Charles Ed back up the hill; call the cops.

Fare shook his head and wiped the puke from his mouth. He had abandoned Charles Ed's body there on the embankment, left him to walk off down the road and call the police. For ten years he had been the one who abandoned things. The old life, the old place, the old people and the places where he had watched them get buried; he had even rid himself of the accent that linked him to them. Now he talked like the man on television, the *American* man. But he could not abandon memory, not entirely, and September was the month of memory and of the strange tormenting dreams. He had lived with it all too long now, at night in dreams, in the daytime, in his fear of life. The hand that ripped the box, that swung the blade, that dropped the hammer was the hand that held the gun. The faces were all the same, vapid and untroubled. Now he would have to live with this new character. This thin, tall, neat and efficient Negro would join the night troupe and the

116 /

sound of the long blade chopping, the sight of it glittering, falling upon the seriousness of William Hughes, who could not read or write; these were in him now too.

The fire door boomed again. Hard breath puffed toward him.

"Where you been, Mr. Odum?" A hand on his shoulder. "We been looking for you in ever hole in that school, didn't know *what* we'd fine."

Crews, the school security guard, was trying not to look at him. Fare wiped the bile from his face and stood up.

"You mean he just, by God, walked in here an unscrewed the thing, just like that?"

The school was shutting down now; the walking line was shuffling out. They all gathered in the office, around the paper cutter. Bray was talking to Holly Mardis, the only inmate in the room.

"I guess so, Mr. Bray."

"Jesus Christ, and nobody *saw*."

Here Arthur, the science teacher, chimed in, "Considering the circumstances, an unfortunate choice of words."

Bray gave him an icy stare. Fare could see that Bray did not know what Arthur was talking about. And Fare was ashamed of knowing.

"Guess not," said Mardis, hanging his head. "Somebody said he had one a them tool belts, you know, like somebody from Physical Plants Division wears."

A voice from the crowd offered, "Maybe they thought he come to fix it."

This got nervous laughter.

"Wasn't broke," said Bray, pacing back and forth in front of the violated paper cutter. "Shit like this goes on they'll close this school down. It's some of them just looking for a chance."

He looked up at the group of teachers. "You all be out of a job."

Fare looked at the paper cutter. The big knife with the hand-formed grip at one end was gone. It lay, now, wrapped

in a towel in the Rock Lieutenant's office. But the bolt that
had held it, the cotter pin and lock washer, lay here neatly
stacked on the cutting surface where the killer had left them.
The crazy good manners of murder.

"Anybody know what this is all about?" Bray was asking.

The men in the crowd said it must have been something
from back in the Rock. "You know how that goes."

And they knew. A debt, a slight, maybe even a contract.
No, not for William Hughes. He wasn't big enough for a
contract.

"You know, Mardis?"

"Naw, sir, Mr. Bray."

"Ain't likely we'll ever know, is it?"

"Naw, sir. Ain't likely *you'll* ever know."

Now Bray retreated to his own small cubicle, examined
paper clips and ashtrays. He slammed a filing cabinet with
his forearm. "Shit," he said. "Just shit! I just say shit." The talking stopped. "I guess you guys can punch out. Odum, I want
to talk to you a minute."

Fare sat in the cool green leather chair, across from Bray,
and did not think about the knife wrapped in the State of
Florida towel. Bray was filling out a form.

"You were closing the windows, go on? . . ."

"Yeah, and . . ."

"How come nobody was there but you and this Hughes, and
this mad dog nigger . . . says here . . . name of Simmons.
This Simmons?"

"Most of the class was out in the hall smoking."

Bray looked up from the report. He looked at Fare the way
his daddy had when he'd messed up some expensive machinery.

"I know. I know," said Fare. "I'm supposed to keep them
in until the walking line forms."

"Why were they out then? If they hadn't been out . . ."

"Because you got to give something to get something. That's
the way things work around here. I give them a smoke, they
play school."

Bray sighed. "*You* gone tell me how it works around here?"

He rubbed his chin distractedly, muttered. "I still got to put something on here. Now between you and me I don't care who cuts who in this bunch of trash that's out here, but it cain't happen in my school." He tapped the form on the desk in front of him. "Now how good you want it to look? You want me to put your whole Goddamned class, ever swinging dick of em, was out waltzing around the fucking hallway?"

"Don't care," said Fare. "Get yourself off if that's what it comes down to." It sounded good to say this. It sounded like the truth. "I can go somewhere else. I can leave."

"You know I'm not asking . . ."

"I know. I know you're not."

Fare got up from the chair to go. Through the cantilevered glass partition he could see the last of the noon walking line shuffling out. His legs were growing tight from the running. Late, hurrying, a sheaf of poems in his hand, Ivory was locking the science supply room door. He turned and before sprinting to catch up, popped a gumball into his mouth. There goes my teacher, Fare thought. It was not true. He could not leave. Not now. This one was the one he could not run away from.

TWELVE

HE WOKE UP. HE CAME OUT OF THE GUILT YOU ARE IN WHEN you sleep in the middle of the day. In a dream, he had worked the night shift in the slaughterhouse near home. All night he had listened to the hogs screaming in their pens, waiting for morning in strange surroundings. He had kept records of all the trucks that came and went, bringing hogs and taking out guts for soap. He had jumped aboard, careful of the hot upright exhausts to ask for names and numbers. From these thirty seconds of climbing, raising his voice to the dark tired eyes in the cabs while the diesels grumbled, he was left with little pools of steaming piss and stacks of shit. The animals answered their fear this way.

The stink accumulated in the night, with the buzzing of insects and the air-conditioner and the coffee turning acid. All these things, under the delicately lashed, weeping eyes of a thousand hogs, blinking at him through the slats, he had dreamt as though they were real, until, when the knocking came fetching far down into the maze of his sleep, he had begun to see a very strange thing. One of them, a fierce, battered old boar with evil curved tushes had parted the milling, packed cargo of hogs in the back of the truck and walked toward him, and had spoken plainly in the voice he remembered from the night and the roadside, "Gasoline."

It was Lester. But the knocking came spiraling down before Fare could reply to this, and as he awoke, he knew that he had formulated the only reply but had lost it. To the knock now, he awoke in the guilt, and he shook to get rid of it. It was not deserved.

She was standing in the dim hallway of the old house. She looked like one of its commonplaces. In her hand, just lowered from knocking, she held nothing, but the fingers trembled in an attitude of grasping. She was shy. Now he remembered. It was time. Of course. She hugged him in the doorway, holding him.

How long since they had been together? He didn't know, but knew she carried within her a tiny device telling her when to come and find him. Without looking, he saw her car parked down below. The back seat, he knew, was filled with yellow chrysanthemums. A little dirt would be spilling over onto the seat covers. Her eyes were asking him, "Won't you please come?" In the doorway now, she held him by the upper arms.

"Come in," he said, "Mother."

He remembered now when he had last seen her. It had been on the day of the packing, when she had loaded it all, finding that it was all so pitifully small and light, there simply was not much left from the life which had been hers, and this had made her cry. He had comforted her that day. Now she let go of him and walked into the room.

He sat on a marble bench. Not far away and a little behind him, she was on her knees making small mounds of earth about the stems of transplanted chrysanthemums. Strange how she cared nothing for her expensive summer dress, or the shredded stockings at her pale edemic knees. She hummed as she worked. All in all, what he heard was a little too happy, the cadence too quick for the occasion. The fall wind brought him a verse of "Red Wing," a song she had sung to make them sleep when they were children. When the wind died he heard only little pulses from her throat.

She was happy. She was in the somnolence of ritual and this was enough—an act in the magnitude of dishwashing. She could lose herself, as a child would, in the monotony of a repetitive task. Around him were the other headstones and footprints and the flowers, some of them real. Some were taking hold, the way she hoped hers would.

She was dressing two graves in fall clothing. His father, his brother. Beneath the surface he imagined them ignoring her little pats and straightenings as usual. Was he really needed?

She was oblivious of him and wouldn't let him help. "No, you sit down right over there and I'll just be a few seconds."

He had forgotten this yearly coming of hers. This bench where he sat and said nothing to the woman behind him. What did you say to your mother, a woman grown old beyond the distance of your understanding? To her he was a strange thing—man and child—a memory to be kept, and flesh here on this bench. He turned to see her sweep loam in wide arcs to the base of a tall chrysanthemum. Still she hummed, ". . . that Indian weeping her heart away." He knew that, back turned to him, she was singing him to sleep again. Him and Charles Ed.

He lit a cigarette. In this country cemetery, not five miles from the home place, lay dead generations of Odums going back to the Battle of Olustee. The influenza epidemic of 1904 was represented by clusters of infant graves. Thirty yards from him in a fresh grave lay his cousin Hart Odum from the Battle of Khaesanh, and near Hart, Uncle Harold's oldest girl, Hermione, nicknamed Leadfoot, a crossroads casualty.

Near his brother's grave lay the blue ceramic football from the Quarterback Club. As a symbol of the power and grace that had been Charles Ed, it was ludicrous. Yet it was from the town, a gift from men who had gaped at his brother's magic, whose sons had gone with him, in fact been carried by him, to the state Class B playoffs.

His mother had had her way for once in the matter of the inscription: CHARLES ED ODUM, FIRST BORN OF BASIL AND INEZ, 1945–1965. FROM THE ARMS OF MOTHER TO THE ARMS OF JESUS. Fare tried to picture it, Charles Ed at six-one, 190, ascending. Near the blue football lay a crystal vase. Purple flowers had years since wilted to powder around its edges. Fare remembered the vase, the day they had packed, and on their way out of the county, stopped to leave it here filled with pansies.

She had given him something that day.

"Take it, Fare. He would of wanted you to have it."

"Naw, Mommer, you keep it. Or give it to the museum."

He knew she didn't want it. He knew also that his father

would have wanted Charles Ed to have it before him. But
Charles Ed would not have given a tinker's damn for it, would
probably have lost it inside of a week.

She held the heavy knife out to him. He had taken it only
to please her, to alleviate the pain it needed for her to hold it
out like that. It was a Confederate soldier's Bowie, or side
knife. He had unsheathed it to read the words embossed on
the knuckle guard. "Death to Abolition." It had probably
been the product of some crossroads smithy, made of steel
from a wagon spring. Its grip and D-shaped knuckle guard
were a single piece of cast bronze. Its steel blade was spear
shaped and double-edged, severely hollow ground, diamond
in cross section. The name Carmack Odum was crudely etched
in the pommel. Carmack Odum, Fare's great great grand-
father, had fallen at Olustee with the First Florida under
General Colquitt. Reading it again that day while his mother
packed, Fare had known that, even though Carmack Odum
had not himself struck the three-word motto, cold and unequivocal as the steel itself, he had given his heart to it in
agreement, and his heart's blood for it in fact. Things had been
so simple then.

"Thanks."

"Thank your father's memory by staying out of mischief."

A woman's fear of accidents. He remembered his father's
easy care with dangerous tools, guns. No axioms, but always
safe. She was newspapering glass knickknacks. His father's
father's mustache cup went under, then some colored animals.
Then her hands balked at the Bible. She turned to Fare. It was
the "new" Bible. After a decent space, she laid it aside, but not
before she stopped herself from saying something.

He had never been comfortable with this part of his father,
the church part. It was a failure. The beginning of all the
failures. Secretly, he knew how it had come about. He knew
more about the change (their people all called it this, some of
them half-reverently) than anyone else. How it had started
with the wish. With the dissatisfaction that lacked a name
growing in the man who was too simple, had neither the

powers nor the vices to deal with it. How his father had become a lay preacher, "heard the call," they said. Some of them had looked down on him. Some of them wanted a seminary preacher, feeling times had changed so that no man could unofficially take up a call. This, the dogged lonesomeness of it, was the one thing Fare did admire.

It had begun the year of the corn blight. They had expanded operations that year, rented land, taken on labor, introduced a new strain of seed. It was going to be a big year for corn. Everyone said so. His daddy, still the big, strong, young man then, had borrowed money for this first big push to get ahead. It was good land, ironsome red clay. But there was too much rain too early that year. Red clay dust turned to dark red mud. Then the fields dried and things seemed fine. Later, at the end of summer, the men gathered in groups in the fields. No one moved to break out the tools for servicing the big gleaners. They laughed in brittle, careful bursts. They laughed clinching their hands against the bottoms of their pockets, giving themselves a bowling pin look, breaking off their talk in midphrase for a distracted searching of the horizon. They sifted and played with the dirt wondering was it, or was the sky, the betraying element. His uncle Harold said, "What the hail *is* spores, anyway?"

One day, the bank vice-president stood on the front porch, pawing with his feet. The word "credit" was mentioned. He was winding his hat around and around in his hands. Later, when the discussion had ended, his father went in to unsheathe the gleaming shotgun and hold it lovingly, thoughtfully in his hands. Fare had watched while his mother came to him and stood with one hand gripping the barrel till her knuckles whitened. Their hands clasped the gun for the time it took to count to twenty. Then, his father walked out, fast toward the west, as if to stay under the last light, and did not stop till his chest hit barbed wire. Then slowly, he stooped to gather red dirt in one hand, sift it to the other, down and down, red smoke in the wind at his denim cuffs. Watching, Fare had not been afraid anymore about rotten corn sighing in the wind at night.

The old man waited until the sun was gone, and the dark seemed to touch the way he could feel the dirt, its colors, and he turned, striding back to the house, his shoes tracked by wisps of red vapor. His father's shoes. Unlaced beside the doorway, or propped, or working the pedals of a little Ford Farmall tractor.

"Keep up, Fare. We got a right smart a walking to do."

"Daddy, I got to take three steps to ever one of yours!"

"Do what you got to do."

They walked to the little church even though they could have driven. His father liked to do things primitive on Sunday. *He* would never have said it that way himself, but that was what he liked. No work, no nonsense. (Somehow, hunting had become nonsense.) Sleep. Good food, and something called "meditation," which was pressing your fingers against both temples and giving off a headache look. Before his father took up preaching, Fare had thought meditation must be something like the wish, and maybe it had been at first, but later, his father had traded the wish for the call. He could not say exactly when, or could he?

Afternoons that year began with the hollow lilt of a piano playing off somewhere. It was the old man, they said, gone off down to the church building. Don't bother him, you hear. He had just dropped his work, they said, and wandered down there. Don't bother him.

But secretly Fare had followed him enough times to know how he was improving on the instrument, how he had gone from pecking to simple chords, to whole pieces, just by ear. How his eyes were changing. Fare had the uneasy feeling that while the music was getting better, something else was getting worse.

It had rained too much that year. That was what started all the trouble, and sometimes because they blamed it, the rain kept them away. They would grab at any excuse, some of them. Sunday night services could get particularly thin, many of them feeling they had done service enough in the morning. They were a small congregation anyway.

One night rain had come at sundown out of a cloudless sky, falling through an eerie orange light. It was a small rain, picking its way into Fare the way locks were opened by thieves, until he felt ready for something. He listened for patterns like those he found sometimes in idling engines. Outside the church, the leaves of a camellia sighed against the windows.

A few came. Stamping their feet on the plank porch, they scattered in the thumping little church, mumbling greetings across empty pews.

Sitting as always in the front pew, Fare felt strangely oppressed and somehow, gladdened by the emptiness around him. For a while, his father's performance reflected no difference. With his first words there were ripples among the scattered, tired forms of his neighbors, a backward rocking from the censure of the voice. It was as though a strong wind had begun to blow. From the high pulpit, he meted out his sermon with the familiar, careful anger. When the call to the altar yielded no comers (who was left here to give himself to Jesus?), he moved to his chair for a repetition of the pattern Fare knew like drawing breath. His father sat, eyes closed, with one thumb pressed tightly on his temple, the other hand gripping the new black book in his lap. The hoarse organ worked through the opening chords of "Stand Up for Jesus," under the spider-walking brittle fingers of old Miss Tift. The first verse was sung. Both congregation and organist were poised before the second, ancient flight of steps, when in a rage of frayed blue serge, the old man leaped from his chair and flung crossed arms outward, cutting the song, like phlegm, from their tired throats. Miss Tift's hands fumbled the lace at her throat. Then, crouching behind the keyboard of the old piano, his father played, and was, for himself only, "A Mighty Fortress."

The room waked then. None of them had ever seen the Reverend play. None of them remembered their hymnbooks. There seemed to be no obligation to sing. The Reverend, eyeing the rain through the open door, cared only for a communion with his music. He played through all six stanzas, working hard at the pedals, defying the muttering rain with clear chords. Watching, Fare saw the muscles in his shoulders leap at the base of his neck. His father's whole body seemed wedded to the song, and now it to all their lips, and each full, liquid chord for an instant in danger of isolation, so that all their mouths sang the coming word just before he gave it to them, sang as though they would sing this once and no more, rise and leave this fortress born again in Jesus. They did not know what else to do.

Fare knew that as long as his father played, he could command belief by the song's authority. The arms, the transported, bobbing head, were the center of a power until all was forgotten in the church but the forces of darkness gathering against its fortress walls.

When the last notes shimmered away in the rain, silence stole in and still the Reverend saw only the lancing drops in the arc light out of doors. His eyes were still wild from the place he had been. Then he stood, called them quickly to benediction, and carrying his book, stalked coldly through the side door. Fare heard two voices behind him, first a woman's, asking, "Sober?"

Then a man's, answering, "Cold."

He followed, under the eyes of the still-motionless congregation, and behind the piano, found his father's sweat-soaked bow tie. On the porch of the house a mile away, wet from the rain, he thought of the music, the press of submissive faces. He sought for some gesture of his own, something more grand than the prints of his small feet beside those of his father across the yard and up the steps. But the black tie in his hand seemed suddenly larger than anything his mind could offer. He stood clutching it in the cone of the porch light, and finally, shivering from the cold and an unnameable anger, turned and flung it into the dooryard. He knew that he alone in the church had not mistaken his father's look of contempt for the glare of an eye seeing God. In his bed that night, he felt himself stop waiting to believe.

The next morning, his father found the tie, a puzzlement. Their eyes did not meet all day. From that day, he felt his own contempt growing, and the lonesome burden of the wish. His father's ache now was for heaven. The old man had fallen off in his hunting and farming and warmed to his preaching and piano.

When his father died and he returned from college for the burying and dividing up, his mother had tried to give him the new Bible. She packed the knickknacks, mustache cup, but at the Bible her hands balked. She thought about it. It was not the family book. She would keep that, and with it, the history. No, this was the special, gold-leaf embossed book presented by the congregation. When it was clear to her he did not want it, she did not ask why.

"Don't much want it, either," she said.

He saw the change come over her that took her when she felt the need for strength. She was moving in with her sister up in Valdosta. Quickly, she pressed the book into one corner of the packing box.

But he took the old knife. He wanted it, not to use, but as something to have from the earliest times, and he carried it with him through school, from dormitory to apartment, storing it here and there, but always taking care to keep it clean.

She was nearly finished with the two graves. They would be going soon. The tall chrysanthemums ringed the graves in two dark trenches. She smiled, lightly clapping dirt from her palms. She believed something was buried here, but he knew now that he did not. There was nothing here, and he would not come back again to nothing. What was left, he carried with him in his heart.

They walked to the car and he helped her in. Driving to his apartment, pushing their shadow along into the evening, they saw, as they passed over a little bridge, a stretch of gleaming branch. Racing its shadow along, came a large, dun-colored water bird. Fare blinked, and his vision kept this ghost's image until it blurred, turned orange, becoming a grainy blot. He felt that the two of them, he and his mother, understood something then. Something about what it was to survive. Should they gaze any longer at these forests and pastures filled with life, nothing within their field of vision would ever move again. They would be exterminators.

He parked the car. Then she stood again in the doorway, waiting sheepishly before him, her mouth open a little, but her hands satisfied. There were things he feared she would say. That they might have, or could have . . . She would go now and her open mouth holding these things unsaid would hang in his mind like the image of the bird, and when he turned, he would see it above the bed and by the sink for only a little while. Then, when he looked from new angles, it would be gone. What could he say to her? Had she ever known them, him and Charles Ed, in their dewy world of collisions, as living remnants of the man who had traded his life to her for hers? Had she ever understood why they turned away from the song she was singing? Why they could not grow up softer than they did? She had been the center—quiet and certain, undemanding. Now she was at the tilting edge of something. A cipher, she had no more identity. She was the former wife of an abstraction, the mother of two memories.

So he said, "Mother I, . . ." not knowing how he would finish this, thinking perhaps he would tell her what he had in mind to do. But she raised two fingers to his lips and pressed them so he tasted dirt, and with the other hand, pressed her own lips to quiet them both. Then, after a pause, said, "Fare . . . " She placed both hands on his shoulders and, kneading them like bread, she lost her way. "Such a big, strong boy. I never knew. I never knew how it happened. That you all got so big. That we all . . . You have your father's shoulders. His collarbones that stick out." He wanted to tell her to go, but now her fingers pressed his lips.

She said, "Tell me, do you like your work? When they ask me what you do, I tell them you work in the prison, and it makes them very serious like you were a doctor or an astronaut. But I tell them it is what you were called to do. That there are many calls and no accounting for what comes to any of us for work in this life. I tell them that you were my work, and that what you are doing, in a way, I am doing too. I tell them we are doing it. I know you are doing good up there. And that means I am doing good too. Some time I want you to come and meet them, some of my friends." She faltered.

Her eyelids fluttered and she brought her hands down to clasp them at her waist. "We talk about our children," she said.

She seemed tired. There seemed to have been a preamble, but now she had forgotten and she shook her head. But she nodded as though she had said it. He looked into her eyes and saw that it was there and that it was that she loved him. "Now I've got to go," and she was already walking away down the stairs, small but steady, brittle but erect. Careful. Fare wanted to run after her, but did not.

Where is the lesson, he wanted to ask. What do I carry inside me from you, Mother? What is my equipment for the time being?

He caught her by the arm in the narrow stair, bringing her face up to his. In it was her perpetual question. She would settle for anything, any platitude, so long as the answer was polite. His face burned; he was clutching her arm too tightly. He said, "Did anyone ever . . . did any of us, the Odums, ever kill anybody?" She dropped her eyes, pivoted slightly; was she struggling a little to free herself?

"Kiss me bye," she said, leaning toward him.

"Mother?" he said.

She looked at him sternly now, "You'll have to ask your . . ." She shook her head again. "But you can't, can you?" Crystal tears rolled down her cheeks.

He said, "Did Neamon? Did any of those . . . louts from your side of the family? . . ."

She smiled. A pale blue handkerchief fluttered up between them. Her face was dry now. "Neamon and that bunch," she said, remembering. "Neamon *was* a rakehell scoundrel."

She laughed. It was a laugh of pleasure.

He let go of her arm.

"Your father used to say . . . But it was mostly talk, Fare. It was mostly . . ."

But he was moving backward, back up the stairs.

THIRTEEN

His class, weary from the weekend in the Rock, dozed over the morning's work. Fare cut a look from the papers he was grading to the clock. Ten minutes. He locked the drawer, took his cup and walked to the supply room.

His back to the door as usual, Ivory sat deeply absorbed in his writing. Beside him, the hot plate ticked red under a laboratory beaker full of coffee. Fare let himself in and waited. A stiffness took the broad blue back at the sound of his entrance. Slowly, as though submerging into a troubled lower world, Ivory contracted his neck and turned.

"Howdy," said Fare.

"So, back you come, and all in one piece." Ivory stretched.

"You think I'd get eat up over the weekend?" Fare was playing with words now.

"Not exactly, but I thought you might be pissed enough at that fool with the sword to cut me from the social register. You know, eat up with the white man's burden. I mean, if one nigger'll run after your balls with a knife, so will another one. But," he cut his eyes to the cup in Fare's hand, "but, I see lust overcomes good sense."

"Well, maybe . . ."

"Well, what else? Exploit the nigger?"

"Invite me to sit down, I got something to tell you."

"Invited."

Ivory put on an asbestos glove and removed the beaker from the hot plate. He poured Fare's cup.

Fare said, "Someday, somebody's gone find out about you in here." He raised his hands like a painter framing an image. " 'Mad spade constructs nuclear device in state prison. Senate investigates enormous crater north of Starke.' "

Ivory shucked the glove with a flick of his wrist.

"Naw, man, just coffee."

They sipped without talking.

Ivory was interested, aware of something. Fare would wait for him to ask the question, make the next move on his own turf.

He did.

"So, uh, what you got to tell me, man? You acting funny?"

"What's funny about me?"

"You puttin on them jive changes, man. The doh opens, and 'Howdy' you says instead of hello. You come on with all this "gone do this, gone do that' shit. Next thing I know, you get up and leave without saying, 'Once more into the breach, dear friends.' Maaan!"

"You onto me, huh?"

"Like stink on shit. Can't pull nothing over on this nigger."

Ivory laughed, a bitter, unhappy laugh. This bitterness was growing in him. Fare didn't want to think where it might take him.

"What do you know about trying to find somebody in this place? Somebody you don't know the first thing about?"

Fare's stomach lurched as his decision took irretrievable shape in words. With words he was committing himself to someone. He was not sure he could trust Ivory, yet these words needed to see light. He could make them as real as possible this way. He considered how the movies handled this moment. In a courtroom somewhere, in his youth, he heard Raymond Burr describe these words as the defendant's first mistake. The small weak place where investigators had first inserted their probes.

"The defendant did, in fact, admit in the presence of one Ivory Rose, to an obsession with finding a certain Lester Macabee." He felt sick.

Across from him, Ivory sat with his mouth open. His face was the surprised face of a child drawn into dangerous play. The bitterness was dispelled.

"What chew mean 'fine somebody' in here? People in here ain't gone nowhere. They been foun."

"Not found enough," Fare muttered.

He was controlling it now. It felt strangely good to have Ivory this way, half-contemptuous, half-eaten up with the curiosity.

"You don't mean that cat in the dream, in the dream you tole me about? That . . . Lester?"

Fare stood and slowly raised his right foot, resting it on his chair. This would be the most dramatic moment. He could not help playing it out a little. His eyes held Ivory's as he slowly rolled his pants leg. As the fabric came up, revealing his ankle and calf, Ivory's eyes let go and he watched open-mouthed as first the gleaming steel tip, then the double-edged blade, and last, the polished brass pommel and knuckle guard of the heirloom side knife were revealed. They both stared at it.

"What's that?" said Ivory.

"That," Fare said, "is a symbol."

He reached down with one hand while the other held his rolled trouser leg, and ripped twice to free the blade from the surgical tape which held it in place. With the first two pieces of tape sticking awkwardly to his fingertips, he ripped the last, which held the grip, trapping the long knife with the flat of his hand before it plunged down into the top of his foot. He hefted the blade in the space between him and Ivory. It felt balanced, utile. He had read that men had been smaller in Carmack's time. The three stripes on his calf where the tape had barbered him felt hot and good. For the first time, he understood the knife as something more than history.

Ivory had recovered a little.

"At's quite a shank," he said. "Sho get the job done."

Then he looked up at the wall, hardly more than a blink at it, where maybe he was seeing some job that *got* done. He blinked down again. He held out his hand casually. Fare let him heft the knife.

"This is contraband, man. You could fall for a five-to-ten spot just for this one little truck here."

Fare knew it was contraband. Knew the risk he had taken to bring it in, but also knew that he needed to play out this little scene. He had to jump in knee-deep if he was ever going to get in up to his ass, and there couldn't be any toe dipping and running back from the water's edge.

"How'd you get this past the detector, man?"

"They let up on me when I'm late. So I was late. Besides, it rings every morning on me for something they can't find. Teeth in my zipper. They figger I'm all right by now."

"You gone take it out the same way?"

Ivory's fist closed around the knife.

He said, "I could put this to good use in here, you know. I could . . ."

Fare took Ivory's wrist into his hand. It was the first time he had touched Ivory.

Never touch an inmate. Any touching is considered provocation and will likely result in retaliation.

Ivory was provoked. He was on his feet. The chair slid as though on greased tracks clean to the opposite wall. Fare held to the wrist.

"Let me go, white man."

Fare saw Ivory's free hand ball up into an ugly chalk gray fist. With his own free hand he drew back. He deepened his grip, and for a moment they Indian wrestled.

"Listen, nigger, I've made up my mind for something. It's gonna go down. I'm gonna join the organization. If I have to, right here."

His words came out as spaced, bitten-off squeaks through the blood pumping up past his knotted tie. He felt years of something chip off like ice from a pipe. He was no match for the Negro. But he didn't care. A little bit, Ivory stopped resisting with his black body, and began something with his eyes. Fare knew that if they did their work on him, then the body would come back at him. He did not say any more. Only he breathed and waited and nothing in him changed. His decision could not anywhere be felt coming undone. A happiness was growing in his eyes like none he had known. For a moment he considered trying, cold-bloodedly, just to see if he could kill the man whose arm he held. He drew back his fist a little.

He sighted for a striking place at the bridge of the flat black nose. The sledgehammer had fallen on the hog that day, long ago, striking it on the forehead where he now focused his eyes.

Then he felt something at the wrist he held. A loosening. The knife rattled on the tile floor.

"Better pick that up, white man. Somebody see it you be in a shitload of trouble."

Faces drifted past the window.

"You pick it up. You dropped it."

Fare stepped back and squared off his feet. Ivory laughed. Not the bitter laugh, but a laugh of real mirth.

"Anything, baby, anything."

What was so fucking funny?

He bent to the knife. From the floor, he quickly tossed it to Fare.

Surprise!

Fare bobbled it. It seemed all blade, alive; its edges writhed as he tried to cradle it where clothing muffled flesh. If he cut himself, the brown uniforms would have to know. At last he had it. Blood shimmered from his palms like an augury. He stared at it, then at Ivory. Ivory stared back at him with a taut seriousness both exhilarated and baleful. They both had shown edges, he and Ivory. Keen edges.

"First thing you got to do is read the motherfucker's file. You got to know what the bulls know."

Ivory sat again. He refilled both their cups. Fare could not, for a second, assimilate what he was saying.

In another movie, he flashed his forged I.D.

"I'm from the State Attorney's Office. Like to see the files on a '65 murder. Lester Macabee. Happened up near Carrboro, South Carolina. You'll likely remember it."

The clerk of records was a little wary.

"I member hit good enough. Them two boys hitching up from west Florida. Who I doan member is you. You new at the State Attorney's?"

Touchy. Should he try a bribe?

"Yeah, started last week. Name's Wilson. Please a meetcha. (Ten in the hand that shook the hand.) Now you don't have to get up. I can find my own way."

"Well, I guess it's okay, but . . ."

"I ain't wastin' these pearls on no swine."

It was Ivory.

"Oh, sorry. Go on. I'm with you."

FOURTEEN

As FARE NEARED THE CANTEEN, HE SAW THE BIRDSHIT brigade at work by the Rock gate. With hoses, push brooms and bottles of disinfectant, every morning and into the afternoon until the job was done, they brushed and scraped and washed under the five huge live oaks which shaded the Rock and the visiting park. Every evening the sparrows flew in to sleep in the trees, making a sound like a sustained note from an enormous police whistle, and every morning the birdshit brigade marched out to clean up what the birds deposited in the night.

In the gutters along the walk flowed a foul, granular sludge, flecked with white and green. When he had taken this walk for the first time, Fare had been shocked by the force of the odor. It struck the nostrils like a fist, bringing a mist to the eyes. His breathing had constricted; he had wanted to break into a run. Now, as a matter of course, he walked holding his nose.

"Mornin, Mr. Odum."

"Mornin."

Fare unpinched his nose. He did not know the man who stood in front of him, leaning on a push broom, shirt wet with sweat. The ammoniac smell of sweat and birdshit hung around them in the air. He tried to pass on down the walk, but the young black man, a man he had seen here and there who sported a shiny gold star in one of his front teeth, stepped into his path so that the broom, shifting slightly toward Fare, became like a weapon. Fare lurched a little to the side. The other held his ground in the middle of the walk. Above them, the birds sang like power lines and the white chalk pattered down.

"Got a message for you."

A smile tricked at the corners of the black man's mouth. Fare watched the glimmering star under the lip that blinked like an eyelid. Two freemen walked past them toward the canteen. Fare waited until they were well past. The tone of voice the young black man had used bothered him. It glimmered like the star; it was a night, not a morning, tone. The man's face held a kind of dirty apprehension.

"What is it?" Fare asked, as brusquely as possible.

"The message is," the man leaned toward him and said, *sotto voce*, "to get you ass down to the main gate right now."

"Who says?" Fare stepped back, lowering his own voice.

"It's a friend."

Fare said the word in spite of himself, "Friend?" He watched the other's eyes. "Friend?" It sounded flat, as though someone in the Rock kitchen nearby had struck a cheap saucepan with a spoon. He recalled that Ivory had not reported to school that morning. Who else?

Beyond them, the two freemen disappeared into the canteen. It struck him that some of them, the others, the freemen, should have been his friends, yet none of them was. There was only Ivory, and for them to use the word "friendship" would have been to beat a saucepan with a spoon.

He pushed past the man, reaching out and moving the broom aside. As he walked toward the canteen, from behind him came the hiss of the broom on the wet concrete and the low voice, "If you doan go, you be sorry."

Fare had entered the alcove which led to the first of the barred doors before remembering that he would have to give them some reason for going out in the middle of the day. Reflexively, he shoved his hands into his pockets. The stomach acid tablets.

He walked to the first door and stood, trying to look impatient. The thin guard looked at him, did a double take, "Yeah?"

"I got some medication out in the car I forgot. Can you let me go out to get it?"

The thin guard turned his wolfish face and looked a question at Sarn Thomas, who stood at the outer door. The Sarn looked at him.

"What kind a medication?"

Gingerly, he placed a hand on his own middle while letting his eyes drop to the Sarn's heavy paunch. "For my stomach." He figured the Sarn would sympathize.

"Aw-ite."

In the parking lot he pretended to rummage in his glove compartment. He had just begun the short walk back to the gate when he saw the Bradford County sheriff's car pull up to the walk in front of it.

Not really knowing why, he hurried his pace. He had signed back in and passed into the inner chamber, when, on the other side, two deputies appeared in the doorway. He stopped to look back at them.

Outside on the steps, he knew, a man would be waiting to endure this passage for the first time. He would be standing outside in street clothing, perhaps his own, perhaps that provided from the stores of the Bradford County Jail. Smoking a cigarette, almost surely a ready-made, he would be looking around him in mute absorption at the administration building, and the quiet, fiercely suburban residences of guards and clerical personnel. But he would be standing there, Fare knew, endowing these things with extraordinary significance because they were the last he would see of the free world for a long time. This was why the two men in the gatehouse with Fare fell silent when the door swung open.

The two deputies looked around inside the gatehouse. One of them approached Sarn Thomas and accepted from him the forms by which the prisoner would change hands. The other deputy stepped back to the gate door, swung it out, and spoke.

"Here we go, Bud."

With the others, Fare gazed toward the door. The new man stepped backward toward the opening, his eyes apparently not wanting to let go of the outside. The broad back of him was relaxed, slouched. He was a fat man with light, curly hair, thick dimpled arms and massive shoulders. When he half-turned, his cuffed hands rose to take hold of the doorjamb, and from his sideways position he delivered the shock to Fare's heart. He swiveled his head fully around while his feet remained planted. He turned his head in a bed of curly hair upon a pouched and slabbed neck with the mobility given to some birds.

Lester walked into the gatehouse with a look in his eyes of pure defiance untainted by fear. Ignoring the deputy's soft push toward Sarn Thomas, a push which did not move him because it was absorbed in his flesh, he walked slowly past an ashtray to the nearest potted palm and in it stubbed out his cigarette. Fare stared at the man who had murdered his brother for gasoline. Lester's eyes passed over him. They did not pause even for an instant, only continued, from the stooped position, to cover the room in a slow, predatory sweep. Fare was sure he had not seen the light of recognition in Lester's eyes. He hoped that he had kept it from his own.

As Lester stood upright from the palm, a hardness came into the face of Sarn Thomas. Sarn Thomas was an old man but he could still summon airs of bygone power into his bearing. His cured old face could make five or six expressions only, and all but one of them, the benign, rested one he used when nothing was happening, were weapons. He stepped over to Lester, who stood now staring at the ceiling, his teeth grinding audibly.

Sarn Thomas brought his hand up in a quick, sweeping gesture that took in everything, all of them. Lester flinched just perceptibly.

"This is my house, plug," he said. Lester did not seem to hear him.

The Sarn moved closer to Lester, and Fare saw that the two, with their hard, single-minded regard for things and people alike, were of the same make. They might have exchanged positions, lives for that matter, but for fortune. The Sarn said, "That sorry thing there is my tree," and pointing to the cigarette butt, "Is that what you call making a start?"

The two gazed at each other, their eyes trading strains of malevolence. Sullenly, Lester bent to retrieve the butt. But he did it with a broad grin, a comic obsequiousness to show that he was not whipped. The two deputies backed away. Jurisdiction had changed hands. Near Fare, the wolfish guard laughed. Ignoring Sarn Thomas' beet red face, Lester cut his eyes to this laugh. Then he slouched to the counter and the ledger book.

He bent to sign his name, slowly, as though his fingers hurt. As he made the words, his defiance seemed to wane. The near-gate guard impatiently motioned to Fare to pass through. He backed through the door. Sarn Thomas was on the phone calling for someone to come and take Lester to Records and Classification. Soon the Sarn would remove the cuffs from Lester's hands and give them to the deputies with a receipt, releasing them. But, because theirs were the only firearms, they would wait until Lester had disappeared into the prison before leaving. As Fare passed through the door, the wolfish guard leaned out to retrieve it and swing it back, and as he did so, he said to himself as much as to Fare, "It's some of them over in the Rock that will teach him some manners."

Fare flattened himself against the fence at the corner of the visiting park, slipping in among the branches of a eucalyptus tree. He watched as a distant Lester walked sulkily beside a guard toward the north wing of the Rock, where he would be processed by R. and C. The Lester he saw and the Lester of the dreams and the memories were not one whit different. It frightened him, chilled him to see this. He had hoped that Lester had grown, changed dimension in his imagination to become more threatening, but this was not true. There was Lester, fat but hard underneath. There he walked, listless, yet in a gust of physical potential. Fare closed his eyes and saw him jump from the car seat again, as though propelled from underneath, saw the door of the old Buick fly open, groaning on its hinges, to bounce back shocking Lester's hips, saw the recovering quickness with which the fat man drew back the bolt of the little pistol and leveled it in the smeary dew of the car roof.

He stepped back onto the walk to make his way toward the school, but turned one last time before Lester's blocky form punched its way through the Rock gate.

Later, sitting in his classroom while the men quietly did the morning's work, he brooded about it. Cutting circles, his thoughts always returned to this: What he really wanted was knowledge. For now at least, he wanted to know about Lester. He wanted this for balance. There must be something, a body of objective fact to place alongside the uncertain knowledge he had from his feelings, from his dreams, fact to make Lester small again.

He knew that somehow he had to obtain Lester's records, had to discover the meaning of the intervening ten years: how and where Lester had lived, under what sad or cunning train of identities, in what fruitless pursuits, and most of all, what his crimes had been, of what he had been convicted before now, and of what he was yet suspected. How long would Lester stay at Raiford? Where would he live in the prison? What would his habits be, his job, his recreations, his friends? His needs?

Fare had been told this was the way of it with the young boys and the men who made them. What do you need—friendship, protection? I will provide it. Later, will come prices. Let us contrive for you a gambling debt of fifty packs. Impossible? Then we will discuss the mode of payment. But Lester was not young. He was a maker, not one of the made.

He knew he had to be careful. He could get the records by saying Lester was his student—it was not uncommon for a teacher to read a student's jacket. If he were caught, he could profess a mistake. But how, finally, to get to Lester? To do this would require help, and there the danger lay. He recalled the message which had been delivered to him: "Get you ass down to the main gate." He had already been helped. Who had helped him?

Later, when he left his classroom, coffee cup in hand, it was with the answer in mind. Ivory. Ivory, and why not? It would only require less love for Lester than for Farel Odum. Not much for either one. Ivory hated white men but cared less for certain types than for others. By stripe, Fare was no less a turpentine peckerwood than Lester, but he had escaped his origins somewhat, while Lester had wallowed all his life in the same filth and ignorance out of which he had sprung. Fare and his kind were more to be pitied by Ivory than hated. Ivory saw them as the hollow men. But, Fare reminded himself, he must not make too many judgments about Lester. For all he knew, Lester was a bigger man, a more formidable man than was suggested by the ownership of a spavined Buick and the questionable friendship of an old alkie named Chuckie. Maybe. And maybe not. More danger if Lester were something rarer than the usual neck. In either case, Fare told himself, he had to know.

Ivory was not in the equipment room. Fare spent the better part of his afternoon break looking for him, and finally found him holed up with two other men in the storeroom of the shoe repair shop. When he entered, making as much noise as he could, and hissing Ivory's name like an idiot because he did not want to catch them at anything, there was a shuffle and the stifled whispering of instructions. He heard the word "shoe."

Slowly, as he became accustomed to the half-light, Fare made out the rookery of eyes. The sweet, licorice odor of marijuana laced the leather-smelling air. His part was to ignore it, he knew, particularly if he wanted anything out of Ivory. But there was a wrong way and a right way to ignore it. He must not seem too stupid or seem to bargain for anything. He must not seem to want it too much. He stood facing the tight half-circle of eyes, the ebony and imperious faces, and said, "Smells like . . . shoes back here. Don't know how you all can stand it."

"S'cording to whether you like the smell of shoes," said a voice, vaguely familiar. Ivory said nothing. Fare guessed he was embarrassed. He had been sought out and discovered for no official reason by a free white man.

Frowning, Fare waved his hand at the smell in the air. "Inmate Rose, I'd like to talk to you a minute if that's all right."

It was difficult to tell how stoned they were, but Ivory liked this a little better. He said, "Right you are, Cappy," sweeping his hand toward a ream of brown wrapping paper.

Fare watched the others go. Moving to take the seat Ivory had offered, he brushed the smaller of the two men, and caught the glow of something in this man's mouth. He thought it must be the gold star, but, in the half-light, it was difficult to tell. The two of them left carefully erect, like automatons walking between the metal racks of shoes and treatment chemicals. They were stoned, all right. He had not been able to make out either of their faces.

When the two had fallen through the white hole at the doorway, a sudden intimacy crowded in. Fare spun the empty coffee cup around his finger.

Ivory reached for a nearby shoe, tipped it upward, then pinched with two fingers into the heel. A match scraped, then flared. All the shiny shoes leapt red and orange.

"Goddamn it," Fare said, swinging wildly to slap out the match.

Ivory laughed. "Smoke wid me, man, that's what you come in here for, ain't it?"

"You know it isn't, and put that thing away. How much do you think I'm gonna overlook?"

"Oh, I don't know." Ivory crooned. "More'n you suspeck right now."

"Don't count on it." He hoped Ivory could not see how scared he was. But it was a vain hope. Like a police dog, Ivory could smell fear.

Ivory's face stiffened, his voice dropped several octaves. "So what you want then? I ain't got all day."

Fare sighed. He stood and backed as far away as he could between the confining rows of metal shelves with their cargo of half-salvaged shoes. He hauled a breath of air.

"You know that fuck Lester I told you about?"

"Yeah, so what?" Ivory's voice was too weary.

Fare could not bring himself to say more. Surely Ivory had sent the message. Yet how could he know? Ivory stood to leave as though this were the whole story.

"Listen . . ."

Fare thrust his hand out. There was an immediate tension. As small as it was, it was force. Ivory stood looking down at the hand on his chest. Then he backed away from it out of distaste, not obeisance.

Fare said, "This Lester that . . ." For a moment he could not go on. "He showed up today at the main gate. Can you believe it?"

To put it into words was more difficult than he had imagined it would be. His voice had broken. Now his eyes melted bits of steely shine from the toes of shoes into wet pools. He backed farther into the shadows.

Ivory sat down again, clearly surprised. Ivory, whose style was absolute refrigeration.

"You sho it was him?"

"Fucking A."

Fare blinked in the darkness, smearing the bright wet pools.

"Couldn't been nobody else?"

"I'm dumb, but I ain't blind."

"Right. Right."

As though he had realized something for the first time, Ivory made a clicking noise in his throat and stood again. He was changed.

"So what you want wid me, man?"

Fare did not know how to say it. He did not want it to sound like something from a movie. He said, "Just some help. That's all."

Even in the darkness, he thought he could see the fierce white lakes of Ivory's eyes. Far away, the bell rang, muffled and irrelevant to the conduct of life. Ivory said, "It's all business, my young friend. Buying and selling. Nobody gets nothing free in this life. Supply and deman."

Fare listened but did not hear words. What he heard was the small but definite sound of acquiescence. For its resemblance to the noise of the striking of bargains, in this moment of elation, he was certain he could not be held accountable.

FIFTEEN

AT THE MORNING BREAK, WITHOUT THE COFFEE CUP, HE
walked to the shoe repair shop. On his way in he met an old
black man whose elephantine, wrinkled face he had not seen
before. The old man stood in the doorway facing out. There
was something furtive, sentinel in his attitude. Fare stopped.
He did not want to be seen entering the storeroom.

That morning, he had found a handwritten note in his desk
drawer. Someone had slipped into the school building during
the night and left it for him. The drawer had been locked—
he was sure—yet the lock showed no signs of having been
jimmied.

> What goes around, comes around.
> Same time, same place.

A childish attempt at some secret code? A joke? The
cryptic tone was Ivory's. Fare had wanted to ask what the
hell it meant, but class had begun.

Now he loitered in the vacant sewing room, hefting some
of the familiar hand tools. When he heard the shuffle behind
him, he did not know why he whirled with an awl in his hand,
raised up like a knife. With surprising quickness, the old man
threw up both hands in a gesture that combined surrender
and defense. Fare's knees were bent, his weight evenly dis-
tributed, his face flushed, his palms moist. Where in the hell
did these things come from? They faced each other that way
for half a second. Then the old man grinned, hissed, "Gone
in."

"What did you say?"

"Ah said, *go on in*. They waitin for you."

Harder than he meant to, he struck the awl back into the
wheemed surface of the workbench. "Sure," he said. It quiv-

ered there, singing faintly. Its noise took the glimmer of scorn from the old man's grin.

The same smell, only stronger. The same rookery of hard, dark eyes waited in the storeroom. No, Fare sensed that only one of these men, the smaller of the two, had been with Ivory the day before. One had been replaced by a bigger, more powerfully built man, who sat sullenly a little distance from the other two, separated somehow by more than distance. There was no shuffle to hide the joint this time. Openly, the three passed it among them. Fare watched as it came to Ivory, who took it, throwing back his head and huffing his cheeks in the greedy, exaggerated way of college kids. When he had finished, he tightened his chest upon the smoke, to force it into his lungs' blood more quickly and, holding his breath, said to Fare in a compressed falsetto, "Good shit. Want a hit?"

Fare panicked. He would write them all up, he thought, turn them in. Why were they doing this to him? He looked down at the crumpled note in his hand.

"What the fuck was this doing in my locked desk drawer this morning when I came in?" His voice, as high as Ivory's, had the panic in it.

"Seemed like a good idea at the time," Ivory laughed. He punched the man sitting close to him, and then handed the joint to Fare. The man laughed. It was a giddy dope-laugh, but even so, Fare recognized the voice of the man who had delivered the message yesterday. Fare took the joint, slammed it down in a shower of sparks, and ground it under his shoe. The man sitting close to Ivory snorted, got up slowly, and knelt at Fare's feet.

"Lift your foot," he said. Yes, he was the messenger all right.

Fare moved his foot. Delicately, the kneeling man picked up the fragments of the joint and ate them. He looked up at Fare with an enormous delight in his eyes, and the gold star glowing between his lips.

Ivory held out a hand to him when he had seated himself once again.

"Oh, yeah," the messenger said. "Minute."

He stood again, working one hand down into a tight trouser pocket. Now he handed something to Ivory. Ivory passed it to Fare. Fare felt the metal of his desk drawer key fall into his hot palm like a drop of cold water. Yesterday, this man had lightly touched him as he walked out. But he had seemed so far away, so stoically, irretrievably stoned. Now they all three giggled the irrepressible, untouchable dope-giggle. Fare noted that the big man, holding his belly, joined in the laughing for the first time, while the pickpocket placed his index finger beneath his right eye, held it there for a moment, and tapped it twice. This ignited them all again. Fare waited for the laughing to stop.

Ivory stopped laughing, turned it off as though it flowed from a valve in his chest. "Seems like you wanted something," he said. "Seemed that way to me."

Fare felt the cold, depressed feeling he had felt that night in the back seat of Lester's Buick, as though he lay trapped beneath the weight of the burnt-out and broken parts of some device whose design was a mystery.

"This is just between you and me," he said. He knew the other two were present for good reason. Still, he said, "Why don't you tell them to leave?"

"He doan tell me nothing," the big man said. " 'Why doan you tell him to leave,' " he mocked. As he spoke, he stepped closer to Fare. A little light caught his face and Fare saw, with the full recollection of all he had seen that day, that this was the man who tore boxes. Ivory shook his head. "He's correck. It ain't nothing I can do for you by myself."

Fare sat down. He told himself to calm down. At least he could give a little of the needle back to them. He had brought this thing upon himself and he *did* want something, after all, though he still did not know what it was.

"So what do you shines want then?" he asked, his voice better.

"Who said we want anything?" Ivory spread his big, limp hands in an elaborate show of guilelessness.

Vacantly, Fare looked at the three of them. Shadows. When you were in it, you could get a little control back. They waited. He looked at them, not sure whether they could see his face, but looked at them, nevertheless, as though they were insects. It was the way they had been looking at him. He tried with his body to communicate this.

Finally, the new man said to Ivory, "Tell him what you want, man. Fuck ease games."

The man who tore boxes had probably not liked the word "shine."

Ivory took out a pack of cigarettes, ready-mades they were, not R.I.P. He offered one to Fare, who took it, nodding thanks. The other two declined.

Ivory said, "This is brother Dealy Drawdy," indicating the smooth, imperturbable man who had delivered the message and filched the key, "but he goes by the name of Taylor County, and this is brother M. D. LaPointe, also known as Mad Dog LaPointe, who chooses to be called Point."

"Hey fuck it, man, get on wid it," said the box man, La-Pointe, who was having trouble with Ivory's style.

"Easy now, brother," said Ivory. "We got to do bidnis wid the white man like the white man do bidnis wid us. He shake you by you right hand and gut you wid his leff. We shakin hands right now."

Fare held out a hand to LaPointe, smiling broadly in the darkness. LaPointe did not gesture in kind. He turned away to the wall, inspecting the toes of a pair of shoes. Fare's memory held a faint recollection of the newspaper accounts of LaPointe's crimes, and now crowded in the more recent image of LaPointe standing at the tag plant loading dock, ripping the boxes effortlessly, and later, standing in the walking line, holding his belly and laughing while Fare knelt puking in the grass.

Ivory took a drag, bringing his features up in a red glow. "Now Point, who don't even like to be in the same room wid a white man, let alone you, Odum, for which he has got a particular hard-on, don't ask me why, and Taylor County,

who is just a live-and-let-liver that ain't living up to his own
personal expectations right now, and me—the three of us, we
got one thing in common and that's what bring us to this shit-
hole here and present company. Ain't none of us wants to
spend another day in this . . ."

Here words failed Ivory Rose. And Fare understood it,
sympathized with it. How could a man of better than fair
intelligence and gift of gab ever come up with a word to
describe this place, this Raiford? Hell was too prosaic, death
was not final enough.

"So what am I supposed to do for these great expectations
of yours?" He felt anger rising, like a need to retch. They
wanted out. All along, he had thought at least he was still
dealing with sane men. Now he knew that Point was mad and
Ivory was deluded.

"What am I supposed to do for you, sing 'If I had the wings
of an angel' . . . wave a magic wand? . . ."

"You ain't got a wand, eunuch!"

Point stood, shoving his big hands onto his hips where there
was little to keep them from sliding down. He was as thin at
the waist as a dancer.

"If you had, you wouldn't be working in this place."

"You let us worry about that," Ivory interceded. "We'll
think of something. What we got to know is whether or not
you got the will. Cause where there's a will . . . But if we
let on about *the way* right now? Well, we just cain't do that,
not till we know."

"So I'm gonna buy a pig in a poke?"

"Not exactly, white folks. You gone get my personal assurance that we ain't axing nothing you cain't pull off and
get out clean."

Fare wanted to ask what form Ivory's personal assurances
came in—were they promissory notes, postdated checks? But
more than this, he wanted to know what was in it for him.
They couldn't get all they wanted on blackmail. He didn't think
they would try. "So what's the other side of this big deal? This
big fucking deal?"

"My, my," said Ivory. "Where does a English teacher learn that kine of language?"

Fare moved for the door. "This must be the end of part one," he said, "and I'll find out in my desk drawer when part two's gonna run?"

"Easy now, white folks. Just sit down. Get into the process. The process is at lease haff of it. Ain't none of us knows what we gone get out the results."

Point snorted, hawked, picked up a shoe and spit into it.

Ivory's voice was conciliatory, mesmeric. Fare would have told himself to look out, but for the feeling that Ivory was talking more to himself, more to some surfacing mechanism of pleasure, than to his audience. Ivory Rose, prison poet, second-rate Eldridge Cleaver, seizing the day five years behind times. Fare had the feeling that Point, standing huge nearby, half-turned away from them, was the only one who was a professional. Ivory, in his own way, was probably as much an amateur as Fare. And who knew about the pickpocket? A two-bit grifter? Point possessed the heart and soul to kill them all and certainly, from the look of his big, tensile body, possessed the wherewithal. Fare was scared of LaPointe, yet felt an ambivalence toward him. The presence of this man, as careless with his size, his strength, his words as with his spit, was like a blood bond—blood promised more blood. If he did this thing, it should be with men who knew how. LaPointe, he sensed, knew how. Had Fare not known LaPointe close up, had he not felt his energy burning in the darkness across from him now, he could have guessed it from that day, weeks before, when he had seen him rip the boxes and later, when their eyes had met. It was the way he looked at things, making no distinction between the living and the inert. But why did LaPointe hang back, fuming, while Ivory played out the part of leader? Ivory's knowledge of Fare did not stand for that much. Who was running things?

Fare sat down for the second time. But this time because he wanted to. No one was telling him what to do. He would get into the process. "Like I said, what's in it for me?"

LaPointe stepped forward. He stood squarely in front of Fare, raising his right hand to begin unbuttoning his shirt. Fare could almost see the tatters of cardboard falling at his feet—this was the same brute, slow movement. When the shirt was spread open to the waist, the glistening muscles, hard, discrete, a woven fabric like chain mail, leapt to Fare's eye, and LaPointe seemed to expand upward out of the trousers. Under the flat pectorals suspended like black buttocks from the yokes of collarbones, Fare could see in the dim light the manila-colored shape of something. LaPointe withdrew it and held it out to Fare. It was a file folder. He took it and with it he took the human warmth that still lived in the paper. His heart crawled at his lungs and he felt spit drying on his teeth. He backed to the far wall but LaPointe came forward holding out his lit cigarette lighter, holding the waving flame up to the white strip of language at the folder's heading. It read: Macabee, Lester Delancy, 046789.

From a great distance, the pickpocket laughed the dope-laugh. "Exter, exter," he giggled, "read all about it!"

LaPointe laughed too, quietly, not much coming out but a broken rasping of breath. "Well, look," he said, "he ain't gone throw up."

Fare stood holding the folder. He looked into LaPointe's strange, blank eyes.

"At's what you wanted, ain't it? Ain't it? We gone get at hog for you, white folks."

SIXTEEN

FARE STOOD AT THE BARRED WINDOWS BEHIND THE LIBRAR-
ian's desk looking down and to his right at the crazy explosion
of bright color and random movement—women and children.
They violated the neutrality of the prison's one color—faded
denim blue—and its tired, careful style of movement. Everything seemed to come undone, all the discipline and purpose
of the place. The oddness of it was this: You could spend so
much time among men dressed as these dressed, behaving as
these behaved, that you came to believe the world outside was
the smaller, the stranger, the less real of the two. And then
came weekends, the invasion of freaks. Their magpie voices,
their cakes and pies slaughtered by the hacks in search of contraband, their stares. The freedom, the abandonment of their
caresses, and the way they plotted territories for themselves,
threw up the partitions of family out there among the picnic
tables, under the canvas awnings. And each man in faded
blue was suddenly again the heart of something.

The library behind him hummed quietly with its current of
careful thought. Saturdays, visiting days when he worked as
substitute librarian, were odd times, interesting and disquieting
too. These days gave him the opportunity to mingle with that
portion of the prison population which did not go to school.
Sixteen hours of dead time during which he was asked only
to rubber-stamp a few books brought him all manner of
strange encounters. Any freeman who was not clearly engaged
in official activity was fair game. A teacher, whose position
was only marginally official anyway, who was a member of an
elite corps of eunuchs among prison officialdom, was especially vulnerable. After all, what could a teacher do to you if
you were not his student? So they came out of the woodwork,

to tell their stories, complain their complaints, and, trapped behind the desk, he listened.

He had long ago purged himself of the habit of saying to these men, when they spoke of some brutality, "I know what you mean." He had seen the looks that came into their eyes, some of them, in these moments. Looks that said, "Fucking A, sure you do!" It was only in a manner of speaking that he said, "I know what you mean," but even so, he had given it up.

When they left him alone, he had often stood behind the desk, located at the extreme west side of the Rock on the second floor, and placed his hands on the many-times-painted bars and known the raw feeling of imprisonment. Or thought he had. Could you know it?

Standing at the window, he could hold the bars in his hands and press his face to the spaces between them, and breathe the air outside. There were moments of vertigo sometimes when inside, the library, suddenly meant captivity, and outside, the chapel, the visiting park, the hospital, the distances of athletic fields, meant the life withheld. His stomach lurched sometimes. That was all. He would turn away and shake his head. Say to himself, Don't play with it. It's not even interesting. It's like being an animal. Your most persistent thought is that confused one in which, by some weird miracle, you become thin enough to pass through the space between . . . and then, maybe you just take to the air and fly.

Now he turned from the window and seated himself at the desk. Slowly, he scanned the faces and bent heads, the backs of necks arrayed before him, looking for . . . for what? Looking for Ivory? For LaPointe? Some kind of sign that something, the next thing, was happening.

He wondered how many times, through how many moments end to end, a man like Ivory or LaPointe had stood face pressed to bars, maybe knowing, maybe not, what a terrible cliché the image was, but knowing truly the difference between inside and outside. Knowing, perhaps better even than he had when he lived it, the life withheld. Fare had stood at the window today looking out, straining to feel it, what it must be like, and had, as usual, felt nothing. Yet when he had left the storeroom the afternoon before, he had felt heavy with the terror of it and light with a new sense of membership. Of being one of them. The lesser one, the least perhaps, but nevertheless a member, endowed with a member's rights. He could make a threat and it must now embed itself in another's mind, whereas before it would either have been something official or nothing at all, as thin as air.

He had never believed in fate. Yet now, Lester was here. What were the odds? It was September. No, the beginning of October. Something like the odds it would take for a single snowflake to drift this moment past the end of his nose. Fate had been nothing but an antique abstraction to him. Something to read about, a reason things happened in old books. He had not, at least since childhood, believed in anything but a profound disorder that sometimes coincided men with each other in ways they could not understand. To keep sane, they proclaimed the existence of a design in things. Fate was the word for this design.

Yet, since he had seen Lester again, and since the meetings with Ivory and LaPointe, he had begun to see that somehow, above the human collisions or near them, must hover an aura of spirit, faintly like a gas, not from but present somehow in human belief and trust and love. He'd had the feeling for a period of hours which had seemed like days, that this thing had been controlling him.

His father's words kept coming back to him. "Fare, to some men it is given to be seekers. Others are called. They are intercepted upon the path of seeking like Saul of Tarsus, and they see a light, and they are renamed, washed and made new, and they undertake to discern God's purposes and to serve him." This was his father's answer when Fare had asked what it meant to be called. It seemed to Fare now that everything had been annulled but the responsibility to Lester. Time had been saved, the experience had been foreshortened. Surely, it had been *given* to him to do this thing. The question now was, how?

He brooded on the two meetings. First there had been the change in his relationship to Ivory, so subtle, yet so abrupt and so complete. And who had been responsible for it? Had he done it, or had it been done to him? Walking into the storeroom the first time, calling Ivory's name, he had betrayed to the others his dependence, revealed the fact that something outside the controlled society they kept in the chemical room existed between them. And yet Ivory had seemed, at least at first, to be damaged by this. If not, why had he required of Fare that they speak in formal terms until the others had left? To the two strangers, the inescapable conclusion was that some form of regard, more or less than the prison demanded, existed between them. But he did not see how this could hurt Ivory.

He had felt, at first, that he had rushed into it. He had seen Lester for the first time in ten years and a half hour later was standing at the lip of a hole poised to jump. He could only guess at its depth.

When he had left the storeroom after the second meeting, he had felt differently. He had gotten himself into it all right. They had set a trap for him and he had stumbled into it and they had closed it upon him as surely as if it had been sprung steel. If he had walked out of there and left this thing behind, it would all have been laid out in front of them, and they all knew it. If he did not report them, they would report him, probably through the old sentinel out in the sewing room.

"Yessir, I saw dat white man go in dat storeroom. Nawsir, I don't know who he wit. Yassir, I found dis here reefer in dere on a flow. Nawsir, I ain't see him smoke hit but . . ."

If he reported them, the questions would be the same. Why had he gone into the storeroom twice? Why hadn't he reported the loitering the first time he had encountered it? Why had he been looking for inmate Rose in the first place? What did he hope to gain by fraternizing with inmates in dark storerooms?

In this second scenario, the old man would be instructed to admit that he had smoked with Fare in the storeroom. He would be a lifer, an old man with nothing to lose. It wasn't fear that had kept Fare sitting where he had sat, but it was close enough.

Then there had been the sudden, complicating emergence of LaPointe. Fare had used the word "shine." LaPointe had not been able to take it. "Fuck these games." The words had exploded from him. Ivory, who was a known quantity, could take that stuff, could even like it for the honesty in it. After all, the black men called each other every dirty thing they could think of, rarely using the words "black man." Ivory possessed a sense of irony, he stood a distance from himself. Irony Rose. LaPointe, the unknown quantity, could not get outside himself, stood in the middle of a burning lake of himself unable to escape. He was dangerous, to understate it.

Thinking about it, Fare had sought for the moment of tilt, the moment when things had pivoted away from certain possibilities and toward others. He guessed it had happened when Ivory had offered them all the cigarette. He remembered this moment for its resemblance to those two other times when Ivory had offered him the joint, to scare him, provoke him, jangle his nerves. But the cigarette had come out without hint of motive. It was the getting-down-to-business feeling of it which made it seem now to Fare the moment of the change. There in the darkness, sitting in that circle, completing it, some part of his mind had entertained just briefly the image of Indians and white men, of the loss of Manhattan Island, and he had wondered who in the storeroom, where the cigarettes were lit in a gesture of goodwill, would end up wearing the feathers.

From the desk in front of him, Fare picked up the newspaper for the tenth time. But before he read it, he moved his eyes across the room again, looking, feeling again the sense of violation he had felt when he had first found and read it. He had known, the moment his fingers had located it, near the bottom of a dusty bundle in the storage area where the old

newspapers were kept, that it was the reason he had looked
forward to working in the library this morning. Again his eyes
completed their survey. He did not see any of the familiar
signs, Ivory's shining bald head, the glimmering gold star, nor
LaPointe's thick neck or blank animal eye. He read the clipping again.

The headline: INTERSTATE KILLER CAUGHT!

There was a bleary black and white picture of LaPointe,
handcuffed, staring the camera down, walking between two
conservatively suited detectives. The text was brief, but you
could not miss the hysteria and the relief in the language. It
was as though something supernatural had been brought to
bay, and prayers, not news, were being offered up.

There had been some slight to M. D. LaPointe, a Vietnam
veteran, something said or done to him in a welfare office, no
one was quite sure what it was. He had drawn a gun and fired
shots at the woman who vended food stamps, killing her instantly, then he had taken a female hostage and made his
escape. Then there had been the wild swath up the interstate
highways from Miami to . . . was it Maryland, where he had
finally been caught with his fifth victim wrapped in a shower
curtain in the trunk of a stolen car? What had given the case
its long life in the press was not the murders themselves, but
the backward trek along the highways during which Mad Dog
had theatrically led the authorities to the burial sites of the
throat-slashed, shot, strangled, bludgeoned victims, most of
them women, most of them hitchhikers (though there had been
a gas station attendant and a convenience store operator),
most of them raped, one way or another, before death.

It was finding this newspaper clipping, knowing he would
find it, somehow; finding and reading it into his memory almost, so many times had he held it before his eyes, that made
him wonder what the history of the last few days really meant.
Could there be any meaning when something as cosmically
accidental as LaPointe was in it, and with LaPointe seeming
to gather more and more control?

Fare walked back to the window. There, below, was the

visiting park. The light of it, its color and quick movement clashed briefly in his mind with the dark characters and furniture of the world in the clipping which lay behind him on the desk.

He stood at the window, in sprays of dust motes, the fall air crossing the barrier cool, the bars cool in his hands, the smell of the sparrows rank in the huge live oaks that stood before the Rock. As usual, the visiting park was a riot of ill-concealed groping love and bolted food, earnest talk, the amazed gazes of lovers. And as usual, the men loitered before the canteen and the chapel, talking in groups of two and three, matching for nickels they were not supposed to possess.

These men who did not receive visitors were by far the larger of the two groups. They lounged on the chapel steps, went to the canteen, climbed the stairs to the library, then began the circuit again, but they had a distracted look about them as though they were waiting for something. It seemed to him that they tortured themselves. Why come so close to the visitors, and then stand with your back to them, your hands shoved into your pockets, pretending you did not give a shit? Why not pass through the Rock's main gate and out to the yard beyond the reach of this carnival's sound? Fare had come to know the men who stood near the visiting park, how they stole glances in its direction.

He did not notice until later, until it had become imperative to notice, that there were three hacks in the vicinity. Two were walking toward the chapel from the direction of the ornamental horticulture greenhouses. Another must have been standing in the Rock gate, or happened to have been passing through it.

For some reasons, perhaps for the suddenness of his movements, a violation of the sultry pace that dominated the crowd of loitering men, Fare's eye singled out LaPointe. Tall, well-built, wearing carefully pressed blues, the usual Afro, spit-shined cordovan shoes and this: an expression of the most bitter, unalloyed hatred Fare had ever seen malign a human face, wearing it fixed like a scar, LaPointe broke suddenly away from a group of three men with whom he stood and walked resolutely, head tilted down a little, straight to the place where three Puerto Ricans stood nearby. He leapt the distance between himself and the nearest member of this group, and punched this man with mechanic quickness and force, a piston stroke, under the right ear. Fare saw the victim's head lay over. The force was such that his left ear contacted his collarbone almost instantly.

The Puerto Rican recovered himself into a street fighter's crouch. The two stood very close together fighting, each kneeing for his opponent's groin, each punching aimed, measured, but still somehow maniac blows begun and ended before Fare could see them. Each held his jaw tightly shut, but each grunted, and these grunts, mixed with the solid, smacking sounds of blows landing, were the only sounds in the cavernous silence that had grown up around the two. At first, everything stopped. All sound, all movement lost in the attempt of two hundred eyes to find and interpret these new images. Then three things happened. The other loiterers were surprised only momentarily and then became spectators, creating quickly, but with the paced sobriety of paying customers, a ring. Before too long, a few began to speak encouragements to the two fighters.

The hacks looked first at the two fighters, and then at each other, locating friendship, and then, each of them in turn slowly turned his eyes up to the visitors as though to say, look at these hogs. These are your husbands and fathers.

And the visitors merely looked away, knowing. Except for the very young, they looked away. A few of them, the young women, took their men by the upper arms and turned them to recreate the circle, to throw back up the partitions even before the fight had entered its second stage.

Which was the part of it that took place on the ground. When the Puerto Rican fell in an attempt to deliver a kick, LaPointe was on him at once, and attempting to sit on his chest, pounded wildly, the effects of exhaustion showing, at the downed man's bobbing, slipping face and throat. Some of the punches struck pavement and Fare saw a red color dominate the blue of their clothing. Somehow the Puerto Rican crab-scuttled backward, backed up under LaPointe's weight, and the two neared the chapel steps. They were on their knees side by side. LaPointe held the Puerto Rican in a headlock, and with the last upright surge his legs could muster, bolted forward three yards slamming the other's head into the stone abutment of the chapel steps. Concussed, unconscious, the Puerto Rican fell back. Fell back because LaPointe, knowing what he had done, had already let go. They lay side by side, the Puerto Rican convulsing, LaPointe breathing the athlete's measured, recovering breaths, his eyes closed to the sky, his winner's face utterly changed, utterly cleared of its scars.

It was not until it was all over that the three hacks converged. Two of them picked the Puerto Rican up by the armpits, trying to make him walk, one of them speaking into his ear, probably saying, "Come on now, Bud. You can do it." But he could not; his legs hung limp in his trousers; he twitched. The other, the third, merely stood above LaPointe, letting him catch his breath, letting him alone the way a man lets a snake die before he tosses it across the right of way. After a space, he leaned down and tapped; LaPointe was getting up even before he opened his eyes. He knew what the tap meant.

The hack, a big man, holding him at arm's length by the muscle of his forearm, led him toward the Rock Lieutenant's office. Then, with a quick effort that almost caused the surprised hack to strike, LaPointe turned full around. He stood motionless alone for a moment, then raised his middle finger to salute the families in the visiting park. Fare was still standing at the window a half hour later, when LaPointe, with his head shaved, carrying a blanket and a Bible, was taken from the Rock to the Flattop.

SEVENTEEN

FARE LEFT THE LIBRARY AND WALKED DOWN THE RINGING spiral stair into the runway behind the Rock gate. In the narrow passageway, like a tunnel under a stadium, men crowded where LaPointe had been led out toward the Flattop. They watched it, the path he had taken, as though it were a solid, visible thing. Cigarette lighters flared like flashbulbs. They smoked as men do after taking a pleasure. There was a lot of loud talk.

He walked toward the sound of the exercise yard. He walked with a stiffness, and felt the electric twitches in his neck and shoulders that came with a sense of something behind him. He parted the crowd, watching the faces as they stepped aside. Their eyes fixed him hard stares from under hooded brows behind hands that cupped cigarettes, or gave him the cool "right through you" look they had for a freeman, a few of them moving aside for him out of genuine deference, and one or two knowing him nodding, "Afternoon, Mr. Odum." He made for the ramp that led onto the yard, impatient to have the white sky drop down behind him.

The yard was a place most freemen didn't go. For one thing, there was no reason to, and for another, it was dangerous. It was simply too easy for one of them in the milling, faceless crowd to slip a shank into you and then melt away. The yard was where most of the killing occurred.

Ahead of him, Fare noticed McLaren, standing with two other men; they were all slight, pale, white men in their middle years with a stooped look about them. They kept now to the perimeter of the yard and, Fare realized, kept to the edges of everything. McLaren had been the English clerk before Fare had come. He did his job well and did not lord it over the other men. He never tried to finagle special privileges, though it was traditional (and illegal) for teachers to pay their clerks two or three packs of cigarettes a week. He and McLaren were a lot alike. Both of them sensed it, and neither particularly liked it.

As Fare approached, McLaren cut him a glance which had recognition in it but conveyed no invitation. Then one of the men with McLaren smiled and broke into a sniggering, nervous laughter, which infected them all, and they turned a little away from him, their shoulders bouncing.

Fuck it, Fare thought, but one of the men nudged McLaren as though to say, go ahead. McLaren stepped out, opening the circle.

"Ever seen anything like that, Mr. Odum?" McLaren asked.

"Like what?"

"That fight," one of the others said. "Wasn't that a mother of a tussle?"

Fare looked at the man. He was a little smaller than McLaren, balding, with a pitted face. Apparently, they were interested in his reaction. He did not feel much like giving it to them. He felt a sudden, awful closeness to LaPointe.

"I was in the library," he said.

"But you saw it," the man said.

He was the kind of little man who'd have bullied others had not nature failed him.

Fare was about to deny he'd seen it, when he had the feeling somehow they knew he had.

McLaren was watching him and, seeing his hesitation, and perhaps sensing that something more than his ordinary reticence was in it, McLaren said, "You should have seen your face."

Fare looked at him. "I should have seen my face?"

"We were standing down by the canteen, in that group there, and Loren here happened to look up at the library window and seen you and he said, 'Looka that.' You had you nose stuck so far between them bars it looked like you was going to come straining on through like applesauce."

The other two laughed at this. They messed their feet around in the dust and flicked their cigarettes. They were saying to him, "See what we live with. You just come to work here; you've got to at least see it; at least do that."

They looked at him. "Yeah," he said. "It was something all right." He saw from their faces that his words disappointed them. They were expecting some pronouncement. He tried again, "That La . . . that big black man is an ass kicker, all right. What's his name?"

"LaPointe," the balding man said. "His name is Mad Dog LaPointe." He looked around at the yard to see whether anyone had heard him say the name. "You must of read about him."

"LaPointe?" Fare said the name aloud, testing the sound of a new word.

They watched him. "He's an ass kicker," he said again.

All around them, men must be saying, "That LaPointe is sure-God an ass kicker." Couldn't the English teacher come up with anything better?

Finally, the third man, who had not spoken yet, broke the silence. He gestured at the yard with a kind of angry yet prissy flip of his arm. His voice was high-pitched, like a child's.

"There's a bunch more like him. About ever third one's like that, or wants to be," he said.

They all looked around them at the yard.

"And look at how many they is of them," the man continued. "A white man ain't hardly got a chance."

It was true. The black faces vastly outnumbered the white. Everywhere, the black men laughed, talked loud and played games with incredible vigor. But the white men, even the rough-looking ones, seemed halt with nerves, twitching the mechanical glances over their shoulders at what enveloped them.

Fare wanted to talk to McLaren. He wanted to get away from these other two.

"You get those papers graded?"

The three stared at him, at the abrupt change of subject.

"No . . . uh . . ."

"Let's talk shop a minute," Fare said, walking away. Soon McLaren caught up with him, looking back once at the other two, and shrugging.

They walked the perimeter of the thousand-yard-square compound dotted with clumps of wounded grass, the white eruptions of anthills and the aimless trails that curled and turned seeking the briefest passage from one boredom to another. When they had distanced themselves sufficiently from the other two, Fare said, "What do you know about this La-Pointe?"

They were walking with their eyes trained ahead at nothing. Here and there, men stopped talking to watch them. There were shouts from the basketball courts.

"Just the usual, what everybody knows, and what I read in the paper."

"Tell me what everybody knows."

McLaren sighed. Fare could feel the man beside him struggling to push his mind to the heart of it, perhaps to make the story brief, perhaps because he wanted to tell it carefully.

"Mr. Odum," he began, "there is a thing that goes on here that you don't have on the outside. It's a way some of them have of getting themselves above the others. It's not that they want what they get, or even that they always get it, it's that they *can* get it and everybody knows they can, and that's what makes all the difference."

Fare looked at McLaren, whose brow was clamped down upon his eyes as he worked at choosing words. His voice was rising as he warmed to it.

"It?" Fare asked.

McLaren blushed fiercely. "Well . . . assholes is what I'm talking about, put it plainly. You see, LaPointe is one of the men here who does a lot of what we call 'rough-off.' He wants to control a lot of men, and the way he does it is by taking their assholes."

Fare nodded, but he did not see. He half-turned, but McLaren held up his hand to stop him.

"What I mean is . . . is a kind of ownership, like . . . like soybean futures. LaPointe don't have to actually put his body together with another man's to own it, he just has to get that man to the point where he knows, and everybody knows, LaPointe can have him, or give him to one of his friends, whichever."

Fare stopped. Mother of God, he thought, sweeping his eyes away and upward from the yard, affixing them gladly to the flight of a red-shouldered hawk. McLaren took this for impatience.

"OK," he said, "let me give you an example. Let me tell you the way Point does it. That's what we call him, Point. It fits, you'll see.

"There was a young man named Bodwalk. Most of them are young. It's the young ones that are pretty, and the little ones that aren't big enough, or it's child molesters and somebody finds it out about them and says they'll tell the others. If they did, if they told the others, a child molester would be killed just like that. Let me tell you, Mr. Odum, there ain't nobody into the right and wrong of things more than this bunch in here.

"Anyway, this Bodwalk was young and pretty, but he stayed to himself and didn't get any gambling debts or anything like that and so they had to get him the hard way. He lived up on the tier with me, up on 2-T, and I knew him well enough, as good as anybody did. He was quiet and comely, and he had a trade. He was a engraver and he worked in the print shop and did the illustrations for the *Starke Reality* and the *Raiford Record*, you know, the newspapers.

"On the street, they tell me, Bodwalk's trouble was he was bad to get drunk. Sober, he worked, and his life was just like yours—" McLaren's eyes had found the hawk's looping flight too "—or mine used to be. Drunk, he went to hell. He called men out into the parking lots of roadhouses and bars, wanting to fight them with knives or pieces of broken glass. He was a regular Jekyll and Hyde, if you know what I mean, but it was all on account of the whisky. He killed a man, in the bed of a pickup truck one night. Some fool nastier drunk than he was. They sent him here where he couldn't get no more whisky.

"Point was patrolling around up there on 2-T one day, which is what he does, he just cruises around looking into other people's business, and this day, he seen through the screen door of Bodwalk's cell and Bodwalk was doing something in there that got up his curiosity. Now I was up there, Mr. Odum, and I seen Bodwalk go into his cell a little before, and I was going to go over and smoke a cigarette with him, and then I seen Point go by and thought better of it. Then I heard them in the cell and I got several men to go with me and I went to look at it. That's just what Point wants you to do, see, is to have people watching, It helps him put the pressure on.

"We was standing at the door, four or five of us, and watching, and Point says, 'Give me that.'

"Bodwalk says, 'What?'

"But Bodwalk is standing in front of his bunk and it's obvious what he's doing is hiding something in it.

"Point says again, 'Give it to me.'

"Bodwalk says, 'Give you what?' or something like that, and Point says, 'All right then,' and he looks at us at the doorway, and I tell you, Mr. Odum, Bodwalk was my friend, but I didn't know what to do, nor how to go about it. Then Point turns back and he says, again, 'All right,' and he starts to cruising around the room and he comes to the picture on the night table of Bodwalk's wife. Now she is a woman of more than common homeliness, Mr. Odum, but I tell you my heart crawled in my chest when I saw him touch it, because Bodwalk did dearly love that woman. He picked it up and Bodwalk turned red, then purple, and he couldn't talk.

"Point stood in front of him, and Bodwalk had dropped down onto the bed by now out of just, what do you call it, he was just tired of it, the hate he had, and Point just stood there rubbing the picture up and down against his trousers in the front, you know against his dick, and smiling and then he started to moan. Then he tossed the picture on the bed and walked out, and said, 'I'll be making my rounds,' or some such as that.

"Well Bodwalk, he just laid there on the bed, and it was like he was staring at a hole in the air. The others left then, and I walked in, and I saw what he was really staring at. It was what was left on the table, a watch, a Masonic ring, I don't know what all, but we both knew that Point was going to come back and steal it all one by one and ever time, Bodwalk was going to go closer. I stood there in the cell with him, Mr. Odum, and I didn't know what to do, so I offered him a cigarette. He was lying there on the bed with his legs pulled up like a little baby, no, I'll tell you what he looked like. He looked like the man I seen once on the beach at Sebastian Inlet, who got his legs tore up by sharks. He looked just like that man, lying the same way, and the same look on his face."

McLaren walked beside Fare. Both of them were watching the hawk scrupulously. It scrolled the hot updrafts, precise and mindless, a part of things.

"Well, he wouldn't take no cigarette. It was like we was losing each other in this big hole of . . . with no sound in it, and so I said, 'What the fuck,' or something like that.

"He looked at me then, and then at the things on the nightstand. 'Yeah, what the fuck,' he said. 'My asshole is what the fuck.'

"Well, after a while I left. It wasn't nothing I could say to him after that. Three days later, he was going around trying to call back all of the debts that people owed him. He was looking for help from some of the bigger men. There was a sort of a meeting right out here in the yard one day. Bodwalk was popular, or else it wouldn't have ever got that far. You see, the men, they liked his pictures that he did for the *Starke Reality*. He engraved these pictures so that you could see the prison like it really was, not like the bulls want people to see it. The men liked him for that. So there was this meeting out here one day, and people talked about it and I guess we did our best, but it wuttin much. The smart ones finally got the better of the stupid ones and we decided that we would have a race war if we tried to group up on them. I say we, Mr. Odum, but you know what I mean is some of them, the rougher ones, decided. There is so many more of them than us.

"Some of them talked about luring Point into a fight and making it look accidental, but nobody would step up and talk about him actually doing it. And it wasn't always because they was afraid of Point. A few of them did not fear him. It was just that none of them could figure a way to do it without getting the hacks involved and getting more charges. I learned something there, I'll tell you. None of them, not even the lifers, would say they had nothing to lose.

"So, what they done was just dropped him. He sat there listening to it, and when it was over and we all just drifted away, he was sitting there with that red, then purple face of his, like the day in the cell. Right over there by the dugouts. A little after that, he came up to some of them, his friends, and took them aside, and asked them, very dignified because that's the way he was, he had honor, and asked them very dignified to help him. He wanted one particularly, Chinaski that lifts weights, to just stay near him as often as possible. But he wouldn't do it.

"So Point come back like he said he would and he would ask for the thing, whatever it was that Bodwalk was hiding in the mattress, and Bodwalk would not give it to him. He would just sit on the bed and watch Point and Point would take out his dick and pee on the picture, or rub it in his asshole, and then he would take something of Bodwalk's and leave. I came in to see him sometimes, and he would be smoking a lot and not eating, and he would not talk about it, and I was glad of that because there was nothing to say. We would talk about this and that, and I was just trying to be a friend, but it wasn't doing him no good. On the table would be the picture, and there would always be something else missing. He took to puking a lot.

"One day Bodwalk walks up to Point in the mess hall and says to him in a very calm voice that he would like to have something in return for what Point is going to get. Point asks him what he wants. Bodwalk says that he would like some buck, to make it go easier, and he knows that Point can get it for him. Points says to him, 'I know how you get when you get drunk.'

"And the two of them just look at each other. Finally, Bodwalk says, 'Please?' and his face gets red.

"Point sent the buck to Bodwalk's cell that night with a messenger, one of his friends named Taylor County. This Taylor County tells Bodwalk that he is going to be the one who will come after lights out. Not Point. Bodwalk just looks at him, calm, and starts to drink the buck. Now that's when I went in there to see him. He was sitting in the cell, on his bunk, and drinking the buck, not even trying to hide it. It was some of the batch they made over in the hospital kitchen out of grapefruit juice. It smelled awful, but it was getting the job done.

"So, we are sitting there and smoking, and Bodwalk is the calmest I have seen him in a long time. So I says to him, 'I guess it's better like this.'

" 'Like what?' He looks at me, strange in his eyes with the mason jar of buck in both hands.

" 'To give in,' I say. 'After all, what can it hurt?'

"He says, 'Yeah,' or something like that. Not yes or no. And we just sat there for some time like that, smoking, and finally he says 'Do you know what it was?'

"And I says no. I don't know what he is talking about, but I figure I'm going to find out. 'Tell me what was it?' I says.

"So he gets up and digs in the mattress ticking for a while and comes out with this packet of something wrapped in silicone-treated cloth. He opens it up and what it is, is his engraver's plates. And there they are, pictures he has been etching for years. I remembered some of them myself; there was the railroad station in Raiford proper over there, and one of the guard towers over by the Flattop. I was surprised to see that that's all it was. So I asked him, 'Why didn't you give it to him in the beginning?'

"He takes a drink of the buck and says, 'It would of just been something else.'

"And I guess he was right about that, but I never been sure. He told me then that his wife was using the etchings on the outside. She was taking them out on visiting days and having the prints made and selling them at art festivals around the state. 'And you know what?' he says to me.

" 'What?' I ask.

"He says, 'She puts her own name on them.'

" 'Why?' I ask.

" 'Because,' he says, 'a incarcerated man cannot be gainfully employed during the time of his incarceration. That's the law. So she signs them and sells them and the income and what she makes working in a dry cleaner's get them by, her and the kids.'

"He looks over at the picture on the table and I see that, since Point had been messing with it, he has turned it to the wall.

"Then, he salutes me with the jar of buck and he says, 'You better get on out of here. It's almost lights out.'

"So I left. But I did not have a good feeling about it. He was lying there drinking and looking up into that hole in the air.

"Next morning before light a man got up for a pisscall and stumbled over him in the doorway. Then the man slipped and fell flat on his face, and the first thing he noticed, he said, was that whatever it was he was lying on was wet, and cold as rocks in a well.

"So he lights his cigarette lighter and there is Bodwalk, lying there with the broken glass all around him and the blood everywhere. They said he was splattered with it and the walls and that it had ran with the tilt of that old building all the way to the north wall of the cell. In his right hand he still had half of the mason jar and he had used the raggedy edges on his neck. He must of wrapped it in a towel to break it quiet. Over at the hospital they said it looked like he had just punched himself in the neck with it a whole bunch of times. One of them said they wasn't a ounce of blood left in him and it looked like his neck had been hit by a shotgun, you know, bird shot, up close.

"Well, I looked around in there after it was all over, and I didn't find those plates, and I figure it happened this way. Taylor Country come back and found him that way, in the door, and had the presence of mind to go get the packet out of the mattress.

"I wondered what Point did with it when he found out what it was in it. Later, I thought about it and I figured Bodwalk could have got the plates out to his wife and fooled Point that way at least. I asked myself why he didn't, and here's the answer I got. He wanted Point to see it was all for a bunch of nothing. But you know, Mr. Odum, Point known that already, and so it wasn't any good in what Bodwalk done. I thought about it a lot, and I figure what Bodwalk was trying to show him would of been like that man up at Sebastian that I seen that time, without his legs. It would of been like that man going back out in the water to talk to the shark."

McLaren stopped walking. His fists were clenched in frustration. In his way, Fare could see, he was trying for poetry, for summation to equal the horror of his feelings, but words wouldn't bend to his will. "You just can't talk to him. Not a shark, you can't, cause he won't listen . . ."

McLaren ground out his cigarette and shook another out of the pack of Winstons Fare had given him earlier that week. Savagely he stuck it between his lips. His eyes roved off above Fare's head somewhere.

"Or there, there! . . ."

McLaren was pointing. Fare turned. McLaren was hopping beside him, as though to rise in the air. The hawk had tucked its wings to plunge. The force of its descent was such that feathers were sucked from its body. The hawk struck in an explosion of dust and feathers, righted itself, then slashed once, twice with its beak, then beat its wings down to rise stretching to full length before pulling the still-struggling rabbit into the white sky.

"It's like that, Mr. Odum," McLaren said. His voice had quieted. He remembered to offer Fare a cigarette. "It's just like that. You go talk to that bird."

They stood smoking, watching the circling hawk, high and rising, a far black dot with its underslung freight, diminishing now over the fire tower at Lockhart.

Fare murmured, "Did Bodwalk know Point? Did he ever? . . ."

"What?" asked McLaren.

". . . do anything to Point? Did he ever slight him?"

"No, sir. N'more than that bunny there did that hawk."

They walked the circuit without speaking. All around them on the teeming yard the big ones were moving on the little ones and on each other. The strong were homing on the weak. In his way, Fare knew, Point was a man of imagination. His patterns, like those of the scrolling hawk, the flesh-eating shark, were intricate in their randomness, remarkable in their efficiency. Perversely, they seemed to lack all but the most primitive intention. By refusing to surrender the plates, Bodwalk had tried to muddy the waters. But the shark had been too stupid to be puzzled, to deadly to swerve.

When they neared the basketball courts, Fare caught sight of Ivory, naked to the waist, driving for the basket through a flurry of slapping hands and jostling bodies, executing a stylish lay-up, clapping his hands together in a loud pop as the ball dropped through the rim. His shirt hung from his trousers. Beneath the yoke of his almost delicate collarbones, his pectoral muscles rolled in perfect colloquy with the movement of his arms.

Fare turned to walk toward the library, but McLaren dogged him.

"That Rose can sure play some basketball, can't he, Mr. Odum?"

Ivory now stood, pausing to rest, bent at the waist with his

hands on his knees. Nearby, two black men put their faces
into each other's space arguing about a foul. Ivory looked up
at them, saw that he was in the realm of imminent danger they
had created, and stepped away a few yards.

"Yeah," Fare said. "And he can type too."

"You like him, don't you?" McLaren was looking at him
with a curiosity Fare had not seen him spend much of.

"He's all right."

"He and Point is homeboys, you know, friends."

"That so?" Fare watched McLaren for some sign of more,
but there was only the flat face, still moved from the story
it had told about Bodwalk, and curious.

"I got to get back to the library," Fare said.

With the still room behind him, he stood at the barred
window staring.

"Trying it out?"

Ivory stood beyond the desk, tucking in his shirt, the sweat
beading on him like mercury. Faintly, Fare could smell it, the
athlete's new, almost sweet sweat, overcoming the mildewy
smell of books.

"Something like that."

The words Fare spoke were convenient, but his tone was
near reverential. It seemed to him a moment of extraordinary
perception. Ivory saw his confusion, his respect for the insight.

"They all do it. *You* all do it. I seen you," he said. "All
the freemen, the ones with any sense. You catch them acting
it out. Someday I spect to find one of them up here taking
a shower." He laughed. "When I do, I'll know what to do."

He handed Fare a book and a chit indicating his turn had
come round to check it out. Fare stamped the book card,
ripped the chit, and checked the signature.

"I saw you playing basketball," he said, wanting to say, I
know what it's like; I'm getting it, but knowing that Ivory
would only laugh.

Ivory walked away to sit at a far table. Suddenly, Fare
wanted to call him back. They were two intelligent, literate

men. Ivory had just checked out St. Augustine's treatise *On the Two Cities*. They could talk about it, about the window too. He dismissed the thought.

You didn't talk about it. If you talked, you didn't know.

Grasping the bars, he turned back to the window, and stared out at the life withheld, at the visiting park where the last couples groped goodbyes, and, finally, at the spot on the chapel steps which bore no mark to distinguish it from any other stone, where an hour before, LaPointe had flattened the Puerto Rican's head.

EIGHTEEN

HE DREAMT HE LAY ON THE PALLET IN UNCLE BATES' HOUSE.
Outside, the old mule, D'Arcy, was walking around in harness
turning the gears of the cane press and Bates was feeding the
green cane into the hopper at the top. Nearby, a cauldron
bubbled with the darkening, thickening mixture that was becoming blackstrap molasses. It was the same cauldron Bates
used to scald hogs and render lard. Up on the porch stood the
collection of washed bottles, all kinds, waiting to be filled
and labeled with Bates' hand-scrawled labels. Bates left the
cane press and walked to the cauldron. He took up a large
spatulate paddle and stirred the smoking mixture. Fare could
smell the too-sweet, burnt smell of the molasses. Now Bates
walked back to the cane press and fed more of the green cane.
The gears ground, the white liquid spilt onto the runway and
ran toward the collecting vat. Bates, always slow moving and
deliberate, looked up at the window of the house and smiled
his wizened, neither approving nor disapproving, only knowing smile, and then bent to pick up more cane.

Inside, on the pallet with her, Fare was happy. If Bates
was outside, he reasoned, then so was time. Inside, here where
he lay with her in the afterward with the sweat drying on
them, and their hearts slowing down to be caught and carried
in a strong rhythmic undertow out to deep sleep—inside was
safe from time. They had all the years that remained to the
old man outside, and after those were used, all the years it
would take Fare to grow up and live in the white house under
the tall pines and learn all the things, and meet her at church
picnics by the river and later, see her and speak to her, but
stand off from her through the years of school until, one night,
she would sit near him in a car and tell him that time had
always intended them. Had intended this.

He turned on his side, carefully encircling her breasts with his arm, fitting his face into the curve of her neck.

Past her throat, he saw something, a shape in the darkness, on the other side of her. A man.

The man had flung his arm across her just so, and had pressed his face to her neck just so, his flesh like a mirror of Fare's. And now he felt her turning a little toward this other face, this other naked length, unsettling their symmetry, and he heard her lips as they began the nibbling motions of kissing this other face, and her voice, "Oh Charlie, Charlie Odum."

Fare sat up. They were locked together. A long, deep savage kiss. He tried to pull her away to him, but she was perfectly mated to the body of his brother. Silently, he watched them. His flesh recoiled from hers. He rose and walked to the window. Outside, Bates stood stirring at the cauldron, his face furled in the dark sweet smoke. He looked at Fare, and curled up the corners of his mouth, and smiled the untouchable, far-off, lonesome smile of unarguable knowledge, and before bending back to the paddle, said. "Time." Behind him, on the pallet, started the sounds.

Fare awoke in the early morning. Bates, the mule, the bottles of molasses, all were gone from the room. On the table, like a summons, lay Lester's file, and beyond it on the bureau, leaning at the angle of repose, was the picture of Charles Ed and him and Clare, dull gray under the glass of a cheap frame.

He walked to the shower. It was still dark outside. Like the old man, he could rarely sleep the full amount he had allotted himself. He remembered the men in their middle years, his father's friends, saying that they could sleep less and less as time passed. Had to get up for the pisscall, they said, or the old clock inside the head woke them and they wandered in the dark making bad coffee and waiting to get started. It was just part of it, they said, all part of it. He had been young, listening to them, but he had known it would come to him, this wakefulness.

But now there was something new. As the hot water coursed over him, lulling rather than waking him, he tried to locate its beginnings. Perhaps it had begun when he had made the great effort in the storage room that day to still the part of his mind which had always, since childhood, screamed its objections. Slow down, it said. Stop, it said. State your business. Ivory had said don't think about it. Do about it. He had tried. It had not worked. Then it had worked, but not well. Now it worked too well. Not for long, but for too long, he had been stepping at every opportunity into the embrace of a shallow, troubled sleep full of anxious dreams. His weekends, those times he only waited to begin again, were spent more and more now in the great hollow of this sleep.

Yesterday, he had walked out of the library at five with the half-formed resolve in him to think again. Driving home, full of what he had seen from the library window, what McLaren had told him, he had made up his mind to forget what Ivory had said. He would not sleep away the space between this morning and Monday. He would look at some things clearly. He would ask himself some hard questions.

Lester's fat mean face was stapled inside the cover of the file. He looked at it for a long time. It was an animal's face, that was certain. But it was too easy to call it a hog's face and leave it at that. What it was, he decided, was the face of an old boar hog, and not a blooded hog either, just one of the survivors from the days when hogs ran free in the scrub. Yes, it was the face of an old boar who had never had enough of anything. Not enough to eat, not enough worming, and not enough of the sows either.

It was the face of the second-meanest boar hog in the lot, who got up only when the big boar hog got down. It was the face of animal frustration, having in it an expression of allegiance to nothing but its own unfed appetites, and a kind of lonesome outsider's pride in its hatred for everything better than itself. Fare stared at the face. He could not rid his mind of the fact that Lester, even as a newcomer to the prison, was more in his element (having never really left it) then he, Fare, would ever be.

LaPointe had handed him the file and said, we are going to kill that hog for you. Kill him for me, he had thought, fine, do it. The thing was to get it done. But something was wrong, and he had known it the moment the file came into his hands, and had known it ever since.

He rose from the table and walked to the window. It was light now, but the clouds were dark and fulminous in the October configurations that promised tropical rain, a rain which could drop six inches of water in a half hour. Like a cow peeing on a flat rock, they had said. But it wasn't cows he was thinking about.

When he remembered it, it usually came prompted by the dark clouds of a thunderstorm. For, just as the clouds fumed and rolled, shaping and reshaping themselves, so it seemed in this memory that people and objects, even animals, became indeterminate. All were the gray color of the early morning ground fog, all were immobile, until, as the eye roved, it detected as it did in clouds, the changing of form, a man's movement to separate himself from another and to become one with an animal or an object.

After the fog had dispersed, there was the smoke, the same gray color encircling them, coming hot and sudden up the denim legs of their trousers, making their eyes water. Later, not more than two hours after it all began in the early morning, this chimera sense of things caused by the fog and smoke could no longer be said truly to exist, but always in his memory, the day was thus shrouded.

It was a thing that had come with the first flush of prosperity. Odd, that they had done things in the old ways only later, in Fare's adolescence, when they could afford the time and money. Earlier, in leaner times, they had taken the feeders to market, and eaten macaroni and cheese, or hamburger purchased in bulk at the supermarkets in Gainesville. But when the small prosperity had come with the boys' coming of age to labor, there had come with it an itch among the older people round about to remember the old ways before they were lost. And, had it not been so much more of something else, it would have been comical, seeing them that first time trying to remember how it was done. The several of them, the older men, each of them having a piece of it, at last able to patch it together into a whole thing. One man taking a job as far as he could take it, then giving up in disgust, appealing, "Now how did Daddy do that?" Someone else, a brother, an uncle, walking over, taking the knife, "I bleeve you cut him like this."

"Wait now! Don't cut his pizzle!"

Then, "Hot-amighty, look what Prat done done; cut the pizzle an run it all on the tenderloin." Everyone laughs.

That first time, after which for Fare there had been few others, as few as possible, had begun the night before Thanksgiving Day, when the old man and Uncle Prat, who was not really an uncle but who was called one, and Uncle Harold (who was) had been sitting on the porch in the cold twilight talking about turkey.

"Turkey hail," Prat had said. (Here, as always, in his condition of perpetual afterthought redheaded Prat looks are there any women present.)

"Shit," he says as though to better affirm that there are not, "let's kill a hog."

There is silence. Fare sits with Charles Ed, dangling his legs off the edge of the front porch. A black cat's head appears between their two pairs of legs, looks up at them. Charles Ed kicks it, not viciously, but matter-of-factly out toward imaginary goalposts among the dark pines. Not a head turns at the yowl. The old man gets up and walks out to the edge of the porch and spits tobacco juice in the spot, a yard wide and black as an oil spill, where he has been spitting it for longer than Fare has lived.

"Hail," he says. "Turkey an roast pork. I wouldn't turn around for the difference."

"Ain't the point," says Prat, staring into the dark beneath the first branches of the pines where, across the hard road in the west eighty, a cow says, "Noooooooo."

They are all up before light. There is the sense of an adventure. Dressing in hushed silence in the warm wool hunting blouses, artillery men's shirts from the Second War. Walking out, past the kitchen where his mother is sitting at the table, picking in a tattered shoe box full of recipes for something different to do with pork. She is not happy about the turkey cooling in the icebox, so breakfast is last night's biscuits sliced, buttered, smeared with gravy, slabbed with salt bacon. Coffee for bellywash.

The next thing is to select the hogs, one for each family table, one from each man's lot. There has got to be competition. Who can get up the best feeder pig? Such things, Fare knows, are moot and interminable; no one will ever acknowledge defeat. He is excited, wanting to get on with it, hoping they don't get into guessing weight. If they do, not only will they have to select three hogs, scare each to the pickup, prod him up the ramp into the bed of the truck fitted with cattle sides, but each will have to get into the truck with the pig, kick him around to look at him one way and another, and then, each will have to heft him, one hundred fifty pounds of squealing, shit-smeared, dew- and piss-wet hog, whose feet, like hammerheads, can break toes, and whose teeth can take a fist-sized chunk of meat from a thigh, tear off a pectoral muscle, three fingers.

With Charles Ed, Fare watches, helps scare up the pigs, hopes for a foreshortening of things, wanting to get on to what is unknown, bored with what is known. The boys are given the job of honing the blades. Fare doesn't understand why there are so many of them: four big butcher knives, as many clasp knives, several of the wicked, hawk-billed linoleum knives used for cutting tar paper.

They do what they are told, spitting on the whetstones, circling the cold blades till they shine like silver.

The three men in the truck cab, Fare and Charles Ed perched on the cattle sides above the three hogs, they drive to Prat's where Prat's nigger, Vester, has got the fire up. Vester is going to get the head for cheese. For this reason, he is, as Prat says, happy as a pig in shit, and they will get

the best day's work out of him they ever got. The sun is just
fully risen as they reach Prat's, smelling the fire before they
see it.

It is smoking gray and smelling the turpentine way that
a good fat lighterd fire smells. It is a small fire built at the
mouth of what looks to be a toppled red brick chimney with
a large iron cauldron spreading at one end, an enormous
hollow-handled spoon lying on the ground. It is simple. There
is fire at the mouth of the chimney. A draft pulls heat along
the low tunnel under the cauldron, upward to be expelled at
the top.

Fare has seen this apparatus before, has asked what it is
for, has been told, but has, in his mind, consigned it to the
category of things—rusted machinery, dead trucks and the
like—left where they have fallen, to be consumed by rain
and wind and the tread of animals. Now he sees it works, for
the water is hot, sending its steam up to mingle with the smoke
and fog.

There are so many rituals. Each must be remembered in
action, which, after all, is memory. Remembering is the point.
There is a table, high at one end, low at the other to the lip
of the cauldron. Fare sees what will happen. The hogs will
be taken from the truck, slid onto this ramp table and down
into the big pot.

The truck comes lurching to a stop. Fare marvels that its
tailgate still matches the table's height. His father gets out of
the cab, leaving the door open, the radio playing ("Hey, good
lookin"), and walks to the cauldron where the other men are
standing now, Prat and Harold, and Vester, at a little distance.
Because it is Vester's fire, and therefore, his hot water, they
are asking him is it ready yet. He walks over close, and resur-
rects an old motion they have forgotten. Fare can see each
of them in his own way take pleasure in its recovery. Vester
stands above the cauldron in rising steam, and reaches down
with one finger, which he strikes across the surface of the
water one, two, three times like a man playing a zither. After
his last stroke, he shakes his hand, waving it in front of his

face like a black lily, but with little conviction. "Nawsir, nawsir," he says. "She ain dere yet. She just ain."

The others smile, spit, nod. They remember now the three finger strokes. Later, it becomes clear to Fare too. He stands at the cauldron, looking down. He can see, on its rusted bottom, bubbles beginning to form, merge, and rise, wobbling upward like knuckle balls. His father walks to the pot, repeats three strokes, shaking his finger with the last. "Whoo!" he says, with not quite genuine pain. He looks at Vester, who grins at him and asks, "Hit hurt?"

"Some."

"Got to hurt more den some, . . . mos likely."

About this time, Fare notices that, while the men are joking and pushing each other around a little from time to time, they each cut an eye to the truck bed, to the hogs, who, it is clear, know something is happening. They have been stirred up countless times in their lives by some human business, but this, they sense, is different. They keep moving, their ears flattened. There is the constant tattoo of their hammerhead feet on the wood of the truck bed.

At last, Prat says, "Try her again, Vester."

Vester's finger goes across one, two, three times, and, shaking, does not quite finish the last stroke. "That's her," he says. "Sho is."

Each of them steps up in his turn, as though to learn it over. Fare's own finger comes up on the third stroke testifying. He shakes it in the cool air, and the men laugh.

Vester: "That's her awright."

Vester goes to the fire now at the mouth of the brick tunnel. He scrutinizes it long and hard. The thing is to keep the water as it is. Boiling water will set the hair. He reaches in, and with a snatching motion a man might use to pick up a snake, he jerks a piece of lighterd out of the fire. It lies where he has tossed it, adding smoke to the steamy air.

The white men, meanwhile, have congregated at the back of the truck. Vester stands behind them at the ramp. Fare sees that there is a hitch in things now, an indecision. Hands are shoved into pockets. Finally, the old man steps to the cab of the truck and returns with a nine-pound hammer. A hush comes over them all. Fare and Charles Ed, who have finished the blades and laid them out on the cutting table, stand at a distance just greater than Vester's from the three men, watching, as they hand the hammer back and forth.

Fare knows that each of them will kill a hog; that is just as sure as it was that each of them would give a hog to be killed. What is at issue now is who will kill the first hog. By their deferential manner, he can see that, partly, it is an honor each of them is refusing. By the more than salutary way refusals are made, he can see also that each wants to pass on the chance to make the first mistake.

Finally, after going around the circle twice, accompanied by hard-edged jokes (Prat: "I ain't got a steady hand no more. Too bad to drink. You take it, Basil." They laugh. Prat is a reformed heller with ten years of righteousness behind him. His hand is steady enough.), the hammer comes to rest where it started, in the old man's big hands. He hefts it twice, then climbs to the truck bed. They lift the cattle gate for him, and he crawls under it, dragging the hammer. He stands in the truck bed and, as though someone has blown a whistle, the hogs begin to squeal and mill. The old man holds his own, kicking and hopping. Finally, they calm.

"Let's kill that Poland Chinee," says Harold.

Fare can see beads of sweat on his father's forehead, shapes of it in the gray cloth of his shirt. It is very awkward in the truck with the hammer. A full stroke is not possible. To raise the hammer too high would be to risk the hogs seeing it above them. They would spook at this. To take it too far to one side or the other is to risk hanging it in the cattle sides. Too short a stroke will necessitate another, ruining Vester's hogshead.

The old man manages to straddle the orange Poland China hog; he sights its head. He practices twice, an abbreviated straight-down stroke which will be little more than a dropping of the hammerhead, assisted by the muscles of his hands and forearms. The moment elongates as everyone stands quietly around, waiting for the hammer to fall. But the old man stands up again.

"Just between his ears, Vester?"

"Nawsir, just a little mo closer to he snout than that. Jus on that bony risin ahead his ears."

The old man aims again.

Harold says, "I could borrow Unc Taylor's twenty-five."

They all laugh in a nervous way, and it spoils the old man's aim.

"Come on Basil, strike a lick," says Prat.

With Charles Ed, Fare watches, thinking about the deliberateness of all this. That is what is so different about it. He has seen a lot of death, but this is slaughter, is business, and sensing in them the consciousness of the need to recover this, he wonders why. There is a growing feeling of disdain in him, mixed now with a strange apprehension. It is as though he will cross a line soon, visible only to him. Beyond it, he will look back at them. They will give up on him.

When the hammer falls the first time, Fare does not see it. Somehow, he has looked away for a moment. But the sound, soft and wet, and the shuffle of uneasiness, quick like the shock of blasphemy, that runs through them all, pulls his eye to the truck bed where he sees that his father has missed. Not badly, but badly enough. The Poland China is down on second joints, its head looping. The old man follows with the hammerhead, trying to get in his second blow, the hammer rolling in orbit with the snot-slinging, bubbling, snorting, wild-eyed hog's head. The hog is more dead than alive, out of control. The men are frozen in embarrassed fascination, watching the death uncleanly executed. They can't turn away. Finally, two big drops of sweat shake from the old man's face as he strikes his second lick. More by luck than design it is a good one, straight to the bony rising on the top of the hog's head. The animal spraddles down, almost perversely quiet this time, and the men spring at it, dragging it barely quivering through the cattle gate, onto the table. They swing it around and stop it for just a moment on the slanted table while Unc Prat stabs straight into the side of its neck with a long butcher knife. He seems to stir the blade at the moment of its deepest penetration, then draws it back out with a snapping motion. It is followed by a hard, pumping flow of blood, maybe three, four heartbeats of a solid stream.

As the men wait, breathing hard now, for the blood to stop, Fare looks up at the truck bed. His father is moving slowly, exhausted; he has put the hammer back down and is climbing over the cattle sides to get out and join the work. His face is sallow; he is still sweating. But his eye is on the work, and there is a pleasure in it. He is a little ashamed of the unclean killing, that is all. A question forms: How do you do it? How do you do a thing like that? Can anyone?

The blood is barely a trickle now, and at some signal from Vester, the men step forward again and shove the hog down the blood-lubricated track into the cauldron where it strikes the surface with a splash and sizzle. The thing Fare remembers most vividly is the way the blood turns instantly brown, to become a thin gravy in the water, and the way, as the three hogs go down the table, the gravy becomes thicker and thicker, darker in color, like caramel, smelling like bean soup, maybe, but more like what it is, which is something he has never smelled before, blood soup. Blood gravy.

In the cauldron, the first hog bobs slowly, once, twice, nobody touches it. Then Vester steps forward and snatches at its back, his fingers coming away with nothing. "Not chet," he says.

But each of them has to try it. Fare is not surprised to see Charles Ed's forearm, muscular already, not much distance from manhood in shape and size, among the others, his fingers grasping a knot of hair and pulling. Soon the hair comes off in large gouts and they are all around the cauldron, heaving the hog, two hands to an ear, back onto the table. They snatch with both hands, all of them furiously like swimmers, trying to get as much hair off as possible before it sets. They are laughing and whooping now, and spitting hair.

Soon the knives come out and the scraping begins, the hair

coming off in long swatches under the knives, then getting more tenacious as the hog dries.

"Fare, get on in here son, what's the matter fyou?"

Then the old man looks at him, looks closely. His eyes ask what's the matter, and then get their answer. As they hold each other briefly this way, across this distance, holding with their eyes, Fare wonders how the old man has formed the answer in words. He hopes for a charity that has no history hereabouts. The old man may not know it. Such categories may not exist in him. What are the words the eyes are saying? Son of mine?

It's all right. He just don't like it. That's all.

Son of mine?

He's a good boy that does his best. He'll work out all right.

Son of mine?

"Fare, gather up the rest of them knives and come over here. Hep us scrape."

It is with an effort of the heart, not the will; it is for his father that Fare finally brings himself to take the hog flesh into his fingers. He works hard, his mind elsewhere. Later, he stands beside his brother, each of them facing a gutted, gambled hog, scraping, endlessly scraping the mottled hides in front of him, ridding them of hair, then of their very pigmentation it seems, repeating over and over again the up-sweeping, whetting motion with the knife, the washing with water, and all the while he hopes his face does not reveal what his heart knows. Staring into the fog that burns away to be replaced by smoke, seeing the long far field, the highway beyond, he says the words, get away, get away, get away.

NINETEEN

RAIN LASHED THE WINDOW. LIGHTNING HUNG TO EARTH AND Fare counted in thousands to gauge its distance from his furnished room. Hearing the boom, he said one thousand twenty-one; that would put it south of Olena, too far south to wet the fields he had toiled in for twenty years more or less. He turned from the window. He had been spending too much time alone, too much time in the room by himself, sleeping to face the dreams. He had not even unpacked his books. He walked over to the cartons, ignoring the file on the table, and with Carmack's knife cut the twine that held them closed. But the bright colors of the bindings, the lettering of the titles were incomprehensible to him. Places he had been and had forgotten about. And how could this happen? He had thought, surely, through all those years, that the getaway had been complete, secure. That he had left no forwarding address, no trace. He could lay the books end to end and they would form the path he had walked out of ignorance. They were story books most of them. His own beginnings, he knew, were to be found in stories. He had not been on the right track, just now. For the day the hog hung before him slick and empty had been a foreclosure, not a beginning.

The beginning of the long wandering that had taken him from hog shit to sheepskin had come much earlier. Staring at the books still in their cartons, he knew it had come with the stories.

In the evenings, in the fallow times, there had been stories. All his life, he had heard the stories about those called his "people." These stories, about his family, the Odums of Alligood County, were delivered in hard-driving rhythms which sprang eloquent from even the most unlettered of his uncles and their children. But he, the bookworm, could not tell a story. His attempts had fallen on silences often enough to make him stop trying.

They told about each other and themselves, their tales peaking abrupt acts and harsh laughter, a thing done hell-for-leather.

These stories came out of the bedrock of his existence; they were the past and the family. The two were one thing, theirs inextricable from the history of the land which they worked to grow things, to become more and plentiful and to create after themselves more history.

Yet even he could see the difference between what came to be told and what really had been. And in the long moments of silence between acts and their crystallization into tradition among his people, he lived in his dream of becoming a story. But all his life, he had been the quiet one, the one dismissed by a strange consent from the duty of action. The voices said, "Oh, Fare, bout same as always." (An eyebrow cocked.) "You know."

Where was his position in the tribal mind? In the boredom of farm living, he formed it in dreams. He became, like them, a good ole boy. His dreaming had no regard for the propriety of night. It worked overtime in the daylight, becoming what they called mooning, "Fare, son, pick up that shevel and strike a lick." From the beginning in the white frame house on the red brick stilts by the grape arbor near the tall tobacco barns, under the live oaks and slash pines, he could not, except in his dreams, make up his mind.

From his earliest recollections he had no memory of ever choosing without agony. In his youth he had dreamt the simple acts of life, things done cleanly where decisions were made skin and muscle deep. His dreams were always real in the way what ought to be is real. As a child he witnessed life's simple equations of act and consequence—a sow would lie slatternly on her pigs, another would lie down gently and not kill—yet his mind could never wholly grasp this great orchestration of cause and effect in nature. So in his dreams he was reckless, a mover. Awake, he deployed himself always in the direction of simplicity, but life only grew more complex. Continually, his moment, the moment in which he was to do something, passed by him. He came to hate his growing up. He saw its moments coming, big moments, but he did not move from one to the next with any of the mute grace he saw in other boys. Always there were questions, never enough answers. No one with the patience. He approached choices slowly, as slow as time was swift. He read books. In the tiny school library, in the dusty stacks, far from the echoic playground, he searched for a tablet which would fall open to a magic code for young gentlemen.

Then later, drawn to the dark heart of the movie house, he waited for his lesson to stream upon the screen. Here he could learn action. Often, he thought he caught some piece of the code, a fast draw, a hard fist, a flesh ultimatum. A feeling of captured direction would last until, in the flat street outside, the afterimages of tall men blackened and broke, like things windblown, sun shriveled.

In his late teens, a high school senior whose large face shone between thin shoulders with ferocious intensity from the first row in the football picture, he understood that he could become words in the mouths of his people only by leaving them behind, and his inwardness began to shine as a virtue. Indecisiveness in this simple island of farmland meant either stupidity or intelligence. Nothing in this boy suggested stupidity; he was not slack-jawed, nor did he chew or drool. The intensity of his blushes alone was sufficient to send him off to college, provided there was money. So the dream dawned in the family's mind.

He would become educated, the only member of his family to go to college. From the first, it was he, among all the children, cousins and nephews. This mantle would descend upon him like a new coat. A coat not handed down.

He remembered that last summer, their defenselessness under the late September sun, the promise of winter in the air. The tall man walking to him across the field. He knew his father liked to see him work, liked it, because now in the summer after his graduation, it would be the last time. Fare knelt nailing insulators to a fence post.

His father stood above him. A scarred ball peen hammer hung from a loop in his denim pants. One big hand down, oddly gentle, turning his collar back, shaping it carefully as though they two were about to enter services.

Him thinking: Old Man. Old Man.

Listen to me call you old. This is what you want to save me from, this electric fence, this bending till bones rearrange themselves.

"Son, you cain't do it any way but bend over."

These barbs that gnarl your hands and thin your wrists until the veins stand out hard and break easy and won't heal. You love this land. See how you walk on it. See how the shock of your step shakes the loose white flesh in your face. But you can't see. No man can see himself changing. You are old by look and not years. You are truly old, your mark erased by these rains, these animals, this sun, and I am here to make you happy. How did you know it was to be me? What made you sure it was me to choose?

"Don't put them insulators up too high now, Fare. We gone to stop these piny woods rooters, we got to hit em in the snoot."

Then the old man sighed deeply and looked off to the north.

"Let's drag up and go to the house," he said, squinting far above the roofs and outbuildings to where the tall trees swayed. A calving cow lowed somewhere, and far off over the sinkhole, like dark stars, doves were falling to water.

"Yes, Daddy."

Sometimes he thought they had chosen him for his quietness, mistaking it for intelligence. And because he could not hold his own in a round of joking. (His friends all stood around talking about pussy they *got* as though pussy was something you could separate from the few unstrung country girls they shared. Or they talked about cutting each other, "if you don't watch out." He had left them behind before any of it, the pussy or the cutting, came true.) But chiefly, he knew it was because his father understood a link they had.

It was not binding upon his brother, though it was understood Charles Ed would stay, would work and inherit.

Fare liked to stand off by himself sometimes and stare at the winter coming in at sundown, making big green brooms of the pine tree tops to sweep the sky clean. He was like his father in this. This quietness which was a straining to see beyond the tops of the pine woods. Which was a crazy, uncontrollable wish to be somewhere else right when it was best to be where you were, right when the winter came low in the sky like a beating of wings. Because your blood was quick in those few days and you knew something. You knew it in your throat, and behind your knees where the hard fibers ached for a run you couldn't point yourself at, whose distance you didn't know. You had things to do, and people to see, new things, new people. All the world seemed to gather to great decisions.

That last autumn he had seen and felt the wind come and felt the wish too, in his throat. They had walked to the house. He had gone to wash, had come out again to call his father to supper. His father stood in the hog pen, holding a flashing bucket of protein pellets. The old man was transfixed, the center of a wild melee of glowing, refractory hog flesh. He stared up, jostled by the milling animals, cupping his vision with one hand at his temple, with moving lips. Fare knew he was wishing the wish.

The sun was so low it winked in the veined ears of the hogs. His father's eyes turned then, down to the hogs, and around to see Fare watching. The eyes were shy and a clear cold blue, suddenly releasing a cold sorry light. The secret of the wish was in them with the blue color of all the regret of his life. Fare alone, in all the family, had his father's blue eyes.

At graduation, his father, wearing a checked sport coat over denim pants that said Lee, had bent to him and told him about the bonds, shares of Coca-Cola. He could have them; his father said shyly, "Fare, we saved them for you."

In his eyes, Fare felt the wet movement of all the things they had needed and gone without. They straightened each other's ties then. Knowing that, in a way, they were both going, searching his father's blue eyes, he had said, "Thanks, Daddy."

"Get on, be late."

He had hurried to take his place in the processional of twenty-four seniors.

There had been the real beginning, standing that day in the hog pen with his father, knowing that an understanding stood between them as palpable as a man, someone to speak the words they could not speak. So, at the end of that summer, which had contained much more than any of them foresaw or wanted, he had gone off to become a creature of the examined life.

Now he sat examining Lester's file, staring at the picture stapled in it, and he felt a ringing impulse of hope. He did not have to do anything. Did not have to pursue this matter further. He could get up and walk out of this place and never come back, and live with the consequences, just as he had done, provisionally, for years.

But this moment was followed by another. He knew that he was parted now, and that part of him wanted to kill the man whose picture he was looking at, but didn't know how. This part had consigned the job to LaPointe. The second part wanted to get away, but didn't know how either. And the trouble was that the first part, which held fast to its course, was his mind. The second part of him, his body, was what continually failed him. For this, he had always suspected that he was inferior to men whose instincts were right. Men who did not think but merely let their sinews rumble them along toward oblivion or salvation. But wasn't Lester one of these? Lester had the quick trigger finger, the eye for the gunsight.

The file was written in the clotted jargon of social workers and lawyers. Between them, they did not tell you much about a man. It said here that Lester Delancy Macabee had been convicted of disturbing the peace in Raleigh, North Carolina, in June of 1968. What would that be, Fare asked himself, public drunk, bar-fighting? How much better it would be to write, "convicted of sucker-punching a man for no good reason."

It said here that Lester possessed a paranoid sociopathic personality with delusionary tendencies and persecution anxieties. What did that mean, that Lester was not fit to live among other men because he saw ghosts and thought they were chasing him? How much different was he, then, from Fare, who sat holding this file in his hands?

They had classified and labeled, and so, trivialized Lester, never realizing that the subject of the file was the unique hatred that lived in a soul which had never made the social contract, which had sent his brother to darkness under the earth forever. Goddamn them, he thought, the pychologists with their seventeen-syllable words for the hard, the mean and the stinking. All of the ugly things and the evil things they had made into sicknesses. Lester was human garbage. Lester was scum. How much better it would be to write, "This man was born without the imprint of humanity on him. He is an animal. Cage or kill him."

The file told him that Lester had been married to a woman who had borne him two children and been abandoned by him, for which he had been brought to the law and convicted of nonsupport. He served ninety days in the Harlan, Kentucky, county jail for this abandonment. The file said Lester survived his parents and had one living blood relative, a Charles Wilson Macabee, his brother. This, Fare knew, must be, or must have been, the drunken Chuckie whose face in the Buick's window that night had said, "What now?" a perfect tableau of righteous indignation.

The file held the Bradford County judge's sentencing recommendation in Lester's last conviction. Judge Harry P. Blackmuir stated that "while the prisoner's offense was not one of great magnitude, it was yet another in a series of like offenses whose repetition clearly shows that the offender, like so many petty criminals of his kind, can not be moved to better himself by means of the ordinary sanction for such an offense. In light of this, more severe measures seem to be indicated." Therefore, it was the decision of the court that Lester Delancy Macabee be sentenced to Raiford Prison at Raiford, Florida, for a period not to exceed five years nor to be less than three.

Fare stared at the judge's words. The judge, the court, the law were satisfied to let the matter rest in its present solution. So could he. Or he could rest it elsewhere.

He dropped the file onto the table. It told him nothing he did not know, or could not have guessed. He walked to the window. The rain had stopped. People were driving home from church. More and more now, he felt disdain for those he had come to think of as ordinary people. When he drove the long road to the prison in the mornings it was like going to war, even though the war was inside him. And when he came home again, and caught the first glimpse of the city streets where people wore bright-colored clothing and did not march in twos, he felt an ever-growing disjunction, a separation from them, their normality, this city where his clothing no longer marked him a freeman among the banished, nor gave him the burden and privilege of a freeman's behavior.

He turned from the window and lay down on the bed. The thing was not to sleep, dream, but to think. He sat up. Briefly, he thought of going out, but there was only time now until Monday, and only this room and the view from its window (containing the enemy) until then.

He stared at the picture on the bureau, knowing it for an accident of the most subtle art. In the foreground in sharp focus stood Charles Ed and Clare, the principals. The far field behind them still supported rows of corn, shrunken, almost white, waiting for the harvester. Behind, in soft focus among the corn stalks, half-obscured by Charles Ed's bulk, the bony form of Fare ten years younger stared out at the world. His young eyes, ignoring the lens, watched his brother. Clare stood beside Charles Ed, accepting the fact of his arm, casual across her shoulders, everything and nothing. The picture's subtlety lay in its clear separation, by means of focus and placement, of known and unknown quantities.

Staring at the three lovers still, Fare lay down again. Was

he, he wondered, like Bodwalk, in thrall for his devotion, or like LaPointe, for his hate. The picture would not say.

It had been fall then and was now again. That fall had been ripe with the promise of harvest, the reward of summer labor. He and Charles Ed and Clare had stood there in the confidence of that time and its purposes, each of them seeming already to have been rewarded. Three good, lucky kids.

Clare had been a rich man's daughter, a pretty girl who would become a beautiful woman, the winner's reward. She had been a way of completing an important thing. But Fare thought he could see in her eyes, even in the small, sunlit eyes in the photograph, the dissatisfaction that had given her to him for a while. She knew Charles Ed was complete as he was, that when the years of football were finished, there would be only losses. After graduation, there would be the gradual passage of time until the stories had been repeated to staleness and the body that had made the stories changed to resemble all the toil-broken bodies of the men who worked the farms. She had been able to see that taking him for what he was, a reckless young hero, would only mean living all the years with the bitterness of loss. In revolt from this, she had grasped at Fare. And this was not all of it, for she had not been merely seeking the best merchandise for the price of her life.

She had a lot of the loner in her too. More than dissatisfaction had brought them together. There had always been those moments, from the earliest times, when he had seen her gaze off into nothingness, going into herself where things were simpler, better. When you asked her to do something, you always felt she considered it, not against something else, but against nothing at all. Then it struck him, watching the picture as though something in it might move, and as the arms not of Clare but of sleep reached out to embrace him; it struck him that he had never asked her for anything. It had never occurred to him except that one drunken time, to try.

TWENTY

FAT RAT JENKINS, THE SCHOOL RUNNER, BROUGHT THE Monday morning memo from Bray. It read: "Last class canceled today, faculty meeting at 4:00. I have read this memo."

Underneath was a list of names, a blank beside each, and the initials of all the teachers who had seen the memo scrawled in the blanks. As the newest, he was the last to see the thing. Glad for something to break up the routine, he pulled out his pen and signed it. He wondered how Bray would operate as the presiding officer at a faculty meeting.

Four o'clock, the inmates shuffling out in the walking lines to spend the last hour before count-in on the yard. Fare gathered his things and walked with the others to the large, air-conditioned math classroom at the front of the school.

Hands cupping mugs of coffee, they took their places in cramped student desks and waited for Bray. Things were getting more military all the time it seemed. Would they all stand and salute and be told "as you were" when Bray entered?

Arthur, the science teacher, had removed a sack of donuts from his attaché case and was arranging them on his desk top. He bit the first. It squirted his cheeks with red jelly. He daubed himself with a napkin, sipped coffee, then dunked the donut and bit it again. Apparently, he had not heard of the fifth deadly sin.

Arthur had tenured here longest. He was fat, his face vaguely lascivious in a Hogarthian way. With the required tie and white shirt, he always wore a suit as well. In the expensive attaché case he carried sweets, handgun magazines, and Bible tracts. Arthur had a mail-order degree from a Bible college and it was said that he preached the local church circuit. From the beginning, Fare had studied him. He was the man who had lasted longest, defied the statistics, and so he must be, Fare reasoned, the best equipped for the work.

His equipment, as near as Fare could tell, was his abiding love of power. He loved to exert it where there could be no reprisal, and where he did not have to look at the results if he did not want to. He had no compassion, was stupid, though glib in the way that preachers who have memorized verses are glib, and he loved his position for its professional status and its supposed links to medicine and law. He was the kind of man who sinks to the sump level of systems like the Division of Corrections, and outlasts better men through sheer insensitivity.

Once, in response to some fatherly statement Arthur had made to him about the profession, Fare had said that teaching, like journalism, was blue-collar work. Arthur had fingered his immaculate white collar and said, "It's that kind of attitude, Mr. Odum, that will make it one."

"Call me Fare, Tom. We's all just folks."

Arthur was a good ole boy on the pulpit and a learned man in the classroom. So Fare's words caused a crossing of the weekend and workday wires in the preacher-teacher. He did not know what to say next. Now, he sat chewing the last donut, while the others tried not to watch.

Bray walked in carrying a clipboard. Like a football coach, he slapped it against his thigh, then put his foot up onto a chair in the front of the room, leaning onto the flat of his upraised thigh. His next words, Fare thought, should have been, "All right men, take a knee," but instead he said, "Right, well, just a few items on the gender this afternoon and we see'f we cain't get you all out a little early. I know Winzinried and his crowd want to get to the Oasis in time for happy hour." Bray looked pleased with himself. Winzinried guffawed. Arthur snorted powdered sugar.

"First," Bray said, "we got a few items from upstairs. It says here that Mr. Lavery over in the tag plant has reported groups of inmates loitering out on the back steps of the school. Now we don't report on him when we see his men sitting out behind them dumpsters cooling their heels, but that is beside the point, ain't it?"

Bray looked at them for approval and they all nodded, a few of them laughing. Bray smiled, but his face got serious, something it did by pinching itself together in the middle.

"Now, we got to keep this loitering within reasonable limits. I know you men don't want to be policing the halls. I know you can't keep track of everybody when there's always new ones coming and you don't know their faces, but I want us to all make a renewed effort to keep this thing down to reasonable limits. Can we agree to do that?"

They nodded. They would work at it for a while, and then slack up, and then have another meeting to be exhorted to work at it some more.

"Now," Bray said, shifting his other thigh up and leaning back down onto the clipboard. "It's my pleasure or maybe it's not such a pleasure for us, but it is for him, anyway, I got to announce to you that Mr. Rustley, there, is leaving us at the end of the month. He's give me his notice, and he's going to take a job, says here, take a job with the Family Services in Gainesville. Is that right, sir?"

They all looked at Rustley, a dapper, reclusive black man called Oreo by the inmates because he did not engage in discussions of radical politics.

Rustley coughed into his hand, smiled, showing his beautiful teeth, and said, "Uh, no. It's a job with the Forestry Service."

"Well, I be damn, says here, oh, right, says here Forestry Service, sure does. Anyway, it's our loss and a gain for them trees, ain't it, men?"

Bray set the clipboard down by his foot on the chair, and clapped for Rustley, nodding his head at them all to follow suit. They clapped. Rustley sat there, smiling the pearly smile.

"Now," said Bray. "Next here, I see a couple of men have come down sick and been took to the hospital and they got it out of them over there that they had been drinking the mimeograph fluid again. Well, naturally, they sume that it's our fluid just because it was ours the last time.

"We all know it's other people in this place who got the stuff and could've had theirs stolen, but they say it's us, so we got to keep a very tight grip on it. These boys that drunk it are going to lose their eyesight, and they tell me one of them might buy the ranch. Now I want you all to sign the ledger every time you run off assignments, so we can account for who's using the machine, and I want all of us to take special care about the key to the supplies cabinet till I can get the lock changed. We can't have nobody getting to that fluid anymore.

"Now last here, I see we are going to have a cultural event. It's going to be a group of actors coming from the university to put on a play, says here, the Harlem Renaissance Players, feature that name, and the play is going to be called, let me see, called Juh-net's *The Blacks*. Must be something for the colored inmates, but anyway, what they want us to do is provide somebody from over here to give a introduction for the play, you know, stand up there and tell the jarheads what it's all about and what it's supposed to mean and why they ought to shut up they mouths and listen for once. Can I have a volunteer to do that?"

They all looked at Bray. None of them raised a hand. Bray looked back at them, frowning, his eyes passing from face to face.

"Thank you, Mr. Odum."

"Wait a minute. I didn't hold up my hand."

"Well, think about it a minute. Who else could do it but you?"

Fare looked around. The intermediate-level English teacher was Harvey Boildeau, who was teaching out of area. His degree was in architecture. He could diagram sentences with the best of them. Boildeau smiled at him and shrugged. Rustley was the elementary-level teacher. He taught reading and writing to the illiterates. He had a sociology degree. Apparently, he knew something about trees. Fare looked at Bray.

Bray shrugged and said, "If you ask me, it's all a waste of time. Shit, you men know how I feel about movies and plays and truck like that by now, but they asked us to do it . . ."

"What do I have to do again?" Fare asked.

"Just get up there and tell them a little bit about this play by this Juh-net, says here, *The Blacks*. Use that Ph.D. of yours for something one time." Bray smiled, the others laughed. Fare said, "Sure. I'll think of something."

Fare walked back to his classroom to secure the wing and lock his desk. He picked up a few scraps of paper, straightened the rows for the next day, and then made his way toward the entrance. Bray, ahead of him in the dark hallway, was locking the door to his suite of offices. Fare hurried up the hallway, seeing that Bray would wait for him before turning out the last lights. As he passed, he nodded and heard the light switch snap down. Bray said, "Wait a minute there, will you, Mr. Odum?"

Fare stood in the doorway, while Bray used the last of his keys on the fire doors. "Got too many damn keys," Bray muttered. "Ever key is another job I got to do. Work me to death."

They fell into step, following the others toward the gate. They were getting out a half hour early.

"Jew mind that about the play and all?" Bray was walking at his usual brisk pace, looking ahead at the gatehouse and fences.

"I don't like to get up in front of people," Fare said, "but I guess I can handle it."

"Teacher has got to get up in front of people."

"Yeah," said Fare, "but I'm getting used to the bunch I got in the classroom now."

"Hard on you at first was it?"

"They newcocked me like everybody else."

They walked in silence for a while. Bray's pace seemed to

slacken. He was coming unwound as they moved along, all of the tension flowing out of him. Fare wondered what he was like on his own time. Was he a fisherman, a yard and garden fanatic, a shade tree mechanic, or was he just one of those sit-in-front-of-the-TV types. Bray was married. He had to be. A good Division man was married, had kids, went to church, had worked his way up from tower guard, and was waiting for one of the state-owned houses to come up for grabs so that he could live on the grounds rent-free.

"So," Bray said. "How you liking it, so far?"

What was this all about? Fare felt the truth coming to the surface, along with the tiredness, and the irritation he had felt at the meeting. But he pushed it back. You couldn't tell Bray the truth. He didn't want to hear it. He adopted his best young-man-on-the-make tone of voice.

"It's coming along fine, just fine. I got a few things to learn about it yet, but it's coming along."

As they passed the canteen, Bray halted abruptly and said, "We got a little time. Let's get a cup of coffee. Unless you chasin Ernie and them to the Oasis?"

"No," Fare said. "I don't go home that way. I go the back way."

Granger was in the back washing dishes and getting ready to close. They asked for coffee, and Granger scowled at the clock on the wall, pouring them the last of what had been sitting on the burner since noon. It had a grease slick on top of it and when you tilted the cup it took a second for the coffee to get the message and come on to your mouth.

They both sipped, then put the cups down. Bray shook his head at the taste. "We used to call this 'Granger's revenge' when I was working in Classification. That was before I had my own coffee over at the school. Granger, he's been in here too long. He's getting to where he thinks he owns the God-damned place." Bray winked at Fare. "Ain't you, Granger."

"I'd gladly take off this apron, Mr. Bray, and walk out of here and never look back." Granger's voice came to them

through the thin Sheetrock wall. They could hear him chuckle
and slosh the dishwater. He said, "How'd you like to help me
get out of here, Mr. Bray, so's you could get you somebody
to make good coffee. If you help me, I promise I won't touch
nare match to the place when I leave."

"I can't help you, Harold. You know that. I ain't much
more than a coffee-maker, myself. Sides, I thought you'd put
all that touch-a-match stuff behind you by now."

Bray winked at Fare. "He was a burner," he said, jerking
his thumb at the wall. "You know, a arsonist."

Fare nodded.

"That's right," said Granger through the wall.

Bray smiled at Fare. Granger appeared at the hole in the
wall that separated the kitchen and service areas. He gathered
up the day's receipts in canvas sacks and walked to the door.

"Pull her to and she'll lock," he said, backing out. Then he
swung his lean form back toward them. "And don't forget to
wash them cups."

"In a pig's ass," Bray said.

They stared at the coffee. Fare picked up his cup, then put it
down again. Bray turned his cup around in the saucer with
his forefinger. Fare saw the cleat marks, round red half-
moons and a few full circles, on the backs of his hands.

"What position did you play?" he asked.

"What?" Bray looked at him with concentration and ill-
concealed delight.

Fare said, "I was just noticing your hands, there. You know,
the cleat scars."

Bray held the hands up in front of him, smiling at them.
He poked a forefinger into one of the deeper holes, turning
the fingertip in the small depression with the motion a man
uses to clean his fingernails with a knife blade.

"Yessir," he said. "I sure got em. Ain't I?" He held the
hands up for Fare to inspect again.

"Yeah. What position?"

"Guess." Bray's voice was proud, and a little shy. All the
good ones, the old jocks, who had been called jocks before

the word became a term of approbation, all of them had this shyness before talking about it. He had learned this early, back when he had played. The boys he met in surrounding towns who said they played football in this same, shy way, these boys were the ones to look out for. They would knock your dick off. He would ask them what their numbers were so that he could suck up his guts when he saw them coming. They were always coming.

"I'd guess tight end, in a running offense, or maybe a pulling guard on a smaller than average team."

Bray smiled broadly and then drew back from the waist in a show of surprise.

"I God, you got it. It's both. It's first one, then the other. They put me at tight end to throw the pee-hole block after I hurt this knee."

They looked at each other. Bray held the hands up again, like pleasant memories, then put them down as the shyness and the delight faded from his face. It was ten of five, the whistle would blow soon, calling them to the gate. Bray looked up at him suddenly.

"So, you think things is going along pretty good?"

"Sure," said Fare, not wanting to go back over it.

Bray cleared his throat. "What I was wondering was . . . I wanted to ask you about something. It's the reason I got us the coffee. I wanted to ask you about you and this Ivory Rose and some of the things I heard. Now don't get upset."

Fare looked at him sharply. He had been lulled by the talk, the quiet gloom of the canteen. Things I've heard, Bray had said. Heard? From whom?

"Don't get upset about it. I want to ask a friendly question or two, that's all, and maybe give you a piece of friendly advice. One old broke-dick ballplayer to another."

Bray was leaning toward him across the table and looking him straight in the eyes in some kind of stare-down manner. Fare looked back at him until his eyes watered. He had to blink.

"So what do you want to know? Because there's nothing to it. It's just . . . he's just an acquaintance."

Bray narrowed his eyes. His face pulled itself toward the center.

"That's just it. That's it right there. You see, a inmate can't be just a acquaintance. And he better not get to be a friend. He can be your helper, work for you, be your gopher, your runner. It don't matter who he is, he can't be nothing but *under* you. It's got to be that way in here."

Bray paused. He watched Fare's face.

"Heard from who?" Fare asked. The name Arthur came to him.

It was not the best response. Bray's face took on that hard, slightly disgusted cast, the expression he used to confront the school's disciplinary problems. The hard cases. Fare was a hard case.

"I can't say who it was told me. It could of been anybody. *I've* seen you in the chemical room with Rose myself, sitting in there, both of you with your jaws chopping at each other ever spare minute."

"I only go in there on my break."

"That ain't the point. The point is, it don't look good. It don't look good to anybody who might come in, one of the Division men, or somebody who could hurt the school with it, and it don't look good to the other inmates to see a freeman giving special favors to another inmate. It gives them ideas. They think they can all start putting on the con jobs."

Fare interrupted. "You think that's what's going on? I'm getting a con job?"

"Well what *is* going on?"

"Nothing is going on. Just talk.We talk about poetry. Rose writes poetry and he asks me to read it. That's all."

"That's all?"

"Sure that's all. And we drink a little coffee together."

Bray looked relieved. He sat back in the chair again. His eyes went to the clock, then confirmed the time at his wrist.

"Just let me tell you something, you know, friendly. There's men in here like you can't imagine. You just can't imagine what they capable of. You new at this, and you doing all right, maybe better than I thought . . ."

Fare smiled at the grudging compliment.

". . . that's why I don't want to see you get into a mess. You remember what I told you that day in my office? That about the print shop?"

Fare nodded. He remembered it. He had heard it from others since then.

"Well that kind of thing ain't rare in here. It happens all the time. They are always waiting to catch you out in something and get something on you and then start the demands to get you in deeper and deeper. I seen it happen to better men than you or me. There was a colored man, one of the first ones they got working here a few years back, and he got friendly with some inmates, and one of them asked him to take out a letter. Nothing but a little ole letter. So he didn't see what it could hurt and he agreed to do it. Well they had put dope in it, sprinkled in some marijuana. When he got to the gate with it in his pocket, Sarn Thomas was waiting for him. You know what they done? They ratted on him, snitched on him just for spite. Just to get rid of him because they didn't want to be looked after by no other colored man. That feller, he ended up with felony charges, smuggling. And all he was doing was a favor, a act of human kindness. Well, there can't be no human kindness in here. Not unless it goes by the numbers. We have got to do it by the numbers."

Bray leaned back, out of breath, a vein dancing at his temple. Without thinking he took a swallow of the coffee, looked around in panic, then spit it back into the cup.

"Scuse me," he said, "but you see what I mean?"

Fare nodded.

"Sure," he said. "I see it."

"Good," said Bray.

"You want me to stay away from Rose, right?"

"Not stay away, just keep it to business."

"Sure," said Fare.

They walked out. The whistle crashed down on them, unbelievably loud, its frequencies plucking the nerves in Fare's head. He walked uncomfortably beside Bray to the gate, parting from him with a nod in the parking lot.

Getting into his car, he watched Bray drive away in a new, red pickup truck. In a way, he wished Bray knew the truth, knew how far it had gone. Bray could tell him how much was too far. Bray could pull him back from the edge. But, going by the numbers, Bray could also flip him to the hacks, if his conscience told him to. His kind were made that way.

TWENTY-ONE

LAPOINTE WAS ON THE FLATTOP AND WOULD BE FOR A minimum of ten days. After that, it was anybody's guess. He would be sitting there, big and insular, on the bare concrete, entertaining whatever thoughts were his to pass the time. Or kill it. Beside him would be the Bible. He would be waiting for his hair to grow back. They would be feeding him baby food. If he asked for a bath, they would run in a hose and turn it on, throw in a bar of soap.

Ivory was something else. He and Fare had not spoken, except as student and teacher, since their meeting in the library. Ivory was cold-shouldering him. Fare had considered telling him about the talk with Bray, but did not want to. Let Ivory approach him. Or let him stay away. Either would do for now, maybe for good.

But Fare had the feeling, watching him give half his attention to the grammar exercises, that Ivory already knew about it. What else could explain the way Ivory had, on his own, decided to show Fare the chilly exterior.

He had to tell himself more and more often now that the others, Bray, Rose, LaPointe, were not mind readers. Nor had they planted listening devices to gather the sounds of his voice. They were just men like himself. It only seemed they knew what he would do before he did it because they had so long operated by the secret rules of this place. They had fitted themselves into the network, made bargains, sold goods and received goods in return. Remember, Fare, you must get highest prices for what you have to offer and accept nothing but the best in return.

And, as the early part of the week passed in the routine of teaching and eating and driving and teaching again, he felt perhaps it was over, had been dropped by mutual consent like a bad idea.

He had read the file. It told him nothing. Less than nothing. It had been another symbolic gesture. They had given him nothing but a hint at what they could do, so he owed them nothing in return. If they reported him, using the old man's testimony, couldn't he fight them? He did not know what he could do, because he did not know what else they could use against him. Had Bray or one of his snitches, Arthur perhaps, seen him leave the storeroom? Perhaps someone had been hiding among the shoes, listening, recording.

On Wednesday afternoon, Ivory waited as he had that first day with the poetry. Fare noticed him and considered hurrying out, considered not speaking. He could say, "It's all over. I don't want any part of it anymore," and let them do what they would. But he had to secure the wing.

And part of him wanted it to go on, wanted to know the next step. He was still undecided when Ivory stood before the desk, smiling in his controlled, unmirthful way, handing him the grammar exercise sheet. The work had not yet been started, much less . . .

"Turn it over."

On the back, in a cramped hand, Ivory had written something. When Fare looked up again, Ivory was sauntering through the door to join his walking partner.

Bray passed, leaning in as usual to tap his watch and nod toward the windows Fare was to close.

"Quittin time," he muttered, padding away as quickly as he had appeared.

Fare looked down at his own right fist, opened it. He unwound the sheet, smoothing its creases, and put it into his shirt pocket. He went to close the windows.

Fare spread the sheet on a table in the restaurant where he took suppers.

LaPointe's on the hard top so things is going to have to quit for the time being. Brother Mad Dog wouldn't take it right if we continued our plans without him to help us. In fact, he's going to get a copy of this letter I'm writing to you. We decided that already. That's the way it is between partners, everybody get the news, and the benefits when they come down. Here a few items of news. First, you will give a little lecture to the bunch of us who going to see a play. Second, you had you a talk with jackass Bray. Ask me how I know I got ways. It just is not that hard to find things out in here if you know how, and you deal with reasonable men in business. All business, remember I told you that? Sure you do. Now heres what I want you to do. I want you to call this number, ask for Jamahl—378-3935. Now ask yourself why should I call this number? (You are a very self-centered white man, and you always wanting to know whats in it for you.) Well the answer is just what you think it is. It is Macabee, Lester (oink) Delancy, 046789. Brother Mad Dog is going to bleed Lester for you to fulfill our part of the bargain. He will do it. All in good time. When we know that you are doing what we ask you to do. He will do it in his own special way. Now, you call the above number, like the writing here says. We can't do much more until Brother Point gets off the hard top. It is in you best interest to destroy this paper after you read it. Do not forget to copy down the phone number first. Well be in touch with you. Be cool. PS By the way, you did real good with Bray, turning him around with all that football jive. If you want to talk to me, go to the hospital on you break to give blood.

The letter was not signed.

Fare crumpled it again, and when he left the restaurant, dropped it into a storm drain, nudging it with his toe and waiting until he imagined he heard it hit water below.

When the bell rang signaling morning break, he walked down to Bray's office to sign the blood donor sheet. Inmate Mardis gave it to him with a solemn nod of approval. "Yessir, Mr. Odum. Let's see, that gives us almost one hunderd percent participation. The only ones ahead of us now is the hospital." As Fare signed the sheet, Mardis scrutinized the list of signatures. "That leaves Rustley, but course he's quitting, and leaves Arthur. I tell you, Mr. Odum, I don't think we'll ever get him to sign. He tells me he cain't on account of religious plications or something, but I think he just don't want

that horse needle plugged into him. What do you think?"
Mardis grinned at him conspiratorially.

Mardis, rumor had it, had filched the mimeograph fluid to
sell it. Fare wondered whether or not the grinning bootlegger
had known what he was doing to his customers' eyes when he
sold them the fluid. Fare said, "It's every man's choice, Mardis.
Every man to his own delight. You know, like who to vote for
or what brand of whisky to drink. It's one thing they still ain't
got set down into law."

"Amen, Mr. Odum," Mardis nodded solemnly. "Amen to
that."

The hospital was one of the oldest buildings in the prison,
and looked it. It had been worn smoother than any of the
others. Its corridors were narrow and labyrinthine. There were
unexpected dips and rises in the floors where additions had
been made, walls knocked out, partitions thrown up.

Windows had become doors, doors windows; insulation hung
from pipes, their plaster of paris and fabric emulsion sifting
down to coat the floors with white powder. The building was
not air-conditioned, and condensation dripped from exposed
pipes. A ripe odor clung to walls despite a chemical coating
swathed here and there by men with mops and buckets full
of a milky white solution.

As Fare passed the wards, he saw patients lying in the old-
fashioned high beds fanning themselves with cardboard revival
fans. One man turned his head as Fare passed. He lay in a
buzzing cloud of flies. His face was covered with scabs. He
snatched at the flies with a fan whose reverse side was deco-
rated with the face of Jesus Christ. Fitfully, the man was
singing about the wings of an angel.

The blood donor's clinic was in the basement. As Fare
walked in, another freeman walked out, his right arm bent
at the elbow. Fare saw a new dressing and a bright dot of
blood. The attendant was refrigerating a plastic container of
fresh blood. Fare could see, inside the cooler, hanging racks
of these bags of gelid red liquid.

"I came to give blood."

A young, slight, high-yellow Negro with an unmarked, almost effeminate face and clean, slender hands smiled, revealing a perfect keyboard of teeth.

"Yessir," he said. "Please fill out this card." Fare took the card. The attendant grasped him gently by the upper arm and sat him down. Expertly, he began to unbutton Fare's shirt sleeve. He produced from a cabinet the rubber and fabric harness to take blood pressure.

As Fare filled out the card, the young man pumped up the apparatus, narrowed his eyes at its gauge, then shook his head, a look of troubled concentration crossing his eyes. A second time, he inflated it.

Fare did not like the cold, tightening feeling. He imagined his whole body in such a casing, its fluids percolating in the cold pressure. All around him hung torture devices. He had always hated doctor's offices. Some of these instruments he had used himself, on animals. Others? What parts of the body were they meant to violate?

The attendant deflated the apparatus, refitted it to Fare's arm, then reinflated it, squinting at the gauge. Fare felt the thing loosening by stages.

"Damn," muttered the attendant. Then, "You nervous bout something?"

Fare looked at him, disliking this intimacy.

"No more'n usual." He tried to chuckle.

The attendant took the card from him and scanned it.

"Got any history of high blood pressure?"

"Not that I know of."

"You twenty-eight, huh?"

"Yup."

"Drink a lot of coffee this morning?"

"Some. Same as usual. So, uh, what's the trouble?"

"Well, I keep getting a high reading."

Fare looked at the attendant, who looked back at him. The young man seemed not so much worried as interested.

The rubber thing grabbed his arm again, then loosened.

"There it is again," the attendant said, shaking his head as though he had tried to give Fare a break but it hadn't worked out. He took the card and, as Fare watched, erased the check from the "no" slot at "history of high blood pressure," and beneath it wrote, "HBP, 160/102." He took the harness from Fare's arm and put it back in the cabinet.

"Lie down on that table there, please, sir?"

Fare tried another joke. "You don't take the water if the pumps ain't working right?"

The young man did not laugh, only gave Fare the confident and competent medical look they give you when something is a little bit wrong.

"Oh, it don't affect the blood at all. Fact, it's a little bit good for your condition to give blood. Reduce the volume of blood, an you reduce the pressure. Don't last long though, builds back up quick."

He smiled at Fare. He removed the several parts of a large plastic syringe from a drawer. Horse needle. The paper covering of the table crackled beneath Fare. It stuck to his arms. "How high is it?" he asked.

"It's high borderline, and it fluctuates some. It don't stay at the same rate."

"That good?"

"Could be. You got to get it took quite a bit, then get a average to know for sure."

"Should I worry about it?"

"You should get it looked into."

Fare was imagining someone looking into his blood when Ivory strolled in, a pass in one hand, in the other a bottle of prescription medicine.

"You ain't got nothing to worry about," he said. Then, "Kutana, brother Morton."

The attendant glanced at the open doorway, then at Fare, and muttered a greeting under his breath.

Rose stepped closer to him.

"I said, 'Kutana, brother.' "

The younger man looked at Rose; his hands stopped their automatic movements with the syringe.

"Kutana," he said with a tired, resigned expulsion of breath.

"There you go," said Rose, fixing him a moment longer with his eyes.

Fare sat halfway up from the table, bringing the paper up with him in what seemed a deafening explosion of waxy crackling. Suddenly there were other sounds, stainless steel clanging in a kitchen somewhere above them, clanking pipes, a murmur of voices. How far away?

Ignoring Rose, who sat in the chair Fare had vacated, the attendant gently pushed him back down. He touched Fare with the firm, impersonal force that barbers and dentists used, but his fingers worked now too quickly with the rack and tubes and bag. Fare closed his eyes. Get on with it.

The attendant straightened and twisted Fare's arm. Fare felt cold alcohol rub the crotch of his elbow. There was a pause, then the alcohol rub came back again, but differently, and he opened his eyes to starched blue, not white.

"I'll bleed this one," Ivory grinned.

TWENTY-TWO

FARE TRIED TO SIT UP AGAIN, BUT IVORY PLACED A FIRM, medical hand on his chest and whispered, "If anybody walk in, I look busy this way."

He winked. Fare let himself be pushed back, but it was preposterous. Ivory was not wearing the hospital white.

"This takes me back," he said, rubbing Fare with the alcohol. He seemed to be enjoying himself.

Fare started to speak, but saw the needle rise up in Ivory's hand to have its plunger pressed all the way down.

"Don't want to get any air into you," Ivory said.

Fare said, "You trying this for the first time?" He did not believe Ivory would really go through with it. Ivory would only stand over him and go through the motions while they talked.

"I know what I'm doing, don't I, brother Morton?"

Fare could hardly make out the attendant's curt, "Yeah," from somewhere beyond the narrow field of his vision.

"See, I was a corpsman in the Marine Corps back in the hot'n heavy days. You remember the Tet, don't you?"

"The Tet?" Fare could not recall it.

"Wasn't I a corpsman?" Ivory said to the presence offstage.

"You was that." The attendant's voice was the same, quiet and dry.

"Whyn't you go smoke a cigarette, brother Morton," Ivory said.

Fare heard an exhalation of breath, then the sound of crepe soles gripping the concrete floor, then nothing, then a voice added itself to the murmur he had heard in the middle distance.

Ivory was still rubbing his arm, hard, with the alcohol. It was beginning to hurt. He could feel the blood in the soft crotch of his elbow passing back and forth under the pressure of Ivory's thumb. His veins throbbed.

"Hey," he said. He felt abjectly vulnerable.

Ivory stopped rubbing the alcohol.

"Got to get it good an clean," he said. "There's a lot of jaundice around. You don't want to turn yellow, do you? Yellow ain't a popular color these days."

"Let's get the blood out of me, will you."

Fare could not keep an angry edge out of this voice. Control yourself, he thought. Just go along with it. He ain't going to hurt you. What good would it do him. Learn something.

"Yessir, this takes me back. It sho does."

He looked up at Ivory's looming, foreshortened features, a chin, its curve imitated by lips, their curve the pedestal for a sharpish, not very negroid nose, and above the nose, the spreading french curve of eyebrows, the fluted, shining hairline. All curves. The "V" imprint of a lost widow's peak still lay on Ivory's forehead.

"Back to what?"

"Back to my shores-of-Tripoli, gung-ho, Sergeant Ivory Rose days. Back when I was going to help the good slopes run off the bad ones so they could build a concrete and plastic paradise just like Perth Amboy, New Jersey."

Ivory tied off his arm above the elbow with a length of surgical tubing.

"Listen," said Fare. He was going to say, "Don't make me any more speeches." He was going to say, "You don't have to convince me." But he felt the needle slide into his arm, balking an instant at the skin, breaking through, then feeling its way neatly to the artery, going too far, then backtracking a sixteenth of an inch and stopping, its mouth taking the blood. Now he felt only the cold of metal and a dull, stretching discomfort. No pain. The blood was flowing through the tube, rushing into the plastic sack, blue and outrageous. He could have sworn that Ivory had done it all by feel. Hadn't he kept his eyes on Fare's face?

Ivory was adjusting the flow of blood to the sack, his deft

fingers turning a small plastic dial. Already, the blue blood was blossoming the deflated sack. Fare closed his eyes to the stream of blue and it went yellow, then white, entering the bag in the photographic negative behind his eyes.

"Pretty good, ain't I?" he heard Ivory saying. "I ain't forgot."

With his eyes closed, Fare found the silence absolute, like the blood flowing soundlessly out of him.

"How come you went as a corpsman?" he asked.

"I was out of high school, dropped out. I got myself into this paramedic program. So naturally, they drafted me and made me a cook. But when I got over there, they needed corpsmen, so they retreaded me. Most of the corpsmen was dudes like you. Whites from the money . . ."

"I ain't from money."

"You white." Ivory had spoken too loudly. Fare waited.

"Anyway, most of them was rich white kids against the war; got they feelings mixed up with religion, and come over as corpsmen so they wouldn't have to fight."

"But you wanted to fight?"

"I didn't know what I wanted. I wanted to do what they told me, like a good house nigger. They told me to be a corpsman. I done it. That was back when all us niggers was going to be war heroes and come home to the movie contract."

Ivory's hands stirred. Fare heard clicks as he adjusted the dial at the plastic bag again, then he reached down to rub Fare's arm a little bit.

"You ain't got good flow, white man."

"Maybe you didn't get the needle in right."

Fare was beginning to feel a little floaty. The dull discomfort which was not pain had a way of compounding itself. It clutched at his stomach. He opened his eyes. The curves of Rose's face wavered above him. Rose was watching him.

"We just about finished," he said. "Be a good troop. Don't fall out on me."

Fare closed his eyes again.

"One day," Ivory said. His voice slipped from its rhetorical

218 /

promontory down to a murmur of reverie. "One day, we was on the fire base. It was in the middle of the Tet, and they was a lot of confusion. We was in a bunker complex next to a mortar platoon and I went out for a walk. It was about night-fall, and getting dark, and I was walking through this big fire base, and I come to the perimeter where the mortar battalion had its big four-deuce guns emplaced. I stopped to bullskate with some of their guys. A forward observer and a fire direction control, a couple of noncoms, smart dudes, like me. They was white, but that was before I got it straight in my head about the third world. I was standing there talking to them, you know, identifying, all of us with the stripes. All of us with a little education behind us, telling the other grunts what to do.

"We was talking and looking out at the perimeter. One of these guys pulls out a number and we was passin it. It was a big fire base. They had set up the wire and floodlights and planted the claymores. Next thing we know, out on the perimeter, here comes this Honda. One of them little ones that you got to pedal like a bicycle to get it started, and on it was one of the boom-boom girls. I guess that's what she was. And she had two little kids with her, a boy and a girl. Both of them was less than ten years old. I stood there bullskating with these two mortar men, and watching the boom-boom girl and her kids . . ."

Ivory slipped the needle from the flesh, and, without look-ing down, pressed a cotton ball into the crotch of Fare's arm. He bent it back up, reaching absently for Fare's free hand.

"Sit up and hold that cotton there for a minute."

"What's a boom-boom girl?"

Ivory looked at him sourly, then humped his hips forward twice, "You know? Boom-boom.

"So, what I didn't know was that the three slopes, that's what we called them back then, the three slopes was doing a very dangerous thing. My two friends, they knew it, and they didn't say a thing about it. Not at first, anyway.

"The girl and her kids was out on the perimeter messing

around in the fire base dump. Now, I couldn't see what was out there, but what it was was a lot of garbage, and a lot of these round, donut-shaped bags of explosive they put into the mortar shells to make them go long or short. You know, one to nine. These guys had been taking the bags out of the shells and dumping them with the other garbage stead of storing them in special containers or neutralizing them some way.

"Ole boom-boom and her kids was picking through the dump. We could hear them talking, high-pitched, like birds. One of them would find something and the other two would come over and poke at it. Then the little girl, she picked something up, and they all got together and pretty soon we seen boom-boom light a match and touch it to all their cigarettes and they stood out there smoking. We could see the glow of the cigarettes coming on and off in the dark every time one of them took a drag. They was just about finished. One of the white dudes says he's going to go ask the boom-boom for some poozle. I guess we was getting ready for that. The three of us, we was going to pull a train on her.

"Then one of these two white guys says to the other, 'Maybe we ought to tell her.'

"And the other says, 'Tell her hell. I ain't going out there now.'

"The first one says, 'Fuck it, you right. I ain't either.'

"The second one says, 'Not for a couple of three dinks.'

"They just ignored me, standing there. I tell you, man, I didn't know what the hell they was talking about, and when they said 'dinks' I just shrugged and let it go by, because it was the Tet and we was right in the middle of it and they was giving it to us pretty bad.

"Then, the whole night was lit white. It was like one of them phosphorus illumination rounds. I felt a hot wind. Knocked me back into the four-deuce hole, and then I heard thunder. Like lightning striking an oak tree and us standing underneath. We all jumped up and looked at each other, and men was running from all around. Some of them started firing their weapons at the garbage dump.

"When it quieted down, the two dudes from the mortar was getting their asses reamed by an officer. But he was just scared. They scared him and he was reaming them out for scaring him. They was standing there kicking the dirt with their boots like two kids. I looked at them and I could see the blood spattered on them. I could see little pink chunks of it, and, all around, pieces of black nylon or silk, and black plastic from the seat cover of the Honda.

"There wasn't nothing left out at the dump but a grass fire. The Honda was up in the top of a tree, burning. A few dudes with weapons slung was poking they boots through the junk. I heard the mortar men telling it to the officer. One of them said, 'It wasn't nothing but a couple of three slopes.' Then I saw him look at the officer like he didn't know how it would sit. The lieutenant said he didn't care who. It could of been worse. It could of been one of his men, he said. 'Instead of a . . .' and he didn't say dink or slopehead. He stopped and he looked over at me. He lowered his voice and he said, kind of half-smiling, 'instead of a colored person.'

"It might of been a man, but it was a colored person."

Ivory lit a R.I.P. and then, slowly, held it out at arm's length. He stared at it. "I can still see them cigarettes. It was the little girl who found them and it was the little girl that threw hers down and done it. She was just a little girl. She took a big toot on it, just like her momma done, then she flicked it away like a whore on Tu Do Street.

"I went back to my bunker and I sat down and thought about it, and I realized I didn't have no business fighting no white man's war against 'colored people.' My bunker mates come in and they told me some dinks had wasted themselves out on the fire base dump. Then one of them looked at me, a blood, and he said, 'Say, man, what's that on you face?' He reached out his hand to pick something off of me, and then he stopped and turned away. Just like that. I reached up myself and pulled it off. It was all over me, on my clothes and in my hair, and the smell of it was . . ."

Fare sat up and dangled his legs off the edge of the table.

His arm was bent upward, awkwardly beside him.

Ivory stood next to him, absently holding the bag of blood. He discarded the tube and syringe, sealed the bag, and moved to the refrigerator.

"Yes?" said Fare.

"Yes, what?"

Ivory stared at him now as though he had invaded some private territory.

"Fuck it. Never mind . . ."

Ivory hung his blood on the rack in the refrigerator. He slammed the refrigerator door.

". . . it was the same stink as ever other thing over there. All of what we done to them for no Gotdamn reason but stinking politics of white supremacy."

Fare thought of several replies, but all were just replies. He did not more than half-believe any of them and did not want to compete slogan against slogan. He sat silent. It was all so sad, so far beyond debate.

"How'd you beat the draft anyway?" Ivory was smiling at him again.

"1-Y."

"What's wrong with you?"

"I got a bad ankle. A football ankle."

"Shit," laughed Rose. "All the white boys with they little notes from the doctor. Don't you think you could of did it?"

"Sure," said Fare. "I could have done it. Physically anyway. They didn't want me and I didn't argue with them."

Ivory walked to the door and closed it, turning the lock. Fare looked a question at him. What if somebody comes?

Ivory's face said, fuck it, let them.

They sat at the small table where the blood pressures were taken. There were shabby scales in the room, flaking cabinets of dressings, the rattling refrigerator. A blinking fluorescent light was suspended above them. Fare felt a sudden self-consciousness. He had not wanted this intimacy. Telling the story had broken Ivory's cool, caused him to show anger, waste time. Yet, all of this had somehow gone to his, not

Fare's, benefit. Ivory sat across from him, staring at him as though *he* had made a war against women and children on Hondas. Maybe I did, he thought.

Ivory thrummed his fingertips on the tabletop.

"So," he said. "You read my pistle and you come down here to talk to me. Or did you want to give your blood for the next brother that get cut on the yard?"

Fare said, "Who is this Jamahl? Why does he, or anybody else, have to get involved in this?"

"Why don't you ask him? He the one that knows. He the one that gone explain it to you. Why can't you stay with the program?"

Feet, voices passed in the hallway. Fare looked at his watch. Fifteen minutes of his hour remained to them.

"You tell me," he said. "I want to hear it from you."

"Before I tell you anything, I got to know if you going along with it?"

"I can't tell you that until I hear it."

"We could make you do it. You know that, doan you?"

But Ivory's smile was only half-sure, as it had been that day when they had held Carmack's knife between them. It was the Ivory smile, but not sure enough.

"You can *try* to make me. I don't think you can get very far with it. You ain't got nothing on me that can do more than get me fired. They won't prosecute me. It wouldn't look good. Anyway, where would you be with me gone? Back to nothing."

Ivory stared at him, holding the smile. "Pretty smart, ain't you? Well, maybe you right. Who knows, but it's what you want that's gone keep you with us, not what we got on you. Ain't it?"

For the first time in many days, Fare felt some of the control passing back in his direction. It felt good. Ivory had as much as acknowledged it. They could not force him. It felt good, but it felt dangerous. He was reponsible for it if it was his.

Nobody else but him. He could become its victim and have no one to blame but himself.

Ivory told him what they had worked out. And told him they would wait for LaPointe before finishing their plans. Fare had to admit, it sounded as plausible as most things he had seen and heard since entering this place. There wouldn't be any bloodshed, Ivory told him, or even any danger of it if things went right. Now just contact Jamahl, Ivory said, and get the particulars.

Ivory sat across from him, smoking, watching him. Fare felt good. He felt like he had used to feel when he had committed himself to a job on the farm, or to tackle a much bigger man on the football field. It was the what-the-hell feeling he had known so little of in his life. The feeling came back to him in a rush, like the rush of whisky to the heart, like memory, or like the pain that came seconds after the stroke that made the wound. He lit a cigarette and rose to leave, but then turned back. "I got something to tell you, Rose. I want you to try to understand it."

Ivory dropped his cigarette beneath the table, stepped on it.

He looked at Fare in the usual, half-condescending way. His was the face of messianic purity.

"I didn't go to that war because I didn't have to, but I wouldn't have gone, I don't think I would have, if they had told me to. I'm not like you. I can't say for sure. I don't always know what's right. But I think I would have told them to stuff it and that's more than you did, because you believed in it.

"I gave my blood because I came down here to talk to you. I had to give blood to make it look right. But if a *brother* gets my blood, then he's my brother just as much as he's yours and if a brother gets cut out on the yard it will probably be another brother who cuts him, and that brother with the knife will be less of his brother than I am if my blood saves his life. What I'm telling you is I ain't taking other people's guilt in with my own. I got enough of it.

"You told me about the abstractions once, the empty words.

Well, you people with your Swahili names and calling each
other brother and your third-rate poetry and cutting each other
and sneaking around butt-fucking the young white boys that
come here, you are just as empty and full of abstractions. I
didn't kill anybody in Viet Nam. You can't put any little girl's
blood on my hands just because she is yellow and you are
black and I am white. If it's on your hands, *you* live with it."

Ivory was giving him the cool stare. He was opening his
mouth to speak when Fare closed the door in his face and
walked away thinking about how it felt to be left in the room
full of cold blood with a heart full of guilt and no one to give
it to.

But he knew how it felt, and he relished the moment. He
would not carry any more of it for the time being. Ivory, like
the town, and like Clare, and like his mother and father, and
all of his people in their ways and amounts, had tried to give
it to him, tried to lock him in a room with it. All his life he
had been saying yes to them and reaching out for it, going
into the room and embracing it. Now, he was refusing it and
it felt good. The only one, he realized, as he walked back to
his classroom, who had never tried to hand him any was his
brother, Charles Ed. It had been the cement between them, an
unspoken article of faith that bonded them, otherwise opposites, to each other.

When he entered the classroom, five minutes late, he smiled
broadly at McLaren, who was frightened of everything irregular, who first looked at the clock and then at him with a critical
eye. Charles Ed had possessed the total audacity given only
to the very few who do not know guilt at all. Charles Ed had
simply not known its name, and this, his owing no one an
account of himself, this had early been his power. And later,
losing it had killed him.

TWENTY-THREE

FARE TRIED THE NUMBER BUT GOT NO ANSWER. HE CALLED
the operator to ask whether or not it was a working number,
and she told him to try it during working hours. He mumbled
that he could not do that because he worked himself, and she
said that was not her problem and hung up.

So he took Friday off, calling in sick.

Bray's voice rattled on the long distance line: "Giving away
that blood get to you, big'un?"

"Naw," said Fare. "I think I'm catching a little cold. Need
the long weekend to come back strong on Monday."

Bray wished him a speedy recovery, but not before reminding him that he had accumulated only one day of sick leave
and this was it.

He dialed the number. A woman answered.

"Drama Department. May I help you?"

Drama Department? The play. His introductory talk. Jamahl.

"May I speak to . . . Jamahl?"

"To who?"

He repeated the name.

"Hold a moment, please."

A hand was placed over the receiver. He heard a distorted
voice, then another or perhaps two voices answering.

"Anybody heard of a Jamahl?" A pause.

"He must be one of the graduate assistants."

"Is that a first name or a last name?" Someone yelling.

"Oh, wait, I know him."

A new voice on the line.

"Hello. Yes. I think he's one of our T.A.'s. Let me take your
number and have him call you."

Fare gave the woman his number, telling her it had to be

today. She said she would write it on the message.

He waited by the phone only a short time. The voice was low, resonant, and had in it a half-concealed black Southern accent. He guessed its owner was younger than he. The voice of Jamahl suggested they meet. Fare said it could be anywhere and, without hesitation, the voice suggested the student union.

The cafeteria was crowded with the lunch trade. Students meandered past steam tables, picking up the demolished gray entrées, and past the ice chests that offered identical Jell-Os and salads equally unappetizing. Fare was not sure what he had chosen for himself when he reached the cash register and began to survey the dining room beyond.

He had been away from the university for only four months, yet he felt alien among these loud, and so young, and so brightly dressed children who ambled or ran past him, sliding on the polished marble floors to tables where they greeted friends. It seemed now not as he remembered it, but as he had wished it to be. There was an air of unconcealed enthusiasm, even of joy, in the room. He felt a strange impulse to put his tray on the conveyer that led to the kitchen and leave. He realized that he missed the prison, disliked missing a day of work there, missed the trustee white, the blue, the occasional freeman's red or green shirt, striped tie and centurion air.

Someone bumped him.

"Toot-toot, man," said a young girl whose breasts swayed beneath the sheer fabric of her halter like the Jell-O on her plate. She churned her arms like a steam engine and smiled at him, "toot-toot."

"Oh," he said, stepping out of the way.

He sighted an empty table and tried to balance the tray and scan the crowd at the same time. He could not find a face or the back of a head whose serious, attenuated attitude suggested a connection to Ivory Rose.

He sat and ate mouthfuls of something that might have been liver and onions. He watched the crowd. Most were very young. This was not the cafeteria in which graduate students ate. Many were sitting in a loose semicircle around a television set, watching the first of the afternoon soaps. A girl was going to have an abortion and wanted a young man to pay for it, expected him to offer without making her stoop to ask. She would think less of him if he did not offer and less of herself if she had to ask. It was a matter of feminism, apparently.

The young man, it appeared, wanted the baby, knew the girl did not, and was afraid to reveal to her his incipient father love because he did not want her to run off and have the abortion in unsafe surrounds. Nor did he want to tie her to the burden of a child. Or so it seemed.

The students watched soberly, spooning yogurt and cottage cheese. Fare scanned their faces, looking for the smirk that bespoke a love of camp. He did not see it. What he saw was literal-minded absorption. It was everywhere. And the yogurt was going up and in. He wondered how many of these young girls sat on top of the twisted wire of IUD's, or carried in their ocher Indian folk art bags the plastic mandalas that dispensed pills that made this soap opera predicament quaint.

The pill. The wire. How easy they would have made things ten years ago. For him, for all of them out in Isle Hammock where there wasn't a hell of a lot to do with yourself on Saturday night. Where the girls had believed only in the near impenetrable armor of stockings and garter belts, Bibles and girdles. How easy and how difficult. He turned his eyes from the young girls and realized that he liked it as it had been, furtive, clumsy, full of fear and mystery and gratitude, and, yes, guilt.

He swept his eyes around the room in a circle that took them all the way to the kitchen behind him. Someone opened the kitchen door. A black woman, thin and unusually tall, stepped out into the dining area, wiped her hands on an apron, then raised it up to wipe her brow, revealing a narrow waist. She found a pack of cigarettes in the pocket of her dress, shook one out and lit it.

It did not take her eyes long to swing to his and fasten. She smiled coolly at him, but she looked taut. She turned back to the open kitchen door and said something to someone.

Removing the apron as she walked, she strolled toward him. She stopped at a table on her way and spoke to a small, moon-faced black man (a boy, Fare had thought when, moments before, his eyes had rested on the round, cherubic face) and motioned the young man to follow her. Watching him as they came, the two of them moved straight to his table as though they knew him. When the woman stood above him, he rose and motioned her to a chair. The cool, abstracted expression on her face was replaced by one of confused anger.

"Sit down," she said. "I don't need that shit."

Fare might have been stung, but somehow, he had expected it. In retrospect, he realized that he had made the antique gesture just to pique her. For some reason, he liked her immediately. She had a faunlike lissomeness which she tried to diminish with the tough walk and the cool smile and the affected way with the cigarette, but the loose dancer's innocence clung to her. Her face was narrow, almost severe, and it went well with her long body. She had a wide mouth, even, starkly white teeth, and her eyes were not the usual dark brown, but lighter, almost caramel or pale amber in color. She flicked the ash from her cigarette onto the floor. He wondered if, later, she would have to clean it up.

Reluctantly, he shifted his attention to the young man, who spoke to him. It was not the voice he had heard on the phone.

"Are you Mr. Farel Odum?"

Fare acknowledged as much. The young man wore a pair of wire-rimmed Trotsky glasses and the flower-print mid-thigh-length smock that was popular with young blacks. There was nothing about the young man's face that aroused interest. It was pan flat. In profile, the nose did not pierce a plane of air beyond the forehead or chin. The young man's eyes were the standard dark brown and perhaps extraordinary for the fact that they were very lively, unlike the rest of him, which did the slow-drag plantation shuffle when it moved.

Closer, Fare could see, mostly from the toughened skin of the young man's face, that he was no boy.

"You must be Jamahl?"

Fare looked at the young man for affirmation, but the quick eyes cut to the woman. She stared at Fare, a cobra mesmerizing a small rodent, occasionally bringing the cigarette to her mouth. After a space, Fare said, "You then?"

She stubbed out the cigarette and leaned forward. Organ music rolled from the television and a man told them to join him tomorrow for the exciting conclusion of . . . She was calmer now. More organ music . . . "Tide gets clothes whiter."

"I don't mind it," she said, "that you automatically assume Norris here is your contact. He is a man and so are you. I get it all the time. What I do mind is the way you leer at me like I was kitchen help. Are you having a fantasy? Are you thinking about boffing the colored girls?"

"Brown sugar, man?" Norris got in his two cents.

The girl cut Norris an eye full of razor blades.

Norris chuckled, but shut up.

Fare recognized her voice now as the one he had heard on the phone. She had spoken more slowly to him in this most recent exchange, and her voice was the abnormally low, husky voice of a young man. He liked it. She was a black Lauren Bacall. All he had to do was whistle.

He said, "I don't have fantasies in public places. Might run amok."

Things were not going as he had imagined they would. For one thing, the girl and the young man seemed to have formed little more than an uneasy truce, and for another, he did not like the way she had used the word "contact." It sounded theatrical. It sounded like a word some black Natasha would use in a smoky café, not a word for a dancer to use here in this sunny student dining room while *Search for Tomorrow* droned into the eyes and ears of America's doubtful future.

The woman looked at him, digging for another cigarette. He held out his lighter as she brought it to her mouth. But she put the cigarette down on the table and looked away. He held the flame, pale yellow in the bright light, in front of her for perhaps ten seconds. He flicked the lighter shut.

"Be that way," he said, smiling.

He watched her light the cigarette. He could feel himself getting a hard-on. The part of him beneath the table was having a fantasy. He hoped they did not suggest going somewhere just yet.

The woman, Jamahl, smoked and watched him, then began talking in the low, unhurried voice. "You are Farel Odum, Ph.D., recent graduate of the University of Florida's vaunted English doctoral program. And now you teach subject-verb agreement to inmates at Raiford."

"Right," he said. "What about you?"

She flicked the ash from the cigarette with an indolent movement of her wrist. She had a lovely wrist.

". . . and your dissertation was entitled *Time and His Times: A Study of Pope's Concept of Temporality* . . ."

"*As It Is Expressed in* The Essay on Man."

"What?"

"That's the rest of it. You left it off, the rest of my subcolonic phrase. Every scholarly study worth its salt has a subcolonic phrase." He smiled at her, his hand killing the tumescence under the table.

"What a lot of crap," she said, expecting him to object.

"Exactly, and what will be the title of your magnum opus, Jamahl?"

"I'm going to call it *The Black Absence: A Study of Contemporary American Folk Drama.*"

"See. You've got a subcolonic phrase."

"What is this bulljive?" said Norris, turning half-away from them in his chair, then looking back skeptically over a shoulder at Jamahl.

"Don't mind us," said Fare. "We're talking like what we are, two scholars."

Jamahl turned to Norris. When she spoke, her voice was sweet, feminine, there was a sound of beguilement in it. She placed her long-fingered hand on top of his fat one. "Norris, honey," she said, "why don't you get on back over to work and I'll come over as soon as I can. All right?"

"Right, babe," Norris was on his feet and walking away. Her hand lay still on the table. Norris had pulled his abruptly from under it. Fare could not read them any longer. He did not know what was going on.

When Norris' squat body had made the doorway, she turned back to him.

"All right," she said, her voice husky again. She leaned toward him. He cut her short.

"So you are a graduate student in the Drama Department?"

"Yes," she said.

He cut in again. "And a part-time teaching assistant, and part-time kitchen help?"

She nodded.

"You lead a schizoid life."

"It's what I've got to do."

"Got to?"

She bent her head a little. The part of her he could see, head and torso, remained erect like a bust on the tabletop before him. He noticed that she had none of the blotchy white scars, the tracks of impetigo and ground itch that marred the limbs of so many black women in the South. Their absence meant that she came from a better-than-average background. He would bet on it.

"You don't have to work in any kitchen. Your daddy is rich . . ."

"And my momma's good-lookin." She fixed him the cool stare.

"You choose to work like this."

She kept silent. It was something she did not want to say, yet the tension in her signaled that she felt it strongly. She fingered the coarse fabric of her apron.

"To atone? . . ." he asked, watching her face. "You are

atoning, aren't you? Aren't you, for the advantages you had and . . ."

He looked back at the kitchen. So did she. Inside, there would be black women, their arms and legs blotched, talking in the argot, living their lives at one level.

". . . and they didn't have? Is that right?"

"It's none of your business," she said. "The less you know about me the better for both of us."

He looked at her. Another line from the black Natasha. He could not keep a sneer from his lips. "The less you know about me the better." Woman of mystery. Dark lady of the sonnets. Ivory's sonnets? Ivory?

"What's your connection to Rose and? . . ."

He stopped himself before he said LaPointe. For some reason he had the feeling she had not been told about La-Pointe, that her frail, romantic commitment might not extend so far as to embrace that animal malignancy. She looked at him in discomfort. *She* was supposed to be running things, her eyes told him. He should let her, they said, and they also said that she would like to force him. Put him on the defensive.

"We are lovers."

She smiled at him. It was the satisfied smile from the womb that says to the questioning male, I am filled. I cannot hold any more. He'd seen it a few times. It had the power, almost religious, of few human gestures. It was the smile he had never seen on the face of the insatiable Clare.

He did not want to say anything flippant, but in the face of the imperative, absolute smile from the womb, he could think of nothing but flippancy.

"Pretty rough, to be lovers at this distance."

"It's not difficult at all," she said, smiling the womb smile, a coronal glow, "when you have been lovers, and when you will be lovers again."

TWENTY-FOUR

THEY WERE WALKING ACROSS THE COLONNADE FROM THE union cafeteria toward the theater. She had stopped twice, telling him not to follow her. But each time, he had asked some question, pretext to let him fall back into step beside her. All around them students were walking to classes, their dull-eyed, ewe faces registering nothing but satisfaction with sunlight and quantities of air to breathe. Passing them as he walked beside her, the two of them tangled in the knot of their hour-old connection, Fare felt like a member of a new elite of the very strong, the capable, sensitized to the nuances of life.

She was nervous, looking around as though someone might wonder what she was doing with him. Clearly, such a prospect frightened her. Their conversation had been circling and returning to its point of origin for an hour now, first at the lunch table, later as they walked to the upper floors of the building and looked at the campus from the balcony, and now, as he followed her against her wishes. He felt there was more to know about her, much more, and that he had to know it before they could talk business. Ivory's word, business. What else to call it? Not pleasure, not compared to this. But more than this, he was fascinated by her.

"Please," she said, her voice slipping up to its high-pitched feminine level as it had with Norris. "We'll talk again later. Tonight if you want. Over the weekend." She looked at her watch, then at the entrance to the theater. "I've got to . . ."

"You don't want to be seen with me, do you?"

She looked at him resignedly.

"Of course not."

"Why?"

He expected her to say it was because they were planning a felony together, she and he, or because Ivory had told her how to conduct things, but she said, "Because you are white."

He was surprised. In the past hour when she had spoken to him in third-world political rhetoric, he had ignored it, or rebutted or ridiculed her sloganeering. And each time, the part of her that disliked slogans (he guessed it was the scholarly part) had seemed sheepish. But he sensed this was no slogan. It came from the deeps.

"You would sit with me at the table there, but now . . ."

"Norris was with us. I was a maid."

She turned too quickly for him to interfere, with words at any rate, and ran to the entrance of the theater building. He stood where she had left him, lit a cigarette, thinking about it and watching people come and go. A group of black males, students he guessed, for they were dressed like students, entered the theater. Several more followed, as the crowds heading for classes thinned. When he heard the bells ringing in classroom buildings nearby, he had an idea.

He waited a while longer, smoking and watching the fat ducks, stuffed with bread and crackers, wallowing on the oily surface of the artificial lake beneath the colonnade. When he guessed enough time had passed, he walked into the building, climbing the stairs to the large, dark theater. He slipped silently into the back row and watched what was happening on the stage.

A man with a clipboard stood in a circle of light staring up at him. The man cupped his hands to his mouth and yelled, his voice echoing in the nearly empty house, "Give me dimmer number five. Good. Now number six. Good. That's good."

Lights were slowly coming on, enlarging the bright circle. The young black men Fare had seen entering the building began to come from the wings and seat themselves in the first row of the house.

As Fare watched, the group rehearsed the play. It was, he guessed, Genet's *The Blacks*, though never having seen it, he could not be sure. The director, a middle-aged, tired-seeming white man, put the company through its paces in an unenthusiastic way, stopping the action occasionally to jump onto the stage and demonstrate movements, how certain lines were to be spoken. Twice, he leapt up with masking tape in his hands, sticking strips of it to the floor so that the actors would know where to stand.

Fare was surprised and somewhat annoyed to see that Jamahl played the part of a man. He wondered if it was because they had so few black actors. Or was something cryptic and illusive intended by it? He did not try to guess at the symbolic content of the gesture. Fuck it. He watched Jamahl.

She was good at it, playing a man. She could manage the masculine, yet light, athletic stride of a black man, a hurdler or flankerback. Her voice was right, when she kept it down, husky and resonant. It carried well, better than some of the male voices, which thinned before reaching Fare at the back of the house. At one point in the play it fell to her to beat another player. She did it with great realism, grunting with the effort, pulling her punches expertly at the last instant.

When the rehearsal ended, the director seated them all again in the first row while he sat on the stage, dangling his legs as he read criticisms from a clipboard. The actors listened, occasionally responding. It was rather desultory, no one seemed to care much. Perhaps, Fare thought, this is professionalism I am seeing.

When the group broke up, he walked quickly down the aisle and introduced himself (as Dr. Odum) to the director, who shook his hand and listened while he explained that he was to introduce the play to the Raiford audience.

"Do you know the work?" the director asked him.

"No," Fare admitted, "but I've just seen you rehearse it here, and I'll read it as soon as I can."

The director furrowed his brow, and began to talk. He could provide Fare a brief bibliography so that he could make the best possible introduction.

Fare thought of the inmate audience with its mean IQ of ninety, and the weird fascimile of understanding it would bring to him as he stood on the stage introducing a play.

He listened to the director, but stole glances at the wings, first one, then the other. It was not long before she appeared, her eyes large, their whites gleaming in the half-darkness behind the curtain. She was watching him. She held one hand to her mouth chewing a fingernail.

A door closed far up in the cavernous house, and footsteps slapped down the aisle. Norris stepped into the pool of light.

He looked at Fare, then at the director, who broke off to speak to him, "Norris, can you give me your design by the end of the week? I want to know how you are going to gel it, and what you plan to do with that long monologue in the second act."

Norris allowed that he would have the lighting design finished as soon as the director got someone to repair the dimmer board. They argued about it briefly, in softly shrill voices.

Fare gazed at Jamahl, who gazed back at him. She had stopped biting her fingernail. The director spoke to him. When he looked back at the wings, nothing moved in the dark but the heavy fabric of the curtain.

She opened the door as far as the chain would allow and peered out at him. He stood silently, regarding the thin slice of her face in the door. It closed, the chain rattled, she swung it open, letting him walk past her into the room. Inside, he turned and saw that she was standing on the front porch watching the parking lot, his old Belvedere. Was she afraid he had been followed? He smiled as she closed the door and relocked it, slipping the chain into its catch.

"What if I have to run away fast?" He nodded at the chain. He realized too late that he had made an implicit reference to Ivory.

"Then you'll have to run through the back door," she said, not returning his smile. Behind him, in the small kitchenette apartment, were only a bathroom and a closet.

She sat at the kitchen table, before a half-glass of dark liquid. She had been drinking it, whatever it was, before he came. She did not ask him to sit with her.

"Offer me some of that, and I'll take it."

"Get it yourself."

He looked around, found the bottle on top of the refrigerator. She was drinking cognac. He poured some into a plastic glass and sat opposite her.

"Why did you follow me into rehearsal?"

He considered saying he had wanted to see the play, or that it was because she had told him not to. The last was partly true at least. But the fact was, he had wanted to watch her move. Why not tell her?

"I wanted to watch you. See what kind of an actress you are. I didn't think they'd have you playing a man."

"Not enough warm bodies to do it with men. Not enough black ones anyway."

"I don't see how it did any harm."

She sipped at the cognac, holding it in both hands and dipping her head to it, her long curved neck amber like the contents of the glass, its delicate veins enlarging slightly with the effort. He could not remember when he had been alone with a black woman. Perhaps he had never been. There had been no maids in his life. He sipped the bad brandy. The apartment, half of a small duplex, was austere and clean. Her clothing, most of it black and severe, hung in the open closet. A few mismatched dishes lay in the drainboard. There was a small bookshelf, the table and two chairs. A bed. The only extraordinary thing within the field of his vision was her body. It commanded attention in these stark surroundings as would a piece of sculpture or an arresting painting.

"How come you live here?"

"It's a place to live."

"More atonement?" He smiled at her, wry but friendly.

She put down the glass and regarded him, much as she had those first moments in the cafeteria.

"Perhaps it is. Do you find it amusing? Ironical? Are you so far from believing in anything that you think I am ridiculous?" Still she regarded him. He picked up his glass, drained it, and walked to the bottle for another.

She was nervous, getting more unsure with him. She spoke

slowly, conscious of choosing words. She seemed to swell with words, and yet she said little. Something about him intimidated her. He was tempted to indulge it, beat her down, purely for the enjoyment he could have in it. But part of him said let up. She's got a friend of yours inside her, she just doesn't know it yet. There was despair to go with this last thought. Chances were small.

"You're a good actress," he said. This judgment hung in the air while he considered the fact that he had no competency to make it.

"No," she said, somewhat more calmly, "not really. I act with my head, not my heart. You have to live in the play with your heart in order to be really good."

"Just the same," he said, "I liked you."

He groped for a word. Why not just be honest? Say what was there at the root of his tongue without a layer of artifice.

"You have wonderful grace in the way you move."

He stood with his back to her holding the bottle. Now he poured it, going back to sit down and look at her face.

What was there was something soft, illusive, contrite, briefly conciliatory, a momentary promise of peace to their children and all of their children's children, but it faded so quickly and was so totally gone, replaced by its opposite, so genuine and pure, that he could not move, could only sit and stare at her face as it changed from the understanding to the hating again. Had he really seen the brief moment of promise? Now he could not be sure. When he could drink, he took too much of the brandy and coughed it into his hands.

"What are you doing?" she asked, changing not one whit in her eyes or face, giving no clue to what she meant. What could be the largest or the smallest answer to the question? He chose the smallest.

"Got it down the wrong pipe. I'm coughing."

He got through the fit, and wiped his eyes on his shirt sleeve, then drank the last of the brandy to get the pipes lined up right again. She smiled at him, cool, abstract, and got up and brought the bottle, half-full, to him. "Here, save you a trip."

He poured them both, but she showed no signs of wanting hers. He could not feel the stuff at all. Maybe it wasn't strong. Was cheap brandy weak brandy?

"No," she said, "you know what I mean. I mean what are you *doing*?"

Fare stared back at her. You could stumble along for years, he thought, and turn a corner into one of these naked collisions, and you had no equipment. There was no code for such things—nobody talked about them. People had politeness for the table, and for meeting each other on the street to say hello. They had law and religion, but there was nothing for this moment here. You collided and you knew that across the gap, inside , naked, was a friend of yours, but you did not know how to help him out. You had to go it on instinct.

"Explain what you mean by that," he said. "I can't answer it. It's too many questions. I got too many answers."

Her eyes cooled him. She did not drink. Or move. Erect, hard, she was the sculpture and the painting, beautiful and timeless beyond price or replacement. He realized that in the early part of the answer, the answer she wanted, there was a question.

"What are you doing?" he asked her. He tried to make it sound not flippant, not evasive, honest. He took another drink. The brandy was not half-bad when you got used to it. She curled her lip a little. Her voice was tainted by the pitch of a sneer.

"Waiting for you to stop sniffing under my tail like a dog in the alley."

So that was what she thought. He remembered the hard-on back in the cafeteria. Could not remember when it had faded, and with it had faded the possibility of its return. He felt nothing between his legs now but an absence the brandy seemed to be filling. Still she sneered.

"I know you can talk better than I can. I know you are brilliant, or think you are. I read your dissertation on Pope and I know that you are sensitive to the subtleties of literature, that I will never write a dissertation half as good . . ."

"Wait a minute." He was confused, but she went on.

"I know you think my politics are sentimental, 'idealistic in the extreme' you would call them, that living here, and working like I do, and getting involved with Ivory Rose, that it's all nonsense and will lead to nothing but . . ."

Fare did not interrupt again. He only sat watching. Her face had not changed, nor had her posture. She was saying these things to him slowly and distinctly, acting from the heart.

". . . but trouble. And now you think I'm going to tell you all about it. You have been trying to break me down, to avoid what we have to talk about, and to break me down, don't say you haven't, so that I'll tell you all about it. Well, I'm not going to do that. You don't have any good reason to want to know. Telling you will only fill up your empty curiosity."

He stared at her. He had been doing it, questioning her, out of admiration and need, and with the hope growing that she held inside her an image of that other human being, part her and part him. Angry, he poured the brandy. He could get mean again. He could feel it starting. She had tried to provoke it.

"All right," she said, standing up abruptly. "All right, dog in the alley. We've got to get past it, don't we? Only I want you to know this one thing. I would never spoken to you. I would never so much as looked at you . . ."

She drank the brandy that remained in her glass. She walked a little way to the only unencumbered space in the apartment, in front of the bed, beyond the table, just free of the closet door.

"Here it comes," she said, cool, smiling again. "Here it comes so you can sniff and get it over with."

She wore a black dress, longer than was fashionable, of nylon or some other clinging fabric. It was neither a tight nor a loose one, yet the shapes of her breasts, their nipples and her stomach's swell, the protrusions of her hips with their twin, delicately fluted bones, and the rise of her thighs below; all the planes of her body were visible in it. All but one. One plane lay shrouded in convexity beneath the black fabric.

She stood facing him, and reaching back. Cocking her hip

to one side, she found the zipper. She tugged at it, and he heard it start to slide and then stop. She stood again with her hands at her sides. She was moving her knees a little forward and then back, one, then the other.

"Do you want a little music, dog in the alley?"

He stared at her.

"Do you want to sniff my tail to music?"

He knew that he should say he did not want her to do it, that it was not necessary, though he certainly would enjoy it. Certain things she had said had come back to him as he sat, holding the brandy glass and watching her. She moved her hips now with her knees, rhythmically, and smiled, waiting for him to answer her.

She had said, speaking of Ivory, "When you have been lovers, and when you will be lovers again." He found that he remembered the phrase, the way she had said it, her voice, her eyes, the attitude of her lips and nostrils, remembered it all perfectly. She had loved Ivory, was his lover, and yet she would do this. With him, Farel Odum. She would do it and love Ivory. Clare, they had told him, had gone off with Charles Ed, you know. He didn't know. How could she? Wasn't it true that what you were willing to do for love could kill love?

"What about the music? Tell me quick. Tell me."

Her voice was a low raspy whisper. He shook his head no. He did not say anything. He found himself thinking that if he did not say anything, then what she did, without his acquiescence, would be hers to live with, not his. Done to him, near him, but not by him. But then he thought, go on Fare, take it. Take your part of it even if it's not what you expected, or really what you want. Even if it's wrong. Just take it. It's what all the others do.

So he cleared his throat and said, "No, I don't want music. I want you to sing. You make the music."

She smiled and the zipper plunged, making its long metal scream.

Later, when he left her that night, after they had "gotten

past it," he could not keep his mind from circling to the moment when the last plane of her body had risen, like a tufted sun, above the falling black cloth of the dress. As long as he had memory, he knew he would have that.

After they had finished, and after they had talked, he remembered his last look at her. As she stood in the light of the doorway, cool and retracted, possessed only by herself and Ivory Rose, his eyes had honed again to that place, that last plane, his mind to the moment when all of her had been reduced to that.

"You make the music," he had told her, and immediately she had begun a strange, brute humming, unlike any music he knew, arrhythmic, atonal, guttering and rekindling as though a wind blew between them. And all the while, her blank eyes had stared at him.

TWENTY-FIVE

TWO WEEKS AFTER LAPOINTE HAD SAVAGED THE PUERTO Rican beneath the library window and walked, head shaved, across the courtyard toward the Flattop carrying a blanket, gray and coarse with the name of the Division of Corrections stenciled on it, and a Bible, Fare stood at the same window while the library mumbled its numb business behind him and watched LaPointe come walking back, thinner, but nevertheless moving like the predator he was, carrying the same blanket and Bible, a nappy black stubble coming in where the black crown of the Afro had been two weeks before.

Ivory Rose stood two windows removed from Fare, holding a magazine in his hand, watching with the same concentration. LaPointe was a natural spectacle. He always drew an eye to himself. Fare had seen enough of him to know this. Even men who didn't know his reputation (if there were any left) turned as a matter of course to watch him pass. He was simply something extraordinary.

Fare turned from the window and sat at the desk. From his briefcase, he removed a piece of paper. It was a facsimile of a page from the ledger book that he and every other free-man signed each day at the gate coming and going. On it, as though their owners had come and gone already in some theatrical future which was already a past, were the signatures of two members of the drama company that was coming next Friday evening. He had been given the paper by Jamahl, who had told him simply to pass it on to Rose. One of the signatures on it was that of Norris Thibideaux. The chubby boy-man who operated the lighting apparatus? The petulant complainer who, in the dark theater the weekend before, had held his ground against the equally shrill director?

The other name was Harrison Petri. There were two names.

That was all Fare knew. The rest he had guessed, or was in the process of guessing. Ivory had instructed him to work again this weekend in the library. He had had to exchange assignments with fat Arthur, whose natural suspicion had led him to ask all sorts of questions. Fare had avoided explanations as much as possible, saying only that he wished to have his weekends free during the coming month and so wanted to double up this month. Grudgingly, perhaps out of some notion of Christian duty, Arthur had given in. But there had to be paper work, always there was paper work. Ivory moved from the window and sat now, staring with glazed eyes at the magazine. *Mechanix Illustrated*. Fare might have laughed, but that capability seemed to have atrophied. He looked at the clock. Five minutes since LaPointe had strode the quad below.

Ten.

He flipped through the pages of a book, not seeing the words. Ivory was watching him? Laughing? He looked at the clock, at Ivory, who, at the same moment, looked at the fancy gold watch on his wrist.

Fifteen.

Walk from the Flattop to the Rock Lieutenant's office. Counted in there, added to the number of residents in the Rock, subtracted from the number in Punitive Segregation. Endure the brief, obligatory lecture from the dust-mouthed Lieutenant Harlan.

"Now, LaPointe, you back again, and it ain't no reason in the world why you cain't make this a fresh dust. I can't see nary reason why you cain't get off to a better dust after this and get you a good dust started today. None of the dust under my command is going to be on you case. We all give you a fair dust. So far as we concerned, you starting out dust again. Dust?"

Maybe a "Right, sir," from LaPointe, with an animal's cunning smile. Maybe just a moment of purely insolent silence.

Twenty minutes.

Ivory passed the desk where Fare sat, tapped twice on its

Formica surface with his index finger, and without looking down, strolled on to the farthest corner, into the stacks. Fare looked around. No one had noticed. A few men browsed or surreptitiously gambled. A quiz show could be heard rumbling along toward refrigerators and new cars in the auditorium. Fare rose and, after a space, followed. When they reached the southwest corner where there was no window and the narrow stacks were dark, Fare ran his fingers along the spines of the books. It was a gesture familiar yet now foreign. He felt a sudden contempt for books. His finger came to rest on a volume, its pages thick and sticky with the dirt of a thousand fingers, *For Whom the Bell Tolls.*

"D'you ever read this?"

He drew the book out from its berth between its mates, *A Farewell to Arms* and *Across the River and into the Trees.*

"Let me see it."

Ivory took the book, glanced at the title, then tossed the heavy volume onto the radiator nearby.

"Yeah," he said. "All that shit in the sleeping bag. You believe that?"

"Guess not."

Ivory looked at him, smiling in the mildly patronizing way that long ago had become his habit with Fare. It was the smile Fare had had leveled at him all of his life by those who knew, or somehow thought they knew, they were better men than he. He had never had it handed to him in a library before. Maybe that was why he had spent so much of his time in libraries.

"Good," said Ivory. "That's one good thing I know about you."

Good, thought Fare, but there is one thing you don't know about me, or do you? He thought of Jamahl, how different it had been from what had taken place in that snow-covered sleeping bag which Robert Jordan had called "a Robe." How far theirs had been from that fairy tale followed by the pistol killing of the mounted *Guardia Civile.* The dirt on the book meant they still read it, these men who had never come within ten thousand psychic miles of what it told about.

An inmate walked past them in the narrow aisle of volumes, his eyes searching the top level of shelves. He nodded as he passed Fare, walking on, then coming back.

"Lo, Mr. Odum. You know where they keep a feller named Henry Miller?"

Ivory was kneeling now, making a good show of searching for the missing volume of Hemingway he had just tossed onto the radiator.

"No," said Fare, "I don't think they got Henry Miller here. But you could check in the M's."

"Where am I?"

"You're in the H's."

Ivory snorted contemptuously.

When the man had moved off in the direction of the B's, Ivory stood. Both of them turned then.

LaPointe strolled insolently, more insolently than usual, toward them in the close aisle. For a few days, Fare knew, LaPointe would be a hero to some, and even more to be avoided than usual by others, and knowing this, he would wear his insolence all the more coolly.

The two of them, Rose and LaPointe, stood on either side of him. Their bodies took a confident, theatrically professional attitude toward his, as though even an accident of position, such as this flanking of him in the narrow space, were planned.

Fare looked at LaPointe for some acknowledgment of complicity, or at least of prior knowledge, but saw in the other's dark eyes only the operation of the undifferentiating radar that knew obstacles but did not classify them, only transmitted the message that something was in the way. LaPointe did not even look at Rose.

"You got it?" he asked Fare.

"Sure," Fare shrugged.

"Let's see then, Gotdamn it!" LaPointe nudged him hard on the shoulder.

Fare removed the paper from the book he had carried with him from the desk.

LaPointe reached for it. Fare shifted it sideways slightly so that LaPoint's pincering fingers missed it.

"You're going a little too fast, aren't you?"

Rose was leaning toward them now, unabashedly curious.

"Fuck do you mean 'fast'?"

For the first time LaPointe looked back at the desk where Fare's absence would soon become a problem. Fare was pleased to see the radar in the dark eyes work harder.

"I mean, what about Lester? I want to know what you are going to do and when."

"Listen, you Gotdamn fucking maggot . . ."

Ivory interrupted.

"He can't tell you when, but you . . ."

LaPointe hit Fare with his shoulder, knocking him backward to clear a space between himself and Ivory. He leaned across Fare's tilted body. "I don't need you to talk to this punk for me." He spoke in a hiss.

Fare could smell LaPointe. It was the smell of zoos, of animals left to sit in their own filth on concrete surfaces for extended lengths of time, the smell of sweat from pacing that space.

The two black men looked at each other hard. It was clear that they were having a difficult time holding together the alliance. Maybe had been for some time. LaPointe calmed, his fuse burning out. Ivory turned away to retrieve the book from the radiator top and put it back into the empty slot, leaving LaPointe and Fare to finish the business.

Fare was going to give them the paper. He had nothing to gain from withholding it. But he wanted to hear the sound of a shark's promise.

"What about it?" he asked. He kept his tone level and calm. He held the paper at his side just out of reach. LaPointe stared down at the paper. Perhaps he considered twisting it from Fare's fingers. But it could tear, they might be overheard.

"I tole you I'd do it for you. I tole you. Ain't that good enough for you?"

There was a strange tone of complaint, almost childish, in LaPointe's voice.

"It's not good enough. I want to know when and how?"

LaPointe shrugged and shuffled, too big and too wild for such a gesture in this confined space. His shoulders rocked the books on both sides of the aisle.

"I cain't tell zackly when. How is however I feel like it when it come the time. It don't matter how. Why it matter how?"

Fare had not thought about it. Suddenly, though, it mattered how. He had been shaking his head slowly all the while LaPointe was talking.

"Can you cut him?" He had the idea. His voice sounded like someone else's, distant and distorted as though curving through a long tube. "Listen," he leaned close to LaPointe, but the words seemed to come from farther and farther away. "Listen," he said. "Have you seen anybody butcher a hog?"

LaPointe drew back as though stung. For an instant, Fare thought he saw shock in the ebony face. He said more, but the tube that carried his voice curled itself as tight as the curl in the tail of a shoat, and he could not hear himself any longer.

TWENTY-SIX

THE AUDITORIUM WAS FILLING. ALONG THE BACK ROWS SAT the white men, quiet, moody, smoking more and laughing less than the black men, who sat in the front. At each exit stood a hack. Fare had not known what to expect in the way of attendance. He knew only that the more men who attended, the greater was their chance for success.

He stood in the shadows just out of sight of the milling audience, clutching a portion of dusty curtain. When he moved his hand, it left a wet smear.

In the pocket of his sport coat, neatly folded, was the introduction he was to read. It was a collection of inanities none of the inmates would understand, but which seemed to have been expected of him. The more inane it was, he knew, the more innocent he would seem, and the better were his chances of getting out of this thing unscathed.

Behind him, in the small backstage area, the company was completing its preparations for the performance. They had brought the few papier-mâché items of a nonrepresentational set, a trunk full of costumes, a few jars of makeup. Fare was to walk onto the stage when his time came, deliver the brief introduction, and then, when the lights dimmed, walk down to sit beside Bray in the first row.

He wandered back to the makeshift dressing area. The men were making themselves up on one side of the small space behind a bed sheet strung up for them. They stood around, stiffly attentive to each other in various states of undress. Fare looked at them, letting his gaze rest for some time on the tall, heavily muscled black man named Harrison Petrie. Petrie looked like a nervous opening-nighter, that was all. Later on, Petrie was to be impersonated by LaPointe. Norris Thibideaux, who was somewhere in the back of the auditorium operating the rudimentary lighting apparatus, would be Ivory Rose.

It was simple, a good plan. Rose and LaPointe would walk out with the actors after the performance, dressed in the street clothing brought in for them among the costumes. They would sign themselves out (flawlessly, after much practice) as Petrie and Thibideaux, and leave the prison in the van which had brought the actors. They would stop, not far from prison land, shift to an automobile which had been left at a prearranged location. In the car they would head south, rather than north as was expected, to Miami or Fort Lauderdale. Rose had it in mind to try to get to Cuba where he expected to be welcomed in revolutionary brotherhood. LaPointe would fly out of Miami too, if he could, though Fare did not know where he planned to go. Certainly, the airports would be closed to the two escaped men, and how much more help could they expect from this group of graduate students beyond what they had already gotten, what it would take to get them through the main gate?

The perversity of the plan, the thing that gave it its credibility, was the fact that it depended upon the basic racial insult Raiford offered its black men. Rose, who did not look much like Thibideaux, and LaPointe, who more closely resembled Petrie, though not that closely, would walk out the main gate, past the night shift, unaccustomed to much coming and going, because, to the hacks who ran things, all black faces were the same face. Rose and LaPointe were banking on it.

Fare watched the shadow figures moving behind the bed sheet. When the troupe had entered the prison earlier, and he had escorted them to the Rock auditorium, it had taken Lieutenant Harlan, walking with them, some time to notice that Jamahl, tall with the lithe, athletic way of moving and with the short Afro, was a woman. Once he had divined that she was female, he had made it clear that there should be segregated quarters backstage. He had sent a runner for the bed sheet to shield the men from Jamahl's view, while Fare wondered how many of them she had slept with. Then, gallantly,

Harlan had offered the small stinking bathroom backstage to "the young lady."

Fare stood near the bathroom door, not knowing why really, smoking a cigarette. He could hear the impatience of the audience now. It was an audience that could turn ugly. The men would jeer if they were bored, but that did not matter. Closer to him, Fare could hear the sounds of Jamahl behind the bathroom door.

The door opened and she stepped out, half-dressed, calling out to someone named Eddie to help her with a zipper. She smiled when she saw Fare.

God, but he was tired of these smiles that did not cross the chasm to him, only widened it. Hers, Ivory's. So many like them. She looked over her shoulder toward the men's dressing room. Apparently, she did not see Eddie. Her eyes came to rest on him again.

"Come here," she said. "You might as well help me with this."

She was wearing baggy men's trousers and there was soon to be a man's shirt, but now she wore only a brief, severe black bra to flatten her breasts. But the breasts were too large to be completely leveled and the tension of the harness turned them a slightly lighter color than the skin of her throat and belly. It moved him.

She turned back to the bathroom.

"Stop staring at me and come in here."

Inside, he stood facing her and she took the top of the zipper in both hands, pulling upward to straighten it. She had gotten the gauzy fabric of her briefs caught in the coarse teeth of the zipper. Fare hesitated to touch her. He did not know why. She looked at him impatiently.

Embarrassed, he began to struggle with the zipper.

Someone knocked at the door; a man's voice said, "Five minutes, Molly."

"Molly?" he mumbled, not looking up from the zipper.

"That's right," she said.

He broke the zipper from its grasp of the panties, shredding them a little as he brought it down, and then began to zip it up. But quickly, like someone trapping an animal, she clasped his hands with both her own and held them to her mound. Then she began helping his right hand into the opening of the zipper. When his fingers were inside the trousers and cupping her, she said, "Go ahead. Go ahead."

He pushed through the hole in the light cloth of the panties, getting rougher without meaning to, and felt the coarse hair. She stepped to one side, then to the other to spread her legs for him, and encircled his neck to pull him to her while he fingered her.

"You are going to do it right tonight, aren't you?"

He tried to raise his head from her breasts but she buried it, fiercely now. She was buying something. Him. He could not break away. He wanted her on him. He wanted the answer too. He had asked her that night in her apartment, then later, when they had met briefly to go over it one last time. Each time she had put him off, saying he could not be told until the last moment, else he might not fulfill his part of the bargain.

"When? What did they do with him?" he mumbled, his face pressed to the flesh of her throat.

"Aren't you?" she asked again, neither petting nor grasping his head.

"Yes," he said. "Tell me."

"Ivory will tell you on the way out. Not till we are in the van. You are going to do this right, tonight, aren't you?"

"Yes," he said.

She let him go on for a while, then gently pushed him away and went back to her dressing. He stood watching her, watching the flattened, translucent bulbs of her breasts disappear under the coarse men's shirt, watching as she tucked the shirt into the trousers. nestling it down around her slim, firm hips, tightened the belt, skewing its brass buckle.

She had something he had never again expected to encounter. She had what Clare had. But then maybe a lot of them had it. Maybe the knowledge of it just took them at certain times as the moon took them, without them choosing it. When his swelling had gone away, he walked out of the little bathroom and stood where he had stood before, waiting for the play to begin. It was only after he had stood outside, recovering himself from the feel and smell and taste of her, that he remembered the little bathroom was the key to the whole thing. In it, Norris Thibideaux and Harrison Petrie would lie bound and gagged while their counterparts walked out the main gate.

Fare sat uncomfortably beside Bray, who kept muttering about the meaninglessness if not outright lunacy of the play, and kept looking back over his shoulder at the audience, which grew increasingly more bored and demonstrated its boredom by loud talking, bursting into laughter at solemn moments, lighting cigarettes and then letting the matches, in clusters of ten, slowly burn themselves out. "Culture!" Bray sputtered, turning fully around as though trying by the force of his scowls to make the men quiet down.

Fare's introduction had gone pretty much unheeded as he had hoped it would. He had kept it short, ended by saying, stupidly, that the play was a better representation of itself than were his remarks. His words echoed around the auditorium to no response, probably because when he had appeared in the spotlight at center stage, the men were still stunned by darkness and he was finished before anyone could think of a catcall.

He did not watch the play. Did not watch it, that is, as a story. He watched it as a thing to exhibit the movement of Jamahl, her grace, the way she assumed space that was hers to tenant and much more. He wondered what Ivory, sitting somewhere behind him with LaPointe in the bank of humanity, thought when she moved the body which he, Ivory, had possessed. He could not imagine. He had never known Rose to show love for anything. He had seen only the cold fury, the detached irony, the dope-giggle, and a few moments of genuine feeling, as when he spoke of the Vietnam War, which were inevitably tainted by rhetoric. Ivory could not be private.

He had to make the connection between his, and the world's, his brother's, suffering. They were opposites, Fare realized. Ivory, who could not suffer or love or hate only for himself, and he, Fare, who was self-obsessed.

Watching the play, occasionally taking in some portion of the story, but mostly sitting in the entrancement caused by Jamahl, Fare noticed that the men in the audience grew less restive when she was at the center of things. Many, it seemed, sensed she was a woman. They too had begun to watch her for her movement, and gradually things quieted. Bray, beside him, seemed more disconcerted by her slow taming of the audience than he had been by bad behavior. He turned back more frequently. Just before intermission, he leaned to Fare.

"You guess maybe these numbers is learning something?"

"Maybe."

"Don't hardly seem possible to me. What in the hell is this show all about anyway?"

For the life of him, Fare could not remember what it was supposed to be about.

"Nothing," he could only say.

Bray looked at him in the half-light of the auditorium, while behind the curtain they could hear the actors wrestling with pieces of the set and behind them the men smoked, talking and laughing in a subdued way. Bray gradually unsquinted his eyes. Fare saw that he was taking it as a joke.

"That sure as hell is what it means to me. Nothing. You didn't waste you time with any of this in that Ph.D. of yours, did you?"

Fare lit a cigarette. He was thinking about what he was going to do at the end, but his mind could not fix upon a coherent version of it; he could not align its separate actions to make out the way. It occurred as a mosaic only, each piece equally important, and all of it mixed up with moments from the play and from the past three months.

"No," he said to Bray at last. "No. I didn't waste my time with anything as perverted as this. This is Goddamn *French*."

Bray turned away from him, looked at the men behind him,

then at his watch, then, out of the corner of his eye, Fare could see him shake his head slowly and sigh, certifying it all as madness, deeper water than any he wanted to swim.

The second half passed with the slow and slower taming of the audience so that when the lights came up at the end and the actors assembled for a final bow, there was a moment of still shock before the men began to applaud, almost decorously, and then with more and more enthusiasm. Rose and LaPointe had counted on confusion and horseplay afterward, but now it appeared there would be this strange order, and Fare knew, when the actors had disappeared behind the curtain, that he had to do something. And so, before Bray could stand or any of the hacks could move to change the course of things, he rose and walked to the stage and stood, moving his hands toward the audience in the damping gesture that told them to be quiet. It was hardly necessary. They were listening to him. There was absolute quiet for an instant.

"The actors have asked me to announce that they will stay a few minutes here afterward if any of you would like to come up front to talk to them. If you'll just file up here to the front and stand in the center section here, they'll be out in a minute."

There was a pause. Bray looked at him with the resentment he reserved for things that violated routine, and then the men broke into applause again, and some began moving to the front.

Then Bray was standing beside him on the stage, gesturing at the noise and saying, "Now listen, men, listen to me a minute here. Thank you. Thank . . . We ask that you stay down in this pit here or whatever it is, you know what I mean, and don't get up on the stage. Let's keep the actors up on the stage and you down here, all right?"

Bray looked around, automatically checking the positions of the several hacks who stood at the exits. Then he looked at his watch again. He leapt from the stage, lurching at the bottom with the bad knee. Fare followed him, glancing at the wings. There, dressed in a twill skirt and vest and coat, wear-

ing a man's tie, knotted hugely and loosely at her long neck,
stood Jamahl. She smiled at him with an excited look in her
eyes he had not seen, even during the performance. The smile,
the eyes told him things had surely begun.

As the men moved slowly toward the front, many more of
them staying behind than Fare had expected, the noise began
to gather. They spilled into the aisles, poured down, disassem-
bling the ruled forms of the auditorium and making the chaos
he had seen before only in the yard.

He lost sight of Bray in the milling crowd at the base of the
stage, but caught occasional glimpses of brown shirts moving
warily among the men, caught glimpses above of the actors as
they appeared one at a time from behind the curtain, sweating,
wiping at themselves with towels, some of them smiling, coming toward this experience, others, grim, frightened. He wondered how many of them knew. All of them? Only three?

He tried not to look for anything, but could not keep
the searching expression from his face as he cut his eyes here
and there behind his hand while he smoked or wiped his brow,
cutting them for the broad, absurdly hard and big shape of
LaPointe, moving through the crowd toward the stage. Twice
he thought he saw it, the enormous wedge of chest and shoulders driven into the thin waist, a figure of comic-book propor-
tion. But he was never sure. At least not until, looking at his
watch after what seemed hours, he noted that only ten minutes
had passed, and noted also that, pretending to illustrate a way
of standing on the stage, a way of holding the body so that
her lowered, man's voice could carry the auditorium, Jamahl
had lured a group of men up onto the stage with her.

It looked so innocent. She, seeming so absorbed in the
teaching, had two of them standing with their legs apart, two
hard cons, totally unabashed, each pressing the flat of his hand
into his solar plexus and bleating as others watched without
the slightest hint of derision, learning how to "project from
the diaphragm."

Fare stood still in complete admiration. What an actress.
Surely she was terrified. She was giving the performance she

had thought herself incapable of. By seemingly accidental half-steps she lured the men closer to the little bathroom backstage where she had dressed. Fare knew that LaPointe and Rose must soon join the group surrounding her.

He searched for the guards and found two of them watching the group on the stage, frowning, checking watches, annoyed at the violation of Bray's edict. How, he wondered, would they ever pull it off.

McLaren said, "Like I was saying, Mr. Odum, I never known you had no drama in you background."

McLaren, it seemed, had been speaking to him. A quizzical look was in his face. He cut his eyes to the black girl on the stage, trying to see what so fascinated Fare.

Fare had to say something about the drama in his background.

"She's something, ain't she?"

"What?"

"Her. That one. The one you been looking at. I ditn even know she was a woman, did you?"

"No," said Fare, making McLaren look at him, not at Jamahl.

"No," he said, lighting a cigarette from the butt of one he held, then offering McLaren one. He was shocked by the smell of her on his hands. "No, it came as a surprise to me too. She sure managed to act like a man up there, didn't she?"

And then, giving up the pretense, they both watched as she turned to LaPointe, who had moved as diminutively as his frame would allow into the circle that surrounded her. Placing one hand on his back, she pressed his belly and said, "You try it. Go on, big fella."

"Would you look at that," said McLaren.

And she made the bleating sound again, like herself in the male role. She did not look at LaPointe, not to speak of, but Fare saw her eyes catch Ivory's as he too moved into the circle, and for a moment, she seemed to lose her mind's, not her hand's, grip. But she caught herself, and with all her strength, pressed LaPointe's flat belly again, bleating, "It's from the diaphragm." LaPointe looked at her with something like misery in his eyes and did his best to reproduce the sound she had made. In spite of themselves, men stepped away from LaPointe. Fare looked for a change in LaPointe. How much had he learned? There were signs, not visible to others he was sure, that LaPointe was near his breaking point. That, so near to success, he could not stand this artifice, this subtlety, that the trip spring in him was coming past its catch. Fare watched Ivory's face for some confirmation of this and saw it, an enormous fear trying to mask itself behind the Rose smile.

Ivory thrust himself forward and said, "Try it on me."

LaPointe almost fell out of her grip to the back of the circle, his flanks heaving with his malignant animus. Ivory had gotten to it, just in time. She took Rose, too rough with ill-concealed love, and pressed his belly, telling him to bleat, her hands lingering on his back, too low at the waist. She spread her fingers, exploring, closed, then opened them again like blackbird wings. Rose forced out a sound, a love song. When she had finished with him she pushed him to the back of the circle. Fare saw what she was doing. The bathroom door yawned behind her.

More men joined them all the time, and forcing himself to turn back to McLaren, take a drag and check his watch, Fare saw that five minutes had passed. How much longer would they let it go on?

He tried to force himself to say something to McLaren, but nothing came.

McLaren said, "Well, shit."

McLaren smiled a weak, accomplice's smile and dropped his cigarette, watched it glow on the concrete between them for an instant and then too savagely put his brogan on it. Fare tried to reject the smile, to relocate himself near the center of what was happening on the stage. But he found that the corners of his mouth ruffled, even now. McLaren shuffled past him toward the door.

Somehow, Rose and LaPointe had disappeared. What Fare believed first was that they had given it up, walked back into the auditorium. But he did not see them, small chance of it, anywhere around him. The smoke burned his eyes. He had sweated his shirt. When he located the hacks again, he saw that they had been lulled by it, the order of what was going on above, now almost entirely surrounding Jamahl.

One of them dug in his shirt pocket for a Camel, yawned, brought out a lighter and lit up, then as an afterthought, offered one. The other caught the yawn and stretched like an old dog before waving away the cigarette.

In the bathroom now, LaPointe and Rose would be dressing in blazers, gray trousers, light blue shirts and blue ties. Petrie and Thibideaux would be bound and gagged, perhaps blooded a bit to make it look good. LaPointe would enjoy it. They would be waiting, the four of them, for the hacks to call it off, send the men back to sleeping quarters. LaPointe, with his hair just coming back in, with his reputation among the hacks, was going to have a tough time of it. For him, it would be close. But, Fare reminded himself, this was the night shift, a reduced force which locked men in at night and left them to do what they would to one another. This shift would not know LaPointe so well. The important one was Bray. Bray knew LaPointe. Like two animals, they had sniffed each other out long ago.

TWENTY-SEVEN

WHEN BRAY VAULTED TO THE STAGE AND RAISED HIS HANDS again for silence, the men behind him mumbled, a few breaking into boos. Bray smiled tightly, his face saying it would not have happened over in the school. Fare watched him carefully, watched his face, listened for some hint in his voice. It was important that Bray leave before LaPointe and Rose had to show themselves. During the packing and striking of set and lights, the two could stay in the bathroom. Among the company of actors, dressing, working, stacking and carrying, Petrie and Thibideaux would not be missed.

Fare had to make it seem as though he could handle it. He had been cast in the role of goodwill emissary, had escorted the group in, and now must see them out. He would appeal to Bray on behalf of the symmetry of it. Bray had never said it outright, that he would leave this to Fare.

Things quieted a little.

"It's about that time," Bray said with mock regret. "I'm sorry, but it's about . . ."

To Fare it sounded like the bark of a dog, or like the expulsion of air that comes from a human breast when a fist strikes down below. He whirled to locate it. He knew suddenly the feeling of going down, arms waving, down the long distance to the dark water beneath the Suwannee River bridge. Yet he had not done it, except in dreams.

She had been standing within the circle of men, all of them pressing closer to her, wanting something unreachable and undefinable. Bray had jumped to the stage. They had seen him, had known this was the end of it. One of them, a young black man, had reached out for her, had tried to take her into his arms as though to dance with her. Fare had seen his face in the instant he had reached for her. It was the amazed, confident face of a lover. She had been standing there, her hands upon a man's belly, teaching him the bleat, saying, "From the diaphragm, right down there." The young man had simply turned her, whirled her into a dance in his arms. Who could say what he had intended to do?

The sound must have come, Fare thought, when the man whose stomach she had held, had struck out, a kind of blind, reflex blow to the small of the other man's back. Now the two were at each other in the center of the circle, and with Jamahl, seeming to dance, falling and pulling, punching and kicking among the chopping feet and legs.

". . . I'm sure we all want to thank this group, and especially that young lady there . . ."

Bray was still talking, but his voice had changed and he was turning too, moving his big frame. Jamahl was the center of more than she had ever intended. Fare moved toward her, not sure what he would do when he got to her, his feet carrying him along. He could see her clean black limbs flailing among the blue legs. She was riding the back of one of the fighters, holding on. She held the waistband of a man's trousers. As this man swung his body, raising up one arm to fend a blow, she held and swung with him, and as though flying from the saddle of a horse, tumbled among the legs.

The auditorium behind them sounded suddenly like a crowded tunnel; there were the rushing sounds of things coming and going, passing each other at high speeds. Fare could feel behind him the heat of bodies crowding to the stage, to look, he did not know, to get in on it. There was the sound behind him far in the rear, of hard-soled shoes battering the wooden seats as men ran away, vaulting as they went.

Bray was near the center of it now. Fare clawed toward him. Each man he touched flinched from him briefly. He could see in their eyes the instant when they saw he was authority and the next when they decided what to do about it. They gave way before him. Each time he touched, he was conscious of the hot, hard muscle beneath the blue fabric, its electricity, and of what it could do to him. The falling sensation turned in his middle again each time he took a man by the shoulder, and with force, but not violently, turned him aside going to the center.

Bray, ahead of him, was on his knees, like a referee. His shirt was soaked with sweat. He reached out now with both hands and tried with a violent, bulging effort to separate the two fighters.

Above the rushing echoing sound around them, Fare could hear his voice saying, "Break it . . ."

A vein leapt in the side of Bray's neck and without a sound, his shirt split from collar to waistline at the center of his back. He flung the two men from under him and fell forward onto the stage floor.

Bray did a leaping push-up, got his feet under him and turned first to one side, then to the other, his eyes fixing the two fighters. Both sat dazed among the legs. Then, in the lull when it might have ended, Fare watched as one man, who was simply anybody, his eyes ablaze, raised his foot and brought it down on the back of the nearest fighter's neck. Bray looked at the man. Fare saw in his face an instant of shock, and then his mouth opened to make the words, "Custodian. Cust . . ." before someone put a foot into it. They were on him, and he was struggling, like a stunned bullock, then he was down under them and some of them were leaping up, breaking their knees in flight and coming down on him this way. Fare could see the scars on his enormous hands turn red as he tried to push himself up.

He could no longer see Jamahl. She was gone from the center of it. All around him came the sounds of fists landing, the tense grunts of men taking punches. He kept taking the shoulders in his hands, pulling himself hand over hand out of it, moving toward the backstage and the bathroom. He pulled one man who nonchalantly turned swinging in the same motion. The fist, with blood on it, was coming for his mouth. He froze, tasting coppery blood. He had bitten his tongue. He was crawling now, with no memory of going down, then crouching and running.

When the fabric of the curtain hit his face, he burrowed under and in the half-darkness, ran on shaky legs toward the bathroom. The door gave a little with his weight, then sprang back against him.

"It's me," he said. His voice was drowned in the noise. The alarm bell was ringing. He wondered when it had started. The door cracked a little, then swung open and a hand took him by the tie and pulled him in.

He stared at them all, the two actors lying bound and gagged, their faces sufficiently bloodied, LaPointe with the mad eyes of all the stomping, kicking men outside bulging in his face, and Rose, back against the wall, holding the sobbing Jamahl, her legs astride the crapper.

He knew it. He knew it, and knew also that he would never again have to stand at any library window to summon it. This was imprisonment. It was here in all its forms, in hate, in love, in belief and in madness. They were all in it together.

Rose put his hand over Jamahl's face, slowly letting his fingers try her eyes, her cheeks, her lips for injury while all the time he stared at Fare. "It wont sposed to go like this, was it?" He was calm. He smiled.

LaPointe was shaking with the need to do something. Rose cut his eyes to LaPointe, then back to Fare. The eyes said, "He cannot be contained much longer."

Fare leaned back against the door. What would the prison do? What would it want? What it wanted was what to do. It would get the actors out, that was certain. "Stay here," he said to Rose, and stepped out, moving onto the stage where it was open season on freemen.

The auditorium was full of men. It seemed that there were more of them than during the performance. Some were standing toe to toe fighting. Others stood in corner phalanxes, fending off the action, smoking calmly and watching. Some were lying prone, stunned, bleeding. One, Fare noticed, lay with his back broken over a row of seats, legs in the aisle, eyes staring upward at the ceiling. Pieces of plywood from the auditorium seats flew like phonograph records through the air. The alarm bell had become ordinary. Near him on the stage, Bray sat, dazed, bleeding from the mouth and ears. Bray's eyes beckoned to him, but someone climbed the heavy curtain down.

It shrouded Bray and Fare began digging him out. When he had Bray's face uncovered, he found they were saying the same thing to each other. "You got to get them actors out of here. Get you a custodian. Get some help in here."

"How the fuck am I going to get out of here through all this?"

Bray looked at him. Closed his eyes, breathed deeply, "I'll do it," he said. He pushed himself up, then slumped. He gazed at his own legs. He smiled. "Give out on me." He was talking about the knee. He rubbed it with his hand, winced. All around them, men fought, white against black now. Sitting beside Bray, Fare could see several large pools of blood on the stage floor.

"Get up to the library. Take these keys. Get on the phone an tell them at the main gate to get down here an get them actors out." Bray tried to get up again. Fare shoved under Bray's arms and dragged him off to the darkness of the wings.

Making it to the library was not going to be easy. The auditorium was thirty yards of skirmish, all of it full of men white and black who would sooner kill him than step on a roach.

He knocked at the bathroom door again. Rose did not question him when he said, "Give me your clothes." As he stripped, fumbling with the knot of his tie, baring himself to the shorts, he was conscious of Jamahl, of the fact that she had seen him this way before. Now she turned her eyes away.

He had made a small pile of his clothes on the floor near her, and so had Rose. Before they dressed, Rose in the actor's blazer and tie, Fare in Rose's blues, they looked at each other. Had he not been so frightened, Fare might have laughed. Here they were, the two of them down to common ground, and it was obvious who should be staying and who going. Fare in his flaccid white flesh, his muscles without memory, was ashamed of himself. He had wanted to contrive a world devoid of these brutal comparisons. He looked for contempt in Ivory's eyes, but saw only the tensile hunter's concentration that waited for him to dress and go, was confident that he would. He picked up Ivory's warm, sweated denims.

In Ivory's blues he skirted the fighting, made the library, and with Bray's key, unlocked the heavy metal door, pushing it inward. By memory he found his way to the phone in the dark. He dialed the main gate.

"Odum? Who is Odum? I don't know nary Odum on the night shift."

Fare did not know the voice which spoke to him.

"I'm a teacher. I'm here tonight to introduce the play. Mr. Bray. Mr. Bray is the one who told me to call. Said to tell you to get some custodial personnel down here to contain this thing. We got freemen down here. That bunch of actors . . ."

There was a pause. He heard a hand going over the receiver, then the awful muffled sound of men talking, first indistinguishably, then the hand removed, audibly.

". . . so listen, Odum, we can't send . . ."

Fare was squeezing the phone tightly. His hand was a claw. It would have to be pried from his fingers. The alarm bell rang. Down below, it sounded like a storm.

". . . it's your motherfucking ass. It's your ass if you don't . . ."

Calmly, the man on the other end said, "Just a minute."

There was the hand over the phone again.

"Hello, Odum. This is Superintendent Peppers. What have you got down there? Say you've got some actors?"

"Yes. Men and one woman. Bray sent me up here to the library. To call you. To tell you to get some hacks . . . cust . . . to get somebody down here to get them out before . . ."

"Just a min . . ."

"Fuck your just a minute. You haven't got just a . . ."

"Where are they? Tell me . . ."

"They're backstage. Backstage waiting. I'll be back down there waiting with them to show you . . ."

"All right, Odum. We're coming."

The phone was passed again.

Far away, Fare heard Peppers, whose name he had seen on a thousand memos, saying, "Never told me a damn thing about no actors."

Fare stood at the library door. It was locked. Outside was chaos. Inside was the library, books, dark, quiet. He could wait it out. No, there was what they had done for him. He had to go back down there. He had to find out what they had done for him. With Lester.

He met a man on the stairs. The man was coming up, cradling three wallets against his chest. When he saw Fare, he turned sideways to shield them. Fare looked back to see him sit, shaking the wallets on the landing like so many wastebaskets. At the foot of the stairs, men were carrying blankets, chairs, mattresses, books, and clothing out through the tunnel toward the yard. It was as though they were working. He could see the glow of bonfires already.

In the auditorium, the fighting was still going on. But there was less of it. Men were escaping toward the yard, toward the fires. There seemed to be less madness in it now, more of something else, something almost merry. There were bodies in the auditorium. He turned his eyes from the stab wounds as he made his way along the walls to backstage. Bray lay unconscious where he had left him. He picked up a handful of heavy curtain and covered Bray with it. He could not forget the stab wounds. They flickered like face cards, smiling in a ruffled deck, each like an eye, staring for a moment. How could there have been so many knives?

Inside the bathroom, he could not talk. LaPointe was rolling his eyes now. Any moment he would bolt. He could do anything. Ivory still held Jamahl, who had recovered somewhat. Still she would not look at Fare. In the close, hot bathroom, he found his voice at last.

"They're coming to get you. We've got to wait for them outside. All of this is shit if we get caught in here with these two." He pointed to Thibideaux and Petrie lying on the floor. The smell was overpowering. One of them had pissed himself. Fare turned and opened the door. They walked into the backstage. They could hear the sound like breakers on a shore-line, men shouting out in the yard; there was laughter, sing-ing. A few words of "Like a Tree Standing by the Water," came to them. Singing. What were they singing for? Moments before, they had been killing each other.

Fare stood with Ivory, LaPointe and Jamahl, and the others, all of them dressed absurdly in matching blue blazers that bore the insignia of their repertory group. They watched the auditorium door. When they heard the shouts of the men nearest the door and saw them begin to panic, they knew it was time.

The brown shirts hit the auditorium door in a charge, screaming like gulls in their terror. Fare did not recognize any of them. Some carried nightsticks. Others, shotguns. They rushed for the stage, parting the inmates who remained with kicks and curses. Some, those who could only crawl, were trampled. As they came, Fare remembered something. He turned to Rose. Where is he? Where did you put Lester? But the hacks were on them.

Rose composed his face so that it was the face of an actor who was being rescued. The hacks had splintered them into two groups. Fare saw LaPointe, his shoulders bursting the blazer, pass through the door. He turned to speak to the first of the hacks, who was obviously the leader of the foray, who wore lieutenant's bars. He held out his arm to point to the group clustered behind him. Stupidly, he was going to say, "These are the ones. We've got to get them out." Then, on his own outstretched arm, he saw the blue herringbone, the unbuttoned cuff of Ivory's shirt, and he said, "These are the . . ." before the shotgun shut his mouth.

He awoke to the sound of the alarm bell. His eyes opened slowly, and he did not try to move. The blood that had run from his mouth had stuck him to the stage floor. With his fingers, he pulled at his lips, his cheeks, until he could free his face and sit up. In the mess where his face had lain were the white fragments of his teeth. His head ached. Each time he drew breath, the broken surfaces of his teeth shrieked until he could no longer distinguish their sound, the sound of his shorn nerves, from the sound of his own voice. He stood leaning against the wall and surveyed the auditorium. Men lay all around, as they had in his last moments of consciousness. The broken-backed man still stared fixedly at the ceiling. The stab wounds gaped dark blood. He picked up a knife, pried it from the fingers of a corpse as he made his way from the stage. It was a long, sharp, double-edged piece of leaf-spring steel with white, surgical tape wrapped around its top for a handle. It had been painstakingly honed on some concrete surface. Near him, a man moaned. He walked to the man and knelt, looking into his face, but no life looked back from the hard, gelatin eyes. The moan had come from his own mouth. He had moaned with the pain of his teeth. Each time he sucked or gave air came the moan. He had to stop it. He did not want to be conspicuous for any reason, in any way. He had to think. He sat in one of the chairs in the front row, staring back up at the stage where Bray lay still heaped beneath the curtain.

He wanted water but knew the cold of it would tear his nerves. He had to think of something. He was not a freeman anymore. He was one of those locked in and he had not the blue, but the brown to fear.

When he breathed, he smiled; it hurt less that way, and he thought how he must look with his bloody, toothless grin. He must look like the others, he thought. Something was working its way up through the roots of his teeth. The pain was coursing in with the air to his teeth, into them, where, like the jangling of a thousand telephones, it rang its way into his brain. His brain was swollen and hot. The shotgun butt had doubled its size. But there was something else coming up the nerves with the pain. The phones rang in his head. "Odum. Who is Odum? I don't know any Odum on the night shift." Stupid fuck. All of them stupid fucks.

But that was not it. The thing coming was something else. The voice that was coming in was different, a familiar voice.

It said his name differently. And it had, he realized now, said his name. The man lying next to him moaned again. "Wha?" asked Fare. But it had been his own, not the moan of a dead man. He could get used to this. He could get used to anything. They could not hurt him worse, could they? He gripped the knife. He sucked the cold blade until it set his teeth on edge, rang the phones and he heard the voice clearly.

It said his name the way . . . the way . . . "Hodum," it said, "you got to do it youself."

Now it came to him, the fullness of it. Ivory had leaned down to him. Fare's eyes were closing slowly as the shock of the shotgun butt rang to his brain, but Ivory's face came down, large, close as it had been that day in class. He smelled Ivory's breath for an instant, sour with will, and his own, sour with fear, hurt. Ivory leaned close, just as the state trooper took him by the sleeve of his spotless blue blazer, the trooper shifting the gun, its butt dripping, from one hand to the other, saying, "Never mine that scum. We got to . . ."

But Ivory resisted the trooper's grasp for only the time it took to say, "There is some things you can't buy, white folks. You juss got the firss lesson in the mouth and now you . . ." But the trooper had pulled him away. And the phones rang and rang until Fare had, at last, answered them, discovering his face stuck to the floor of the stage.

He shoved himself up from the chair, and stuffing the knife into the loose waistband of his blue trousers, made his way out toward the glow of the fires.

TWENTY-EIGHT

IT WAS COLD OUTSIDE. THE BONFIRES, FOUR OF THEM, BECK-oned. Fare remembered that there had been the madness, then the merriment. Now, as he surveyed the yard, strewn with broken chairs, clothing, plastic crockery, gutted mattresses, flattened basketballs, piles of books from the library, it looked as though madness had given way to despair. As he stood on the ramp before descending to the yard, he glanced to his left and right, up and down the sides of the building. Not far away, in the shadows to his left, a man squatted, shitting. Beyond him, within the stink of him, three men pushed another to the wall. The victim was a young man, whose head lolled. A crude bandage covered an enormous lump at his temple. One of them held a knife to his throat. The man with the knife poked it upward once, twice, and Fare could see in the darkness that the young man tried by clawing with his hands at the wall to raise himself upward from the knife. The other two men stood on either side. The squatting man said, "Let him down a little." The blade lowered slightly, and the boy whimpered, catching his breath. They began to remove his clothing. The man who had been relieving himself stood, glanced at Fare, turning his head half-around without moving his shoulders, buckled his trousers and walked over to join the others.

Fare walked toward the fires. He looked back once. They were over the boy, one of them giving up the knife to another. He saw the white flash of pumping buttocks in the darkness.

As he neared the fires, a few men turned to look at him, none of them for long, all of them turning back to the glow and the warmth. They were taking everything from the Rock that would burn. From the great round heaps of ash that skirted each of them, Fare could see that the fires had been burning for some time. He stood holding his hand to his mouth. His teeth howled. He did not want them to know that he was hurt. He had seen what they did to the hurt. He heard thudding sounds above those of muted conversation. He turned. Men were throwing mattresses and wooden furniture from the upper floors of the Rock's T-tier down to men on the ground, who carried them to the fires and threw them in. The white men had situated themselves around one of the fires. The black men stood around the other three. He could see the white buttocks pumping against the wall.

Then, as when streetlights are turned on at nightfall, all around the perimeter of the yard lights began to blink on. Pairs of them.

"Cars?" someone murmured. The boy at the wall covered by the pumping buttocks cried, "No!" But no one turned. A growing murmur ran through the men. Some of them jumped as though physically touched by the light. It paled the firelight, leaving the men somehow unprotected. It seemed to make Fare's teeth howl louder. Then, as he looked with all the others toward the fences, they heard the latching, the thuds. Men got out of the cars, stepping in front of the lights to show themselves, to allow themselves to be counted by the men inside. In the ground fog, across the three lines of fences, their bodies seemed to shimmer and dance. Each of them, a dark stick figure in a corona of halating light, carried at high port, or straight up from the shoulder, or nestled in the crook of an arm, a weapon. Fare could see that some of them wore glistening helmets, others the campaign hats of the Florida Highway Patrol. One of them lit a cigarette, his face a white glow in the distance, disappearing. There was absolute silence except for the hiss and crackle of the fire. Then the boy behind them cried, "No!" again, insistently, and in an accent somehow familiar. It was a cry of pain as though something had pierced the heart of him. Still no one turned. They watched the lights. A cold, metallic sound, a little wet with the night dew, came ratcheting across to the men by the fires. It was the sound of the loading of guns. One after another, the bulls in the headlights beyond the fences pressed shells into magazines, pumping "slack-slack" each to get one round into his chamber.

"No!"

Fare could no longer help it. He uncovered his mouth. He touched the knife at his belt and turned. Against the wall, the four men who held the boy stood looking up in the dark shadow in the lee of the building. Above them men dropped the last sticks of furniture, pieces of dismembered desks and shelves from T-tier. One of the men, Fare was somehow sure it was the man who had been squatting some time before, stood now buckling his trousers a second time. They let the boy go. He slumped down to the base of the building, resting on his buttocks for a moment, then cupping his hands under himself and turning to the side. "No!"

The howling of his teeth brought water to Fare's eyes. He watched the man buckling his trousers. He snapped the buckle and, swiveling his head strangely to the side and upward, he called out, "I'm gone blight the next man of you that drops a stob on my head!"

Now, the man walked toward Fare, toward the circle of firelight, into the beams of the headlights. He was thinner, yes, and looked a little taller for it, but there was no mistaking that it was Lester. Fare noticed that the others, the men with him, walked a little behind and watched him for his body's signals.

"No!" The boy was crawling along the wall.

Nearby, staring at the lights, a man said, "Fuck me." He said it softly, in a tone of absolute resignation. Fare stepped away from him. Other men began to look about themselves. The lights bordered them now on three sides. The Rock behind them was theirs, but gutted, all its comforts burnt. Then from the direction of the main gate came the booming click of a bullhorn. The voice was Peppers': "You men will form into ranks and come to the main gate. You will walk with your hands over your heads. If any of you are carrying weapons, drop them where you stand. We are going to give you one minute to form yourself into a column of twos."

Slowly, Fare edged to the outside of the circle, gauging himself to be a little left of the spot where Lester and the men with him would join it. Those around him stood looking at each other. Someone said, "Come on, column of twos."

Another said, "Fuck him."

Suddenly it was as though the formation of a column, a thing they had done many times every day, some of them for years in this place, was impossible for them. One man gestured toward a nearby fire, "I ain't lining up with no niggers."

There were a few catcalls from the upper levels of the Rock. A man shouted, "Boooo!" Another, "Fuck you, Peppers!" to ripples of uneasy laughter. Some of the men began to shuffle in a confused way, not changing the shape of the circle much, but trying, nevertheless, to let it be known to others that they wanted to line up. In the shuffling, Fare found Lester had come near him, stood not two feet behind him, lighting a cigarette.

It seemed to Fare, that now, here, in these shadows, in these ungovernable circumstances the light of recognition must come into Lester's eyes. He gripped the knife. He unbuttoned and pulled up a portion of the shirt from his chest, stuffing it into his mouth to quiet the howling. He could no longer distinguish the ringing of his own lines from the alarm far off in the Rock. He faced Lester. "You got another one of them?" he asked. Lester looked at him, decided he had spoken to someone else, and looked away.

"You have one minute. I'm telling you men to form a column of twos and walk with your hands over you heads to the main gate. Leave your weapons behind you. No one will harm you."

Fare spit out the cloth of the shirt. It was stained dark. He turned away for an instant and sucked the knife blade. "I said, have you got another one of them?"

Lester looked at him with boar hog's eyes, bared tushes, looked around to see what other men were doing. Then back at him.

"No!" the boy sobbed. He was hopping along the wall now, trying to pull his trousers up as he went. A light erupted from atop the main gate. When the light struck him, the boy sprinted. "No!" he screamed, again and again. His pants, flying from one ankle, tripped him and he fell, but he pulled himself up immediately. He sprinted for the gate, left the ground in a long, arching leap and dug his fingers into the wire. His trousers hung down wet from his white legs and bleeding buttocks. He hung there for a moment, screaming, and Fare saw a length of flame from somewhere beyond the gate, heard immediately the hard, flat "slap-pop" of the report. The boy hung an instant, shaking his head wildly, then poured down the fence like liquid. He lay at the base of the fence for a moment, then turned toward them, in the headlights' glow, lifting his blinded monster's face.

The sound of the bullhorn came again, "Your time is . . ." but it could not be separated for long from the sound of the firing. The guns began booming, first somewhere far off, their flashes the toy emissions of toy guns, the shot sprinkling among them, but as it caught on and they felt themselves raked by the first pellets, the men panicked.

Bodies behind him pressed inward to shield themselves from the stinging shot, then flung themselves toward the center of the circle. But in the center was the fire, and soon Fare could hear the screams of the men who had been rolled into it by the force of those on the outside.

He was never sure whether Lester struck him intentionally or was himself struck from behind so that they fell, and the two of them lay at first struggling separately toward the center, then, when the madness took them, with each other.

At the sound of the first far-off shots, Fare had drawn the knife. He had held it to his side as he rolled. His teeth howled and jangled and he repeated again and again the same senseless phrase, "a cigarette, a cigarette. You got another one of them?" They slugged each other, Fare conscious of his advantage but not revealing it. All around them men screamed as the little pellets embedded themselves, and they rolled in the smell of sweat and urine and the burning flesh of the men in the fire. Wildly Fare punched and kicked and kneed Lester, saying again and again, "You got another one of those?"

No more would he be ignored. He was a force. He would be reckoned with. He would see the light of recognition. As Lester flinched from him, turning sideways, Fare scuttled onto his fat back, imprisoned his legs and gagged him with an arm. IIe brought his mouth close to Lester's ear. He was conscious of the other's smell, of the feel of the curly hair, of the mortal resilience of the pouched fat at his shoulder.

He whispered into the ear. He spoke as he had not spoken since he had lain with Clare. He did not know what he said until he got hold of himself. He said, "This is for a boy. It's for a boy named Charles Ed Odum who you shot with a pistol in South Carolina. Do you remember it?"

A tremor went through Lester. "What's for . . ." He struggled wildly to free himself from Fare's grip. Fare could feel himself losing Lester. He could not wait to say the rest, to see the light. It was not so necessary as he had supposed to make Lester remember. Why did he have to know? He brought the knife up.

In the last instant as they writhed together, Lester must have seen it glint, for he moaned, "No." Fare did not draw it. He put it into Lester's neck at the side, where the big artery would be, and with all his strength whipped it back out to pluck the artery like a chord. When the blood sang out warm and unspeakably dark in volumes unimaginable, he held while it spurted, held while it flowed, held while it trickled and while the last shudder went through the body he embraced. Then he pressed close again to the ear and whispered the one thing he knew would not be misunderstood, "You ain't riding for free."

As the last shots boomed around him, he shoved the fat body away, dropped the knife, and stood up with the others to form a column of twos.

PART

TWENTY-NINE

THROUGH THE PERFORATED ALUMINUM SHIELD THAT SEPArated the seats, past the epauletted shoulders of the Bradford County deputy in the front seat, Fare gazed out across the hammock land. Through a long corridor in the pine barrens he could see far off the first rust-streaked Spanish orange tower. An obelisk of cold, flat January light rolled across the corridor, flashing the blue windows of the tower, then passing on to be followed by the shadow of a cloud carried like driftwood on the gray stream of sky. He sat back, closing his eyes to let it unfold as he had known it would, his memory summoning the fences, the upper floors of the Rock, the tall live oaks, before his eyes could see them. The two deputies, Neely and Pettigrew, looked at each other. Neely glanced back at him, a question in his eyes.

Standing before the judge's bench at the sentencing, he had been asked if he had anything to say. They had given him three to five at Belle Glade. There had come a sharp look from the man standing beside him, his lawyer. It had been the last of many cunning, strategical glances to come from this man through the two weeks of the proceedings. Fare was tired of it. He did not even know why, when he had refused counsel, they had not let him do without one. But they had given him the benefit of this cunning standing next to him in the vested doubleknit winter-weight suit, and now he was asked to say something, and the lawyer shot him the for-your-own-benefit-be-quiet glance. He knew his own benefit.

"Do you ever let a man request where to go?"

He could not so much see as feel the lawyer wincing in impotence beside him.

"I'm not sure what you mean." The judge leaned toward him.

"I want to go back there, to Raiford. I don't want to go to Belle Glade."

The judge looked at him for a moment, then smiled. It was hard to read the smile. It might have been a smile of simple mirth; it might have denoted satisfaction in the knowledge that Fare was going to get what was coming to him.

"That is a request I will grant," the judge said.

Later, Fare turned on his heel and walked out in step with his lawyer. In the anteroom, the lawyer turned to him, raising his hand, about to say it, that he shouldn't have.

Fare stopped walking. He stood with his hands at his sides. He had been feeling more and more lately, the strange drug of calm. His hands did not want to get into his pockets. They hung content. His eyes could rest. He examined the bridge of the lawyer's nose where the eyeglasses had trenched. The lawyer's eyes seemed to vibrate. Fare could not affix them to his own.

"I'll appreciate it," he said, "if you don't talk to me anymore about it."

The man frowned, sighed professionally. They were about to part. But Fare reached out and pulled his coat sleeve. The other turned, looked at his watch, pulled his sleeve away.

"I did a bad thing," Fare said. "Not confused or sick or stupid. Bad."

He might have said more about it, about bad things in good causes, but he did not. He was certain only of this: He deserved his punishment just as Lester had deserved his own, and he would get it just as Lester had gotten it. He did not want the benefit of legal trickery. The world was no longer a place of relativity. It was a place of some few, but definite absolutes. Evil was one of them. And anyway, what could the lawyer do but prolong things. It was, as they said, an open-and-shut case. After lying in his own piss for twenty hours Thibideaux had raved the story to anyone who would listen.

* * *

When the car stopped with a little lurch in front of the main gate, Fare reached up to the door handle and was surprised again. Where one hand went in the manacles, so did the other. No matter, he would have them off soon. There was no door handle anyway, only a smooth stud.

Deputy Neely stepped out and hitched up his pistol belt. His right hand brushed down the butt of the pistol to the strap fastened to the holster. There his thumb pressed briefly before he opened the door.

"Right, Bud," he said, not looking at Fare, stepping back to keep his distance. When Fare stood up, the pants they had given him fell down.

"Get you trousers."

"Yes, sir."

They waited on the walk for Pettigrew to join them. Neely took him under the left arm and started walking him toward the gatehouse, then let go. When they neared the steps, Fare turned and looked around him. He could feel a little wash of panic, not coming from inside himself so much as toward him from in there.

"Deputy Neely?"

"Yeah, Bud?"

"Could I have one of your Camels?"

It was awkward lighting the cigarette with his hands in the cuffs. At last, Neely did it for him. Neely put the matches and the pack of cigarettes back into his breast pocket and buttoned the dark green flap, smoothed the shape of the cigarettes beneath the fabric. Fare took a deep drag, feeling the drug in the smoke. He closed his eyes.

"Say, Bud?"

"Yes, sir."

"You ain't gone fall out on us . . . ?"

Fare guessed he had reeled a bit.

"No. I'm fine."

He was wondering whether Sarn Thomas was on duty in

there. There was no reason why he shouldn't be. What would he say? Nothing probably. It would all be in his eyes. All about what a sorry spectacle it was.

He'd about finished the cigarette and was going to have to turn and go in. Neely and Pettigrew had been standing at a safe or respectable distance, depending upon how you cared to read them, but now they were coming close to take him in. He turned toward them, sweeping his eyes across the land around. There beyond the road was the prison laundry, there were the "suburbs," and farther, there were cornfields in a cover of whispering gray chaff. He said, "Bet there's quail in those fencerows," but Pettigrew (or Neely) put a hand on his shoulder and the heat told him the cigarette was too short to be any more excuse. Then he saw someone sitting in the cafeteria. He exhaled gray smoke and so did the image sitting there in the smoky glass. She set down her coffee cup and rose. She walked with a rolling gate to the door and opened it. And as they turned him, rather roughly, so that his trousers dipped again, she raised a hand. He was not certain it was a greeting. Maybe it had been to touch her hair. But it was *her* hair.

The Rock, he had learned, had two voices. In the daytime, there was the babble of a thousand jiving transistor radios, the clatter of plastic crockery, the clank of Olympic bars in the weight rooms, the patter on walls and floors and ceilings of handballs and basketballs, the shuffling of cards, the prayerful evocations of luck, the clattering of dice, the naming of bets and threats with details of accompanying mutilation, the whisper of love and confidences and a thousand thousand misuses of heaven. At night, there was the voice of its dreams.

At times, during his first month on T-tier, it had been a comfort to lie in the strange, drugged calm and listen to it. It was as though he lay rocking on the breast of some huge singing beast.

Now he lay on his bunk trying not to listen. He was waiting for the two fingers of the clock on the desk nearby to come

together across an eternal fifteen minutes to one o'clock. He
had done nothing but wait since before dawn. At one o'clock
on Saturdays the visitors came. On the desk by the clock lay
the letter:

> . . . saw them taking you in, I thought, doesn't he look a mess.
> Where did you get you those britches anyway? Off a Portagee?
> You looked just like old Moke, you remember old Moke?

Old Moke had been the swarthy dwarf who had helped out
at tobacco time. Some of them, joking, had called him a
Portagee. He'd smoked Kools since he'd been old enough to
light a match, and had gone around singing the Kool jingle:
"You ain't moking koo, koo, koo enough, till you moob up to
Koooo." Sure, he remembered ole Moke. He lay in his bunk
on T-tier as the two black fingers inched toward each other at
the top of the white circle, thinking about her coming, about
why, what they would say. Since getting the letter, he had
begun to lose the effect of the drug. He had been tense and he
resented it.

> . . . remember Moke? He used to have a pair of britches just
> like that. You going to be wearing the same ones when I come
> to see you next Saturday? And your face. Look to me like you
> bought you a new one and got the wrong size.

He had paid two packs to have his best blues laundered and
pressed, but there wasn't much he could do about his face. The
doctors had told him it was something in the nerves. They were
stuck, or *it* was, with one side drooping down a little. You
didn't get cosmetic surgery in the Bradford County slammer.
He'd get rid of the plastic caps and get new teeth when they
got around to him, but that wouldn't be for a while yet.

He'd stood at dawn that morning at the cell window in his
best starched blues. Now they were matted to him, and he
smelled himself. At the window, he'd watched the moment
when daylight took hold, breaking like a plucked string from
the horizon across carefully overlapped pools of electric light

falling from the tall poles along the fences. What was she doing? Was she awake too? No. Not yet.

Between the fences, the dogs left their houses, scratching themselves and peeing their boundaries into good order, each moving to the end of his sector to wait for food. He had stood and listened to the night voice of the Rock.

It was a strange thing. He had first heard it soon after coming back. He had stood many mornings at the window, after waking early from a sleep without dreams, lightly swaying in the movement of all their dreams, each man of them eternally dreaming his complaint or his longing. It was a deeply humid, slurred rolling, like the sea swell before weather. Out there in the sea of dreams sometimes trouble was agitating to make its presence known. Other times, he heard only the fretful, gentle swell and roll of the sleep of the housed two thousand. It was as though he stood in the murmuring heart of one troubled man. And for the first time in his life, he'd had neither longing nor complaint. That is, until he had gotten the letter.

The night he had gotten it, he had dreamt again. In the dream, she had come to him, sliding the barred door open soundlessly and without effort, and when he had sat bolt upright, she had raised one finger to her lips. She wore no clothing and the moonlight that sluiced through the bars above his bunk spattered first at her ankles, then gently rippled her golden body as she walked to him. She held something in her hand, gripped tightly. As she neared, he saw that she was wet, streaming, and he knew somehow that she had been to the river. She came to the bed and he could not bring himself to reach out to her. Instead, he shrank from her, cold against the wall beneath the moon-wet sill. She sat on the edge of the bed and held her hand out to him and he reached out, unable to refuse her now, and slowly, he unwrapped her fingers from around the ring. She held it out gleaming gold and seeming enormous in the flat of her hand and they both watched it for a moment. Then she fixed him with fierce, hungry eyes.

"He said to put it on me."

Fare was going to ask who, who said? but he had awakened, just before dawn, and there had been the letter on the table by the bed. To reread it, he had to wait until the lights were switched on in the hallways at five-thirty, a crackle of fluorescent tubes in the hollow quiet. Outside, men could be heard shuffling to sick call. The loudspeaker clicked behind the mumbling of lights, then whirred like a scratchy record with the day's first announcements: "Spates, Edward C., report to the control room immediately. Spates, Edward C., Oh-Niner-Niner-Three-Seven-One . . . Lascowitz, Thomas D. . . ."

The sounds thickened. The great swell was breaking as men quit their sleep. The murmur of protested awakening could be heard now among the other sounds. If there was no fog, they would open the yard gate at seven. He read the letter again quickly. He would eat and then walk the yard until the library opened at eight.

In the library it was not much good. He picked at *The Compleat Angler* for a while, but could not understand the words. He tried reading a chess manual, thinking he would pick it up, but could not understand the words. Finally, he sat watching the clock.

At eleven he walked through the chow line thinking, asking himself questions he could not answer.

"What?" said a man near him.

"Nothing," he said.

"Right. Nothing."

It was beans and greens again. On the bolted benches at the row tables he sat as far from the others as he could get in the crowded, noisy mess hall. The sense of being inside a percussion instrument increased with every mouthful. The clatter of trays and plates, the cymbals clang of pans in the kitchen, the sweat and steam, all seemed to get into his mouth until his plastic teeth were mauling the metallic sound of the place.

When he looked up, LaPointe was straddling the bench, half-standing. Fare nodded, knowing that LaPointe had not really asked.

"Odum, my man. You looking healthy. Looking like my dream."

He felt Point's eyes touch the bad side of his face.

He took a mouthful of metal food. Stay pleasant, he told himself.

"How you liking it here? How it look from this side?" La-Pointe was smiling, still staring, examining it. Fare swallowed and looked over at him. He wanted to ask how LaPointe had managed to beat him back to Raiford. He checked himself. "It looks about the same as it does to you, I magine." A moment later. "Expecting Rose any day now?"

LaPointe's face clouded some. "They ain't gone get my man Rose."

"Hope not," Fare said, finding that it was true.

They ate in silence for a space. Then LaPointe stood, leaving most of his food. "Be checkin you."

He ambled off, a wedge of muscle wrapped in a black T-shirt and hammered into a wide leather belt, a comic book swaying in his hip pocket. Fare put down his spoon. Somewhere on down, he knew, LaPointe would want something. It was going to take it all not to give it to him.

Since he had found LaPointe waiting for him here, he had kept this out of his mind, had used the past to hold it away from him, but the past was only a path to crossroads where he had learned as much as he would ever know about such things.

Lester was past now, a mad accident which had washed him up here more or less intact, leaving other people more or less injured than he. And what had he learned? What truth had he discovered? Only this: The day after he had finished Lester, he might have dealt better with LaPointe. Running the obstacle course alive did not mean that you possessed competencies, or that the next maze would be laid out like the first. Experience could guarantee you nothing, not even the knowledge of what you could endure.

Since coming back, he had tried to keep himself apart, to have no truck with other men, to make himself capable of living without them. He took care to possess nothing anyone could want. He had kept clear of gambling debts, of politics, of cults of personality, had been polite and well-disciplined but never obsequious before authority. Even his body had been made, in the course of that other accident, undesirable. And where had all of this care gotten him? LaPointe was sniffing around again.

He had sifted it, and in his half-comic scholar's way, classified what he had learned under two headings, the doctrine of the accident and the doctrine of the first movement. That night long ago, when accidentally they had gotten the wrong ride, his brother had moved away from him first, perhaps to lead him, perhaps to draw danger from him, or perhaps to abandon him to it; he would never know. He would know only the graceful image, ever repeated, of his brother walking that light, earthsprung, athlete's gait down the shoulder of the road, away.

And his own first movement that night had been one of the throat, of the voice, lost in the noise of the pistol shot. In the doctrine of the first movement, the word was properly subordinated to the act, defeated by the mechanic quickness of the gun. After the useless word, his flesh had run away, leapt down the embankment, for already Lester was turning the gun as methodically as any exterminator.

That night by the fire in the yard, his first movement, as the guns boomed, had been right but accidental, perhaps some stubborn remnant of heritage, briefly reencoded in the blood. Would the trait cycle back into his life again?

He turned in his tray and walked to the yard. There was nothing else to do. When he emerged on the ramp from the west gate, he stood for a moment in the sunlight.

What did it mean, he wondered, "Be checkin you?" Just accidental language? Something benign? No, Point would be back, wanting something somewhere along the way, the long way, three years at least.

He walked along the wall of the Rock letting the heat of reflected sunlight strike the drooping nerves of his jaws. There was one thing, one thing he had going for him now. It was the way Point had stared, long and almost professionally, at his face. Now he wished he had turned to Point, played the scene more fully, asked, "Is this the way it starts again?" He should have stared back, fixedly into Point's strength, those blank eyes which gave nothing away, which by dint of pure stupid instinct were fearless. He should have said, "Point, what's on your mind? Do you want something with me?"

Next time. Next time. He would always keep the bad side to LaPointe. The side of him that Point knew nothing about, the side which was his mystery now. Turn it to him and by its grotesqueness, not by bulk or power, but by mystery, show that he was different now. He had put it in the way of danger, had given its blood. Let Point guess when and how and why, and this would delay things, would be his strength. And then, when it would, let the accident happen.

As the black fingers met at the top of the white circle, Fare rose from the bunk. He had just made the door when the announcement came, ". . . inmates for the visiting park will form a walking line at the east gate. Inmates . . ."

They formed the walking line in the dark hollow at the mouth of the east gate. Fare looked around him at the men who were going to meet visitors. They were clean as a Sunday school class. And they had made themselves into individuals. One man had slit the waistband of his blues, sliding a belt through so that only the buckle showed in front; another had snipped off the loops, cutting new ones in the band; a third had sewed snaps to eliminate the belt.

Anything, Fare thought, standing in his matted uniform. He had seen men at visiting time receiving these materials as gifts, elastic for waists, colored piping for cuffs, bigger buttons, smaller ones, even rhinestones.

Some had special starching arrangements with friends in the laundry. Others, the iron freaks, cut parts away, sleeves to reveal nineteen-inch biceps with leaping tattoos, pockets to give a pectoral definition. Anything for vanity, or for deception. Men wore sunglasses in places so dark they stumbled. Illiterates carried plastic penholders in their breast pockets stuffed with pens and pads of paper to obscure the name tags stitched above.

Penitence was here too. In stifling heat, men wore their shirt collars tightly buttoned, their sleeves rolled down, coats in summer, sleeveless undershirts in winter. They wore tight chains around their necks as symbols of bondage. They inflicted daily punishments upon themselves, trying hard to be hard, to deserve what they were getting. But there ran in them also a strong counterimpulse to be soft, pretty, the male in his plumage. Fare laughed softly as his hand went to his face.

He stood beside Langely, his walking partner in the callout line, while Sarn Edwards checked the count against his clipboard. Langely dug for a pack of R.I.P. in his shirt pocket and automatically offered Fare one. Fare took it, accepted a light from Langely's Zippo, which was still wrapped in black tape from Viet Nam days. Next time, it would be Fare's turn to offer. He would not forget.

THIRTY

THEY BEGAN WALKING TWO ABREAST WITH THE SHORT, SHUF-
fling steps of paratroopers toward the visiting park, while
ahead of them in a disordered dribble, the visitors, carrying
what they had brought with them, were beginning to flow
through the main gate. Fare arched to see over the heads of
the other men. Soon they would enter the human world of
bright street clothing and polite talk. Every second word
would not be "fuck."

He did not see her among the ones coming. Farther off, he
saw the spaced, luminous traffic making for the parking lots,
heard the distant sigh of tires on the New River Bridge. They
entered the visiting park.

. . . I thought you were acting a little more put-off than usual
that day you came by the house, but I sure wasn't expecting
anything like this. You gone and —— up good and proper,
haven't you?

He put the letter back into his pocket. There was a hole
where the censor had cut out whatever it was he had done
up good and proper. The paper was beginning to tear from
all the handling. He did not know why it fascinated him. He
had spent far too much time looking for significance where
there was none. The letter was nothing more than typical
Clare, an over-the-back-fence conversation.

In the park, he did not know what to do with himself. The
men broke from the line, walking more slowly now, individu-
ally, toward the far end of the park to meet the women and
children, brothers and fathers as they entered. Fare watched
them meet, or collide, some of them, grabbing each other
roughly, yet somehow shyly. It was never clear who was
drowning and who was the lifeline. Some of the women looked

taut, as though they had been imprisoned outside the wire, waiting to get in. Some of the children, beholding their fathers, looked as though their lives were just now beginning; others had in their eyes an elaborate casualness, too adult for their little faces. To these, Fare could see, it meant the most. Without meaning to, he found himself drifting to the edge, a fence, azaleas. Clusters of visitors and visited formed near the middle of the park, sat at the tables. Cakes and pies emerged, sandwiches wrapped in wax paper. As the middle filled, the few whose visitors were late yielded, as Fare had done, to the sides, lining the fences, waiting too casually. We are like those children, he thought.

To have something to do, he fished for a cigarette and matches, then noticed Langely standing near, Langely had been a Green Beret they said, had served two tours in Viet Nam. Fare held out the cigarettes. It was awkward. Langely already had one. But it was short, and he smiled, ground it underfoot. "You gonna kill me quicker than I thought."

Fare lit them both up. "Be something," he said, "wouldn't it? To go through it all and die from cigarettes?" It sounded stupid, he knew it, but anything to keep from standing there gazing toward the empty gate. By the tone of Langely's voice, he could tell he felt the same way. Jesus, thought Fare, what we are reduced to. After what he's been through . . . And then he thought, me too. I have been through it too. A war. Langely picked a piece of cigarette paper from his lip and used the opportunity to glance at the gate. Fare looked away, to help out, but too late. A little color drained from Langely's face. "Well, Goddamn her, I guess she ain't coming." He turned and walked quickly back toward the Rock. A few yards away, he held up the cigarette, not turning back, "Thanks for this."

"Yeah, sure."

Fare stood alone now. He wished Langely had not walked off so quickly. Given the chance, he'd have joined him. To do it now, he'd have to hurry to catch up. "Goddamn her, she ain't coming." Something in the way Langely had said it told him "she" was not a mother or a sister. She was a woman.

There was a litter of cigarette butts at Fare's feet, and he leaned down to pick them up before one of the roving hacks told him to. He would deposit them with the letter in the shitcan on his way back to the Rock.

He did not feel much of anything, certainly not bitterness. He felt a little of the calm coming back, the drug beginning to rise in him like whisky. Then he saw it, a rolling brown, white-crowned shape coming along the fence line past the first guard tower; something white flung up, and closer, he could see it was a horse, a woman riding, her hair bouncing in time with her elbows. She waved again at the second tower.

He had to smile. He walked to the far side of the park and stood, watching through the fences as she neared, how she kicked the horse into a sprint the last two hundred yards, leaning down to put her face almost on its neck. Damn her, but she was original if nothing else. She was that at least.

When she made the gate and dismounted, leaving the horse standing with its flanks heaving, the reins trailing to the ground, she walked into the office. He looked for her inside the gate, but instead saw her emerge again outside, followed by two hacks with whom she seemed to be having an argument. After they had pointed toward it several times, she walked the horse to the parking lot.

He was waiting for her at the gate, another cigarette in his hand, wondering what they would do. His gladness was such that he hated to worry about anything like the proper gesture, but he did. Would they embrace, shake hands? (No, not that.) What else was there?

She stood before him in riding pants, narrow-kneed, bagged at the thigh, a white blouse with rolled sleeves, high, laced boots. There was a film of sweat on her face, and he could smell the horse. All around, people stared at her. She smiled, looked him up and down, her eyes stopping at his face, blinking, then going beyond to the others, watching them. She whirled suddenly on one heel, then back again, her hands daintily upturned at the wrists. She was impersonating a model in a fashion show.

"Feature me. Ain't this uptown or what? They took my crop, the shitasses. Have you ever heard of *parking* a horse?"

His lips were stuck together, the cigarette between them smoking up into his eyes.

"Uptown," he managed to say. Yes, feature you.

She came to him, took his hand, turned him and began searching the place like a woman looking for aisle twelve in the Winn Dixie.

"Can we go in that canteen?"

"If you brought money, and if there's room."

She dropped his hand. It burnt. He knew her smell would be on it. Her hand went into her pocket and came out with a wadded twenty. She smiled, " 'If you got the money, honey, I got the ti-i-i-me.' " They started toward the canteen.

"Hank Williams," she said.

"I know."

"Clara Belle Carnahan singing Hank Williams tonight at Larup's, folks. Two shows, midnight and one A.M., nickel beer for the gents, free for the ladies. . . ."

She said it under her breath, but some of the nearest heard her. He could see in their eyes the sense of her violation. He was thinking hard. She never called herself Clara. And why did she mention Larup's? Why start off with that?

There was one table, near the cash register. They sat, and he said, "They got a floor show at Larup's now?"

"Shit," she said. "They ain't even got any Larup's at Larup's now. It's a 7–11. Sells ice chests and beer to the Yankees that stop at the fish camp."

"It wasn't nothing but a cut and shoot dive anyway," he said.

"Yeah," she said, "but I had me some good times there."

She looked straight at him, a hard look. He had not imagined it going this way. Her coming here to look him in the eye and remind him of it. What good? What possible good?

"Look," he said, "what? . . ."

"Can I take your order?"

Granger stood over them, tall and fat at the middle, and with the burner's glint in his eyes, and something else. By the way he steadfastly looked at Clare, asking her too politely what their order was, Fare could tell he resented it, having to serve Farel Odum, the teacher turned fuck-up. But weren't they all turned something, formerly better, formerly free? He looked at his cigarette while she ordered them steaks, home-fries and mustard greens, apple pie a la mode, the most expensive items on the menu.

When Granger walked away, he was going to go back to it. What good is it to? . . . But her eyes had changed, and her hand, bringing with it the smell which was, he understood now, what this imprisonment would take away, came across the table to him, and took his chin, turning his face to the side while she looked at it. She turned it a couple of times side to side as though it were a horse's face, and once said, "Smile," which he did, and she whistled at the five lower and four upper plastic spacers.

He did not know when he closed his eyes, but knew that he had done so to concentrate on the smell, and knew that it was a great sorrow that there was so much leather in it from the reins and saddle.

She said, "Who did that to you. What son of a bitch?"

When he did not answer her, did not open his eyes, she said, more contemplatively, almost to anyone, "You don't look so young anymore, or so pretty either."

He could feel it, that very soon his hand would come up and take hers and bring it to his lips, which was something you did not do in the canteen.

"Fare. Open your eyes."

"Yes." She sat across from him as before, the film of sweat still on her forehead and at her upper lip, and her green eyes alight with a fire somewhat like the arsonist's.

"What were you doing? Just then? With your eyes closed?"

"Feeling sorry for myself," he said, knowing that it was true.

"I don't know," she said. "Maybe it'll go away."

"Not for that," he said.

"Then what for?"

"Because I'm going to be stuck in here for three years and your hands are going wherever you take them."

"My hands?" she said. "That's dumb." But she smiled and laughed deep in her throat, a kind of whinny.

"To me, right now, it's not dumb at all."

"Three years?"

"At least."

She aimed him a business expression. There was the old appraiser in there, poorly hidden. She leaned forward.

"What you want to help that LaPointe get out for? I read about him."

He had thought about what he would tell her, if she asked. It was not so much that he felt he owed an account (she was not one to keep accounts), but that some of it belonged to her.

"I made a bargain with him."

"To get what?"

This was what he had been calling "it" consciously for some time, and from time almost out of mind, unconsciously. This was it. What he told her could determine a lot. How she felt about him, which mattered, what was left of it anyway. How she felt about herself, as a cause. If she thought of herself that way at all. He was not sure. He looked into her eyes. Why not be honest with her? She had never been anything else with him. But what was it, honesty? Was it to tell her, or to make something up?

"A hold of myself. To get a hold of myself." Let her be satisfied with that if she would. If not, let her signal him. She must show him she wanted it.

She shook her head, staring. "Horseshit."

Contempt was coming into her eyes now. "That's not it. Tell me."

He did not want contempt. He'd had too much of it and always, a bitter ration from her for the fact that he had been only half of what she could love.

"To get revenge," he said. He leaned toward her and whispered. "He was going to kill a man named Lester."

"What Lester?" she asked, whispering too. "Why him?"

He could say anything. Let her believe it or not. Or, he could say, because you wanted me to. You always did. But instead, he said, "The man who shot Charles Ed. He came here and Point was going to get him for me."

As he watched, the color left her face. Her tongue licked the corners of her mouth twice quickly. He could not tell whether she had the appetite for more or not. He stopped.

"Gone," she said, "I want to hear it."

"But he couldn't, so I did it myself. That's all."

A smile came to her mouth. Crawled there, slowly, and curved itself like a snake.

"You ought to be in here for killing, not . . . not . . . for conspiracy or whatever it is . . ."

"No," he said, firmly. "Not killing. I did not do murder. I did extermination." He stopped himself, breathing deeply. His thoughts whirred and lagged. "Oh, it was a bad thing, and I'll do three years hard time because it was bad, but it was not as bad as . . . if ever there was one who deserved what he got."

He stopped. It sounded half-right to him, half-wrong. A speech, somehow rehearsed. "I don't know," he said. "I just don't know. I don't think I ever will."

He looked at her fiercely. "Do you know? Tell me."

He realized that he had always thought of her as someone who knew. She knew, he thought, in her flesh and bones and blood better than a mind could know. But now she looked at him as though withered. She wasn't a cause. She simply *was*.

"Is that how you got that?" She meant his face.

"No," he said.

"Well, what'd you do, fight a circle saw?"

"A trooper hit me in the face with the butt of a shotgun. He thought I was rioting."

"All by yourself? You rioting? You mean he thought you were part of it?"

Goddamn her. She was smiling again.

"Yes."

Granger brought their food. Fare lit another cigarette and leaned back away from the heat of it. She picked up her fork and then put it down again.

"Damn," she said, and then looked around them. When she looked back at him, she was making an effort not to get back on the horse and sprint.

"I saw you mommer."

An item checked from a list?

She forked a piece of steak into her mouth. She looked up at him, guilty, or seeming to be, as though she thought he'd dislike her doing it. He was glad.

"Did you tell her?"

"No," she said quickly, "and she don't need to know it either. It wasn't in the papers up there."

Fare knew exactly how long he had to figure what to do about his mother. He had until she came down to take care of the graves.

"Did you and her have a good talk?"

"She cold-shouldered me pretty much. She don't like me any more'n my mommer liked you."

"How'd she look?"

"She forgets things. What she just said, and she says it again, or what you said. She asked me three times if I'd seen you lately. Kinda like she used to . . . when I wasn't supposed to see you. I didn't stay very long. Out to lunch. That's all."

"I'd give you the guided tour, but they don't allow it."

They were sitting on a bench with another couple, haunch to haunch. It was as private as they could get.

"I don't need no guided tour," she said, looking at the Rock. "I can imagine it."

She looked at him again, her eyes stopping to appraise the left side of his face. It unnerved him. She wasn't pretending to get used to it like most people did.

"You smoke too much," she said.

"Yeah."

She had eaten the entire meal, enjoying it. He had left most of it.

"You know what I see when I look over there?" She nodded at the Rock.

He shook his head.

"A lot of lonesome jerking off."

She took his hand and placed in on her thigh. With her hand on top of his, she made him take the flesh and squeeze it.

"They say you don't know what you've got until you lose it."

She was looking into his eyes and making him squeeze her. He felt some of the energy, the audacity which had seemed to bleed away in the canteen come back to her. He was asking himself whether the "you" in this most recent chunk of philosophy was he or she. He knew now that during the long process of the meal she had been thinking, making up her mind. She was trying to shock him now, something she did when she had settled herself. "Look at my hand," she said, and he did. The nails were broken, the fingers calloused, there was dirt in the quicks. It was a horsewoman's hand.

"I'm farming," she said. "I decided to kick them shitasses out of the peanut field. Who needs any Blue Pines Estates anyway? You ever seen a blue pine tree?" She looked at him earnestly, making him squeeze.

He was feeling the dreamy calm again, with her hand doing what it was doing and a dull point growing at the center of him. "What about your momma?" he asked.

Her eyes held the same unalloyed earnestness, something he had not seen much of. He had seen it that night in the parking lot when she had said she couldn't help it.

"I won," was all she said.

"You a winner, all right," he laughed, "and I'm . . ."

"Fare," she said.

Her hand suddenly convulsed over his and the pain was such that he almost cried out. He could feel the unsubsided strength in it, the roughness of it when she interrupted him, "Fare, come back and farm with me. Mommer died."

A tear broke from the corner of her eye and as quick as

it began to roll she grabbed it, using a gesture much too large. She was ashamed of crying. He put his arm around her, but felt the shoulder of the man on the other side. He lifted her, and started her walking toward the far end. People were packing up now, lingering. Holding her, he looked out across the wire at the hammocks and pine barrens, the cypress islands. He could see her sitting on the rotting dock his hands had built, the lawn sloping up behind her to the old house, her mother gone from it; it hers alone now, and across the lake, nothing but the red scar where the earthmovers had been. A farm wife? His?

"You know I . . ."

"My old daddy's ghost, . . ." she said, with a sudden and lonesome passion, "our family's still got some kick and push around here. I can . . ."

"You go on," he said. He thought his eyes might be starting too. "It's time. They're going to blow the whistle."

"Fare?" She birthed another tear.

"We'll talk about it."

She stepped away from him. As though it were something coming at her, she snatched away the last tear.

"All right, shitass," she said, but smiling. "You know best."

He smiled the same, their old smile back at her.

The sky had darkened, lowered. He thought of her riding home, galloping in thunder and driving rain, her wet hair flying behind. He would watch her to the gate, then across the parking lot to the horse, his eyes keeping her for all that lay ahead. He closed his eyes and saw her wanting her third jump from the bridge, streaming wet, naked legs rocking her under Charles Ed's rented white coat. They had stopped her and she had called them shitasses. He had raised a can of beer to her that night. He would raise a hand to her soon and salute as she cut sod off to the west.

But something about a clean way of doing it occurred to him and he turned away sooner than he had expected. There were going to be days and nights. There was going to be the voice of the Rock, the sea of dreams numbing him, waking him early to stand swaying in the heart of the big singing beast. There was going to be LaPointe. He opened his eyes as the rain began falling.

In the dark hollow beneath the library he fought the impulse to climb the steps and watch her from the window, flying white in the saddle, whipping the horse out low and long to charge the far tower.

He remembered the last dream. Her words. "He said to put it on me." She has it on her, he thought. Only she doesn't know it. It's the dirt, those callouses. She's wedded.

He passed the spiral stair, fought successfully, and walked to the yard where he would earn his freedom.